THE ENIGMA

Loup-Garou Series Book 1

Sheritta Bitikofer

Moonstruck Writing

Cover art by Covers by Combs

Print ISBN: 978-1-946821-56-0

Ebook ISBN: 978-1-946821-55-3

This story has been one that is near and dear to my heart. I have to thank everyone for helping me through the ordeal of writing, editing, revising, and countless reediting. I couldn't have done it without the support and love of my family and friends. Also, a big thanks to my husband for rejoicing in my quirky obsessions. I can always count on you to be by safe harbor, someone I can speak freely with about my stories without fear of rejection. Your support has been invaluable.

CHAPTER 1

DECEMBER 6, 2007

The cold December wind whipped at Katey's long, chestnut brown hair. Her chin rested atop her folded arms over her bent knees, clear green eyes staring into the expanse of forest ahead of her. From the steep, grassy slope behind the Crestucky library, she studied the way the morning light filtered through the swaying pine branches, attuned to every slight movement in the underbrush. Here, in the quiet and away from the rest of the world, she found a tiny sliver of relief. She hoped it would rekindle some part of her spirit that had begun to slowly fade over the last several months, but no such luck.

She filled her lungs with the Florida winter air and sighed. Any girl might have been ecstatic for her eighteen birthday, but Katey felt nothing. For years, she waited for this day and now, it felt so anticlimactic. She had fantasized about when she would age out of the foster care system and finally be on her own. Social workers had prepared her for the reality of this milestone, and she researched her options. Though Katey had some time before making the leap, since her foster mother agreed to let her stay under her roof until the end of her senior year, the excitement couldn't touch her now. It was as if she were in a bubble, her senses dulled to the world around her, unreachable and disconnected. Each day, she put on her mask, complete with a fake, cheery disposition, but inside, she was dying.

Once more, the aching emptiness stole her breath and reminded her that something was missing. Ever since she was a child, she knew her life could never be normal. Jumping from foster home to foster home taught her that nothing in life was as good as it seemed, or nearly so permanent. Yet, more recently, the loneliness got to her. She used to pride herself on being so strong. The adults called it "resilience." She considered it the refusal to cry when they told her to pack her clothes in a black trash bag for the fifth time.

Katey's fingers gripped the sleeves of her hoodie as she willed herself to stay grounded in the moment. If she allowed her thoughts to slip into that dark hole, she may not be able to crawl back out again.

The rumble of a car engine in the parking lot behind her brought her back into the present. She pulled out her phone to check the time and cussed under her breath. The first period bell would ring in five minutes and there was no way she'd make it before the tardy bell. She jumped to her feet and bolted into a run for her jeep.

A sprawling town centered on the crossroads between two highways, Crestucky had been Katey's home all her life. She thought few foster kids could say that. She and her friends blew so much smoke, saying that as soon as they graduated, they'd leave this small town and find some place more exciting. Independence was just around the corner, and though Katey was more than ready to leave, she didn't have a solid plan. Not yet.

As predicted, the high school parking lots were full and Katey had to snitch an empty faculty parking stall, nearly all the way on the other side of the campus from her first period class. With her messenger bag banging against her hip, Katey sprinted her way toward the main building and down the vacant halls until she reached Mr. Dubose's classroom.

She paused, her hand on the door handle. It was so unlike her to be late and she dreaded the way everyone's eyes would turn to her the minute she walked in. She didn't really care what the other students thought of her, just what her teacher would say.

"No point in delaying the inevitable," Mr. Dubose called from inside the classroom. "You're fifteen minutes late."

He must have spotted her through the narrow door window as she walked up. Katey braced herself and entered. Mr. Dubose's classroom resembled a chemistry lab, with rows of eight-foot tables set up in two columns to serve as desks. Along the back wall were sinks and cabinets for storing supplies and equipment. Mr. Dubose taught environmental science during this period, but she wondered if he taught chemistry or biology throughout the day.

At the head of the classroom sat Mr. Dubose's desk, neatly organized with an open laptop. A projector screen hung behind his desk and concealed a blackboard that he never used. Her favorite teacher leaned against the front of his desk, arms folded over his broad chest as he watched her with wise brown eyes. His dark hair was cut short, and unlike his full beard, showcased the subtle hints of age with silver threaded around his temples.

His button-down shirt, tucked into a pair of dark slacks, and sleeves pushed up to his elbows showcased a body better representative of an athlete than a middle-aged high school teacher. At the beginning of the year, she heard other students mutter about how ripped Mr. Dubose was, and how he must have worked out after school or played some sort of contact sport over the weekends. Katey, however, couldn't imagine him in any other setting. His professional attire never suggested him to be the kind of guy that would exert himself like that, leaving his physique an ongoing mystery.

Above all, Mr. Dubose conveyed an air of authority that may have intimidated some. To her, it was comforting. His classroom was a safe harbor, a place she felt she could run if she needed help, though the situation never arose. Here, even under his disapproving stare, Katey's tight chest slowly decompressed, and she could breathe easier.

He jerked his chin toward desks in the very front row. "Take your seat, Miss Katey."

Mr. Dubose's accent sparked even more whispers amongst the class. His voice held a distinct, yet recognizable British accent. During their orientation, he answered the usual probing questions he received every year, telling his prospective students that he came from a place called Warminster in Britain, but would disclose no further details of his childhood or past life in the United Kingdom. Katey burned with curiosity, but refused to test his limits and ask, as so many did in the first couple of weeks of school.

Beside her sat Beth, one of her oldest friends from junior high. Environmental Science was the first period they shared since freshmen year, and she hoped this would give them a chance to rekindle their friendship, though their lives seemed to divert in two very different directions. Beth had quickly fallen in with the goth crowd, and her daily choice of dress showed it plainly. Though they shared similar interests in music, Katey wasn't bold enough to plunge into Beth's kind of lifestyle. She doubted that she could pull off the thick, black eyeliner and studded jewelry in the same way that Beth could. Neither could she judge Beth for her choices. At least she found a place to fit in. Katey preferred to stay unnoticed, unimpressive, and slip between the rigid, defined lines of high school social groups. If she didn't plug into a clique, then it'd be easier to disengage when the time came to leave.

As Katey dropped in her chair, she let the mask settle into place. The soul-crushing darkness lurking beneath her calm expression couldn't be brushed aside, but she could veil it for the day. Like tossing a blanket over clutter on the floor or draping a towel over a puddle of vomit, Katey could pretend that the mess in her soul didn't exist, just for a little while, and no one else would know it either.

Katey met her teacher's stare and noticed a shift in the way he watched her. His dark brows pinched together ever so slightly, as if in concern for something he couldn't understand. Katey stiffened, trapped under his gaze like a mouse caught between the paws of a cat, for what stretched like an hour. What did he see? Was it about her being late or did she wait too long to don her mask? Something in his eyes demanded honesty, demanded a full explanation for whatever it was he thought he saw. Part of her was willing to give it. The other wanted to run back out the door.

Don't say anything. Don't say anything, she mentally begged him. It was too early and her nerves too raw. If just one person, especially him, were to ask if she were okay, she was liable to break down in tears.

As soon as that strange look appeared, it was gone, and Mr. Dubose turned back to the class, allowing Katey to release the breath she had unconsciously held. No longer the subject of his intense interest, Katey had the time to smother her depression even further. She bolted her mask firmly in place and tucked away the edges of her sadness so it wouldn't show to anyone else who cared to look too closely.

Katey barely paid attention to Mr. Dubose's review of the subject of population change until he turned on the projector hanging from the ceiling and a slideshow faded into focus on the dropdown screen behind his desk. About that time, he took up a yardstick that he often used as a pointing aid during his lectures and turned to regard another senior in the front row on the other side of the room. He slowly strode toward her, like a lion stalking its prey, and Katey noticed the way her head was bent low and the faint glow of a screen on her face. The student was furiously typing out some message on the phone hidden in her lap when Mr. Dubose smacked the flat end of the yardstick on the tabletop in front of her. She jumped and the class laughed at her expense.

"Kindly pay attention when I'm talking," Mr. Dubose said in a humorous tone. "It might be more important than your relationship drama."

The girl gave him a sheepish look and snapped her phone shut before slipping it into her pocket.

Mr. Dubose returned to stand beside the projector screen. "As I was saying... In nature, groups or families of certain species live in tight-knit units, looking after each other as a whole and the individual. But when resources become short or environmental conditions grow intolerable, that bond can be broken easily."

He pointed his remote to the projector and clicked for the next slide. The image of a dueling pair of wolves appeared over the blue slideshow background. Some in the class made disapproving sounds at the bared fangs and bristling hackles.

"For example," he continued, "In a pack of wolves like we'll see on the video, the alpha male will kill the omega wolf for food for the rest of the pack." He paused and swept an expectant look across the class.

Unsure of what possessed her to do it, Katey spoke up. "No, they wouldn't. Even though the omega wolf is the lowest in the pack, they wouldn't kill them." All eyes were fixed on her and she could feel her stomach knot under their scrutiny. "The omega is an important part of the pack social order, isn't it? That's what the video said yesterday."

They had watched part of a documentary about the importance of a wolf pack in Yellowstone National Park the day before, as part of their lesson on the importance of natural predators and prey and their impact on the environment of a region. Not usually one for documentaries, Katey was entranced by the dynamics of a wolf pack and how it was so much like a family, so much like the one thing she never really had.

Mr. Dubose's face split in a wide grin. "Very good, Miss Katey. I was hoping someone would catch that. Apparently, you were the only one paying attention." He clicked the remote again and a giant red cross overlayed the fighting wolves. "No, wolves do not harm others within their pack unless it's to reaffirm dominance amongst its members. In other situations in nature, the bigger, stronger animals will eat the younger, weaker ones to eliminate competition for space and mating."

A junior in the third row raised her hand. "Wouldn't the stronger animal get weak if they eat a sicker animal?"

Mr. Dubose leaned against his supply closet door and crossed his ankles. "No, because most predators such as wolves will eat a sick, older caribou and their immune system blocks out that sickness." Mr. Dubose clicked his remote and the slide changed to a picture of a crowded subway train. "And in just the opposite situation, when conditions are too good, the population may explode. With this overcrowding in the ecosystem, competition grows. And what happens when competition grows?"

Once more, he waited, but no one volunteered an answer. "Come on kids, it's not that early in the morning. You're not zombies..." He waited a moment longer, then said, "Stress levels go sky high!"

A few students snickered when he tapped the tip of his yardstick against the drop ceiling panel above his head. "Competition for space, food, shelter, and other resources can bring out the worst in animals and humans. Fighting will, inevitably, break out. Immune systems within this high-stress environment tend to degrade, making the most insignificant of illnesses deadly. As a result, populations decline. What do we call it when the fittest do not survive?"

It was so silent, Katey could hear a student in the back shift in his seat.

"Natural selection," Mr. Dubose answered, sounding out the words as if he were teaching them to a toddler. With a sigh, he continued his lecture, and Katey once more tuned out much of it, her attention drifting to the pictures above Mr. Dubose's shoulder.

They were part of a larger collage of photos pasted on his red supply closet door in front of her desk, the majority of which his body blocked from view at the moment. The photos seemed to have been taken in Europe and Asia, following Mr. Dubose's past travels over several summers. Katey liked to zone out during the lectures and study the places she had never been, and would likely never visit. Snow-capped mountains, a glittering river snaking through a tranquil valley, ancient monuments and ruins, and architectural marvels from foreign countries captured her imagination. She had heard how some high school graduates went backpacking overseas the summer before college. Could she do something like that one day?

Mr. Dubose cut off the projector and made his way toward the other side of the room to turn on the television set up in the corner. "Now that I have thoroughly bored you, we'll finish the Yellowstone documentary from yesterday." He had his back turned to the class when he said, "Miss Stephanie, if you can't keep your hands off your phone, it's mine until the end of the period."

Katey looked to the girl who had been caught texting earlier. Her head was up, and Katey only saw her hands buried between her thighs, which was the only hint that she might have had her phone in her hands.

"But, Mr. Dubose—"

"No buts." He turned and held out his hand, flicking his fingers in that universal sign that said he wanted what she had. "Give it."

Stephanie complied and forfeited her phone to the teacher. Katey wondered how he could have known that she was on her phone. Then again, Mr. Dubose proved from the first day of school that he had a sort of sixth sense about things like that. This wasn't the first time he had busted someone for pulling out their phone or passing notes in class. Each time, it seemed as if there was no logical explanation for how he knew what was going on halfway across the room, but he did. Katey wanted to think it had something to do with how long he had been a teacher, but some days, she wasn't entirely sure.

Katey settled back into her chair and watched the remainder of the documentary with as much fasciation as the day before. A few stolen glances toward Mr. Dubose sitting behind his desk made her stomach twist. Either he happened to look at her at the exact same moment, or he watched her more closely than she watched him. Was he searching for some sign of what he noticed earlier when she sat in her seat? She steeled herself and tried in vain to not look his way again, hoping that her mask wouldn't slip under his inspection.

The bell rang all too quickly and Mr. Dubose cut off the documentary as students rose to their feet to make their exit.

"Don't forget about the meteor shower tonight!" he called out as they funneled out of the classroom. "Get a good seat in the park around midnight. Be good and don't miss me too much over the weekend."

Katey couldn't keep in the tiny smile at how he always ended a Friday lesson. However, he had mentioned the meteor shower nearly every day for the last couple of weeks. Katey thought it completely ironic that something so rare would choose to show up for her birthday.

Once more, she caught a glimpse of Mr. Dubose's eyes on her as she walked out, but turned to Beth instead.

"How do you think you did on the test?" she asked, desperate to think of anything else but the way her teacher watched her walk out.

She and Beth chatted until they had to part ways in the hall on their way to separate second period classes on opposite sides of the campus. Alone, but surrounded by throngs of teenagers, Katey made her way toward what was considered the "Senior Hallway." The majority of the teachers on that hall solely taught senior students, and many of the senior lockers lined the walls between the classroom doors. The hall served as a separate building, connected to the main building by a breezeway, as if its construction were an afterthought or a later addition.

Katey felt herself almost drowning in the mass of moving bodies. Laughs, shouts, the shuffle of feet, and clanging of locker doors rang in her ears like the chaos of a battlefield. Breaths came heavy through her nostrils as she forced down the panic that threatened to spill out. Once she was inside Mrs. Kimbrough's English class, and she could feel empty space around her, she finally relaxed. But, when she looked to the empty desk beside hers, Katey's heart sank.

Besides Beth, Lily was one of Katey's dearest friends and nearly her polar opposite. Lily was the epitome of the peppy, teenage girl. She was popular, well-liked by most of the student body, and for whatever reason, she chose to cling to Katey. Despite their differences, they became fast friends and there were times when Lily was able to pull Katey out of her shell. They met years ago at the inaugural meeting for the new ballroom dance club. Now, they both worked as part-time instructors at the local dance studio on the weekends, something Lily roped her into the previous spring. Despite herself, Katey was a natural in classical style of dancing, and she had Lily to thank for the job that steadily bulked up her savings in preparation for her inevitable move away from Crestucky.

It took a moment for her to remember that Lily had some family engagement that morning, and would completely miss the test on the Shakespearian play, *Romeo and Juliet* that day. Katey had finished reading it the night before, and felt wholly unprepared for the quiz, but Mrs. Kimbrough granted them a little time at the beginning of class to study. Though she would have liked to have taken that time to study with Lily, she remembered that they would see each other after school. The meteor shower Mr. Dubose had mentioned, had given the senior class another reason to throw a party. She hadn't planned on going, but Lily promised she would be there. With someone to talk to, Katey made plans to go. It wasn't as if she had anything better to do.

When the dismissal bell rang, Katey grabbed her things and didn't have far to travel to her third period class, since it was conveniently right next door to Mrs. Kimbrough's room. She stood by the oak panel door and waited for Mr. Keith, who was quite possibly the most infamous teacher of the senior class.

The only reason she had to wait outside the locked classroom door was because the administration had arranged for his second period to be all the way across the bus ramp on the other side of the campus. He had five minutes to travel the distance between one classroom and the other, and he rarely made it on time. This gave stragglers an advantage and Mr. Keith hardly ever had to administer tardy slips. However, Katey wondered if he purposefully made himself late. She caught him walking once when he was in a hurry, and even at a brisk walk, the man was pretty fast.

Mr. Keith was a close second favorite to Katey, though they were almost nothing alike. Mr. Keith was much younger than Mr. Dubose and had a more vibrant personality. There was nothing calm about him, and his attitude to learning was far less rigid. This was his first year teaching, and he approached it as if it were a fun game, rather than something to be taken too seriously.

The tardy bell rang and Mr. Keith still hadn't arrived as a pack of students formed around his door.

"You're all tardy!" Katey heard his booming voice call from down the hall.

Everyone laughed and parted to let him through. Katey watched him struggle to unlock the door while adjusting the strap on his backpack that was thrown over one shoulder. He always talked about appealing to the administration to either fashion him a new key or install a new doorknob that didn't give him such a hard time.

"Mornin', Katey Kat," Mr. Keith greeted as he opened the stubborn door.

"Good morning," she replied with a feigned cheerfulness. Katey didn't know why he liked to call her that. It was a cute name that stuck ever since they met at orientation, and she thought she heard a certain accented lilt to the greeting, but couldn't place it. He had no distinct accent in his usual speech.

If Katey was a few inches over five-foot, then Mr. Keith had to be at least a foot and a half taller than her. A thin layer of dark stubble covered the lower half of his face, offset by a pair of dark emerald eyes. His hair was a deep brown with refined black highlights, always gelled into a stylish tousled look. Like Mr. Dubose, he looked as if he could hold his own in a fight, though his body was only slightly leaner due to his height.

The most significant thing about his appearance was that he dressed like one of the students. His wardrobe varied between baggy cargos, ripped jeans, hooded jackets, Hollister and Abercrombie shirts, and leather jackets. No matter what the situation, he always wore tennis shoes or boots, and never anything resembling the sort of business casual attire expected of other teachers. His rebellion against professionalism made him well liked among the students. This was his first year of teaching, but everyone already knew his name even if they didn't have a class with him.

He talked like one of the students too, using slang and translating complicated sentences from the textbook into a paraphrase everyone could understand. Human Geography became much more interesting than Katey ever thought it would be. She admired him for his self-assured attitude, just as she valued the safety of Mr. Dubose's presence. Like with Mr. Dubose, she knew Mr. Keith, regardless of his carefree attitude, could be trusted when all hell broke loose, and would likely crack jokes through the whole ordeal.

He finally managed to twist the knob in just the right way and the locking mechanism yielded to his efforts. The classroom was a little smaller than Mr. Dubose's, with a carpeted floor instead of tile. Unlike Mr. Dubose, he used his dry-erase board on a regular basis, and only pulled down the projector screen for the infrequent slideshow or to show off a neat video he had found on the internet. The windows across from the door overlooked the front parking lot of the school. His desk, much more cluttered and disorganized than Mr. Dubose's, sat in the far corner of the room. A counter and set of cabinets lined the opposite wall from the windows and tucked out of sight from most of the students was a mini-fridge. Katey only knew about it because she was Mr. Keith's student aid for her fifth period and she sat at a space on the counter near the fridge to grade papers.

Once everyone was in the classroom, Mr. Keith threw down his backpack, clapped his hands, and rubbed them together. "All right, who remembers where we left off yesterday in our religion lecture?"

The class was silent before one boy in the back offered, "Buddhism?"

Mr. Keith snapped and pointed at him. "Buddhism! Right. There's a fun group of people. All about the Nirvana and burning incense and stuff." He made his way toward his laptop to start up the slideshow and projector. "Who can tell me the origins of Buddhism?"

Katey folded her arms over her stomach after she set out her notepad and pen for taking notes. For the first quarter of an hour, she jotted down some points she thought would be useful for the upcoming semester exam, but her thoughts soon strayed from the classroom. Her mind came back to the idea of Nirvana in the lesson. To Buddhists, it was the ultimate goal of enlightenment, a release from the constant cycle of suffering through reincarnation. It was a state of blissful peace and joy that apparently few obtained in their own lifetime.

Nirvana sounded pretty damn good right about then to Katey. She let out a muted sigh that ended in a fit of anxious, imperceptible rattling. Her chest constricted in that all-too-familiar grip of panic that visited her weekly at the worst times. The pen in her hand froze, her body fixed in place as it tried to ride the wave instead of fighting it. She closed her eyes against the intrusive thought that maybe she'd never be free of this darkness that plagued her. Maybe turning eighteen, graduating, and leaving Crestucky would give her no reprieve from the loneliness. No amount of traveling, as she had fantasized about in first period, would produce the answer to true contentment.

There, staring her in the face, was the reminder of the possibility of absolutely no future, no hope, no life for her after aging out.

"You staying awake, Katey?"

Mr. Keith's voice interrupted her downward spiral just long enough so she could claw her way back to the surface. A heavy, but gentle hand settled on her shoulder. The warmth from Mr. Keith's palm seeped into her skin beneath her hoodie and spread down her chest and arm. With the warmth came a radiating calmness, like cold water added to a pot to soothe out a dangerous, rolling boil.

The panic subsided and Katey scrambled to put her emotional mask back in place before she met Mr. Keith's curious stare. It was that same look Mr. Dubose had given her, only swirling in shades of green instead of brown.

Half dazed as the last of the numbness dropped from her, Katey nodded. Mr. Keith's mouth pulled into a tight-lipped smile and he removed his hand to tap on the notebook on the desk.

"Keep taking notes. This'll be on the exam."

Without another word or look, Mr. Keith moved back toward the front of the classroom. Katey braced herself, half expecting his absence to summon back the panic, but the effect of his grounding touch lasted for the rest of the period.

It wasn't sexual or sensual. Katey felt no weird arousal at his attention, but something totally unfamiliar. It was something she only saw in movies and TV shows when family members offered comfort to one another during times of crisis. Did Mr. Keith sense her distress just like Mr. Dubose glimpsed what lay beneath her mask? How could she be so transparent all of the sudden?

How was Katey supposed to feel about that? Creeped out? Scared? Grateful? Mr. Keith seemed to keep a wary watch over her for the rest of the class, and when the bell rang, Katey wasn't sure whether to be relieved or disappointed. The moment she stepped out of his classroom, a measure of her anxiety returned but she had enough clarity of mind to fight it more effectively than before.

Fourth period calculus was in the main building. Her teacher, Mr. Myers, was unlike either of her other male teachers. Of average height, with hair the color of coffee grounds that curled at the ends and whiskey-colored eyes, the man had an edge to him. He hardly smiled, made little to no attempt to befriend the students, and like Mr. Keith, this was his first year teaching. That point was obvious in the first couple of months of school and Katey wondered how long he'd last through his stumbling lessons. A few times, she was almost sure that Mr. Myers barely had a grasp on the subject. But now, he carried himself with greater confidence, like a newborn colt learning to walk on gangly legs for the first time. Still, he was quiet and reserved. She never saw him chat with the other teachers, or saw him anywhere outside of his own classroom. He was a lone wolf, and seemed to prefer it that way.

Mr. Myers was a born and bred country boy. It was plain in his thick Southern accent and his occasional use of jargon straight out of a *Gone With The Wind* knockoff script. When Halloween came, and students and teachers alike were allowed to dress up, Mr. Myers dressed in a long duster, cowboy hat, and a bandana around his neck like a western outlaw. With his strong build and stoicism, she could easily picture him as a brooding gunslinger.

When she entered the classroom, Mr. Myers sat at his desk, wearing his usual khakis and dark polo shirt and peering at his laptop, deep in concentration. She slipped across the room to her desk by the wide window that overlooked a part of the faculty parking lot. Beyond the cars and blacktop was a buffer of trees that separated the school campus from a hidden shopping center.

A strong wind made the pine boughs sway and Katey stared as she slowly lowered into the chair. Transfixed, she caught herself imagining what it'd be like to stand among the trees, soft soil beneath her feet and doused in the heady scent of bark and leaves. For a fleeting moment, like that morning before school, she searched for some reprieve.

The slam of the classroom door threw her out of her head.

Mr. Myer's deep voice drew her eyes to the front of the class. "Y'all settle down and put your books away. It's Friday, so you know what's comin'."

He gave a test every Friday on the week's lessons, and Katey appreciated the predictability of that curriculum. She knew what was coming and could study accordingly, if she chose to at all. Mr. Myers passed out the tests and the class fell into a hushed silence for the next hour.

About halfway through the test, Katey ventured a glance upward. Mr. Myers, likely bored, had wandered to the window and leaned his shoulder against the space where the wall met the window jam. Unsure what compelled her, she watched her teacher as he stared out over the parking lot and forest beyond.

Seconds ticked by and Katey thought she spotted something odd. It may have been a trick of the sunlight, but Mr. Myer's eyes appeared to lighten from their usual brown to a richer, deeper amber color. She squinted and tilted her head by the smallest degree, but there was no change. Even when he blinked, that dark golden hue remained.

It was only when she leaned forward to get a better look that her desk groaned under her shifting weight and betrayed her movements. Mr. Myers snapped his gaze in her direction and eyes were brown once more. Katey froze as she had in Mr. Dubose's class earlier and waited for a tense moment. Unlike with Mr. Dubose, a shot of cold ran down her spine and she didn't feel safe at all. He didn't glare or frown, or do anything to express displeasure with her. The foreboding came from some unseen energy that passed in the space between them.

However, just like all those other bizarre occurrences, the intensity dropped and Katey sank back into her desk, willing herself to appear smaller. Mr. Myers lifted one dark eyebrow, as if amused by her behavior and then turned away to casually stroll back to his desk. He might have been willing to forget it happened, but Katey couldn't. Why did all of her teachers decide to be so weird on the same day?

CHAPTER 2

The rest of the school day passed by uneventfully. After fourth period, she ate her lunch alone since Lily was still inconveniently absent, and Beth had skipped out to have lunch with her boyfriend off-campus. Fifth period as student aid for Mr. Keith was also smooth. She kept her head down and helped to grade papers for his freshmen classes and he didn't ask her about her panic attack from earlier that day.

Her sixth period study hall was just as lonely as second period had been without Lily. She didn't expect her to be absent this long. It wasn't until after school was over and Katey was on her way to her locker that she heard from Lily for the first time all day. She pulled out her phone and answered it quickly as she knelt down to spin out her combination.

"I thought you'd be back by now," Katey said as she shoved the books into her locker.

"I know!" Lily groaned. "But this thing is taking a long time. Sorry if you missed me."

Katey didn't want to admit it, but she did miss her friend. "Are we still going to meet up before going to the party tonight?"

A long pause on the other end of the line made Katey sit back on her heels and grimace. "Lily!"

"I'm sorry! I can't get out of this. I would if I could. But, hey, I'll send you the directions. You should go anyway. It'll be fun."

Katey rolled her eyes to the ceiling. She hated parties. They weren't fun. Not without a friend to cling to. She already knew Beth wouldn't be there, and without Lily, she didn't see the point. All she would do is lurk around the edge of the party, talk to no one, maybe take a few sips of some sour beer from a keg that someone's older sibling brought, and leave after half an hour. Some of her classmates may have been eager to dance and drink, but Katey just didn't care for it, especially now when her heart still felt dead in her chest.

"Promise me you'll go and try to have a good time? I want you to tell me all about it tomorrow at the studio anyway."

After a moment of debate, Katey gave in. "Fine, I'll go. But under protest."

The party wasn't until nightfall, a few hours away. Katey decided to kill some time at the school library and get ahead on some reading for English class. Not a reader by choice, Katey preferred it over the idea of going home. She knew who would be there and that was another reason to give the party a try. Ambling through a mass of drunken teenagers was better than the ticking time bomb at home.

When the library shut its doors to students, Katey made her way to the faculty parking lot where she hastily pulled in that morning. A scene just a few stalls down from her red jeep slowed her progress, like she was suddenly wading through water. Crouched next to the front tire of a silver sedan, was Mr. Myers. She recognized his broad shoulders and the back of his head, a view she became familiar with over the months spent watching him write out formulas on the whiteboard.

As she came closer, she saw the tire he examined nearly rested on its rim on the asphalt. Mr. Myers let out a restrained curse and ran his fingers through his hair.

Before she realized it, her feet had steered her in his direction and stopped a couple of yards from him.

"Hey, Katey." Mr. Myers didn't even turn to look her way. "Surprised you're still here."

She started. How did he know it was her?

"I stayed behind to study." She cautioned a step closer. "Flat tire?"

"Flat as a tick." Mr. Myers stood and a heaviness settled in her stomach. She had forgotten how tough her teacher looked and felt the unwarranted urge to check if anyone else was around.

In a way to make up for her momentary skittishness, she offered, "Do you need any help?"

Mr. Myers' hand was buried in his pocket, presumably to pull out his phone. The mix of emotions that passed over his face looked so alien on him. Confusion, hesitance, these were not typical of her stoic math teacher.

"My foster mom has tires of about the same size. She has me keep a spare in my jeep for emergencies. I've got tools and a jack too."

Mr. Myers glanced between her and her jeep not too far off, indecision still warring behind those eyes that seemed to change color earlier that day. Perhaps the memory of that moment was what made Katey a little more reticent, but she knew she couldn't walk away without at least trying to help him. It seemed the right thing to do.

"Ya want extra credit or somethin'?"

Katey shook her head. "No. You can just give me a new tire when you can."

Her teacher took a deep breath and finally nodded. "All right. Suppose that'd be easier than waitin' for a tow truck."

They went to Katey's jeep and opened the hatch. Before she could reach for the tire, Mr. Myers seized it and hoisted it onto his shoulder. Katey's eyes went wide. She was no light weight and the tire was a heavy load for her. Mr. Myers heaved it about as if it were a feather pillow.

With a mental shake, Katey snatched up the tool box and car jack, then hurried after her teacher. He wouldn't let her give any further assistance beyond that. He did everything from lifting the car with the jack to tightening the lug nuts once the new tire was set in place with the tire iron. It seemed to take him much longer than what may have been considered normal to tighten the nuts to their max. Either there was something wrong with the lug nuts, or he was much stronger than he looked.

"Much obliged for the help," Mr. Myers muttered as he gathered up the tools.

Katey forced her lips into a thin line to keep herself from grinning at his choice of words. "No problem."

Her teacher deposited the tools into the back of her jeep and slid into the driver's seat of his car. Just as Katey's feet had carried her to Mr. Myers in the first place, they refused to retreat. Most of the trepidation that held onto her moments ago had melted away. She stood there, perhaps expecting something else from him, but she didn't know what.

Mr. Myers looked up to her with his cool brown eyes, and he seemed to wrestle with the same problem. They were both willing to linger, but the moment was far too awkward to stay. Something in her finally affirmed that Mr. Myers, like Mr. Keith and Mr. Dubose was safe. Regardless of how standoffish and grim he seemed, he could be trusted. A tiny part of her hoped that he felt the same way about her.

"You take care," Mr. Myers finally said with a nod and then closed the car door.

As if the spell released her, Katey scuttled back a few steps as the sedan rumbled to life and Mr. Myers drove out of the parking lot. Making her way to her own jeep, she watched his car until it was out of sight, and that comforted feeling of security left with him.

The party was everything Katey thought it would be. Several dozen students from the high school gathered in a clearing a quarter of a mile off the main highway. Headlights from jacked up trucks and cars blazed trails through the thick darkness, illuminating the teenagers that loitered around tailgates and danced to thumping music blaring from a pair of massive speakers. Katey stood just on the edge of the light and could smell spilled beer and cigarette smoke heavy in the air.

She stayed for maybe ten minutes, and merely looked around for faces she recognized so she could tell something of the truth to Lily the next day. If she at least gossiped about who was making out with who, that would likely satisfy her.

Back in her jeep, Katey let out a long breath. She still didn't want to go home. It was just past dinnertime, and she suspected that if Mary was home, she'd already be halfway hammered. Katey would rather wait until her foster mother was completely blacked out before sneaking in. That was hours away.

She started the jeep and made her way back to the main road, another destination in mind. Where she would go, no one would dare bother her. Katey made her way back into town and turned off onto a sparsely populated road. It wound for miles until pavement became dirt and trees closed in on either side, only her headlights cutting a path through the night.

A few miles more and she found herself at a dead end and a cemetery. It was a place she had been to a few times before, but not for the reason most visited there. This seemed the most logical place to find peace, among the departed. Her spirit felt as dead as the corpses that had been laid to rest in the ground.

The sky was clear and the moon gave enough light that allowed Katey to distinguish the outlines of the headstones in disorderly rows across the fenced-in acres. When she slipped out of her jeep, she took a deep breath of the cool, crisp night air. The earthy smell of the woods that surrounded the cemetery reminded her of how her imagination had run away with her during calculus class. This is what she had pictured and experienced in her mind, what she thought she needed. This graveyard wasn't monitored or gated, allowing anyone to visit at any time of the day or night. She wouldn't be bothered by a single soul.

As she passed through the brick pillars that marked the entrance to the cemetery, her steps slowed along the well-worn footpath that snaked around the graves. She could just barely make out the inscriptions on some of the stones. One burial plot was for a couple who had died early in their marriage, another for an infant who was born and died on the same day. Another was for a child who apparently died of cancer at the youthful age of five.

Such tragedy, such loss. Sometimes Katey wondered if she'd become insensible to it all. There might have been a time when she felt her heart ache for the deaths of these people. But now, she felt nothing and it was that nothingness that scared her the most. When had she become so numb to anything but her own suffering?

She crossed her arms over her middle as the air grew colder and a persistent breeze played in her hair. Mechanically, she found her way toward a corner of the cemetery under a shading elm. A stone bench sat in front of a particular grave of a boy who died during his eighteenth year. The engraving captured her curiosity the first time she read it. "*Good night, I love you. See you in the morning.*"

The identity of the boy, as well as the quote, were equally mysterious, but she thought it somehow fitting that she'd sit here with him on her eighteenth birthday. A piece of her wished she'd end up beneath the sod by the end of the night.

Katey let herself sink to the bench and the darkness that stood at her doorstep. Maybe now was a good time to give in, to submit and allow herself to feel the raw emotions that she'd been trying to repress for months. Months spent fighting, resisting, cutting her thighs to relieve the ache in her soul, giving a little ground only to struggle to take back what sanity she could before it drowned her. Maybe, just maybe, if she let it out here, she could fully face it and find a way to truly cope. It had to happen eventually, so why not here and now?

Her eyes drifted shut and she tilted her chin back to feel the icy wind on her face. The voices in her head came screeching through her consciousness.

You're not enough. You'll never be enough.

No one even cares about you.

You're nothing but a burden to the families that took you in.

No one loves you and no one ever will. Why would they? You're a mess.

You'll never have a real family now. You're alone. Completely alone.

The brutal emotions clenched in her chest and her eyes stung with impending tears. She let herself believe the voices, let herself relive the moments when people told her such things, perhaps not in words but in actions and decisions. Her whole life had been dictated by those who were willing to say, "We'll take her," only to be turned over or yanked away to someone else. There were no constants, no security, nothing but her and a broken existence that felt so worthless.

Strangely, as soon as the voices rang through her mind, they began to die away. Their insults and accusations melted into whispers, and then silence. The darkness receded like the ocean tide, but did not lash back with vengeance as it had sometimes. Instead, Katey felt airy, like the chains of her sadness had been lifted somehow and she could move freely.

A tiny spark of light flickered to life inside of her and the night didn't feel so hollow and cold anymore. A smile touched her lips, the first genuine smile in what seemed like an eternity. This feeling of total peace plumed and tingled through her limbs, a refreshing sensation after being bound for so long.

What happened? What changed? Did she just need to release for a mere moment to break the curse? What revived her dying soul so effectively without her conscious effort?

"Someone you knew?"

Katey gasped and spun to see the figure of a man standing not too far from the bench. She hadn't heard him walk up, nor any sound of a car pull into the parking lot. Had he been here the whole time and she didn't notice? Her heart rabbited in her chest and her body tingled with shock. The moonlight overhead shadowed out his features, leaving him little more than a silhouette in the dark.

"What?" she asked once she recovered.

The stranger gave a soft chuckle and motioned to the headstone. "Was he someone you knew?"

Katey glanced at the grave and then shook her head. Fear wanted to wrap its talons around her heart, but some force resisted it. She should have been scared. She was alone in a cemetery, her phone in her jeep, and facing a stranger that may or may not have meant her ill.

"Then, why are you just sitting here?" The stranger's voice was deep, but smooth.

"Why are you here asking me why I'm staring at his grave?" Katey felt a rush of boldness take over. "Was he someone you knew?"

The man shrugged. "No, he wasn't. I was just curious if you did."

"How long have you been standing there? I didn't even hear you walk up."

He gave another soft laugh and her body quivered at the sound, so masculine and yet calming. "Sorry, I didn't mean to frighten you."

As if watching in slow motion, Katey saw him come toward the bench and try to sit down beside her. Reflexively, she jumped from her seat and darted toward the tree, well out of reach from the stranger.

From this perspective, she could see him much more clearly and she studied his face, just in case she would need to identify him to some police sketch artist later.

His hair was black as the night sky above with thin highlights of blonde weaved through the black, as if they were completely natural. Yet, the color combination was so peculiar that it couldn't have been natural.

In the moonlight, his almond shaped eyes appeared light blue, almost gray, a striking contrast to his dark hair and tanned skin. A slender tapering strip of dark facial hair traced along his bold jaw. He was hot, and Katey's belly tightened at that realization. To have him looking straight at her like that gave her unimaginable thrills. He looked like someone off of a rock band poster, dangerous and yet undeniably attractive.

The man's smile was tainted with a hint of embarrassment. "Wow, I'm sorry. I'm being a bit forward, aren't I?"

Katey snorted. "Try creepy and forward."

As if to fix his mistake, he stood and offered out his hand. "My name's Logan. And yours?"

Pairing the outline of his silhouette to his more defined figure now, she knew he must have been well-built, like a football player. That much couldn't be concealed underneath his dark leather jacket, black shirt, and faded jeans with tears at the knees. He wore a black and blue paisley bandana around his neck, the colors matching his eyes and hair almost perfectly. No one wore stuff like that anymore unless they were trying too hard to be edgy.

"Why should I tell you?" Katey challenged.

"Because I was kind enough to tell you mine and it'd be rude to not give me your name as well."

There was an old-world character about him that she couldn't quite place and it didn't make sense with his modern style. It was in the way he smiled, the way he looked at her, his mannerisms, and vibes. There was a genuineness to his words and actions, no matter how off-putting, that made Katey feel valued for the first time in a long time.

She took a steeling breath and replied, "My name's Katey."

Logan retracted his rejected hand and she thought she caught a glimmer of recognition in his expression. "I'm assuming that's short for Katherine?"

"What would it matter?"

Logan grinned. "Boy, are you the edgy one."

Katey bristled at the accusation. "I kind of have a right to be. You just showed up out of nowhere and I'm all alone out here. For all I know, you could be a murdering rapist or something."

Logan's smile faded and she thought she saw something like disappointment. "But, I'm not."

"How can I know that?"

"If I was, I would have done something already."

He had a point. There were no witnesses, no one to put on a show for. If he wanted to do something to her, he could have snuck up on her so easily and did what he wanted. Instead, he decided to be polite and friendly.

Katey stepped forward and extended her hand to him to absolve her previous rudeness. He gave her a friendly grin and shook it firmly.

"It's a pleasure to meet you, Katey," he said.

"Yeah, you too, I guess," she replied, trying to hold in the smile that was threatening to show on her lips. Her palm tingled with an inexplicable energy long after their hands released. "So, what are you doing out here? Visiting someone?"

Logan shook his head. "No, not really. I just come here some-times to relax and get away from things. A graveyard is the perfect place to be alone, don't you think?"

That's exactly how she felt, but she wasn't about to admit it. "Except right now. Neither of us are alone."

Logan huffed a laugh. "I suppose so. Why are you out here then?"

Katey paused, wondering what she should reveal and what she shouldn't. "I just left a party and I came here instead of going home."

"Why didn't you stay at the party?"

She shrugged. "It was boring and I didn't know anyone there. They were all just dancing and drinking. Not my kind of scene."

Logan gave another deep, throaty laugh that made her insides melt. "But graveyards are?"

Katey felt flustered, somehow wanting to save her image in front of this guy she just met. "Well, no... Not really... I don't know."

"Sorry, it was just a question. Didn't mean to rile you."

Katey scrunched her shoulders together to fight off a cold gust of wind and looked away. "I guess I came here for the same reasons you did... I spend all day being around people and sometimes I just need to get away and be with myself for a change."

He nodded thoughtfully. "Well, then let's be alone together. Follow me."

Logan then turned and walked off toward the center of the cemetery. He had a peculiar walk; smooth and graceful, yet mascu-line and commanding. He stopped and looked back at Katey with an encouraging smile. "It's okay."

Katey gave in, despite her better judgment, and followed him, keeping several feet of distance between them. Logan may have seemed like a nice enough guy, but she couldn't ignore the blaring alarms in the back of her mind just yet. She didn't know him, and each reckless moment may have been bringing her closer to some tragic end. Still, something in her spirit told her that Logan would not hurt her. What exactly gave her that impression, she wasn't sure. Maybe that's why she decided to follow him. She had to know why.

She followed him to an unoccupied plot that she had passed by earlier. The space, reserved by a bed of pebbles held in by a perimeter of concrete, was just big enough for two to lay down beside one another. Logan stepped over the little concrete wall and onto the pebbles, his heavy boots crunching against the rocks with each step. Katey watched and waited as he laid himself down on the bed of stones.

He let out a contented sigh, folded his hands over his stomach, and looked at Katey with dazzling eyes. She could see that he was extremely physically fit. His waist was trim and from the way the light hit his tight, black shirt, she could see the ridges of his rock-hard abs underneath. His broad chest steadily rose and fell with each breath in a fascinating rhythm.

Katey raised an eyebrow.

"Okay, I know it looks weird and I know what you're thinking, but I'm really not the kind of guy to hurt someone. At least not on purpose..." A shadow passed over his expression, a fleeting haunted look that came and went within the same second. "But this is pretty relaxing and it's a perfect view of the sky."

It was reckless. It may have been dangerous. She shouldn't do it, and yet, Katey was drawn to Logan so enigmatically. It was a strange shift from just a few minutes before, and she didn't have the clarity of thought to refuse the urge to lay down beside him like he asked.

She joined him on the pebbles, keeping at least a foot of distance between them. The tiny rocks bit into her flesh as she gazed up at the night sky, letting it fill her vision. She'd never realized how the stars shined so much brighter out here, away from the lights of the city.

With each second that became the past, Katey's tense muscles released and she felt she could breathe easier. Katey felt, for the first time perhaps in years, at home. Combined with her earlier breakthrough of peace, she marveled at the difference between this moment and just an hour ago.

"Do you feel it yet?" Logan said softly.

"Feel what?" she asked, her voice sounding loud even in her own ears.

"That weird sensation of peace like the world is all right."

"Yeah," she replied with a grin. "How'd you know?"

"Because I feel it too."

Katey grinned at the absurdity of it. Just moments ago, she wondered if the darkness would drag her into an abyss so deep and consuming that she could never claw her way out. Now, each breath felt new, fresh, and invigorating. This stranger did what she could never do. His presence, the depths of his blue eyes, and the timbre of his voice brought her back to life somehow.

She turned her head and stared at how the moon shone bright in his eyes. "How is that even possible?" she whispered. "We don't know each other. How could we both be feeling that way?"

A gentle, disarming smile touched his lips. "I know. It's crazy, but... maybe it's best not to question it. Just enjoy it while it lasts?"

Maybe he was right. Katey let go of that mental ledge and fell willingly into the ridiculousness of the moment. "But... who are you?"

"I told you."

"No, I mean... I've never seen you around school before. Or do you go to the community college?"

His lips parted, but the answer came slowly and gracelessly. "I've been homeschooled, but I'll be attending public school next semester."

Katey gave an amused huff. "You look so much older than most of the seniors I know."

Logan gestured toward his unique pattern of facial hair. "Must be the beard."

She smirked. "Maybe." Her gaze lingered and Katey hoped that he assumed she was only searching for another explanation for his mature looks.

"You go to the high school?" he asked.

"I do. I'm a senior."

"Almost free then, huh?"

Katey looked back to the night sky, the voices echoing at the reminder. Now harmless, their words didn't have the same impact as before. "Maybe." The reply came out so softly, but Katey didn't mean to be so candid.

"What's that supposed to mean?"

Katey crossed her ankles and shifted as if she were uncomfortable in this conversation. "I guess it depends on your definition of freedom."

Silence stretched between them. She hadn't expected him to answer so she flinched a little when he did.

"Freedom is the chance to go where you want, do what you want without having to answer to anyone. No one watching and waiting for you to slip up. No one telling you what you can or can't do."

There was a sharpness I'm his speech, as if he knew all too well how terrible an utter lack of freedom could be. A quick glance revealed a bitterness flashing in his eyes.

"I don't know if anyone is that free."

Logan met her thoughtful gaze with one of his own, waiting for an explanation.

"Everyone is accountable to someone," she said. "If nothing else, we're accountable to ourselves... but in the end, I think there's always going to be someone or something keeping us from doing everything we want... My whole life, people have made decisions for me. I thought today, of all days, I'd feel the kind of freedom you're talking about... Instead, I don't feel free at all."

Logan peered at her. "Why today?"

Katey hoped she wouldn't have to divulge so much, but it came pouring out anyway. "I turned eighteen today and I'm... I'm a foster kid, so it's supposed to be a big deal. A bigger deal than for any other eighteen-year-old."

"Why?"

She was a little surprised at the absence of pity on his part. Whenever she told people she was a foster kid, their immediate reaction was often one of sympathy and sayings like, "Oh, that must be so hard" or "I'm so sorry to hear that." It was refreshing not to hear it from Logan.

"Once a foster kid turns eighteen, they age out of the system. My foster mom won't get any benefits for taking care of me and I won't be eligible for any either. I'm totally on my own. Most foster kids get to wait until they graduate before they're kicked out. Some are on the streets or at the mercy of a friend's family a lot sooner than that. There are organizations and programs to help with the transition, but most don't take the help. Too jaded by the system to even ask for help."

"Will you get help?"

Katey looked away to the twinkling stars above. "I don't know... I do know that it'll be hard once my foster mom kicks me out. That may be next spring or it may be next week, knowing her. I won't have her or some social worker telling me what to do. It'll be just me against the world, I guess, but... that much freedom is a little overwhelming to think about right now."

Only the sound of wind rattling pine forest followed her confession. She hadn't told anyone how she really felt about aging out. Not even to herself. The calm that Logan gave her went beyond her spirit and permeated her mind. Everything seemed a little clearer with him lying next to her.

"I hope that whatever you decide, you make the best choice for you and what you want your life to look like."

Katey allowed herself a small smile. "Oh, I can guarantee that much." She turned her head and the concentrated look in Logan's eyes made her breath catch in her throat. It took her a second too long to recover. "So, have you heard about that meteor shower that's supposed to show up tonight?"

Logan stammered, as if he, too, had to recover from some trance. "Yeah, my... my friend told me about it. He said it would show up close to midnight." He pulled out his phone and hit the power button to illuminate the screen. The features she had seen only by moonlight became more defined and stunning by the bluelight of his phone. "It won't show up for a few more hours."

Katey caught a glimpse of his lockscreen photo. It looked like a pencil sketch of some animal, maybe a big dog or a wolf. When he slid the phone back into his pocket, her eyes needed a few seconds to adjust to the darkness again. She hadn't realized just how little light there was in the cemetery.

"Did you plan on staying out until it came or was this supposed to be a quick stroll amongst the graves?" Katey meant it to be funny but couldn't keep the sarcasm out of her tone.

"I wasn't sure how long I'd be out here. Were you going to wait for the meteor shower?"

"Maybe. That'd be a long time to lay here, though, and it's getting cold."

Without even asking, Logan sat up and shrugged off his leather jacket to hand to her. "Would this help?"

Katey didn't move at first. The way his arm muscles filled out his sleeves and how the moonlight caressed the strong curve of his shoulders distracted her. When she did sit up and slip into the jacket, his scent and warmth enveloped her, making her a little dizzy with feelings she could hardly make sense of.

"Won't you get cold?" she asked, jerking her chin to his bare forearms.

"Nah. I don't get cold easily."

They laid back down, Katey now toasty warm in his jacket. Yep, this had never happened to her before and likely would never again.

Logan groaned. "Damn, I'm so rude. Happy birthday, Katey. Sorry I didn't say that sooner."

She burst out into a laugh, the loudest laugh she had in what seemed like ages. "It's okay. You're not very good at conversation, are you?"

"Apparently not. I don't talk to many people outside of my pa... outside of my family."

She wondered if it had anything to do with being a home-schooler. She had heard some of those kids were a little on the awkward side. Not all, but certainly enough to create a stigma.

"You said you'd be enrolling at the high school next semester. I assume for senior year?"

It took Logan a moment to catch up with what she said. "Yeah."

"What made you decide to do that so late? Why not just finish up with homeschooling?"

Logan's throat worked, as if unsure how to answer. "Just bored, I guess. My... family was hesitant about it at first, but I managed to convince them."

"Why would they be hesitant? It's just school. Unless they're the ultra-conservative type?"

Logan smirked. "I guess you could say that... but I think it's more that they weren't sure how I would handle myself in public school."

Katey's eyes narrowed. "They don't trust you?"

A dark emotion sparked in his face before he willed it away. "You could say that too."

If Katey didn't know any better, she might have thought Logan had a mask of his own. While her mask concealed sadness, his covered a hot rage, and that rage was targeted toward his family. She burned with curiosity for the story that laid behind such anger, but it wasn't her place to pry on such a delicate subject, even though she had overshared already.

She gave him an empathetic look. "I think you'll be just fine. It's not as dramatic as the TV shows make it seem. If you want any help finding your way around, come find me. I've been there for four years and know all the good hiding spots where the hall monitors won't look."

After she said it, she realized how insinuating that was. By the appreciative nod, he seemed to not register how her offer could have been taken any other way. "I'd like that."

Heat crept into Katey's cheeks and spilled down her neck. She looked away and hoped he didn't notice her blush.

A moment passed and Katey brought the back of her hand to her mouth to hide a massive yawn.

"Getting tired?"

She rubbed the moisture from her eyes that always seemed to come whenever she yawned. "Looks like it. It's been a long day." The emotional and mental strain of dealing with the darkness and keeping her mask in place always drained her, but this day had been especially tiring.

"You can nod off if you want. I'll wake you when the meteor shower starts."

"I thought you weren't planning to stay for that?"

She heard the grind of pebbles beneath Logan's body as he shifted. "I don't mind staying. I have nothing better to do."

"You won't get in trouble with your parents?"

"They can wait."

She passed him a dubious look. It wasn't a real answer, but she wouldn't press him.

"Your foster mom won't wonder where you are?"

Katey snorted. "I doubt she even cares where I am right now." Before Logan could probe further, she asked, "Promise you won't do anything?"

Logan's face morphed with confusion. "What would I do?"

Katey turned sheepish. "You know... I'd be asleep and..."

Logan's eyes widened. "Oh, God. No! I thought I'd just make sure you wouldn't miss the meteor shower or end up sleeping out here all night. I swear I'd never do something like that."

A bit of shame colored Katey's face. She should have known that he wouldn't, but distrust was a hard beast to shake off. As Logan said before, if he was going to do anything, he would have done it to her already.

"I promise, you are completely safe here with me," he said. "I won't leave before you wake up." His voice was warm with sincerity, enough to make Katey believe him.

She closed her eyes and inhaled deeply. She drifted through the dark, her senses sharpening to the world around her. The hissing December wind in the trees, aroma of the pine forest and cemetery grass, and Logan's calming presence seemed the sweetest lullaby to lull her quickly to sleep.

Time passed in a dreamer's blur before Katey felt Logan gently pat the back of his hand against her elbow. His tender whisper pulled her back to the land of wakefulness.

"Katey... Look."

She opened her eyes just as slivers of light careened across the night sky. Their tails left long trails of stardust behind them, burning white hot against velvety black.

Through the thin fog of grogginess Katey grinned at the cascade of shooting stars. For several long moments, they flitted in and out of the atmosphere, like a passing stampede of horses. Katey's heart skipped with thrills. All at once, she relived a totally unfamiliar feeling that only came a few times in her teenage years. Watching the meteor shower with Logan, she felt happy. Pure happiness. What a change had come over her that night. The darkness gone, her mask unneeded even in front of a stranger, and feeling not so alone anymore, a tiny shard of hope for the future pierced her soul. Maybe aging out wouldn't be so terrifying.

Katey didn't really believe in a higher power or anything so metaphysical, but something like a miracle took place that night and she wouldn't question it, lest it slip through her hands like sand through a sieve. She wanted to hold onto this bit of magic forever.

"It's beautiful," She breathed.

When she looked to her side to ask if Logan thought so too, ice water flooded her veins. He wasn't there. The impression of his body in the pebbles was still clearly visible, but Logan was gone.

Katey bolted upright and frantically searched for him, but she was alone in the cemetery again. She called out his name, her voice echoing in the emptiness. No reply.

Through sheer force of will, Katey leapt to her feet and darted in a number of directions, desperate eyes combing the moonlit cemetery for any sign of him. Not one. He couldn't have gone far within the minute or two since he woke her up. Why didn't she hear him leave? It would be impossible not to make some sort of noise on the bed of rocks. For a second, Katey called her own sanity into question. Surely, she hadn't just been visited by some ghost?

Her breaths came quick and panicked, all happiness disappearing like a puff of smoke in a windstorm. Of equal concern to his sudden disappearance, was the fear that the miracle would evaporate and leave her just as broken as before with him not around. Like testing a new bruise, Katey checked herself. As far as she could tell, the darkness hadn't returned and she forced herself to calm again.

With no reason to stay, Katey timidly made her way to her jeep, constantly looking around and over her shoulder for Logan. The only proof that he really existed and was not a figment of her imagination, was the leather jacket that swallowed Katey in his delicious scent.

CHAPTER 3

Katey parked alongside Mary's beat up Toyota in the driveway. It was well past midnight, but she had no missed calls, voicemails, or texts from her foster mother. Mary clearly hadn't tried very hard to reach her, so she didn't expect her to ask questions. With luck, Katey could slip into her room without being noticed. Mary would be gone in the morning, on a flight to visit her long distance boyfriend in Ohio for a couple of weeks to celebrate an early Christmas with him and his family. Katey would have the house to herself and maybe it wouldn't feel so much like a prison in Mary's absence.

When she entered through the garage-to-house door into the kitchen, her muscles tensed. The television was on a cooking channel, the only source of light in the house. She spotted Mary's outstretched legs and a dangling arm, as she sat in her usual recliner. Katey waited for any sign of movement. Not a word or a twitch. Mary must be asleep.

With an easy, quiet gait, Katey crossed through the kitchen and living room, careful not to disturb the piece of trash on the floor or accidentally bump into any furniture along the way. She cast a glance toward Mary and confirmed that she was asleep. Her foster mother's head lulled to the side, mouth hanging open. In the hand she hadn't seen before, was a half empty wine bottle.

Katey turned away and hastened her steps toward her room.

"Where have you been?"

The hairs rose on the back of her neck and her stomach churned at the sound of Mary's scratchy voice that had become hoarse through years of chain-smoking.

She slowly turned on the balls of her feet and locked stares with Mary. Had the woman only been pretending to be asleep? Despite her bloodshot eyes, she seemed scarily lucid and awake.

Thinking on her feet, Katey replied, "Me, Lily, and Beth got something to eat and went to a movie." Through a few years of practice, Katey learned to keep her tone level when answering these sorts of interrogative questions, whether from foster parents or the endless procession of social workers that came in and out of her life.

"What did you eat?" Mary's voice was cold and clipped short, and Katey wondered if she was still drunk at all. That would have been unusual.

"We just got some burgers."

"Whose jacket is that? I haven't seen it before."

Katey had completely forgotten about Logan's jacket. "It's Lily's brother's jacket. He joined us at the movies and offered it to me when I got cold."

"What movie did you see?"

Katey wasn't up to date on any of the new releases in theaters, but she knew Mary wasn't either. The few seconds it took her to think of another lie gave her away.

"You're lying. Where have you really been?"

"I told you already. I was at the movies with my friends." Katey heard her voice rise in defense and knew this wouldn't end well.

"Then what movie did you see?"

"I can't remember the name of it. Lily picked it out. Some cheesy romance. I wasn't paying attention for most of it."

Mary's steely eyes narrowed as the television cast flashes of color across her ashen face. "Why didn't you tell me where you were?"

Katey crossed her arms. "Why didn't you try to figure out where I was? Doesn't seem like you cared."

"What if a social worker came by to see you and you weren't here? I know what day it is."

"Yeah, the day you stop getting those nice checks in the mail to help you pay for your booze."

Mary stormed to her feet and stalked toward her. "How dare you talk to me like that! I didn't have to take you in. I didn't have to put up with your shitty attitude for the last two years. I could have let you stay in that group home. I took you in out of the kindness of my heart and—"

"Oh, please," Katey snorted. "No one is here for you to impress. We both know you're only taking care of foster kids for the money and the tax breaks."

Not wholly unexpected, Katey saw Mary's hand fly at her, landing squarely on her cheek. Her skin stung, flesh gone numb under the impact. She'd been hit harder before. Maybe Mary was still a little drunk.

"Keep this up and I won't wait for you to graduate." Mary's threat came in a fierce, ominous whisper as if she were trying to keep her voice down for the sake of the neighbors. "I'll order you out of this house by the end of the year. Do you hear me?"

Katey touched her cheek with her fingertips. She weighed her options. Keep up the fight or back down to fight another day. The fire in her chest roared against rational thought. She needed a roof over her head for just a few more months, then she could be rid of Mary. But, oh, how she wanted to throw every insult at this woman's face, lay to bare all the hateful words Katey had bottled up for months, too scared to say them aloud in case Mary would make good on that threat. She couldn't afford to call her bluff now. Not yet.

"Yes, ma'am."

Mary's nostrils flared at the potent disdain in Katey's answer. "Good. Now, go to your room. My flight leaves in the morning. I've left a list of chores for you to get done before I get back."

Glancing around the darkened living room, Katey suspected Mary would want her to do a deep cleaning of the whole house while she was gone. Mary turned, swiped the remote off the coffee table and turned the television off, plunging the house into total darkness. Katey grabbed her chance and hurried to her room.

She pulled out one of her smaller duffle bags, one that a previous foster parent had given her upon her departure from their home and began stuffing it with what she'd need for work the following day. There was no way she wanted to be there in the morning to see Mary off. It was likely her foster mother would want a ride to the airport or use Katey as a verbal punching bag for all her problems and complaints like she usually did. After that night, she seriously contemplated the benefits of leaving Mary's home by the end of the year. Enough was enough. She'd wait maybe half an hour to make sure Mary was really asleep this time, and then make her escape.

So, that was the Katey the guys always talked about. Logan had never met her, but he knew plenty about her before they ever locked gazes. Her confession about being a foster kid and the fact that today was her birthday were no surprises. He also knew, from the bits of conversation before he left to roam, that she did not have the best of days. Everything else was new and captivating. The light behind her emerald green eyes called to him and his wolf, begging him to stay when common sense told him to run.

Being in Katey's presence was like coming up from a dark, murky ocean for air, bursting from the surface to take greedy gasps before he was dragged under again. Only, after spending time with her, Logan found it easier to tread the waters. It had been ages since he felt this strong, this solid and sure of himself again. He had to know her more, to bask in her essence without constraints or restrictions.

All the way from the cemetery to the long driveway leading up to their home, Logan concocted a plan to achieve just that.

His motorcycle rumbled down the mile-long dirt path that cut through the dense forest of their expansive property. He knew the erratic pattern of potholes and dips in the ground so well that he didn't need his headlight to find his way in the dark.

Ahead, the drive opened on a cleared lot, two acres squared. In the center was their two-story home with a large, attached carport. He counted three vehicles; Darren's white car, Dustin's red truck, and Ben's silver sedan with a fourth tire that didn't match the other three. Light streamed through the downstairs windows. Inside, they quietly waited for him. They were likely to have heard him turn off the highway onto their unmarked driveway, despite the distance.

Logan circled around to his usual spot at the head of the cars so as not to block them in and cut off the engine. Hardening himself to the conflict to come, Logan entered the house through the back door by the carport. He kept his strides even and relaxed through the darkened billiard room and down the hall to the kitchen. If he turned left, he could slink his way up the stairs from the living room. If he kept walking ahead, he'd pass through saloon doors that connected to the formal dining room and sitting room where his pack waited.

A moment of indecision proved a mistake.

"Come here, Logan." Darren's stern voice, flavored by his British accent, grated in his ears.

He sighed and obeyed his alpha.

Darren sat at the head of the dining table, his laptop closed in front of him next to a stack of graded assignments. Brown eyes stared disapproving beneath dark brows, incongruous to his leisure posture in his chair. In the adjoining sitting room, Dustin sat on a loveseat, elbows on his knees, his looks a note less severe. He may be the pack beta, but he didn't constantly wear that role, only pulling on his dominance when it was necessary. Ben was the one that gave him no mind, but only because the Georgian lay asleep on the opposite matching sofa, fingers laced over his stomach and head rolled to the side on a propped-up pillow.

"I told you not to wait up," Logan said, crossing his arms over his chest as if that would assert that he was in the right.

"We still expect the courtesy of a text," Darren chided. "That's why we gave you a cellphone."

Logan shrugged. "I lost track of time."

"Where's your jacket?" Dustin asked from the sofa, one brow cocked in bemusement.

Logan hadn't thought of an excuse for that. He knew he needed to leave Katey quickly, not one for simple goodbyes, but he couldn't very well ask for his jacket back.

The uptick in his heart rate gave him away.

"What happened?" his alpha demanded.

Logan's wolf bristled with agitation before he had the chance to censor his response. "What's with the damn third degree? I've been out this late before."

His packmates were not disturbed by his sudden burst of aggression. Over the years, the decades, they were used to it from Logan.

"This is not an interrogation," Darren answered coolly. "We're only concerned."

Logan's hands balled into fists as he breathed deep through his flared nostrils. He took a moment to settle down and to come up with a lie. Once he knew he could speak without growling, he said, "I went to the club and fought a few rounds. I left my jacket in the locker room."

He kept his heart rate steady this time, knowing they could sense such things if he wasn't careful. A few beats passed and he met their gazes as if in challenge.

The slight drop of Darren's shoulders told him they must have accepted his excuse. But he wasn't out of hot water yet. It wouldn't have been an unusual thing for Logan to pass time at the fight club. They knew he needed to blow off steam somehow and though it wasn't conventional or safe, it was all he had, unlike them.

"Were you careful?" Darren asked.

"Of course."

"Win anything?" Dustin's inquiry held a tone of suppressed enthusiasm. Out of the three, he took the greatest interest in Logan's fighting hobby. They even shared some moves in the past. Dustin participated in, and started, his fair share of fights in his days wandering Europe before he was brought into the pack.

"Some." Logan turned to his alpha and straightened, ready to change the subject to something more urgent. "Can I make a request?"

Darren's stony expression softened with intrigue. "Though I hardly think you're in a position to make requests right now, what is it?"

"I know we agreed I could give school a try next fall, but can I enroll sooner?"

The ripple of suspicion across their faces warned Logan that he treaded into dangerous territory.

"How soon?"

The follow-up gave him hope. In other situations, Darren might have shut him down without further discussion. "Monday."

Mild curiosity exploded into open shock.

"Monday?" Dustin exclaimed loud enough to rouse Ben from his sleep. He jerked and peered at his pack with amber, wolfish eyes, face twisted with repressed annoyance.

"Why so soon?" Darren asked.

Again, Logan shrugged. "Call it a trial run. Wouldn't it be easier to cut out after a few weeks or a couple of months in the middle of the semester rather than stick it out for a full school year if it's not going well?"

He wasn't sure of the soundness of his logic. Darren was more knowledgeable of such things, and they hadn't discussed this option. The original plan had been to let Logan try a year as a senior in public school and then let him carry onto college if he proved himself. That was what they had agreed on and what would have been more convenient for everyone. Everyone, except for Logan, given the new circumstances.

"You can do that just as easily as if you started at the beginning of the school year." Darren shook his head. "Besides, it's not a simple matter of walking into the school and signing a few papers. There are protocols in place, documentation needs to be processed. If you're going to continue with the story that you are a homeschooler, then we have to fabricate eleven years' worth of assessments and—"

"Weren't you going to get someone to do that anyway?" Logan interrupted, too impatient to wait for the end of his lecture.

Darren sighed and rubbed his face. "Yes, but that isn't something they can do overnight."

By that time, Dustin had joined them at the table, hands gripping the back of one of the chairs as he studied Logan.

"Just tell him it's a rush job," Logan offered. "I'm sure he's had to do them in the past."

Darren glared. "Yes. For those who have suffered a tragedy and have to go into hiding quickly. Not for those who simply changed their minds about how soon they want to enroll in school. Do you think your request is more important?"

The embers of rebellion in his chest flared into a hot flame. His fists tightened, nails biting into his palm.

Before he could act on the building rage, Dustin asked, "What's going on, kid?"

The beta became a new target for his wrath. "Nothing's going on! I stay cooped up in this fucking house all day while you three are off playing human and I'm bored, okay? It was easier with at least one of you home, but now all three of you work."

Darren raised his voice. "Then we can find you a job until next year, if you're so bored."

"Oh, no," Logan sassed, donning his best, exaggerated impression of his alpha. "We can't have you working, Logan. You're much too volatile. You may wolf out on aisle nine at some grocery store and kill half of the town!"

Darren slammed his hands on the tabletop and stood to his full height. "Enough, Logan!" he bellowed. "Continue with this ridiculous tirade and you won't enroll at all."

Like a dam had burst, dominance flooded the room. The force of his alpha's will crashed into Logan, wrapping around his throat and chest to bring him into submission. To his shame, his knees began to shake and jaw clenched against the powerful energy. If he had his tail out, it would have been tucked between his legs.

"Let him enroll, Darren."

Ben's voice in the storm was unexpected and all eyes turned to him on the sofa. He was in the same relaxed pose, legs stretched out over the cushions.

"He can have classes with us in the morning. Don't put him in any electives and throw him into an English class with Bobby Kimbrough's wife. She knows Logan by association and knows what to look for if something goes south. We can get the paperwork goin' and in the meantime, his assignments don't have to count for nothin'. We can make it official for next semester if he likes the next few weeks."

"You're suggesting Logan attend classes... off the books?" Dustin asked, just as nonplussed as the rest of them.

Ben nodded. "Sure."

Logan never expected Ben to go to bat for him like this. He held no rank or authority against Darren besides what personal loyalty and esteem afforded him. In situations like this, it was more likely that Dustin would stick up for him, given their close relation.

Perhaps out of surprise for Ben's entrance into the conversation, or because of his logic, Darren seemed to think seriously about the idea. The alpha's dominance drained from the air, letting Logan take a full breath again. He said nothing, lest a mis-timed word trigger Darren into a new invective.

The room was quiet for several long moments as they waited for Darren's final verdict.

"Fine. I'll make a few calls to get the process started." Darren held up a cautionary finger to Logan. "You attend classes at my discretion. Do you understand?"

Logan knew that all too well. Everything was at his alpha's discretion, and it had been that way nearly all his life. Darren must have thought it would make Logan grateful for every scrap of privilege thrown to him. It only made him resentful for the unfair hand he had been dealt since his birth. The little speech he gave to Katey about freedom was born from years of experience as a prisoner in body and soul. But perhaps, if he could find a way to attach himself to Katey, that would change.

He only nodded to his alpha in acknowledgment. Darren sat back in his seat, Ben pushed himself from the sofa to leave the room, and Dustin moved toward the kitchen door.

As Dustin passed by Logan, the beta lifted his hand to smack him on the shoulder in a sign of good will, but something stayed the gesture. Dustin ducked his head and took a deep whiff, and then chuckled as if he finally understood the punchline of an unspoken joke.

"What is it?" Darren asked as he opened his laptop.

Dustin waved him off and patted Logan's shoulder. "I'll tell you later. Come on, Logan. I saved you a steak from dinner."

Did he smell Katey on him and suspect the truth? Logan thought the ride home would have erased every trace of the girl. Then again, Dustin was a good tracker. Perhaps he hadn't been careful enough. With luck, Dustin wouldn't tell Darren too much and ruin his scheme.

A heavy tapping against her car window jolted Katey out of her fitful sleep. For a moment, her head throbbed with the unexpected wakeup call.

"Katey?"

The deep, familiar male voice sounded muffled from outside her car. Eyes squeezed against the late morning light that streamed unchecked through the glass, Katey's hand absently felt for her phone on the backseat floorboards.

Last night, after Mary was completely unconscious, Katey snuck out of the house and drove to downtown Crestucky. Just around the corner from the ballroom dance studio on historic Main Street seemed the best place to park for the night, knowing that few cars ever wandered down the lamp-lit streets after ten o'clock in the evening. Prepared with a blanket and pillow, Katey had curled up in the backseat of her jeep and tried to catch what little rest she could before she had to be at work.

Groggy with sleep, she squinted at the time on her phone. She had just ten minutes to clock in for the day, but her first scheduled lesson wouldn't be for another hour.

The firm knock on her window startled her again and she lifted her head just enough to see Forrest's icy blue eyes staring back at her beneath pale brows. Sunlight made his shock of red hair all the more fiery. He gave her an expectant look and took a step back so she had enough room to open the door for him.

With stiff, aching movements, Katey pushed herself up just enough to reach the handle and swing the door outward, but she remained sprawled awkwardly across the seats.

"Did you sleep here all night?"

Katey only nodded, aware that her brown hair must have looked like a mass of tangles. It wasn't the first time she had slept in her jeep, but it was the worst in a long while.

"Dare I ask why?"

This time, Katey shook her head. She didn't want to form words into sentences before downing a good cup of coffee from the café down the road.

"Do you... need help?"

Katey was vaguely aware that Forrest had edged closer as if to peer past her into her jeep. He'd see her overnight bag, empty take-out bags, her backpack, and Logan's jacket. Nothing condemning, but Katey aimlessly swatted in his direction to keep him back.

"No. I'm fine," she grumbled.

"Clearly, since you chose to sleep in a cramped jeep all night instead of a warm bed." Katey liked Forrest's wit, but not this early in the morning when she ran on just a few hours of sleep. "Anything you want to talk about?"

She let out a breathy sigh. "Get me coffee and I might."

Forrest chuckled. "Fair enough. The usual?"

She nodded, turning her face into her pillow.

"Should I close the door?"

"No," Katey groaned. "I'm getting up."

"You sure you don't want five more minutes?"

"No, mother."

Forrest laughed again and the morning light and air swept in to fill the void his body left when he walked away. If Forrest was around, it was likely that Lily was too. Those two were inseparable outside of school. Forrest graduated years ago, and Katey couldn't count the number of times older people had accused him of robbing the cradle when he began to date Lily in her freshman year and he was much older. Some said he was only after Lily for a good time, but the constancy of their love for one another proved them all wrong.

Forrest had been instrumental in helping both Katey and Lily get their part-time jobs at the ballroom dance studio. As an instructor himself and close friends with the owners, he was able to put in a good word that convinced the manager to hire them. He was a valuable friend and the absolute best thing for Lily. Though total opposites, they balanced one another in temperament and personality. Forrest knew how to check Lily's mood swings and keep her down to earth, while she livened up his world with her infectious smile and vest for adventure. Katey could only hope that she'd find a guy like that one day.

That thought had her blindly reaching for Logan's jacket. She took a moment to breathe in his scent, her nose buried in the collar that would have brushed the nap of his neck. She let herself smile at the pleasant memory of the night before when they lay under the stars. It was like something out of a cheesy chick-flick, but his mysterious disappearance was something out of a horror movie. Still, she couldn't regret the effects of the night. Katey had never felt more alive and ready to face the future. She had no explanation for it, but something in her heart knew that the change was all Logan's doing. Even if she never saw him again, she could be grateful for what he did for her.

A little more awake, Katey made some attempt to straighten out her hair and clothes, grabbed her bag, tossed Logan's jacket over her arm, and made her way to the studio not a block away. Inside, Lily stood at the podium on the other side of the open dancefloor, laptop open and likely preparing a playlist of songs for that day's lessons.

Lily's hair was pulled back into a smooth, high ponytail, waves of golden blonde falling behind her. Always stylish, Lily dressed in a loose-fitted, flowery blouse, tasteful and stretchy slacks, and a pair of simple high heels. Blue eyes lifted and lit up when they landed on Katey.

"Katey, you look terrible!" Lily abandoned the podium and hurried to meet her halfway across the studio, her heels thudding loudly against the hardwood floors.

"Good morning to you, too."

She endured Lily's welcoming hug and they continued toward the back where Katey could change in the single-toilet bathroom.

"Did you go to the party last night like you promised?"

"I did, but not for long." Katey wondered how much she would tell Lily before Forrest showed up with her coffee.

"Oh, come on! Was it that bad?"

Katey entered the bathroom and Lily waited outside. "You know I hate parties like that. How long did you think I was going to stay?"

"I don't know. Long enough to maybe meet someone?"

The insinuating lilt in her words tipped Katey off to Lily's possible true motives for making her go. "I did meet someone, but not at the party."

Lily's audible gasp from the other side of the door amused her. "Oh, my god! Where? Who was it? Anyone I'd know? What happened? Is that why you look like you slept in her car or something?"

Clearly Forrest hadn't told Lily that he had found Katey in her jeep before leaving for the café.

"I'll give you all the details when Forrest comes back with my coffee."

Instead of giving her a moment's peace, Lily went on to tell her about the day before and why she hadn't been at school. As Katey shed yesterday's outfit and donned her work clothes, she could have sworn the speech sounded a little rehearsed and rushed, but thought little of it. She combed out her hair and touched up her makeup before exiting the bathroom to rejoin Lily.

"Believe me," Lily said, "I would have much rather been with you at that party."

Right about then, the front door opened and they turned the corner to see Forrest carrying a takeout drink tray with three to-go cups. One was her iced mocha, the other likely his herbal tea, and a hot coffee with five sugars for Lily.

She hadn't gotten a good look at Forrest earlier, but now noticed he wore a pair of black slacks to match Lily's and a button-down shirt that matched his eyes almost perfectly. With the top buttons undone, he looked more at home on the cover of a modeling magazine than in a small-town dance studio. Guys with a body like his were more graceful in a gym than on the dance floor, but Forrest had a natural grace about him that surprised many.

"Did you know Katey met a guy last night!"

Forrest's gaze shifted from his girlfriend to Katey, then to the leather jacket draped over her arm. A faint trace of confusion touched his expression, but was smoothed away before smiling at the girls. "Really? Do tell."

They met at one of the round tables toward the front window of the studio and Katey took a moment to check herself in the floor-to-ceiling mirror that covered one of the walls on the dance floor.

"Do you want to hear why I was sleeping in my car, or about meeting a guy?" Katey slung her bag on the ground, but wouldn't surrender Logan's jacket just yet.

"You slept in your car?" Lily screeched. "So, I was halfway right?"

Katey coyly shrugged and sipped her mocha, savoring the flavor of the extra shot of espresso.

Forrest leaned back in his chair next to Lily and hung his arm over her shoulders. "Why don't you start at the beginning and work your way forward?"

So, she did. Katey began her story when she left the party and concluded with the fight between her and Mary. Lily's mouth hung open by the end and Forrest's eyes were locked on Logan's jacket, deep in some concentrated thought.

"Which leads me to something I wanted to ask you, Lily." Katey took one more sip, her mocha almost gone. "Do you think your parents would let me stay with y'all until the end of the school year? I can't pay rent or anything. My paycheck from here goes straight to gas and insurance for my jeep, but I'll probably start looking for another part-time job in the evenings after school. Maybe at a fast food place."

That shocked them both even more than her fantastical tale of disappearing hotties in a cemetery.

Lily stammered for a moment before finally shaking her head. "I don't know. We have a spare guest room, but I don't know what my dad would think about it. My mom likes you enough, so she'd probably be okay with it."

"Can you ask and get an answer for me pretty soon? Mary comes back in a couple of weeks and I want to be gone by then."

Forrest sat forward. "Don't you think you're moving a little fast on this, Katey? It was just one fight. Why bug out now when there's only one semester left?"

Katey squared her shoulders. "I've already made up my mind. I'm sick of living with that bitch and I'm tired of the abuse. I want to start the rest of my life better than where I am right now."

Somewhere between Logan's arrival into her life and the moment Mary slapped her, she had found a new sense of courage and renewed determination to actually give a damn about what happened to her. The darkness was gone for the moment, so now was the time to make the right decisions, not months down the road when things could fall apart again. She had to lay the groundwork for the kind of future she wanted, not what she could settle for.

Lily and Forrest looked to one another and they mutely communicated as only long-term lovers could.

"If Lily's parents have a problem with taking you in, I'll see if any of my friends might be able to give you a place to stay." Forrest didn't seem wholly confident in the scheme, but she could appreciate his willingness to help.

She gave them both grateful smiles. "Thanks, guys."

"Are you absolutely sure you want to do this?" Lily asked.

Katey's lips faltered for only a second. "You're making it sound like I'm planning to commit a crime or something. I'm eighteen. I can make my own choices now."

"Yes, you can make your own choices," Forrest replied, "but we just want to make sure you've thought all of this through. This is a big step. Neither of us want you staying with Mary, especially after what she did, but setting out on your own is a big deal."

Always the voice of reason, it seemed unfair that Forrest had accumulated so much wisdom for a guy that was just barely into his twenties.

"I've thought this through," Katey affirmed. "And whatever happens, I'll take the consequences. Good or bad."

Lily stood to give her another hug, this one tighter and longer than the one before. Forrest slipped once more into some consuming train of thought, but said nothing. If nothing else, Katey took heart in the knowledge that she had friends willing to catch her if she failed miserably. There was bound to be someone in this town that would take her in, whether it was Lily's family or someone in Forrest's rather wide circle of connections. She'd find another temporary home, but unlike before, it'd be with someone she might be able to trust, at least for a little while.

CHAPTER 4

L ogan lay across the living room sofa, arms folded and ankles crossed. Fully dressed, he had succumbed to a short nap after his early breakfast. For the first time in recent history, Logan had risen that Monday morning long before his packmates. Any other day, he might have slept for hours after they left for work. Today, he couldn't have slept in if he tried, too excited for the promise of what the day would bring.

He stirred at the first footfalls of his packmates above his head in their bedrooms. Absent-mindedly, he tracked their progress across the second floor as they independently readied for work.

After so many years, he could distinguish one gait from the other. Darren moved like a true alpha, his steps sure and steady, opening and closing drawers with routine efficiency. Dustin shuffled from bedroom to bathroom and back again, sleep weighing down his feet. Ben, disturbingly enough, walked the softest of the three, barely making a sound across the floor. He heard their muttered remarks as they passed one another in the hall and did not open his eyes when Dustin descended the stairs, feet dropping heavily on the treads.

"Well, look who's up early," Dustin teased. "It's almost like you're eager to go to school."

Logan flicked his middle finger at the beta. Dustin laughed at their inside joke. Over the course of the weekend, it became clear through his snide comments that Dustin may have suspected Logan's real reason for wanting to enroll in school so early. As far as he knew, they were the only two who knew, and their alpha was still oblivious.

As if summoned by thought, Darren was the next to come downstairs as Dustin continued into the kitchen.

The alpha regarded him curiously. "How long have you been down here?"

Logan checked the clock on the wall. "About an hour."

Darren jerked his chin in surprise. "Breakfast?"

"Eaten."

"Lunch?"

"Packed in the fridge."

"Your supplies?"

Logan reached down and lifted a battered backpack from the floor next to the sofa. The thousands of scents it had collected from their many summer trips to Europe had faded, but the scars of overuse were permanent. He had no textbooks yet, but threw in a handful of pens and pencils, and a couple of spiral notebooks.

Darren nodded his approval. "Very good." He propped his hands on his hips. "Your classes will be with other seniors so that should minimize any suspicion. You will have first period with me, second with Mrs. Kimbrough—"

"Third with Dustin and fourth with Ben. I know. You gave me a mock schedule and map already."

Darren did not reprove Logan's attitude. "That's another thing. You'll address us by our last names as any other student."

Ben passed behind their alpha on his way to the kitchen. "That'll take some gettin' used to."

In the kitchen, Dustin began to prepare their breakfast of pan-seared sausages, bacon, and eggs. Three glasses of water had been poured and set on the glass dinette table in the windowed nook to the right of the kitchen. Logan could watch them across the bar counter that separated the kitchen from the living room.

"You'll meet us in my classroom for your lunch period," Darren continued, "and then come straight home."

Logan had other ideas, but gave him the thumbs up in agreement after dropping his bag.

"I want you to walk the campus and familiarize yourself with all the exits before the first bell of the day. Take some hunger pills with you just in case your breakfast wears off before lunchtime. Third period is my planning period so if you need anything, Dustin can dismiss you to come to me, but don't hesitate to leave if you suspect—"

"Darren, I'm not a five-year-old."

"Could have fooled me," Dustin wise-cracked from the stovetop. Ben snickered and a low warning growl rumbled in Logan's throat.

Darren sighed and went to join his pack in the kitchen. "Just use your common sense and keep your head down."

"I promise not to eat anyone," Logan answered with a sneer.

"You'll do just fine, Logan," Ben said from the counter. "It'll be crowded in the halls between classes, but if ya hurry through it won't be so bad."

"But not too fast," Darren added. "A brisk walk. No faster."

The thought of crowds tainted his masked excitement, but not enough to make him back out. Not now when he was a mere hour or two away from seeing Katey again.

All weekend, he replayed their conversation, remembered every detail of her beautiful face in the hours before dawn when he could allow himself to feel with abandon, and not worry about his packmates sensing anything. He knew so little about her, but he knew how his soul, black and damaged as it was, mended little by little in response to her nearness. He tried to convince himself that was all he wanted, to be close to her. He'd cast aside his pride and trail after her like a lost, starving dog if she'd let him. But he couldn't deny that this need was paired with something deeper, more meaningful, but equally selfish. He suffered these stirrings before, but never with such intensity and not for an incredibly long time.

He had to see where these feelings led him, and if her healing presence could work a miracle. If that meant putting up with his alpha hovering over him like a mother hen, so be it.

Katey's lips spread in a shameless grin as she remembered Logan's words again. *"You are completely safe here with me"*.

Safe. Maybe that's what chased the darkness away. All weekend she picked apart that night, analyzing piece by piece, minute by minute, and tried to find any tangible logic to it. She had nothing but the way he made her feel. As irrational as it seemed, something spiritual must have taken place between them. If only she could fast forward through the rest of the semester to January so she might have another chance to spend time with him. Only then could she test that theory.

Plenty would happen between then and the end of the year. Though neither Lily or Forrest had followed up on their search for a temporary home for Katey, she knew the next few weeks would be a flurry of busyness in preparation to move out of Mary's insane asylum and into a safer, better place.

Katey walked down the hall, one finger lazily tracing along the groove between the painted concrete blocks that made up the interior walls of the school. Anyone that passed her by may have thought her a little out of her mind with that goofy grin. Maybe she was.

Far ahead of her, the glass doors that led out to the bus ramp opened to release a batch of students into the hall. The drumming of rain against the metal awning outside echoed louder than the many sneakers squeaking against the slick tile floor.

Katey looked up to the crowd and her legs nearly went numb and boneless beneath her. Amongst the students, she spotted a tall figure, clothed in a black hooded jacket over a dark gray shirt with the hood up to shadow his face. A pair of ragged jeans hung dangerously low over his hips, only held up by a leather belt that had seen better days. His stride, commanding and fluid, was all too familiar.

With one smooth motion, he swept back the hood and revealed black hair with thin streaks of lighter brown pulled back at the nap of his neck. Icy blue eyes met hers instantly and Katey's heart skittered.

One corner of Logan's mouth curled upward, a look of silent victory in his smug smile. He must have noticed that Katey wore his jacket, carrying a piece of him with her days after they first met. Her world spun out of focus and insides melted.

What was he doing here? There were still a whole two weeks before winter break, and then two weeks before the start of a new semester. He didn't need to be here, not yet.

The world slowed around them and Katey couldn't register her feet hitting the floor anymore, though she continued to move in his direction. The spell broke only for an instant when Logan glanced to his left, down the hall toward where Mr. Dubose's class was, and his smile dropped.

Katey gave herself a mental shake and blinked to bring herself back to earth. Once Logan was away from that hallway junction, he looked back to Katey and gave a muted nod of greeting. Heat plumed from her collar to her hairline and she bit her lips together to keep the giggles from bursting forth. She shyly cast her gaze to the tile floor ahead of her and let him pass her by. She could still feel his stare hot on her when she turned to her right, toward Mr. Dubose's class.

When she glanced up, she saw her teacher standing in front of his door, arms crossed over his barrel chest like a bouncer standing idly at a nightclub. He, along with the other teachers, stood in the halls between classes to monitor the students. But there was an air of seriousness about Mr. Dubose that she hadn't seen before. He almost seemed angry about something, and it made Katey edge closer to the wall to make herself inconspicuous.

That, however, was impossible when he looked straight at her. His brows furrowed and his stare took on a pensive quality, like something about her set his mind to work on a puzzle only he could see. Instinctively, she scrunched her shoulders and all giddiness evaporated under his searing glare.

Instead of greeting him, she hastened to slip into his classroom to escape. Beth was already in her seat, heavy black combat-esque boots propped on the table and cellphone in her hands, likely texting her boyfriend. Katey sat beside her, leaving the third seat at the end of the table empty as usual.

"Did you notice Mr. Dubose?" she whispered to Beth. "He looks pissed."

Beth looked up as if she hadn't even realized Katey had sat down. "No, I didn't notice." She glanced behind her toward the classroom door, but Mr. Dubose was out of sight. "What do you think's up?"

Katey shook her head. "I don't know, but he gave me the weirdest look in the hall."

The miracle of seeing Logan became temporarily overshadowed by this new mystery with her teacher. She had almost forgotten it until Beth plucked at the leather sleeve.

"New jacket? It's a little big on you."

The blush renewed and Katey thought to tell Beth everything while they still had a few moments. She gave her the cliff notes version, leaving out the fight with Mary and her new decision to find a place to stay by the end of December. When she was done, Katey happened to glance toward the classroom door again and found Mr. Dubose leaning in the doorway, his back to them, but striking an imposing figure nonetheless.

"Did you get his number?" Beth asked.

Katey shook her head. "No, but I just saw him in the hall a little while ago."

Beth's eyes widened. "No way. Did you talk?"

"No," she admitted. "I think I was so stunned to see him that I didn't even say hello." That wasn't the whole truth. Katey might have been stunned, but she couldn't think straight when those blue eyes held her attention so directly.

"Maybe you'll see him again."

Before Katey could confess such a hope, the bell rang, and Mr. Dubose slammed the door so forcefully that every student in their seats might have jumped out of their skin. If she thought he looked mad before, he was fuming now. If this were a cartoon, steam would be shooting out his ears and his eyes would glow a murderous red.

Katey sank in her seat, willing herself to be as small as possible. What was his deal?

The class became so silent, every student motionless as if they had been turned to stone by Mr. Dubose's quiet fury. Only their heads turned to follow his progress down the center aisle to his desk at the head of the room. Once there, her teacher took such a deep breath that his chest rose and fell by a noticeable degree. In the same few seconds, it was as if the air returned, and students were released from that invisible vice of tension.

Katey heard footsteps outside the class and the door opened. She kept her focus on Mr. Dubose long enough to see his reaction to the arrival. The fury was tempted to return, but he maintained his composure, save for the half-hearted glare fixed on whoever came in.

"Class, we have a new student... Mr. Logan, You're late."

Katey spun to watch Logan close the door behind him. A dagger of ice pierced her chest while heat kindled in her stomach at the sight of him.

Logan faked an apologetic look for the teacher's sake. "Got lost."

They were the first words she had heard from his lips since Friday, and they had just the same effect on her heart. His blue eyes found her and his soft, subtle smile made her core quiver. This was too good to be true.

"Take any open seat."

Behind her, Katey heard Mr. Dubose go to the bookshelf in the corner beneath the television and grab a textbook. She took a quick assessment of the classroom. There were only three open seats, two in the very back and one on the other side of Beth. It only took Logan a fraction of a second to make his decision and he strode straight for Katey and Beth's table.

Forcing calm upon herself, Katey turned back to the front and begged her pulse to slow down. Mr. Dubose tossed the book to Logan as he settled in his chair and dropped his bag to the floor.

Her mind spun out of control and for a moment, she wondered if she was dreaming. But the events of that morning were all too lucid to be a dream. Logan was really here, not six feet from her.

Mr. Dubose seemed to stamp out the last bit of his aggression and conducted himself as he usually did during his lectures, though she caught onto the fact that his attention wandered back to Katey and Logan a little too frequently. She, too, caught herself stealing glances in Logan's direction, desperate enough to carefully lean around Beth to spy on him. Most of the time, he didn't seem to notice. Other times, he cut his eyes to her at just the right moment and her mouth went bone dry before she snapped away.

To Katey, Mr. Dubose's voice might as well have been like the adults in a Charlie Brown cartoon, without meaning or significance as he lectured on, about pollution and its impact on population change. Her thoughts were locked on Logan, conjuring questions and theories that she dared never to confess to any-one. Questions of Mr. Dubose's anger, Logan's sudden appearance, and how they were linked, if they were at all, consumed her for the duration of the class. Would she even get the chance to find out what was really going on? How could she even begin to ask?

By the time the bell rang, Katey was no closer to a real answer. Logan shot out of his chair and to the door, the first out of the classroom. Katey jerked as if she had been slapped. Why so eager to leave? Didn't he want to stay behind and talk to her? It made little sense, unless he wanted to escape from Mr. Dubose for some reason.

"Was that *your* Logan?" Beth whispered.

Katey blinked about to say that he was, when she came back to herself. "Not *my* Logan, but that is the Logan I told you about."

Katey and Beth rose to leave and she gave Mr. Dubose one last look. In his hand was his cellphone and he furiously thumbed the keys as if he were trying to send a long text in a short amount of time. At least his glare was turned to something insensible of his anger.

"He's hotter than you let on."

By the way other girls looked at Logan in class, Katey suspected Beth wasn't the only one who thought so.

"If you see him again, you have to get his number."

Katey reddened at the idea. "I don't know."

If Beth had suggested it a day ago, Katey would have whole-heartedly agreed, but things were different now. All the girlish joy became tangled up in confusion, now that Logan was back in her life much sooner than she anticipated. It was what she wanted, but not like this.

They entered the crowded hall and she found herself uncon-sciously searching for Logan's unique hair.

"You already have his jacket. Why not get his number too?"

Katey's face wrinkled at the uncomfortable idea. "Isn't it just weird how he's suddenly here and we have a class together after what he told me on Friday?"

Beth grabbed her sleeve and pulled her aside at the junction between two hallways. "Do you think he's stalking you?"

"What? No... Well, maybe."

Beth gave her a look that beseeched honesty.

Katey hated how flustered she became at such a simple question. "All I'm saying is I don't know how to feel yet. I was so sure before now."

Her friend seemed sympathetic. "Well, think about this. If you don't get his number and make a move, some other girl will... How does that make you feel?"

That thought gutted her. Katey never supposed that she had some claim over Logan, but the mental image of any girl besides her hanging on his arm splintered her self-control. It must have been transparent in her expression.

"Uh huh. Just remember that the next time you see him." Beth softened. "I don't mean to upset you. Just wanted to give you a bit of perspective."

Katey straightened and nodded. "I understand. Thanks. Hopefully I won't see him until tomorrow so I'll have more time."

They parted and Katey went to Mrs. Kimbrough's class, but found that she had spoken too soon.

At her desk, sat the subject of her new anxiety, grimacing at his cellphone as if he were reading something displeasing. Katey stood in the classroom door and felt the blood drain from her face. If things seemed weird before, they were insane now.

Lily was already at her desk one row down from hers and out of Logan's line of sight. She waved at Katey in a mildly distressed way and pointed exaggeratedly at Logan with a tight smile. She couldn't read if the blonde was excited or panicked. Knowing

Logan may look up at any minute, she refused to react and slowly moved to close the distance between them.

Logan finally tucked his phone away and looked up. "Funny seeing you here." He grinned as if this was some happy accident, but Katey wasn't so sure that it was anymore.

"You're in my seat," she said, carefully void of emotion so as not to encourage him.

Logan didn't buy it and his grin evolved into a triumphant smirk. "My mistake." He grabbed his bag and moved back one more desk to sit behind her. Unfortunately, that desk was normally empty, so Mrs. Kimbrough wasn't likely to correct him.

Katey sat down and tried not to think how he had warmed the seat of her chair.

"You like my jacket that much?"

Logan's hot breath on the back of her neck sent tingling sparks down her spine that burst low in her belly. Her breaths went ragged for a second before she rotated in her seat to face him.

She opened her mouth, but nothing came out. The tender look he gave her made up for all the crazy contradictory feelings from earlier that morning. Like Friday, he had an uncanny way of disarming her with a simple look. She wanted to hate it.

Katey took a breath and gathered herself together again. "You left so quickly that night I didn't have a chance to give it back. I was going to return it whenever I saw you again... If I saw you again."

"You can have it. I don't mind."

She glanced down to the black leather sleeve and held it up for his examination, as if he didn't know the jacket as thoroughly as she did. "Are you sure? This is real leather, isn't it? I didn't recognize the brand, but it must have been pretty expensive."

Looking at what he wore now, she wondered how he could own such a fancy jacket in the first place. The tears in his jeans and the weathered condition of his belt looked to be from natural wear and tear, not purchased that way like some designer clothes.

He waved her off. "I'm sure. And yes, it's real leather."

Katey let her hands drop into her lap, but stayed turned in her seat. Maybe for the next few minutes, he could help fill in the blanks. "Why did you leave so suddenly, anyway?"

"I told you that I'd stay until you woke up, and I did."

He was right. Katey had considered that explanation, but it wasn't enough. "I hardly heard you get up to leave, though."

He shrugged and sat back. "I can be pretty quiet when I want to."

She gave him a dubious look. "I could barely move my arm without making a racket on those pebbles."

Logan glanced toward the classroom door a few seconds before Mrs. Kimbrough came through. A strange nod of acknowledgement took place between them and she went to her desk without a word. What was that about?

"Did you leave after I did?" Logan asked, drawing her back into the conversation.

"Pretty much." It was then she realized there might have been some listening ears around them, including Lily's. They hadn't bothered to whisper and she hoped nothing they said would inspire some weird rumors. Then again, who would ever suspect anything scandalous could take place between her and Logan? He was way out of her league.

That thought reminded her of the conversation with Beth. She readied to ask him for his number when the bell rang. He didn't seem bothered by it and tilted his head, expecting her to say something more. Katey didn't get the chance when Mrs. Kimbrough spoke.

"The assignment is on the board. When you're done, you may read quietly."

Katey turned back to the front, noted the textbook pages, and pulled out her supplies to begin. Mrs. Kimbrough was one of the most strict English teachers she had and she wasn't ready to be on the receiving end of her brand of discipline.

"That includes you, Logan. There's a spare textbook under your desk."

Katey bit her lips as his desk creaked against his movements to pull out said textbook. As in Mr. Dubose's class, she could hardly concentrate. She was so aware of every movement, and even strained her ears to listen for his breaths. A bit of her anxiety washed away, leaving only a thin film of uncertainty over her spirit that only he could scrub away. She needed more time, but this was hardly the class to do that in.

With fifteen minutes to spare, Katey nearly jumped when she felt a light tap on her shoulder from behind. She turned her head and Logan's face was just inches from hers.

"What were you going to ask me?" he whispered.

His breath tickled the sensitive skin of her ear, words so soft and intimate. Her whole body trembled with a spasm of thrills and she thought she'd collapse in her desk.

"Logan," Mrs. Kimbrough barked. "Reading quietly means no talking. That is your first warning."

Something like a low, guttural growl vibrated the air between Katey and Logan, but she was sure no one else would have noticed it before he sat back.

Katey closed her eyes and took slow, concentrated breaths to recover from the moment. No one had ever been that close to her. No one ever tried, and it was unlikely she would ever let anyone invade her bubble like that. To have him so near, where between one moment and the next their lips may have touched, thrilled Katey in inexplicable ways.

She shifted in her chair and wanted to forget it. He probably didn't even realize what he had done, and she'd never tell him either.

The bell rang and instead of dashing out the door, Logan stood and waited for Katey. She wasn't so sure her legs could carry her, but she managed to get up and slung her bag over her shoulder.

"You were going to ask something?" Logan repeated.

Katey passed a look to Lily, who mutedly pleaded for her attention. "It's nothing."

She turned to go to her friend at the front of the class, but Logan stepped closer as if he were going to block her way.

"No, really. What was it?"

Katey didn't like to be cornered, not by anyone, but she didn't bristle with Logan the way she might have with someone else. Another look in Lily's direction, and she could tell her friend had admitted defeat. She made the universal sign for "call me" and turned to head out the door.

With a sigh, Katey moved slowly to show that she wasn't eager to run out on Logan. "I was going to ask... if you got in trouble with your parents for staying out late."

In the moment, she lost the courage to ask for his number. This was safer and made more sense with their previous conversation.

Logan appeared a little confused, but shook his head. "No, not really."

They stepped out of the classroom and Katey turned immediately to stand next to Mr. Keith's door. As usual, he wasn't there, and some students began to gather along the hall to wait. Logan, too, stood with her.

After a few moments of waiting for him to walk away, she asked, "Aren't you going to be late for your next class?"

He shook his head and motioned to the door. "Third period human geography, right?"

Dumbfounded, Katey barely knew how to answer. "There's no way we have three classes together."

Logan gave a huff of a laugh, as if he were in disbelief too. "Imagine that."

Katey stared at him, jaw slack. One class may have been typical, two might have been coincidence, but three classes seemed downright intentional. "And your fourth period?"

"Calculus with Mr. Myers."

Feeling the onset of a headache, Katey groaned and leaned her forehead against the cool wood of Mr. Keith's door.

"Really?" Logan laughed. "I'd ask for your fifth and sixth period, but I don't have any classes after lunch... You okay?"

"Oh, just losing my mind," Katey mumbled.

That earned her another chuckle, but none of this felt funny. She lifted her head and met his gaze with renewed defiance. "I thought you said you weren't going to start school until the next semester? That's not until January."

Logan peered at her and cocked his head to the side like a confused dog. "Did I say that?"

"Yes, you did. I remember very well." Admitting that may have been a mistake. Now he might have suspected that she obsessively replayed their conversation in her head, which she did, but he didn't need to know that.

"I must have misspoke. Not 'next semester' but 'next week.'"

She didn't believe him. Not a bit, but if he wouldn't tell her the truth, then she wouldn't push.

About that moment, Mr. Keith approached with his keys. "Hey, Logan! How's your first day going?"

The effusive greeting threw her off. Did they know one another or was Mr. Keith just being friendly?

"Not bad. No homework yet."

Mr. Keith gave a hearty laugh. "Challenge accepted! Good mornin' Katey Kat."

Katey muttered her usual reply as she looked between the two, searching for some explanation.

Their teacher unlocked the door and let them inside. "You can sit at the desk next to Katey," he said to Logan. "I think that one is empty."

Terrific, Katey thought.

CHAPTER 5

In Mr. Keith's class, Katey could get a better eyeful of Logan. He reclined in his desk, casual and at ease with long legs stretched, twirling and spinning a pencil between his hands. With a furtive twinkle in his eyes, he watched Mr. Keith as if he knew something no one else did. A couple of times, Mr. Keith seemed to mirror that look.

The first part of the lesson was taken up by a review of the religion section of their current chapter, then Mr. Keith projected that day's "Free Response Question" or F.R.Q. as he called it. Students were given a question to answer as thoroughly and analytically as possible on the subject. They were given half an hour to write about the effects of religion on the creation of civilizations, plenty of time to come up with even a half-assed answer. Katey couldn't focus on anything else, but the way Logan concentrated as he wrote out his response in neat cursive. Who wrote in cursive anymore?

"Time's up," Mr. Keith announced with a loud clap of his hands. "Who wants to volunteer?"

Katey despised this part. She never liked reading aloud to the class, especially anything she wrote. Hopefully Mr. Keith would have mercy and leave her alone.

When no one spoke up, Mr. Keith pointed. "Logan. What have you got?"

That was hardly fair. Logan hadn't been there for even half of their lesson on religion. How could he have a worthwhile response?

Logan sat up and smoothly read his answer. It was so well articulated, so deep and insightful that it might have belonged in a college textbook. Maybe he already learned this in his homeschool curriculum.

When he was done, Mr. Keith whistled. "You wanna get up here and teach, kid?"

Some students snickered and Logan leaned back, a little peeved by the comment.

Mr. Keith called on a few more students to follow Logan's performance, but thankfully passed over Katey. She'd have to turn in her work and was less than confident that she'd get an adequate score.

The bell rang and Katey tried to move quickly to catch Logan before he sped out the door, but she had no hope of catching him. How could he move so fast?

On her way out, she saw Mr. Keith watching her with amused curiosity. This day became more and more strange with each passing hour, and Katey warred against the impulse to overthink it again. She would go insane if she lingered too long on it. Maybe it was all coincidence, or some clerical error, that he would have all of his classes with her. But what was with the way her teachers reacted to him? Mr. Dubose seemed furious with him, and Mr. Keith acted like they were already good friends. Mrs. Kimbrough's behavior wasn't too unusual, if not a tad over-critical. What would she witness in Mr. Myers' class?

Her teacher was neither in his classroom nor standing outside of it, but Logan sat in the seat right in front of hers. Of course.

As she sat, her stomach growled angrily. The Poptart from her breakfast that morning had worn off too soon.

"Hungry?" Logan asked, turning in his seat to face her.

Katey leaned down to rummage in her bag for the granola bar she had packed weeks ago and never ate. It was a little crumbled, the gooey honey adhesive failed to hold the nuts and raisins together anymore after being crushed beneath her textbooks and binders at the bottom of her bag. Mr. Myers was a stickler about food in his classroom, but she thought she could scarf down enough to hold her until lunch before he showed up.

"Was my stomach that loud?"

Logan stammered as if she had caught him doing something he wasn't supposed to. "Oh... no, not really. I just barely heard it. I wasn't even sure it was your stomach or something else. Lucky guess."

Katey gave him a look as she broke open the packaging. "I didn't have much for breakfast."

"Why not?"

"Why does it matter?" Katey plucked a chunk of granola and popped it in her mouth.

Logan shrugged and crossed his arms over the back of his chair, his fingers wrapped around his biceps that made her mouth water. "Just making conversation."

After chewing, she looked down at her snack. "I'm not a big breakfast person." She pinched another cluster. "You and Mr. Keith seemed to know each other already."

Logan didn't answer. His hand shot out to grab the partially eaten granola bar and swiped away a few crumbs from her desktop.

"What the hell?" she exclaimed, eyes wide with shock.

A few seconds later. Mr. Myers appeared in the doorway and the bell rang.

"Who's eating?" her teacher asked, cold eyes skimming over the heads of the students in their seats.

Logan held up the pathetic hunk of wrapper and broken granola. "Want some?"

Some of the students laughed, but Mr. Myers was less than pleased. He also didn't seem convinced that Logan was the culprit, as his glare shifted between him and Katey. "I'll give ya some grace because it's your first day. No eatin' in my class."

Katey looked between Mr. Myers and Logan. How did he know that she'd get in trouble if she was caught with food? Why did he take the fall? And above all, how could he have possibly known that Mr. Myers would walk in just seconds after he had grabbed the granola bar from her?

When Mr. Myers crossed the room with a small trash bin for Logan to toss away the snack, he passed her a reproving look. Did Mr. Myers know it was really hers and not Logan's?

Katey hung her head in her hands and willed herself to stop questioning all these crazy things. She must have just been reading into something that wasn't there, just like Mr. Dubose's anger from earlier that morning or Mr. Keith's friendliness with Logan. There had to be logical explanations, or no explanation was needed at all.

Logan had become a little too careless. The comment about her empty stomach may have been too much, but she didn't seem to suspect anything. He couldn't say the same about the rest of the morning. She was far more observant than he gave her credit for. That's why he knew he had to stay out of sight while he eavesdropped on Katey from outside the lunchroom. If he concentrated hard enough, he could pick out her unique scent, the one he got drunk on all morning. A mix of lavender from her shampoo or body wash, and hints of something sweet in the fragrance she wore, with an utterly feminine and irresistible scent beneath it all that called to him every time they got too close.

Just as he had hoped, being near Katey again lifted the heavy weight he had carried his whole life. Anger died in his chest like sparks on damp wood. Dread and fear were refused at the door of his heart. Dare he even think it, he might have been happy. Hearing her voice, gazing into her eyes, so green and flecked with gold that glittered in the light, and just knowing that she was close to him did wondrous, miraculous things for himself and his wolf.

He needed more. He needed more conversation, more smiles, to touch and know how it felt to hold her close. Logan wanted to know just how far these feelings would take him, and he began to realize they might lead him down a dangerous path. When was the point of no return? Had he already reached it? He knew beyond a shadow of a doubt that he couldn't go back to the way he used to live after today. Katey had completely ruined him, and he loved every minute of it.

She had turned down his invitation to go off campus for lunch. The pack would be expecting him in Darren's classroom but after the biting text after first period, he had no interest in facing his alpha.

He leaned against the wall and closed his eyes, sifting through the cacophony of voices to get a bead on Katey and Lily.

"So that was the Logan who gave you the jacket?" Lily asked.

Logan smirked. He knew there was a possibility of running into Lily that day, but he didn't think he would share a class with her too. A forewarning text to Forrest was enough so Lily wouldn't blow his cover, but that earned him a lecture from his old friend about his impulsive behavior on Friday. How was he to know he and Katey had a mutual connection, in Forrest no less, someone he had known for as long as he knew Darren.

"He is," Katey answered as they sat down with their lunch trays. "And you won't believe it, but we have four classes together. "

"That's crazy!"

"You don't know the half of it." Katey then went into telling Lily all about the little things she noticed about Logan and the guys. Yes, he had been careless but so had the pack. A few more hints and she would know the truth soon enough.

That thought knotted his guts. If she put the pieces together, if she knew...

He opened his eyes when he sensed Dustin storm around the corner to find him. The beta stopped and gave him that beckoning gesture.

"Come on, Logan. You know what's coming."

He did and he didn't look forward to it. Together, they went across the school to Darren's classroom. The alpha was already there, arms folded and mad enough to rip a throat, though Logan knew he never would, no matter what he did. Ben sat at one of the long table desks with a container of cooked strips of thin flank steak, half eaten.

Dustin closed the door, locked it, and pulled down the shade to cover the narrow window. Logan slung his hands in the center pocket of his jacket and met his alpha's eyes with all the nerve he could muster.

"You lied to us." Darren's voice was hard and low, and he mercifully kept his dominance to a minimum, unlike earlier this morning.

At this point, there was no denying it. Katey wore his jacket without understanding what it would do to him. Even after a couple of days in her possession, it still reeked of him and the pack. They would have known it was his even if they were blind.

"You didn't go to the fight club. You were out with Katey, at a cemetery of all places! I heard her tell her friend the whole story this morning."

Dustin sat atop the end of one of the tables. "A cemetery... that's... different."

"Yes, I lied," Logan said evenly. "I was out in the woods around the cemetery, but I didn't plan on meeting Katey. She was there and I just... I went up and talked to her. That was all."

Darren hoped he wouldn't ask why his charge had been out in the woods in the first place. It was unimportant. It wasn't as if anything happened. Nothing ever did, no matter how hard he tried.

"I'm not as concerned about you meeting Katey. I'm more upset that you thought lying to us was necessary."

"Wasn't it?" Logan hissed. "What would you have done if I told you I stayed out there with her for hours? Wasn't I reckless? Wasn't I putting her in danger with each minute unchaperoned?"

Darren almost looked wounded by his accusation. "Logan, you haven't hurt a fly in over eighty years. If we ever thought you were a true danger to society, we wouldn't let you go wandering off every now and again as you did on Friday. Did you stop to think about that?"

"But it was Katey." Logan spoke slowly, making sure to throw emphasis on her name. "You three have talked about no other student half as much as you talk about her."

He didn't need to remind them. They all knew and had declared that for whatever ungodly reason, that they thought of her as part of the pack. She wasn't like them, had no family like them, and yet, they all felt this inexplicable reason to protect and care about her.

"And now you understand how we feel, don't you?" Dustin asked. "That's why you wanted to start school sooner... To be with her."

Darren's nostrils flared. "Did you suspect that the whole time and never mention it?"

The beta gave him a helpless shrug and lifted his palms upwards like a kid who got caught rifling in the cookie jar. Darren sighed and shook his head.

"Yes, I get it now," Logan answered. "And... I'm sorry I lied. I didn't know how you'd react, Darren."

"I'm not sure how I would have reacted either, but you know I appreciate honesty above all else. I need you to trust me just as I need to be able to trust you in return. You should know that by now."

Logan cast his gaze to the floor but would not duck his head in submission to the alpha.

"That goes for both of you," Darren added, pointing to the other two of his pack.

Dustin slapped a hand on his chest as if he had been struck. "Me? I didn't lie."

"You did not tell the whole truth. I suspect you knew Logan had met Katey and that's why you suggested his schedule."

"Thanks for that," Logan muttered. He hadn't expected to see Katey for the entire day, but it was a pleasant surprise.

Ben wiped his mouth with his napkin. "I didn't do nothin'. Why are ya lumpin' me in with them two?"

Darren's brows puckered in a frown. "You were the one that offered the compromise so Logan could enroll sooner."

"I just did that so y'all would stop arguin' and I could go back to sleep. I didn't know anythin' about Katey until I saw her in Logan's jacket today."

It hardly seemed the time to ask, but Logan had to know that everything was out in the open. "Will you make me drop out after one day?"

Darren looked at Logan with calculating eyes. After a long, silent moment, he shook his head. "No. You may continue with school."

Logan tucked his chin. "Can... Can I spend more time with Katey?"

They weren't her guardians or her family, but if Logan were to hope for any future attachment to her, he knew that his pack would be the ones to stand in his way.

"Why?" A soft growl underscored Darren's query, and his lips curled ever so slightly as if he were ready to fight as a wolf in a man's skin.

"Isn't it obvious?" Dustin said, suggestion laded in his tone.

Another pensive moment passed before Darren understood. For a man who was so much older than all of them, he seemed the most unfamiliar with the ways of the world.

He swung on Logan and hardened as if he were ready to uncork his dominance, but thought better of it. "What do you hope to gain from courting her?"

Logan's eyes widened. "Courting? I didn't say anything about that."

"And they call it 'dating' these days, Darren," Dustin quipped.

Darren sneered. "I know what they call it, but there is a difference. Courting has a fixed objective. Dating does not."

Dustin swung one of his legs. "Depends on what that objective is."

The alpha waved off his beta's words. "My point is that if Logan is to get close to her, then she will have to be told the truth eventually. And if she is told the truth, there is no going back. She'd know about us and she's been through enough."

No one could argue on that last point.

"I just want to get to know her," Logan pleaded. "That's all... Please?"

Dustin blew out a breath and turned to the alpha. "An apology and a 'please' all in the same hour. Maybe Katey's a good influence on him."

Darren deliberated, staring a hole through Logan as if that would reveal his true intentions. Finally, he said, "Very well. You can stay in school and also spend time with Katey, but within moderation."

Logan released the breath he didn't know he had been holding, and within the same few seconds, Darren squeezed his eyes shut and grimaced at some invisible pain. He shook his head briskly and jaw tightened. In that moment, they all felt it through their pack bond, a tiny prelude to what their alpha experienced. It wasn't enough to elicit a response, but it was still noticeable.

"It's your night, ain't it?" Ben asked.

Darren nodded. "I've been a little off all day and almost forgot."

Dustin hopped down from the desk and went to fetch his and Logan's lunches from Darren's desk. "Not like I had any plans this evening."

Logan did, but he wouldn't tell them. It wasn't as if they would miss him. When it was their night to shift, all of them went out to run, except for Logan. Darren's speech about honesty did not fall on deaf ears, but he would take a page from Dustin's book and omit the truth. For some things, he knew it would be better to ask for forgiveness than permission in the end.

The school day was finally over. Katey hadn't seen hide nor hair of Logan since before lunch. He had told her that he had no fifth or sixth period, but part of her braced every time she turned the corner as if he'd magically appear anyway. With the final bell rung and students boarding buses to go home, Katey thought she'd breathe a little easier. No such luck. Part of her wanted to see him, one last serendipitous time.

She crouched in front of her locker, depositing the books and binders she wouldn't need that evening to do homework. In one swift motion, she slammed her locker shut, stood and turned on the balls of her feet. She shrieked when she nearly collided with a solid wall of Logan. He caught her arms before she could fall back against the lockers.

"Whoa, there!" he laughed. "You all right?"

It took a moment for Katey to get her feet underneath her again. Logan's firm hold on her sent her heart skipping and she was sure it'd burst from her chest. "I didn't hear you come up behind me."

"I guess I should start wearing a bell around my neck, huh?"

A laugh bubbled up from what felt out of nowhere, but it felt good. "For real."

They stood there for a while, Katey still in Logan's grasp before she cleared her throat to make him realize it. In a perfect world, she would have never wanted him to let go.

He released her and took an awkward step back. "Sorry about that."

"It's okay." Katey tucked a strand of hair behind her ear. "I thought you'd be long gone by now."

"I went home for a little while, but came back."

"Why's that?"

Logan's smile widened. "I wanted to see you... and ask you something."

Katey could no more fight the blush that rose up her neck as she could hold back a tidal wave. "Ask me what?"

He took a breath, as if she were the one way out of his league and about to throw all his cards on the table. "There's a cemetery farther north of here, just beyond the Alabama border. It's a bit of a drive, but it's really old... I wanted to know if you'd like to go there with me. We can sit by a stranger's grave and talk."

Katey bit her lips together. Was he asking her out to a cemetery? She looked into his gorgeous blue eyes, so raw with hope and something she didn't expect. Was he afraid? What did he, a guy probably strong enough to wrestle a horse to the ground, have to be afraid of with her? If anything, she should have been afraid of him. In truth, one word from him, one look into those deep, soulful eyes, and she forgot all the crazy theories from earlier that day. Lily talked her down at lunch and convinced her that Logan couldn't have been stalking her, and those little interactions with the teachers were meaningless. She was thankful for her friend's rational advice, but Katey could have used a little more right now.

If she accepted, what did that mean for them? Would one date lead to two or three? Or would this end in flames and leave them both broken? Katey had never been in a serious relationship and didn't know how to behave, but something told her that Logan likely felt the same, though with his good looks that seemed completely unlikely.

Feeling a little cheeky, Katey lifted her chin and asked, "Why?"

Clearly, he wasn't expecting that, and his expression fell. "Why not?"

Katey bit her lips together and pondered it for a moment. It wasn't a real answer, but it was a damned good one.

"As long as we can drive separately."

CHAPTER 6

Seeing Logan on that sleek black motorcycle made him twice as hot in Katey's eyes. It was cliché and shallow, but there was something glamorous in the way he rode ahead of her, his hard body leaned forward and face masked by a helmet.

They had driven an hour and a half to the north, over the Florida-Alabama state line. The cemetery was just outside a town slightly smaller than Crestucky, but much older, indicative of the turn of the century houses and abandoned railway line. She failed to catch the name of the town. The only way in or out of the cemetery was a lonely dirt road that wound through an endless forest of tall pines.

A large white sign nailed to a stone wall was so vandalized in graffiti and faded with age that she couldn't make out the words. The cemetery yard itself was shaded by many trees and dotted with rusty iron benches.

Sliding out of her jeep to meet Logan by the gates, she noted what a fine late afternoon it turned out to be, despite the heavy rains earlier that morning. The sky had cleared and bird songs drifted on the chilly winds. Katey was glad for the breeze as it cooled her flushed skin.

They settled into an easy stroll down the grassy trails between the grave markers. All were ancient, capped in moss and shadowed in decades or centuries of grime. Weather and age smoothed out the stone, obscuring the inscriptions so thoroughly she couldn't read the names or dates at all. However, some markers appeared as new and cleaned up as if they had been erected over the weekend, or maybe diligently maintained by some loving descendent.

"So," Logan began, "how was your day?"

Katey drew together the edges of the leather jacket while her hands stayed deep in the pockets. "Can I be honest with you?"

"Always."

"I think neither of us are the type for small talk and shallow conversation."

Logan laughed, a deep, throaty melody that made Katey grin. "All right... How many foster homes have you passed through?"

Her smile wilted and stomach seized as if she had been electrocuted. "I guess I deserved that... How about we take turns asking those hard questions?" When he agreed, she said, "Eight. I've been through eight homes. Ten, if you count the group homes I stayed in for a while."

The sympathy Logan had withheld the night they met finally made an appearance. "That must have been hard."

Katey pulled out her mask one more time and concealed whatever bit of emotion dared to leak through as she spoke. "I made a game out of it after a while. I'd make bets with myself on how long it'd take for them to get fed up and turn me out. A few times, I acted out on purpose so I wouldn't lose my own bet. I got good at it. When I didn't like my new foster family, I made sure they wouldn't like me either. Sometimes I did that even when I did like them."

She wouldn't meet Logan's penetrating stare. "Why would you do something like that? Didn't you want to have a stable home?"

Katey held up a finger. "Nope. It's my turn, and don't you dare dodge this question. It's been bothering me all day. Why do you have all your classes with me? It can't be a coincidence."

Logan took a fortifying breath. "Okay. You caught me."

Katey stomped in triumph. "I knew it!"

"But you were not the reason for the way my schedule turned out. The teachers were."

She cocked her head in confusion, waiting for an explanation. She didn't ask the question with her mouth, but her eyes. He must have seen it and gave in good-naturedly, but there was something guarded in the way he answered her.

"I wanted classes with those specific teachers because... I know them outside of school. My turn again," he hurried. "Why wouldn't you let yourself settle in one home?"

Katey pouted, hating the agreement already. She was so close to getting to the bottom of the mystery. "It was just easier. Staying meant getting too attached, and sometimes foster kids get yanked for no reason. There is never a guarantee that you'd get adopted. Why fall in love with a family that can't be permanent?"

"I'd imagine that having a good family for a short time is better than giving up something good for the unknown. I've almost made that same mistake a few times."

The dark gleam in Logan's eyes made her change her mind about her next question. There had to be a story behind what he said.

Before she could open her mouth, Logan cut her off. "By the way, that counted as your question so it's my turn again."

"What? That's not fair! It was rhetorical."

"Be more careful about what you say, then." Logan shot her a clever grin. "My turn... What happened to your parents?"

Katey swallowed back the surge of emotion she didn't want to feel, and couldn't allow him to see. "They died when I was a baby. Bad car wreck on interstate 10."

They both intuitively paused in silence for the departed. "So, you never knew them?"

Katey had to turn the tide in her favor and stuck up her nose. "Oh, no. My turn for a question. How do you know the teachers?"

Logan chuckled, having a taste of his own medicine. "They're friends of the family. I've known them for a long time. We thought having classes with them would ease the transition. Those periods were the only ones with available seats."

Katey couldn't remember a single time that she had seen those teachers in the same space together, but wanted to believe Logan anyway. The secret lives of educators outside of school were none of her business, and she heard once that some teachers didn't like it when their students or students' families approached them in public places like restaurants or the supermarket.

"And that's why Mr. Keith was so friendly, but that doesn't explain why Mr. Dubose seemed so angry with you in first period." She was mindful to keep her tone as a statement rather than a question.

"I heard he's been going through some trouble at home," Logan said. "Maybe a bit of that followed him to work."

She thought she caught something like a look of mischief in his smile. "And to answer your question, no. I never knew my parents. I've been in the system my whole life."

They rounded the first corner on their tour around the cemetery and passed under the shade of a barrier of trees that separated the graves from the wilderness beyond. The wind played in the branches, leaves rustling above their heads.

"I won't ask you any more about your parents." Logan gave her a tight-lipped smile as if he were repentant for his nosiness.

"It's fine. I don't mind."

"I don't want to upset you."

Katey snorted. "Do I look upset? It happened a long time ago. Doesn't matter anymore."

Logan paused before answering, likely choosing his words carefully. "Just because it happened a long time ago doesn't mean that it doesn't have power over you anymore. Things like loss and grief never go away. They just change over time and sneak up on you when you're not expecting it."

Struck speechless, Katey only continued on at their ambling pace, though her mind raced with the implications of what he said. Just like his earlier remarks, he talked like he knew about such things as mistakes and grief, but it got her to think a little deeper. Maybe the depression, which seemed a lifetime away now, had been some lowkey side effect of grief that she had never settled. Turning eighteen, aging out of the system, and an unknown future might have dredged up old feelings she didn't know she had about the parents she never knew.

When she was younger, she wanted to hate her parents for dying and leaving her alone in the world. Age and counseling taught her that their deaths were an accident, unintentional and not meant to hurt her. The same couldn't be said for all the foster kids in the world whose parents abandoned them, abused them, or could barely take care of themselves, let alone a child. Katey might have had it lucky, starting off with no strings attached and no relations to worry about once she was out in the world on her own.

Did the thought of her own impending aloneness, the absence of her parents, the many unspoken and unfulfilled fantasies of having a family at all, trigger the darkness?

"You look far away."

Katey fought through the fog of her own thoughts and turned to Logan. Oh, she both loved and loathed the way he could look at her with such compassion like they were so much more than friends.

"Whose turn was it?" She had to take the focus off of her, just for a minute to catch her breath.

"How about we forget taking turns?" Logan stuffed his hands in his jean pockets, tugging down the edge of his waistband by a fraction of an inch below the hem of his tight, gray shirt. That sudden flash of skin quickened her pulse. "Tell me about yourself. I'm sure there's more to you than cemetery visits and foster homes."

Katey winced. "I always hated that sort of question. What am I supposed to mention? Favorite foods? Movies? Hobbies?"

"All of the above."

"Fine," she sighed. "But you have to return the favor."

"I think I can do that."

They turned again, following the edge of the cemetery.

"Favorite food, French fries. Favorite color is blue. I don't really have a favorite movie or genre, but I refuse to watch sappy chick flicks like The Notebook. So overrated... I like most rock bands like Linkin Park, Evanescence, Three Days Grace, Disturbed, Simple Plan, Five Finger Death Punch, bands like that."

Logan beamed. "Me too. About the music, I mean. What about Breaking Benjamin?"

"Totally! Favorite song?"

Logan thought for a moment. "Probably 'Unknown Soldier'."

"I like that one too... So, hobbies. I guess the closest thing is ballroom dancing. I work as an instructor at the studio on Main Street on the weekends."

A look of something like realization flashed in Logan's eyes and he nodded. "That's... interesting."

Katey rolled her eyes. "Go on. Say it. I don't look like the kind of girl who would dance. I get it all the time."

"That wasn't what I was thinking, but now that you say it..." His gaze swept her in an appraising way, and she playfully smacked his arm, earning her another laugh.

"All right, now you tell me about yourself," she insisted.

Logan rubbed the back of his neck as she waited. "Let's see... hmmm..."

"Did you forget to study for this test?"

"Oh, hush," he teased with a smile. "I love steaks, the color black, old whodunit flicks, and I'm a regular competitor at the fight club outside of town."

Katey grinned. "Wow. A real beast, huh?"

Logan stopped dead in his tracks and blanched. "What?"

She stopped too, and sobered at his strange reaction. "It's just a turn of phrase. The motorcycle, rock music, fight clubs... You make yourself sound like some dark, brooding, feral kind of guy... like a beast."

Logan visibly relaxed. "Oh... I've never heard that before."

"All except for the movie thing. What are 'whodunit' flicks?"

Logan flinched. "You know, those murder mystery type of movies where the whole plot is around solving some crime."

"Oh, like Sherlock Holms stuff?"

He wagged his head. "More or less. But I like the older whodunits. It's a little basic, but I like *The Maltese Falcon*. But an even more obscure one I'll watch over and over again is *Laura*. They just don't make pictures like that anymore."

Katey smiled at his enthusiasm. "Yeah, you might as well be speaking a foreign language right now. Never heard of them."

He groaned and tilted his head back. "Oh, you've got to watch them sometime. I think you'd like them."

They fell in step again and Katey could imagine them, at some point in the future, curled up on the couch together watching some old black and white films. She'd let him prattle on and on about the film and she'd enjoy every minute of it, even if she wasn't into the story. Just watching him get this excited was enough for her.

All excitement, however, faded as they approached one particular grave. Logan slowed to a stop and stared at the name carved into the headstone. It was old and not well maintained like the rest. The name of the man that was laid to rest here was Robert Croxen. There wasn't a birth date, but the death year was a few years from the turn of the century. The last name sounded vaguely familiar, but she couldn't place where from. Below the death year was the inscription, "A loving father and valiant leader".

Logan stared at the tombstone with a solemn look in his eyes.

"Someone you knew?" Katey inquired, a taunting lilt to her voice. There was no possible way he would have known someone who died in the nineteenth century, but the question echoed the first words he ever spoke to her. She wondered if he'd get the joke, but his reaction said it plainly enough.

He shook his head. "He's just usually the one I sit next to if I come here."

"Why's that?"

Logan took a deep breath and began to walk on. "I like to think about the epitaph and imagine him as he used to be... What he did to earn it, if it was justly given."

Katey blinked at the depth of his response. He talked as if he really did know who Robert Croxen was. Perhaps a local folklore hero? Something about it told her not to pry.

"How did you know this place was here?" she asked, shifting the subject.

"I actually used to live in that town we passed on the way."

"Really?"

"Yes. But it was a long time ago and we didn't live there long."

Katey seized the chance. "You talk sometimes like you've been through some shit. Did you move around a lot?"

Logan shrugged. "I guess you can say that. I've definitely lived in a lot of places."

"Military?"

"Huh?"

"There are a lot of military families in this county. Is that why you moved around?"

She saw Logan fumble with his answer. "Well, no. Not really. I mean, someone in my family was in the military, but that's not why we moved around. We just... We're kind of a nomadic bunch. We don't like staying in one place for too long."

Katey's brows furrowed. "Why's that?"

Logan inhaled. "I've never really known anything different."

"How long have you been in Crestucky?"

"Not long."

All of the sudden, she got the feeling that he was purposefully deflecting her questions. She watched him, but she realized he must have had a mask just as effective as hers. His face betrayed nothing. She wondered how much more she could poke this bear before it bit back.

"Do you have a favorite place you've lived?" she asked. They had come back to the front of the cemetery and started back on the same loop they had completed.

"Not really. I learned a long time ago that I had to be content with where I was."

"If you've been to so many places, do you claim a specific one as yours? Like when someone asks where you're from, you answer with…"

Logan shrugged. "No one's really asked me. I don't claim to be *from* anywhere."

"So mysterious," Katey taunted and she thought she saw a bit of color rise in his cheeks. "Well, when you're done with school, do you think you'll stay in Crestucky or keep roaming?"

"That's not really up to me." Logan kicked at a stray rock in their path, sending it skipping across the grass.

"Is that a hint to that thing you said the other day about freedom?"

"A little. What about you? You're out of the system. What will you do after graduation?"

Katey sighed. "I'm not sure anymore. I'm pretty sure I don't want to stay here. I've lived in this town my whole life and I can't wait to leave."

Regret shone in Logan's eyes. "But, don't you have friends here? Won't you hate leaving them behind?"

Katey thought of Lily, Beth, and Forrest in particular. Leaving them would be hard, but what else could she do? Staying didn't feel right either. "Probably, but I just keep getting the feeling that I don't belong here, you know? Like there's some bigger, better... something out there for me."

Silence reigned as Logan delicately formed his response. "I think we don't have to go out finding some place we belong. We can make ourselves belong wherever we want. It's a mental thing, not something physical."

She regarded him with wonder. "Yeah, you definitely talk like you've lived a hundred lifetimes or something."

Logan didn't laugh at that, or offer any sarcastic quip in return, and she got the feeling she had said something entirely wrong.

"Sorry," she muttered. "You're trying to encourage me and I'm popping off jokes."

"It's fine. Do you want to sit?" He gestured toward a rusty iron bench a little further ahead on the path.

"It looks like it'd be blown to pieces with the next storm," she laughed.

"I think it's strong enough to hold us for a little while."

Katey tested the seat, pressing her fingertips into the metal. Not entirely convinced, she gingerly lowered herself onto the bench and looked to Logan, still standing with his phone in his hand. His face puckered in that scowl she had seen earlier that day.

"Something wrong?"

He shook his head and held down the power button. "It's nothing," he grumbled before sitting next to her. The bench groaned in protest against his weight and Katey braced to stand as if the whole thing would collapse.

"See?" Logan smacked the armrest. "Totally solid."

She gave a breathy laugh and eased back as a stiff wind tossed her hair. "That reminds me, though. I made a promise to a friend. Can I get your phone number?"

Logan chuckled. "Yeah, sure."

She took out her phone and created a new message to send to his phone, that way he would already have her number stored. "Thanks. If I showed up tomorrow without it, she'd be pissed at me."

"Is my number for her or for you?"

"Oh, it's for me, but she gave me a hard time about being too scared to ask for it." Mortified, she resisted the urge to slap her hand over her mouth. She had said far too much. "But, I'm sure I could sell your number to the girls in our class and make more money than I do in a month at the studio."

"What do you mean?"

Her brows arched. "Have you looked in a mirror lately? Or better yet, have you seen the way the girls in class were looking at you?"

He seemed to pause, as if thinking about it, then shook his head. "No, not really. Why? Is there something wrong with the way I look?"

"No, nothing's wrong and that's my point. Every girl in class couldn't stop staring at you today, giving you goo-goo eyes and all."

"Huh?" Logan's face contorted with utter confusion and Katey had to laugh.

"Don't play dumb. If you ask any girl in that high school to go out with you, even if they're taken already, they'd snag you up in a heartbeat." If that wasn't blunt enough, Katey didn't know what would be.

Logan stretched out one leg and let his stare trail ahead. "Well, I wouldn't ask them out anyway, and if they asked me I'd have to say no."

Something snagged in the way he said that. "You'd *have* to?"

He shrugged. "I wouldn't feel right about saying yes."

"Why not?"

Logan glanced at her. "I think I want to take turns asking questions again."

"Getting uncomfortable?" Katey leaned forward, one elbow propped on her knee and chin rested in her hand as she watched him, utterly fascinated with the way the sunlight played on his features.

"Maybe a little." Logan turned and met her stare, several heart-beats of pregnant silence between them. The world fell away for what seemed like the hundredth time that day, and all that existed was the two of them. "Do you believe in fate?"

Thrown off by the question, Katey didn't look away, but didn't answer immediately. "Not really," she replied. "I don't think anything is really predestined. We all have choices, and those choices shape our lives for better or for worse."

The faintest of smiles touched Logan's mouth. "Just like you had a choice to come out here with me today."

She nodded. "And just like you had the choice to approach me on Friday. You could have ignored me like everyone else does."

He seemed to ignore that last part of her comment. "You made the choice to be there, too. Would you have gone to the cemetery that night if you knew I was there?"

She didn't need to think long to know the answer to that one. "Yes... Would you?" Her words came out breathy and intimate.

"I still would have." He matched her voice, tone for tone, whisper for whisper.

Katey tilted her head. "Why?"

"Because it's been a pleasure knowing you so far."

Her smile widened. "And if I turn out to be a jerk?"

"I don't think you will." His voice softened and instantly stole Katey's heart with his sincerity.

"And why is that?"

"This is going to sound corny, but I can see it in your eyes. You're not mean spirited by design."

Never had someone looked at her with such warm, raw emotion as Logan did now. He didn't say those three words every teenage girl wanted to hear from their crush, but she somehow felt a lesser version of the sentiment laced somewhere underneath all this talk about fate and choice, about grief and belonging. Beneath his stare, her spirit was light, her heart bursting. Katey thought she had experienced a miracle on Friday, one and done, but here with Logan, she felt another miracle descend and bless her with a wealth of feeling she never thought possible.

"You're right... That does sound corny."

"Where the bloody hell is he?" Darren growled, teeth bared and hands gripping the edge of the kitchen island counter.

The shift pushed against his body more urgently as twilight darkened into night. He wouldn't be able to hold it off for much longer. Every loup-garou's shift was unique and took a different pace and course. For some, a pelt rolled out across their skin in a wave of dense fur first. For others, the form and features of the wolf in their faces. It always ended in that half-wolf, half-man creature that looked more monster than human to most. But for all, the golden eyes displaced their human irises, the very first sign that the wolf would take dominion. It was only a matter of time.

Darren's pack ran together, shifting four times a month. Three times by choice and once involuntarily. They dressed in sweatpants and went shirtless, but a fresh change of clothes and towels were packed in a bag they took with them to the woods. They were only missing one member of the pack, though they all knew his attendance was unnecessary. It was merely the principle of the thing that Logan would either be there, or safe at home.

"I've been trying to reach him." Dustin held up his phone as he joined Darren and Ben from the living room. "I haven't heard anything since that last text saying he would be out late." He dialed for Logan again, but all three heard it go straight to voicemail.

Darren lifted his fist to strike at the counter, but Ben's hand shot out to seize his alpha's wrist.

"I'm not keen on replacin' the countertops again."

At least someone had enough sense. Darren unclenched his hand to reveal long, tawny claws where neatly trimmed fingernails had been. Tiny cuts in his palm healed, leaving smears of blood on his skin. Fangs would come next, and his tongue probed along his teeth to test their sharpness.

"How much do we want to bet he isn't coming home until well after midnight?" Dustin leaned against the counter and crossed his arms.

A low, furious growl rumbled in Darren's throat as he began to pace the length of the kitchen like a caged animal.

"Nah," Ben said. "He knows better."

"That was before Katey."

Darren snapped a look to his beta. "You think he's with her?"

Dustin shrugged. "It wouldn't surprise me."

Rage swelled in Darren's chest and tore through his body as fiercely as the shift. His nerves were always volatile on the day of the shift. If he wasn't careful, it showed all too plainly at school as it had that day. With Logan's enrollment and now Katey a step closer into their circle, Darren was uncharacteristically negligent in managing his temper.

Katey was not his responsibility. She did not belong to a pack, and yet he felt a pull to protect her. He hadn't felt so possessive over a human for whom he had no real connection in a long time. He knew Logan wasn't likely to hurt her, as he said earlier that day, but Darren could come up with plenty of other scenarios in which he could put Katey in real danger. He couldn't allow that.

She didn't need to know what they were or how they lived. That was too great a burden for any one person to carry. Only women who mated to their kind, who were fully committed to the pack, were permitted to know, and Logan couldn't be so foolish to think that was possible... Could he?

Anger became disrupted when Darren's joints below his hips snapped and buckled. Sinew stretched and blood sizzled in his veins. He bit back the shout of pain. His pack was there to catch him from dropping to the floor. With great effort, he tightened his muscles to squeeze his joints back into place, resisting the shift like a reticent pup.

"We can't wait around for him." Dustin was the last to release as the alpha steadied himself back onto his feet. "Logan's a big boy. He can take care of himself."

"It ain't like he'd be comin' with us anyway."

Ben was right, another reminder that the alpha had failed Logan.

Another seizure rattled his limbs and Darren relented. With Dustin's support, the pack made their way out of the house and into the forest. Darren willed himself to push aside Logan's act of rebellion and allowed the wolf to swallow him and all his human troubles for another night.

***

Even miles away, Logan felt the twinges of his alpha's change through their pack bond. He shook it off, too engrossed in one of Katey's stories of how she tormented one of her former foster families when she was barely five years old. Night had fallen, but he hardly noticed. They left the cemetery to grab dinner at a drive-in diner in Morrisville, and had sat for hours in their outdoor seating area, just talking.

When they moved to Crestucky, he vowed never to step foot in this town. Too many memories. The streets looked nothing like what it did when he was younger. The roads were now paved, the buildings newer, the shops he once knew were no longer there, but replaced by modern businesses and restaurants. Still, the ghosts cried out to him from every corner, shimmers of a long and bloody night that he could never forget.

Yet, with Katey, the visit was not so painful. They talked of her job at the ballroom dance studio and he regaled her with stories of his fights in the ring, careful to leave out incriminating details. Almost predictively, she didn't shy away or cringe at some of the gorier aspects, though he noticed the way she inspected his face and hands for any signs of scarring. She'd find none.

She ate her fries and he nibbled on the grilled chicken sandwich, minus the bun and toppings. When she asked, he only claimed to have a sensitive stomach. There were plenty of gluten intolerant people these days to make it seem completely normal to forsake bread. When she asked about the slices of lettuce and tomato he slipped to the side, he made her giggle with, "If I wanted a salad, I would have ordered one."

Logan couldn't remember when he had such a great time with anyone, pack or not. With his phone turned off, he was free to enjoy Katey all to himself. As the moon rose higher into the night sky, and more businesses began to shut down along the main strip, he realized that he couldn't have her forever. Time couldn't stand still for them, and it passed by all too quickly.

Katey pulled out her phone to check the clock and gasped. "Damn, it's getting late."

"Do you have a curfew?"

"No. My foster mom is out of town anyway. I have the house to myself, but we have school tomorrow."

Logan's stomach clenched. "You're home alone?"

"Sure. I'm old enough to take care of myself. It's not a big deal."

To him, it was. Like the rest of his pack, Logan instinctively need-ed to protect her, guard her like she was some helpless newborn pup who hadn't opened her eyes yet. Humans were so fragile, though Katey hardly seemed it. Ten homes in eighteen years. He heard that children could be resilient, but Logan couldn't imagine such a life without some stability, someone or something to fall back on in times of need. He didn't appreciate the pack and his alpha at first, but he had learned to see the value in their loyalty and constancy. Though, the way he behaved lately, it might have seemed as if Logan were ready to forsake all of that for Katey. Perhaps he was. He knew, after tonight, Darren might not be so forgiving.

"Thanks again for the food and company." Katey began packing away their takeout trash.

The thought of parting made his heart lodge in his throat. His wolf roared and demanded that he do anything to make her stay. Possessive and greedy, both he and the wolf wanted her, needed her. He couldn't go home after tonight, not just because he'd catch hell in the morning, but because he knew he'd be a howling, whimpering mess, alone in that house without Katey by his side.

"It was my pleasure." Logan paused. He rubbed thoughtfully at his lips and chin, weighing the consequences of what he would do next. "Can I ask for something?"

Katey froze. "For something?"

Logan stared into her eyes, gaining courage. "May I escort you home? Just to make sure you get there safely?"

"I could just text you when I get there."

"I turned off my phone to conserve the last bit of juice. I won't be able to charge it until I get home, but if something should happen and you need help…"

Katey gave him a simpering look. "I think I'll be all right, Logan."

His core vibrated at the way she said his name and he had to plant his feet on the ground to keep himself from crossing the picnic table to reach her. She might have been all right with him, but he wouldn't be. "Humor me?"

Swayed by the pleading gleam in his eyes, she sighed. "Fine. You can follow me home."

CHAPTER 7

Katey hadn't noticed how severe her trembling had become until she reached for the keys to turn off the ignition. Logan's motorcycle pulled up alongside her in the driveway, three bright headlights glaring against the white garage door. All the way home, she wondered how she could have caved so easily to his request to see her home. It was totally unnecessary, totally inappropriate, but part of her didn't care.

The evening had been so perfect, and she never wanted it to end. Just *how* it would end, she didn't know. All she knew was that Logan was so unlike anyone she had ever met. Wise, but dark and mysterious, funny and yet so grounded. He was an old soul, a bit of slow easiness in a fast and chaotic world that she didn't want to return to. For whatever unfathomable reason, he wanted to stay with her for just a little longer. In the end, she resolved that she couldn't have turned him down, even if she wanted to. Hopefully, he wouldn't ask too much of her.

She half expected him to give her a friendly salute and back out of the driveway as soon as she angled out of the driver's seat. Instead, he had killed his own engine and slipped off his helmet.

"Home sweet home," she mumbled, frost in the words she didn't mean.

Again, Logan surprised her when he walked her to the door. The porch light was dead, but a tiny beam of streetlamp light helped her see the way to the door. She fumbled with her keys in silence.

More trembles. She wanted to shake her hands to ward off the nerves, but Logan was watching, standing so close that she was sure he could hear her heartbeat thrum hard against her ribcage.

She pushed open the door and amber light from the streetlamp fell across the stained carpet.

"I guess this is goodnight." Katey turned to face Logan for whatever sort of goodbye he was willing to give.

Logan, however, didn't seem to pay her any attention. He stared into the darkened house, a pensive look in his shadowed eyes.

"What's wrong?"

Logan let out a long sigh, brows knitted together in concern. "I'm really sorry I'm about to ask this, but would you mind if I stayed the night? I don't believe it's right for you to be here alone like this."

Shock barreled through her at the question, soon chased by something akin to excitement that made Katey quiver on the doormat. Was he serious? And why was her heart so ready to let him in? They had only known each other for a few days, but being away from him for longer than a few minutes seemed suddenly unbearable.

"I told you I could take care of myself, didn't I?"

Logan looked behind him at the rest of the neighborhood. It wasn't exactly the worst in town, but there were certainly better. Some yards were overgrown, lined with chain-link fences. Homes were at least three or four decades old in need of repair or remodeling. Most of the cars in the driveways or tucked beneath carports were just as old. Katey had heard a rumor that some guy sold drugs a few doors down, but he was only a little eccentric from what she could tell.

"All I know," Logan said softly, "is that if I left you here by yourself, I'd be worried all night. If something happened to you, I'd feel guilty that I wasn't here to help."

Katey adjusted her backpack strap on her shoulder. "Look, I've been left by myself for days on end since I was, like, eight years old. I'm not scared. Besides, what about your family? Won't they be expecting you home? You said your phone was nearly dead. What if they try to reach you?"

"Do you have a spare charger?"

"I do, but, Logan... I..." She gazed up into that sad puppy dog look he gave her at the diner in Morrisville. After a long moment of battling her own common sense, Katey cursed under her breath. "You win, but you're sleeping on the couch."

Before she could change her mind, she hurried inside and flicked on the living room lights. She had cleaned up over the weekend, but likely not to Mary's standards. The trash was picked up, floor vacuumed, and surfaces dusted, but not even those efforts could make the place look decent. Old secondhand furniture, soiled carpets, and dark tongue-and-groove paneled walls made the home look dated and less than cozy.

She dropped her bag by her bedroom door and went to the hall closet to pull down a spare blanket and pillow to throw on the couch. It was likely Logan wouldn't sleep well on the thin cushions, and she wouldn't get rest because of the creaky springs if he tossed and turned. When she came back, Logan had closed the front door, but hadn't ventured more than a couple of feet into the living room. He seemed to be inspecting the place, his studious gaze roaming from one random point to another.

"I'm sorry if it stinks. I can't get the smell of booze out of my foster mom's recliner." Katey motioned with the folded blanket toward the well-worn armchair.

"It's fine. I've seen worse."

"That's comforting." Katey tossed the bedding on the sofa and checked the clock on the wall. "It's pretty late, so I'm just going to go to bed. You're welcome to anything in the fridge and the bathroom is down the hall there." She pointed in those respective directions and Logan nodded.

"And that charger?"

"Oh, right." Katey went to the kitchen's junk drawer and pulled out the spare charger, then directed him to the nearest outlet to the sofa.

Logan set his helmet on one of the small tables beside the sofa. "Thank you for letting me stay. I know this may be uncomfortable for you, but I promise I won't get anywhere near your bedroom, if you were concerned about that."

Was it that obvious? Katey shook her head. "I know you wouldn't. I... I think I trust you, as crazy as that may sound."

He smiled as if she had just paid the biggest compliment of his life. "I appreciate that."

They stood, not a few feet from one another, in awkward silence with only a lone dog barking somewhere in the distance and the ticking of the clock on the wall. Katey never had a friend over and didn't know what was polite or customary. She certainly never had anyone over when her guardian was away. All the jitters that plagued her seemed to melt away the longer she stood there, acclimating to the vision of him in such a private space. They had been this alone before in the cemetery, but so much more could happen behind closed doors than in a wide open graveyard. That thought made her head a little dizzy.

She swallowed hard and gestured toward her room. "I'm... gonna go now. If you need anything, just let me know."

Logan nodded, evidently just as lost as her. "I will."

Her thigh nearly found the corner of a table when she turned to leave, but stumbled sideways before she could crash into it. With hastened steps, she grabbed her bag and shut herself in her room. She stayed there for a moment, fingertips pressed into the rough door. Just a piece of wood between them and she felt like her soul would split.

This was insane. This was straight-up lunacy. She hated that she liked it so much.

While she readied for bed, Katey played back bits of their evening as she had done every day since they met. There wasn't a single part that didn't make her ridiculously happy. She didn't know where all of this would lead, or how to truly describe what they were, but Katey decided to cherish it while she had the chance. Maybe in six months this would turn into a bittersweet memory, but that was something to worry about later. For now, she took comfort and glee in the knowledge that Logan was here and she was safe.

Dawn cast a silvery blue glow on Katey's small backyard. He stood on the pathetic excuse for a concrete patio just outside the back door, thumbs hooked in his belt loops as he breathed in the morning air. It wasn't as clean and fresh as the air around the pack's home. The odors of rotting garbage, dogs, persistent car exhaust from the busy neighborhood streets, the pungent stink of drugs a few houses down, and sun burnt grass made him wrinkle his nose in disgust. He didn't know if outside or inside was worse. Though Katey claimed she tidied up over the weekend, the astringent odor of bleach, artificial lemon and lavender, and cleaning product made his eyes water. Between the smells, the uncomfortable sofa, and the fight to keep his promise not to invade her space, Logan found little sleep the night before, though he hardly felt tired.

He pulled out his phone and turned it on for the first time since the afternoon before. Twelve missed calls, about as many texts from the pack, and three voicemails. He didn't bother listening to them. He knew what they would say. He had screwed up, again, but it was worth it to just soak in Katey's presence for those extra hours. It didn't take too much effort to filter through all of the distracting scents and noises to hone in on Katey while she slept. Her rhythmic breaths, the way her scent changed through the night in response to her emotions, thrilled him and gave him one or two sweet dreams in whatever sleep he could grab before morning.

The pack would have been back to the house by now, Darren's body released by the wolf and the other two shifted back into their human skins. Facing the inevitable, he dialed Dustin's number, expecting more benevolence from him.

"That was a dumb-ass move, kid." The betas voice was low, as if he had taken the call in secret. Logan wondered if he had to dash out to the edge of the wood beyond their field to escape the keen ears of their alpha.

"I know."

"Where are you?"

"At Katey's."

Dustin let out an oath, tinged with a sardonic laugh. "Wow. You don't waste time, do you?"

"Nothing happened."

"Oh, of course not."

"I mean it. Nothing happened. Katey's foster mother is out of town and I didn't feel right about leaving her home alone."

"She is not your responsibility."

"And I'm not yours, so why the calls and texts?"

"Damnit, you are our responsibility, Logan! When you just disappear, we get worried. Don't you get it?"

Logan brushed the bottom of his shoe against the rough, stained concrete. He understood. Their reactions to his escapades in the past proved that enough. They had had this argument before and they didn't need to rehash it for the hundredth time.

"How much shit am I in?" Logan asked.

"Oh, deep shit. Darren tried to hold off the shift to wait for you."

He winced. His alpha never did that and always chided them if they tried. "What should I do?"

"Grovel, probably. I hope she was worth it."

Logan shifted his weight from one foot to the other. "I think she is. Dustin... I've never met anyone like her. I just lost my head and knew I couldn't leave her, you know?"

Dustin sighed. "I know what you mean, but it's been a long time since Darren knew that feeling. You won't get any sympathy from him."

"I figured... I've got one more thing I want to do and then I'll head that way."

"Fair enough. Darren's a little out of it, so that'll give him time to get his head back on his shoulders."

Logan disconnected the call and looked back to the patches of sod and sand beyond the concrete pad. It broke his heart that Katey had to live in such a home, in such a neighborhood. She deserved better than some piece of trash in the middle of the city. A plan formed in his mind, a dangerous and potentially insane plan that his pack would likely shoot down in an instant. But, if he had enough time to make his case and present it to the pack, grounded in logic that appealed to their better natures, perhaps it could work.

Katey opened her eyes to see she was standing in the cabin again. It was the same cabin every time. She turned and gazed around at the catastrophic mess that someone or something had made. Tables were overturned, broken glass lay scattered about the floor. She could smell smoke and the iron-like stench of blood. Upholstery had been

ripped to shreds, showing the white cotton stuffing underneath. Anything that had once resembled wood furniture was broken into splinters. There had been a fight here, some epic battle to the death... but who won?

Katey paced carefully through the clutter, watching, and wait-ing. She always appeared right around now. Sunrise poured through the windows, shedding a rosy light upon the disheveled cabin. Katey looked up to the open front door and saw her.

The woman stood there, radiant and ethereal. Her long blonde hair cascaded in loose waves down her back and smokey gray eyes glittered with mischief and adventure. What struck Katey the most was her extremely fair skin and dazzling white gown. The beautiful woman glowed in the morning light, like something from another world.

Katey took a cautious step forward, but as soon as she did the woman turned and walked away. Katey burst in a run after the woman, knocking over anything that was in her way. She was determined to catch her this time.

"Wait! Come back!" Katey leapt through the cabin's front door and into an endless white void that engulfed the scene. The woman in white seemed to walk slowly, but Katey never seemed to be able to catch up. Her steps were sluggish and heavy.

"Follow me!" the woman called back to her. Her voice echoed in Katey's ears, as melodious as a trickling stream or shimmering wind chimes. Katey ran faster.

Tears stung at the corners of her eyes as the image of the woman began to fade from her view, disappearing into the white void.

Katey's phone alarm interrupted her dream, the opening notes of a rock ballad blaring through the darkness of her room. She bolted upright, her face damp with perspiration and heaved for air. She snatched up her phone and disabled her alarm. She cursed under her breath, desperately wishing her dream had continued just a few minutes longer. Maybe then, she would have been able to catch the woman in white.

It was always the same dream with the same beginning, and regretfully the same end. The first came when she was a child, maybe four or five years old, when memories seemed to stick. Katey remembered waking up crying when she couldn't catch up with the woman, and her foster mother at the time was of little comfort in her distress.

The dreams came more frequently in the following years, becoming more vivid and urgent with each vision. She had them at least every few days now. Katey tried to think of what they meant, but the explanation always eluded her. Who was the woman? Where was the cabin? Each time she found herself in that place, she tried to search for any hint, but there was no distinct clue that told her anything specific. This was the first time she had the dream since she met Logan and it seemed all the more vivid and real somehow.

After she took several long moments to gather her senses, she reluctantly rolled out of bed, and stumbled her way into the living room. Wearing her usual flannel pants and oversized shirt for pajamas, she half expected to see Logan rousing from his own sleep, or perhaps already up and getting ready to leave.

Instead, she found the blanket neatly folded atop the pillow she gave him, and no sign of him or his motorcycle helmet. The man had a talent for disappearing into thin air, only to reappear just as suddenly.

Logan may have been gone, but she smelled something else coming from the kitchen. There, on the small dining table, was a plate of toast, eggs, and sausage patties. An empty glass and fork completed the place setting. Tucked beneath the plate was a folded piece of paper. Katey snatched it up and greedily devoured Logan's immaculate penmanship.

Katey,

I'm sorry we couldn't have breakfast together, but my family need-
ed me home. I know you said you weren't much of a breakfast eater,
but it would make me happy if you ate something more substantial
this morning. I'll see you in first period.

Logan

She smiled, her heart warmed by the sincerity and thoughtfulness of it. Her usual routine prevented her from eating much at all,
giving herself just enough time to get ready and eat something on
the road. But, she hadn't denied Logan yet, and didn't plan to start
now. She poured herself a glass of orange juice and noticed that
he even cleaned up after himself in the kitchen. Everything was
cooked and seasoned to perfection, much better than if Katey had
tried to make it herself. Logan could stay the night every night if
he'd cook for her.

Katey made her way to first period, her walk a little faster than
usual, knowing she'd see Logan in mere moments. Outside the
classroom, Mr. Dubose monitored the halls. Despite his strong
stance, Katey noticed the dark circles under his eyes as If he
hadn't slept. His face and energy were devoid of the anger from
yesterday, a welcome relief. She remembered what Logan had
mentioned the day before. Maybe the drama in his household had
been resolved.

"Good morning, Mr. Dubose."

"Good morning, Miss Katey." He did not return her smile, but
only nodded as she passed by to enter the classroom.

Any other day, she might have been injured by his disregard, but
the promise of seeing Logan again made it less cutting.

He was among a handful of students already in the classroom, seated at their table, back turned to her. There was something tense in the set of his back and shoulders, as if he were struggling to keep some emotion bottled. As she drew closer, some of that stiffness eased, but didn't completely go away.

"Hey, Logan." She sat beside Logan in Beth's assigned seat. Her friend wouldn't mind, knowing the connection she and Logan already had. Logan wore an army green canvas jacket over a plain black shirt, and a pair of jeans not unlike those he wore the day before. That morning, she debated on wearing his jacket, but decided for a large gray hoodie and jeans, a comfortable and warm combination, as the weather had turned particularly chilly.

There was a hardness in Logan's expression as he glanced at her and then back to fidgeting with a pen in his hands. "Hey."

Such a cold greeting made Katey shrink. "Are you okay?"

"Yep."

Katey frowned. "You got in trouble with your family?"

Logan heaved a sigh. "Yep."

"Grounded?"

"In a way." Logan glanced over his shoulder to the door.

Katey followed his gaze but didn't notice anything beyond the steady flow of students in the hallway. "I'm sorry. I should have tried harder to make you leave last night."

A wince marred his face and he waved his hand at her as if he didn't want to continue the conversation. "It's all right. Let's not talk about it. Did you sleep well?"

Katey settled in her chair and pulled out her binder for the class. "Yeah. And thanks for breakfast. It was great. I normally don't eat that much and I probably won't be hungry for lunch."

The faintest of smiles crossed his lips. "I'm glad. That you liked it, I mean."

The class began to fill and Beth barely acknowledged that her seat had been confiscated when she sat in Katey's spot. She saw a cunning look on her friend's face, as if she had her own lurid theories of what must have taken place in the last twenty-four hours between Katey and Logan.

"I hope you'll make an effort to eat three decent meals a day and take care of yourself."

Katey tucked her hair behind her ears, unafraid to show the bit of blush rising to her cheeks. Other people had told her something similar, but it seemed more meaningful coming from Logan. Yet, something in his tone conveyed regret. Combined with the words, she wondered if it was a prelude to some coming goodbye. It had a familiar ring to the many goodbyes, both sincere and counter-feited, from foster families and social workers. They may not have been sad to see her go, but wanted to impart some offhanded platitude that she take care of herself, mostly because that was no longer their responsibility.

Fear pricked her heart. It was too soon for it all to end. Maybe his family had forbidden him to see her again. It made sense, given that she was the reason he went missing from them for two nights. But, if that were the case, why wouldn't Logan see it, instead of admitting that he had only been grounded? Her pulse hastened and she tried to tell herself that she was just reading into something that wasn't there.

Logan's head swiveled to her, eyes a little wide as if she had just let out a blood curdling scream. "You okay?"

Caught off guard, Katey nodded and reflexively lied. "Yeah. Are you?"

She saw his eyes shift as if he were studying her face for some-thing. Before anything more could be said, the bell rang and Mr. Dubose came in from the hall.

"That is not your assigned seat, Miss Katey. Please switch with Beth."

They obeyed, but the distance hurt like a stiff muscle being stretched beyond its limits. Logan's sudden concern added to her fear, but she willed herself not to jump to conclusions. Still, the anxiety that they both tripped over the starting line was strong, and she hated how she'd have to wait nearly an hour before talking it out.

Mr. Dubose announced that they would continue their lesson on population change with a focus on climate's impact on evolution and the environment, a controversial topic. Katey resigned herself to take notes from the slideshow presentation and tried to ignore the twisting in her guts.

Not ten minutes into the lecture, Mr. Dubose snapped a glare toward their table.

"Logan, this is your first and only warning. Put the phone away or it's mine."

That harsh threat was usually reserved for problem students. She wondered if Logan's family told the teachers about everything that happened. That might also explain Mr. Dubose's coldness before class.

She glanced Logan's way just as her phone vibrated in her pocket. One buzz to indicate it was a text. Logan's upper lip twitched as if he were about to snarl at Mr. Dubose, but thought better of it and shoved his phone in his bag hanging over the back of his chair without a word of protest.

Katey was careful to wait several moments until Mr. Dubose had his back turned. Like she was handling a fragile glass figurine, Katey slid her phone out of her pocket and checked the message. It was from Logan.

Please don't worry. I'm just on lockdown. School and home only. It's not your fault. Wait for

The way the sentence ended, she guessed that was when Mr. Dubose caught him, but Logan felt compelled to send the message along anyway. What did he want her to wait for? Whatever it was, she would. The mawkish thought occurred to her that she'd wait forever for him. Her lips tightened to hold back the smile.

The bell rang and, under the assumption that Logan might have tried to ask her to wait for him after class, took her time packing up her binder and textbook. When she looked up, Logan was gone.

"It sucks that Mr. Dubose won't let you sit next to Logan," Beth muttered. "He's never been a stickler about the seating chart before."

Again, Katey wondered if it had something to do with the trouble Logan got into with his parents. In that case, Mr. Dubose would not be an ally, which made sense. As unfair as it was, Katey understood. It changed nothing about the way she felt toward her teacher, though the last couple of days had certainly produced a very different Mr. Dubose than she was used to. Hard, and a little mean, she wondered if that was Logan's doing or something else.

A quick glance to her teacher awarded her a look she couldn't quite read. Halfway between sympathetic and reprimanding. Yeah, he definitely knew something.

"Did you ever get his number?"

Katey and Beth made their way toward the door and she questioned how much she should tell her friend. To say that she and Logan went on a date might be enough, but to mention his impromptu sleepover might have given the wrong message. Nothing happened, even though there was a short-lived moment in the early hours of the morning that Katey almost wished Logan would break his promise and come to her door.

"I did. I'll have to tell you the whole story later."

"Oh, a story. I like the sound of that." Beth's insinuating tone made Katey's face go hot with embarrassment.

"Nothing like that!"

She was ready to tell her at least a few details to whet her appetite, but when they stepped out the door, a hand lightly wrapped around Katey's arm. She started but calmed instantly when she saw Logan standing there off to the side. Before she could say anything, his grip tightened and gently pulled her out of sight from the door, a finger to his lips. He acted as if he needed to steal her away in secret for something. A muted glance to Beth communicated enough and her friend gave her a cute finger wave before walking away.

Katey allowed herself to be guided deep into the crowd of students in the hall. They were around a few corners and outside in the breezeway between the main building and the detached senior hall when he finally spoke.

"Sorry about that. You read my text?"

Katey nodded. "Yeah. We're you going to ask me to wait for you?"

"Yes. I wanted to ask you something, but not in there."

Katey adjusted her bag. "Does Mr. Dubose know you're in trouble with your family?"

"Yeah." Logan looked over his shoulder as if he expected one of their teachers to pop out of the crowd and snatch them apart.

Katey screwed up her face. "Today's gonna suck, huh?"

Logan stepped closer, the heat of his nearness warming her chest and face, even as the December cold began to numb her fingers. "It'll suck a little less if you'd join me for lunch?"

"I thought you said you couldn't go anywhere but school and home? Or are you talking about eating together in the lunchroom?"

Logan's mouth curled in a mischievous grin. "I know a spot on campus where we can be alone for a little while."

"Only here for two days and you find your own hideout." The thrill of it made Katey copy his smile. "But, I didn't bring a lunch. I'd need to sneak out of the lunchroom and—"

"I should have enough for the both of us... Will you?"

They didn't have much longer to talk before the tardy bell rang, but Katey only needed seconds to nod in agreement. "As long as it won't get you in more trouble."

"I promise. It won't."

CHAPTER 8

After fourth period, Logan asked Katey to wait outside the classroom while he talked to Mr. Myers. Through the din of the hallway, she couldn't make out most of what they said until the end of their conversation.

"I ain't gettin' in the middle of this. You go talk to Darren."

Katey couldn't hide the confusion in her face. Who was Darren? What was Mr. Myers talking about?

Seconds later, Logan emerged, looking peeved. "Sorry. One more pitstop. Can you wait for me by the doors that lead to the bus ramp?"

Too puzzled to argue, she nodded and they walked in opposite directions. As the halls emptied of students, most either leaving campus or retreating to the lunchroom, Katey wondered if Logan got caught up in something unexpectedly to leave her waiting. Several moments passed before Logan appeared from a nearby hallway, frustration plain in the way he moved. From his hand dangled a large blue lunchbox, and by the way it bulged, she could tell it was well-packed.

"I'm sorry," he grumbled. "That should not have taken so long."

He held open one of the glass doors, letting in a gust of winter wind, and stepped aside to let her out.

"What did you have to do?"

"I just needed to let Darren know where I'd be during lunch and he gave me a hard time about it."

They stepped out onto the deserted bus ramp and Katey followed his lead beneath the metal awning that covered the walkway along the building. "Who's Darren?"

The slightly startled look told her he must have regretted what he said. "Oh... I guess I never told you, did I? That's Mr. Dubose's first name. Darren Dubose."

Katey felt as if she had just been let in on some dirty secret. Not many students learned their teacher's first name. "Now you have to tell me the rest of their first names."

"Oh, but should I?" He slid a clever glance her way and stroked his chin.

She elbowed his ribs. "Come on, it's not like I'm going to use it against them."

"You're not one of the Fae, are you?"

"Huh?"

Logan laughed and guided her toward a set of doors off the bus ramp. "You've never heard of that before? Fae, or fairies, can use a human's name against them to make deals and do all sorts of nefarious things."

Katey grinned. "No, I didn't know that."

He opened one of the doors and she entered a large, spacious room with a high ceiling and concrete floor. It gave the feel of a warehouse or storage room, if one wall hadn't been covered in plated mirrors, not unlike the ballroom dance studio. Toward one side of the room was a pair of vending machines for snacks and drinks, a few folding tables, three stacks of plastic chairs, and an old beat-up couch that looked to be straight out of a living room from the 1970s. On the other wall, opposite the doors, was a pyramid of rolled up mats towering several feet high. Skinny windows along the top of the wall allowed in sunlight, brightening the room well enough to see inside with the doors closed. The place smelled of plastic foam and sweaty socks.

"I've been going to the school for four years and didn't know this was here."

Logan closed the door behind them. "My best guess is this is where the wrestling team practices."

"By the smell of it, I think you're right."

He gestured toward the sofa and Katey sat down heavily, the cushion dropping beneath her so that her knees were higher than her lap. Her arms reflexively shot out to prevent herself from falling through completely and Logan chuckled. The sofa handled him just as badly.

"You sure this will hold us both?" she laughed.

"If it doesn't, we can sit on those mats or the floor." Logan pulled up his lunchbox and unzipped it to take out two containers, two plastic forks, and a bottle of chilled water.

"You were counting on me agreeing to eat with you?"

"I figured I had a fifty-fifty chance. Might as well be prepared." He popped the lids to uncover thinly sliced steak sitting in its own juices. "Sorry it's cold. It's fully cooked."

Katey didn't take it immediately, though the meat smelled great, like something someone would order at a high-end steakhouse. The seared exterior was coated in a crisp layer of seasoning. "What is it?"

"Steak... Don't tell me you're a vegetarian."

Katey took the container and the fork offered to her. "I'm not, but I meant, what kind of meat." She stabbed a sliver of steak.

"Oh. Deer."

A little shocked, the laden fork paused halfway to her mouth. "Deer?"

"Yeah. We do a lot of hunting and get it butchered into steak cuts and sausages."

That shouldn't have been a surprise. This was Florida, but this part of the state might as well have been as country as Alabama.

There were plenty of people who waited for deer season with just as much anticipation as football season.

Katey bit into the piece of steak and had to stifle a moan. It tasted incredible. "I've never had deer steak before. This is really good."

Logan beamed, as if relieved that he packed the right lunch for them. "I'm glad you like it."

After a few mouthfuls, she leaned against the back cushion, sinking in so far that she might as well have been lying flat. "So, tell me the teachers' names."

Logan copied her. "Well, if you're going to twist my arm..." He swallowed the meat he had been chewing. "Darren Dubose, Dustin Keith, and Ben Myers. I think Mrs. Kimbrough's name is Lisa, but I'm less acquainted with her. I know her husband better."

The names bounced off the walls of her mind, echoing them in her thoughts and nodded in approval. They looked like their names, she supposed.

"I won't tell them that you told me... Why did you have to tell Darren where you'd spend lunch?"

"They're keeping an eye on me. I was supposed to sit with them during lunch."

Katey's face pinched in befuddlement. "Are your parents that controlling that they would rope the teachers into keeping watch over you?"

Logan huffed a mirthless laugh. "You don't know the half of it."

"Is that where all that talk about freedom came from the other night?"

The cap of the water bottle cracked as Logan opened it, then handed it to her. "Yep. You take the first sip."

"To make it sweeter?" Katey teased before taking a swig. It was a cheesy line; one she had heard in exchanges between Forrest and Lily on a number of occasions. Katey rolled her eyes each time she was there to hear it.

"I wasn't thinking of that, but sure."

Katey handed it back and licked her lips. "One of my past foster families was like that. Controlling, manipulative, paranoid. I was twelve and they interrogated me after school, convinced I had spent the day smoking or out with guys or something just as condemning. I lasted three months in that house."

Logan gave her a wry look. "At least you could get out. I can't."

Bitterness sharpened his words, but Katey wouldn't leave it alone. "I assume you're eighteen. You could leave. Stay with a friend?"

That reminded her of earlier that day when Lily gave her the bad news, via a note in second period, that her family wouldn't let her come to live with them before the end of the year. Lily gave her no details, but Katey suspected it was because they were not fond of her or her friendship with Lily. There was still hope that Forrest could find someone, but she wasn't likely to hear of the news until Saturday at their monthly social party, which she was obligated to attend.

"It's complicated." Logan grumbled and jabbed a piece of meat a little viciously.

"Anything I can do? I know I'm pretty much the reason you got in trouble, but if I can help—"

"It's not your fault, Katey," he snapped. "Never think that. They're just... being unreasonable."

Her eyes fell back to the other untouched half of her lunch. "I was worried they had forbidden you to see me after what happened last night."

"Was that what scared you this morning?" His voice turned gentle and soothing.

She turned back to him, tilting her head back. The stuffing on that part of the cushion was so thin that the back of her skull touched the wooden frame. "Was it that obvious?"

"I'm just perceptive... Honestly, I was afraid of the same thing."

Their gazes met and a myriad of feelings squeezed at her heart. She wished she could capture this moment, the way his eyes caught the sunlight, the warmth of his nearness, the dissonant smells of the wrestling gym, the musty sofa, and their meaty lunch in their laps. She wanted to remember this long, quiet moment forever.

If this were some sappy teenage romance movie, they would be making out by now. Katey would have scoffed at the very idea weeks ago, but now, sitting here with Logan, it didn't seem so silly anymore. Some nameless need mingled with the quiet bliss of being in his presence and she shifted to try and ease her discomfort.

"What are we?"

The thought escaped into the open without her conscious effort. As soon as they were out, she wished she could have snatched the words from the air before Logan heard them.

Regardless, he heard her and heaved a sigh. "At the very least, I'd like to think we are friends. Anything else is... too complicated right now."

"Because of your family?" Her whisper trembled, nerves tangled.

Logan nodded. "Yes, but there's more involved. Please don't ask me to explain it. I can't just yet."

Mouth dry, she nodded.

What did any of that mean? What else held them apart? Was anything that complex that it couldn't be explained? And when could he explain it? Next week? Next year?

Logan was the first to break away and continued eating. Katey did the same and fought the impulse to be wounded by such disappointment. Equally difficult was resisting the self-deprecating thoughts. She wasn't stupid, wasn't fooling herself, and wasn't being played. The regret in Logan's voice was real. The pain, palatable. He wasn't brushing her off. If he could tell her, he would. If they could be more than friends, he wouldn't hesitate. Neither would she.

A tap on her arm brought her back to reality. Logan held out the water bottle. After a second of hesitance on her part, Logan said, "I promise I don't have cooties."

Katey cracked a smile and took another drink, savoring the unique flavor on the rim of the plastic opening. This may be the closest she would ever come to Logan's lips, but she hoped not. Maybe, if they could hang on until after graduation, they could both be free enough to take things to the next level. Then again, what was the next level and could Katey wait that long?

Logan finished his steak and returned the container to the lunchbox before he reached into a small pocket of his backpack. He withdrew something wrapped in a thin black cord with two earbuds dangling.

"Any plans for winter break?" he asked as he unraveled the cord from the mp3 player. "Will your foster mother be back by then?"

"She will, but I'm hoping she'll find some excuse to stay with her boyfriend until the end of the year. It'll give me more time to find a new place to stay."

Logan went still. "New place?"

Katey nodded and dropped the fork in her empty container. "Yeah. I won't stay under her roof any longer than I have to. She's already threatened to kick me out. Might as well beat her to it."

"Like with all your other foster homes?"

Katey sat up straight to watch him turn on the mp3 player. "Only this time, I get to choose where I go next. Sort of. My first choice was to stay with my best friend but her parents said no. So, I'm waiting on another friend to find a place for me. Only until I graduate and then we'll see."

Logan went silent as he scrolled through the long playlist, a thoughtfulness in his eyes, and she wasn't sure if he was trying to find a specific song or if what she said distracted him.

"What about you? Any plans?"

He blinked and nodded. "Yeah. Every year we go to Alaska for about a week. Something like a family reunion."

"Alaska? Is that where your family's from?"

A smirk told her that she should have known better than to ask. Like every other topic that touched on his private life, he wasn't likely to give a lot of details. "Not really. It's just an easy meeting place for everyone."

"Alaska's a pretty long way away."

He shrugged and handed an earbud to her. "It's not bad."

She took the earpiece and waited a bit for him to continue about Alaska. When he didn't, she said, "Is this your way of trying to end a conversation?"

"Maybe," he replied with a playful look.

Heavy guitar and drums streamed through the speaker, but Katey didn't recognize the rapid beat and grinding rifts immediately. It wasn't until the lyrics came screaming through that she smiled. "Is this Avenged Sevenfold's new album?"

"Good ear."

They listened to a few songs from the album on shuffle, her gaze set on a crack in the concrete just beyond the tip of her shoe. A rogue glance toward the wall of mirrors revealed Logan staring at her, eyes fixed on her and only her. Her skin prickled with excitement and heat trailed down her spine.

One song, tempo quick and racing but lyrics slow and ballad-like caught her attention. She looked at the screen of the mp3 player. The song was entitled "Unbound (The Wild Ride)". The words sang of life, death, the inevitable transition from dark to light, or good things going wrong, and not taking either for granted. Something in the song spoke to Katey and in the span of a few verses, she braced herself for a potential mistake.

"Logan, can I tell you something?"

The song faded and another began, nothing like what they had been listening to. Slow and swaying with a feel of casual jazz, Katey knew it but not enough to remember the words. Logan unplugged the earbuds, and the music drifted around them.

"As long as you can tell me while we dance." He offered his hand to her.

She held her breath, staring at his hand, palm up and fingers steady as a rock. He may not have been scared, but she was terrified. Searching her memory, she couldn't recall a single moment when their skin touched since the night they first met. Always through sleeves or cloth. So much had changed since then. If they touched, would she be able to control herself? Could he? Suddenly, the thought that they were completely alone, that they could do whatever they wanted without being caught, seemed like an open invitation to do something they might both regret. The thought never hit her that hard, not even when he stayed the night in her living room.

His hand recoiled. "I don't mean to make you uncomfortable."

"You don't make me uncomfortable." She couldn't say that a day ago. Katey thought she could laugh at the absurdity of it. Logan had become so much more to her than a friend, but she'd never confess it.

This time, she held out her hand to him and begged it to stop shaking. Though unconvinced, Logan curled his fingers around hers. Fire sparked through her nerves, and she had to rely on him to take the lead. Her feet couldn't be trusted to move while her whole soul became seized in pleasant shudders.

They rose from the couch and Logan guided them to the middle of the open space. His free hand settled just below her shoulder blade as he assumed the proper position for a waltz. She often had to correct new students at the ballroom dance studio that correct posture did not involve groping at their partners waist or hip. Her hand artfully rested upon his bicep, the curve between her thumb and index against the hard muscle beneath his jacket. The fabric of their jackets just lightly touched as she kept their elbows barely apart. They formed the perfect frame, something she didn't expect out of him at all.

His masculine scent of the wild forest, a mix of pine and damp soil, made her head dizzy and she couldn't look into those eyes that would make her legs turn to jelly. She lifted her chin and cast her gaze over his shoulder to the wall of mirrors. The vision of his back consumed nearly every inch of her.

Her mind groped for the switch, the one she had to throw during each lesson so she could stay in the moment and focus on her partner and the music. No feeling, no emotion, just shallow indifference and calculated precision. It was necessary during such an intimate act as dancing. But this wasn't just any student. It was Logan.

The music continued, lyrics proclaiming undying devotion from one lover to another. Were these words he wanted to tell her but couldn't put into words? Or was it a promise of days when they could feel that deeply and freely? They made her want to weep and she could already feel her nose sting and throat close with impending tears. She had never cried in front of anyone, but didn't mind being so vulnerable here with Logan.

Katey shook her head and stepped away. It was too much, too fast. She'd never get out what was in her heart if he kept stealing it from her chest.

Logan instantly let go. "What's wrong?"

Katey covered her face with her hands to hide her embarrassment. "Nothing. Nothing's wrong. I just... Can I get out what I want to say before I lose the nerve to say it?"

The music stopped and Katey took a steadying breath before straightening to face Logan. Confused and perhaps a little distressed by her rejection, Logan watched and waited. She crossed her arms over her stomach that wouldn't stop churning beneath her skin.

Thinking it would be easier to spill her guts, she closed her eyes and refused to open them until she had finished speaking her truth to the dark.

"Before I met you, I was struggling with a lot of shit. I was... in a fog. No... Standing over an abyss, ready to jump and let darkness swallow me up. I couldn't feel, couldn't bring myself to care about anything or anyone, not even myself. I'm just a kid nobody wanted, and I tried not to be so... so broken over that, but I was. I put on a mask... every damn day to hide it from my friends, my teachers, the social workers... But underneath the lies and the fake smiles, I was dying. Some days... I just didn't want to live anymore. Official diagnosis would say it was depression, and I guess that would be right, but this felt so much deeper than that. Deeper than sadness, deeper than hopelessness. It was just this constant hollow feeling that I could never escape."

Katey took a shuddering breath to keep herself from reliving the memories, the suicide attempts, the voices, the feeling of being so lost and alone. "That night at the cemetery, I was ready to give into all that darkness inside of me. I didn't care what happened."

She finally felt brave enough to open her eyes and met Logan's troubled stare. "And then you came. I don't know how, and I don't know why... and I hope that this won't scare you away, but when you showed up, the darkness left. It was like dawn broke and you chased away the shadows in my head... Ever since, I've been okay. No black thoughts, no depression. I went from stuck to feeling again." A tiny, unbidden tear streaked down her hot cheek. "Even if we only have a few days or a few months, I'll be forever grateful for that night."

She swallowed hard and waited for him to laugh, to tell her that there was no possible reason why a mere man could break a depressive episode just by showing up. He did neither. Logan's face softened and he stepped closer. His hand cupped her cheek and brushed away the tear with his thumb.

"Thank you for sharing that with me." His voice was low, husky, and achingly intimate. "And no, you'll have to try a lot harder to scare me away."

Katey guffawed and laid her hand over his, leaning into his palm to treasure his touch.

In a move that she didn't expect, he bent his brow against hers, eyes shut, their faces dangerously close. His breath engulfed her, sweet and balmy against her skin. Her whole body tensed and then relaxed, afraid in one second and then wonderfully enraptured in the next. Friends didn't do things like this.

"Believe it or not," he whispered, "you did something similar for me, too. I'd never trade that night for anything as long as I live."

Katey smiled. "How is that possible, though?"

He shook his head, making hers move with him since their foreheads touched. "I don't know, but I'm not going to question it... Not now."

They stood like that for what seemed like an eternity and Katey braced for what might have naturally come next. It wasn't a declaration of love, but it sure felt like it. How could they be just friends after this?

In one jarring motion, Logan broke away to look toward the gym doors.

Katey flinched back as if she had just awoken from a dream. "What is it?"

"I think lunch period is over."

She blinked and eased away to catch her breath. "I didn't hear the bell."

"I did." Logan glanced between her and the sofa where he had left the lunchbox. "I'll walk you to your next class."

Just like that, all tenderness was gone, as if a timer had gone off and they were back to their own reality. He walked away and the cold rushed in to take his place, leaving Katey bereft. Her mind groped for a lifeline. She just bared her secret to him, and in much fewer words he confessed his own feelings. How could he walk away like that?

As if realizing his blunder, Logan rushed back to her with their things. "I know I can't leave home after school, but I want to try something. I just have to go about it the right way." He brushed the back of his fingers against her arm in a warm show of affection. "Meet me after school by your locker?"

His caress made her forget why she was upset. It was a sign he still cared. "I can." He offered her bag, and she took it, unprepared for the weight of it. "You're staying at school until the end of the day even without classes?"

He grimaced. "Yeah. Another one of those conditions on my lockdown. I have to talk to Darren first, but then I'll come see you, okay?"

This whole arrangement between his family and the teachers still struck her as odd, but Katey nodded. She'd wait for him.

It was just a text. A simple message to the pack. Yet, Logan spent the better half of the hour trying to find the right words. It shouldn't have been this hard.

He slammed the phone on the desk and rubbed at his face as if to wash away the frustration.

Katey's heartfelt testimony had to be proof that they belonged together. There was no other explanation for how they could both be healed in the same way. The misery in her eyes as she told her story broke his already damaged heart even further. He never wanted her to suffer like that again. He knew that kind of sorrow, that overwhelming darkness that sucked every bit of light and happiness from life. He knew what it was to see the world in shades of gray and prefer the emptiness of death over faking contentment every day. In those dark times, he had his pack to pull him out of the mire and clean him up. Katey had no one.

It took him only seconds in the wrestling gym, as he watched the tear glide down her cheek, to make his decision to totally commit himself to mending the wounds of her past. Whether that was through friendship, love, a promise to never leave her side, or bringing her into his world of shifting and pack bonds, he'd do it. He just had to find a way to convince the guys that what he intended for her was a good plan.

"It might be easier if ya asked for help," Ben said from his desk.

His planning period gave Logan a place to stay while he waited for the end of the day. What he had told Katey was mostly true. He was on lockdown, not permitted to be out of sensory range from the pack or unchaperoned in some way. He wasn't even permitted to drive to school on his own, but hitched a ride with Dustin. It took a fair deal of arguing with Darren to be allowed to have lunch with Katey away from their supervision.

Logan flattened his hands on the cool desk top. "I doubt you could help with this."

"Try me."

With a sigh, Logan sat back. "I want the pack to meet in Darren's classroom after school. I want to talk about something... and get approval for it."

"This involves Katey, doesn't it?" Logan nodded and Ben made a doubtful noise. "Today? Don't ya think you're pushin' it after ya got your ass handed to you this mornin'?"

Darren hadn't touched a hair on Logan's head, but the dominance was strong enough to crush his bones, even while his alpha recovered from his shift night. The punishment wasn't unexpected, but was totally worth it.

"It's important."

"So important ya want to fall through that thin ice you're treadin" on?"

He didn't care if Darren beat him within an inch of his life if it meant he could help Katey. "I have to try."

Ben sighed and stood from his desk to come up beside Logan. "Let's see what you've got."

"Katey, can I talk with you outside for a second?" Dustin placed his hand on the back of her chair. His fifth period class busily worked on their assigned F.R.Q., granting him a little freedom to have a word with the girl that had turned their household upside down.

A whiff of peppery fear seeped from Katey, but she nodded.

Once out of the classroom, he assured, "You're not in trouble. I just wanted to talk about you and Logan."

Indignation displaced her fear and Katey crossed her arms defensively. That morning, Logan told the pack exactly how much he told her about his connection with the other three. He had to be mindful of what he said and how it could be misinterpreted. However, he couldn't sit aside and be silent while the drama went almost unchecked. They could discipline Logan as much as they wanted, but there was no one to make Katey understand. As much as Dustin had reluctantly taken on the role as beta from the beginning, he was the ideal enforcer in this conflict.

"We know that you two have gotten pretty close."

Fire sparked in her eyes. "Are you going to tell me to stay away from him too?"

Dustin had to smile at her spunk. It was a welcome change, and if he guessed right, it was a change Logan inspired. "That's not my place. I'm just your teacher, but I'm more to Logan and its part of my job to keep the peace."

"No disrespect, but I don't see how. I don't get why his family is so strict and why you and the other teachers have to monitor him. He told me all about that during lunch."

Dustin picked his words carefully. "I can't expect you to understand and I'm sorry you're stuck in the middle of this. What I need you to chew on is if you think this thing with Logan is worth the trouble it may get him into with his family. We don't want some Romeo and Juliet tragedy on our hands."

Katey shifted her weight to one leg, still in defiant mode. "We're both eighteen. We can make our own choices, and mistakes."

Yes, Dustin remembered what it was like to be eighteen and in love. Those memories were sharp, but for Logan and Katey's sake, he let himself be sliced deep so he could empathize. The heat, the passion, the fun, the thrill of sneaking around behind the backs of their friends and family to snatch a moment alone. Those days were rosy and full of hope. Dustin refused to go beyond the short-lived marital bliss, knowing what nightmare lay on the other side of the wedding reception.

It might have been too much to assume that Logan and Katey were already in some whirlwind romance, but nothing could be left to chance. He also knew how to keep secrets, and Logan was good at hiding his true thoughts and feelings from the rest. And if he suspected right, so was Katey. They could be neck-deep in some heady lovefest and they might never know it.

"We just don't want either of you to make the same mistakes we made." Dustin reined in his tongue. "All I ask is that you tread lightly. Take it slow. Logan can get... enthusiastic, to put it lightly. That's what's gotten him in his current trouble, why his family likes to keep a finger on his pulse, and why he neglected to let anyone know where he was last night. He knew they would have kept him from staying the night with you, so he just didn't ask. That was what got him in hot water. We... They didn't know where he was, and it caused a lot of grief. They might have let him stay if he had just told them what he was up to, but he lied and betrayed their trust, which has been rather fragile in the past."

His words finally banked the fire in Katey's eyes. "We never meant to make people worry or break anyone's trust."

"We all know. Logan is on lockdown until further notice, but that doesn't mean he can't see you. Like I said, take it slow and be patient. I know all of this is confusing, but it's in the best interest of all parties involved... We good?"

After a moment of thought, Katey nodded. Dustin gave her a heartening smile and patted her on the back. "That-a girl. It'll turn out all right."

As Katey returned to the classroom, Dustin's pocket buzzed with a text message. Checking it, he groaned. "Now what are you up to, kid?"

CHAPTER 9

Logan found Katey waiting patiently by her locker and let out a breath of relief. He didn't doubt that she would wait for him, but just the sight of her made the last couple of hours without her worth the fretting. He knew Darren, Dustin, and Ben were already waiting for him.

When she spotted him in the crowd of students, she grinned, green eyes dancing with the same renewed delight he felt. Seeing her again reminded him of that moment in the wrestling gym, when they had been so close and intimate. Even now, with a hundred students watching, he wanted to wrap his arms around her until all the fragments of her soul were pieced back together. She didn't look so broken now, but he wondered if that mask she mentioned ever lay quite out of her reach.

He resisted the urge to touch her as he closed the distance between them.

"So, what were you going to ask Darren?" Hearing her call his alpha by his first name gave him a little hope. Perhaps she'd transition easily.

"I'd like to see if I can take you home with me, if that's all right?"

"I guess it'd only be fair I see your house since you saw mine. But why ask Darren about that? Shouldn't you be calling your parents?"

Logan realized he might have said too much. "It's a bit of a long story, but that's another part of what I need to talk to him about. Just wait here. It might take a while."

Katey shrugged. "I've got nowhere better to be."

In an unguarded moment, Logan leaned down as if he were to give her a parting kiss, but reeled himself back before he could get too close. Katey jerked and blinked. How long would it take for Logan to reset his boundaries after what they shared? Could he? He wanted to be so much more with Katey. If this meeting went even halfway well, there was some chance, but he couldn't assume that the pack would get onboard immediately.

"I'll be back as soon as I can with word one way or another."

She only nodded and he hurried away around the corner to Darren's classroom. The door was open, and he could already sense the growing tension from inside. Ben already had an idea what the meeting was about, and if Darren and Dustin had any sense, they would too.

Gathering up his courage, he strode in and shut the door behind him.

"Lock it," Darren instructed.

He did as requested, muffling the noise from the hallway, and went to stand in the aisle between the rows of tables. Ben and Dustin sat on either side of him, Darren at the head of the room as he had been yesterday, standing as a judge over a trial.

"What did you want to discuss, Logan?" the alpha asked, voice edged with aggravation. Yeah, he already knew what this may be about, but none of them could guess his full intention.

Feet shoulder width apart and hands clasped behind his back like a soldier, he decided to jump straight into it. "I want to make Katey part of the pack."

To say the men before him were shocked would have been an understatement.

"You've only known her for less than a week," Dustin pointed out.

"And you've all known her for months. You would know better how well she would fit."

"The only way to make her part of the pack is for her to be mated to someone within the pack, or to be loup-garou herself." Darren folded his arms. "Both options are out of the question."

Logan shook his head and braced for their reactions. "I think both are possible."

"You've lost your damn mind!" Ben exploded.

"Keep your voice down," Dustin snapped. "There are still kids out there."

Darren glared. "You have no idea what you ask, Logan."

"I do. I want her in the pack and I'm willing to go either way to make it happen."

Dustin slipped off the desk and waved his hands as if he were trying to pat down smoldering embers. "Hold up. There's no way you're going to mate with Katey this early in the game, and you sure as hell aren't going to turn her. You know what will happen, right?"

"I don't think it will happen. She's strong. She's—"

"She's a girl, Logan!" Now it was Dustin's turn to raise his voice. "Females do not survive the bite. They die. Every fecking time, they die."

Darren came forward and put a steadying hand on his beta to pull him back. "Calm down. No one is going to turn Katey. It's impossible, Logan. I don't care how strong you think she is. She is just as female as all the others who took the bite and died before. She would be no exception."

Logan clenched his jaw, willing himself to keep his temper under control. "But you've all admitted she's special. I see it too. What if that something special is a sign that she would take the bite and survive?"

"Are ya willin' to take that chance?" Ben asked.

They fell silent and received their answer. Logan knew there were no female loups-garous for a reason, though the knowledge had been lost to them. Only sons with loup-garou fathers were born like this, and daughters were completely human. And yes, he had heard the stories of girlfriends and wives being bitten, and none of those stories ended happily.

The very thought of Katey dead pierced his soul. She wasn't so weak, not so submissive. She had battled the darkness and a life practically alone. Death couldn't take her. Not by the bite, nor by natural causes. That idea, of course, was lunacy. Logan knew death came for everyone eventually, even a loup-garou. Yet, he couldn't bear to think of Katey lying lifeless in some cold grave. Turning her, if it worked, could delay such a fate, and give Logan many more precious years, winning her trust and her heart. It was that possibility, that slim one-in-a-million chance that she could be with him for the rest of his life, that made him even consider turning her.

Logan swallowed hard. "All I'm saying is that Katey... She needs a pack. She needs a family. She's alone and I can't stand it, knowing that maybe we could do something about it."

Darren sighed, though a brief glimmer of sympathy shone in his eyes. "It's not our job to make sure that every lost soul has a place to belong."

"I know that, but maybe Katey could belong with us."

"You mean, belong with you," Dustin corrected. "I know what you may be feeling, but dragging her into our world is not the answer right now."

"Why not? What if bringing her into the pack is what she needs to help get her on her feet. She told me today that she's looking for a place to stay before the beginning of the year, but hasn't had any luck. Couldn't we—"

"Let a girl live with us?" Ben laughed. "That's all sorts of wrong. There ain't no hidin' what we are if we do that."

"Ben is right," Darren added, but paused in thought. "Yet, I understand the dilemma. I don't suspect Katey is safe where she is, but our home isn't the ideal place, not when she doesn't know."

"Then let's tell her." Logan couldn't keep the urgency out of his tone. "She's waiting out there right now. We can bring her in and explain everything and—"

"Nope," Dustin interrupted with a shake of his head. "No way. We have never told anyone what we are and today is not the day to start throwing that kind of information around. It's too risky. If she blabs to the wrong person, we're all in deep shit, and you know it."

Logan balled his hands into fists and turned to pace a bit, struggling to keep his cool. This wasn't going the way he wanted it to.

"What do you want us to say, Logan?" Darren asked, oddly calm.

He swung on the pack, eyes gleaming gold. "I want you to let me have a bit of goddamn happiness! After all this time, I'm entitled to it!" He charged at his alpha, but Dustin's arms shot out to restrain him by his shoulders. Dominance blasted against him, but he fought it fang and claw. "All three of you have had something I couldn't even begin to dream about. Now that I have a chance for it, you deny it from me."

Darren's eyes had also gone gold and narrowed, but he never flinched from the unmitigated aggression from his youngest packmate. Ben was on his feet and ready to assist Dustin if Logan should try to throw off the beta. Alpha and subordinate stared one another down, wolf meeting wolf, and Logan let out a strangled pulse of his own dominance to combat Darren's. It was weak and unrefined, nothing compared to his, but it was enough to show that this wasn't some act of rebellion against him. Logan meant every word he said.

Finally, Darren took a slow, deep breath. His eyes returned to brown and he withdrew his dominance. "Fine."

Dustin and Ben turned to their alpha, brows arched in surprise. Logan pushed away from Dustin and straightened his jacket.

"You can't be serious," Dustin muttered.

"I am." Darren never took his eyes off Logan. "And I'm likely as curious as any of you to find out why Katey has this hold over all of us. We will not bring her into the pack, but we will let her into our circle. If she knows our truth, perhaps we can discover hers in time... But, not today. We need time to find the right way to tell her. We must be strategic about this."

Logan took several breaths to push the wolf back into its cage. Soon, blue eyes returned and his heartrate slowed to something resembling normal. It was a small victory, not the way he planned, but it was better than what he almost settled for.

"If you intended to spend the afternoon with Katey," Darren continued, "I'm afraid you're still on lockdown. You can, instead, spend that time thinking of how we should tell her. We must all agree on the method and words, and only then will we take that next step."

Stunned, Ben and Dustin gave their muted consents, while Logan tried not to seethe in his impatience. Even one afternoon apart felt like a death sentence, but he'd take it.

"Don't get your hopes up that it'll happen anytime soon, but you have my word that it will happen. As far as giving her a place to live to get out of her foster mother's home, I'll make some calls and see what we can do. No promises there."

Darren granted Logan his leave and he darted out the door. The crowd had thinned considerably and he could hear the diesel engines of the buses rumble away from campus outside. Excitement for the plans he'd make for Katey mingled with the dread of how she'd react. He had already imagined a thousand different scenarios. Would she faint? Would she go insane with the knowledge that wolf shifters existed outside of the horror movies? Or would she take the news gracefully and eagerly? He didn't know how to feel if Katey had a curious mind for what he was. All the questions she may have, and all the answers he didn't want to give.

When he rounded the corner to Katey's locker, she wasn't there. Testing the hair, he knew her scent like his own, but it was faint, buried deep beneath the millions of other scents in the hall. Too many students had passed through. All he could tell was that her strongest scent trail led from her locker, to Darren's classroom, and out the bus ramp doors.

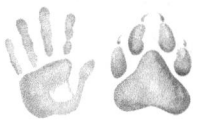

Eavesdropping was a mistake. Katey knew it as soon as intelligible words burst into angry shouts and raised voices behind the classroom door. Now she heard too much but knew next to nothing. Logan wasn't just talking to Darren, but Dustin and Ben as well, and they weren't talking about anything as innocuous as whether Katey could hang out with Logan after school. The words "bite", "turn", and "kill" were thrown about too much for that. She could have stuck around to learn more, but terror made her retreat.

Gripping her steering wheel at the red light, Katey tried to order her thoughts and fill in the gaps. Their conversation slapped of something out of a horror movie. There was one she and Lily watched a couple of years back. *Cursed* had been about werewolves, the main characters turned by being bitten by the monster. They went to see it for the cast and out of curiosity, but the plot was predictable and not the sort of monster movie they expected. Still, the images of gnashing fangs and partial transformations couldn't be shaken out of her head.

That was just a movie. It was pure fiction. Logan wasn't a werewolf and neither were the teachers. They certainly weren't vampires either, unless that sunlight thing was a myth.

Katey banged her hand on the wheel to snap herself out of that train of thought. *They. Are. Not. Monsters.*

What frightened her enough to run wasn't the talk about bites and turning, but the long silence from Logan after Ben asked if he was willing to risk Katey's life. He didn't deny it.

How could he be so heartless to become her friend, to save her from the crippling loneliness, and yet be willing to kill her for some mysterious endgame? Did she mean anything to him or was it all some cruel, murderous joke?

She pulled into her driveway, but didn't get out right away. Was she safe here? From the sound of it, the teachers were not on board with whatever Logan wanted. If they were something... not human, they at least valued her life. Would they keep Logan away from her? Was that why he was on lockdown? Did his parents know all along and that was why they were so controlling?

She leaned her forehead on her knuckles and whined. What the hell was going on?

Her phone vibrated in her pocket in that long, constant pattern that told her someone was calling. She checked the caller ID. It was Logan.

Nausea tickled her stomach and she bit her lips to keep them from quivering. All she could think was, *How could you do this to me?*

The screen went black. A moment later, a voicemail notification buzzed. She gulped back her nerves and listened.

"Hey, Katey. It's Logan. I thought you were going to wait for me. I guess it doesn't matter too much. We can't hang out this afternoon anyway... If you want to talk, feel free to call me... I hope you're all right and your disappearing doesn't mean anything... Regardless if you want to talk, can you text me when you get home safely?... If I don't hear from you, I'll see you tomorrow... Take care."

Katey could have wept. Logan was a great actor, if he could be okay with killing her, yet wish her well at the same time. She certainly wouldn't call him, and she wasn't sure she would text him. He didn't really care if she got home safe. How could he? It was all a farce. Nothing more.

Anger and disappointment swirled in her chest. She wanted to scream, to break something, to cry into her pillow. The one time she thought she could have some shred of happiness and it was torn from her hands before she could truly appreciate it. Before Logan, she had known what loneliness was, and came to accept its familiar ache. But now, she knew what it felt like to really lose every last scrap of hope in a single devastating moment.

Logan sat at the dining table, his phone face up in front of him, hands laced against his lips as if in prayer. Right about now, he wished he could supplicate to some higher being. Not a word from Katey and it had been two hours since she disappeared.

Darren was at the head of the table, laptop open with two piles of graded and ungraded papers. He suspected his alpha stayed close merely to keep him company. Dustin and Ben were in their third game of billiards on the other side of the house. They had invited him to play, but he refused. He could think of nothing else but Katey and her sudden radio silence. It didn't make any sense.

"Staring at the phone will not make her call."

Logan let out a low growl, but would not move. His eyes burned from not blinking.

"You may benefit from pouring your efforts into how you plan to tell her about us instead."

That might have been smart, but something in his gut wouldn't let him rest until he had some sign from Katey that she was all right.

"Somethings wrong," he mumbled. "This isn't like her."

"And how would you know that?" Darren asked between taps on the laptop keyboard.

Logan didn't have a good answer. They hadn't known one another long enough to have a full text or call conversation, but to hear absolutely nothing from her was not right. After what they shared in the wrestling gym, they should have been beyond any timidity, unless it scared her off. "I just know. She wouldn't have taken off like that without a word."

"I'm sure there is a perfectly good explanation and once she finally calls, you'll feel silly for worrying."

Logan abruptly stood from his chair and took to walking about the sitting room, desperate to burn off some of his anxiety. If he could have shifted to work out the nerves, he would have. The rest of the pack did it all the time. Though the shift was never anything less than agonizing, he didn't know which was worse, turning into a beast or waiting for Katey to return his message.

Dustin came in from the kitchen and leaned in the doorway, his pool cue in one hand and the other holding up a lazy, thoughtful finger. "Something just occurred to me... You said she was waiting for you, Logan. Was she outside the classroom?"

"No, she was at her locker down the hall."

Dustin rubbed at his stubbled chin. "What's the likelihood that she followed you to the classroom door?"

Logan shook his head. "She didn't follow me."

This notion got Darren's attention and he closed the laptop. "Are you suggesting she might have heard us?"

The beta shrugged. "We did get a little loud."

"I didn't sense her outside the door," Logan argued.

"Neither did I, but how well were we paying attention?"

Darren sat back, his stare distant as if he were thinking of all the ways this could have gone terribly wrong. "I can't recall if I sensed anyone either. Ben?"

From the kitchen, Logan heard their other packmate pouring a glass of water. "I didn't hear nothin' but I was just as distracted as y'all."

Dustin pulled out a chair from the table and set his cue stick in the corner. "With how many students were in the hall, maybe she slid past our notice. That may explain why she skipped out on you."

"But how much did she hear?"

Darren's question hung in the air like a funeral dirge. They all mentally recapped the meeting, wondering which part was the most condemning. They tossed about a lot of pack jargon that never should have been uttered in mixed company. Then, there was the part about their bite and how it could kill her.

"I'm going to check on her." Logan rushed out the sitting room doors and into the foyer.

Ben, dashing with his superhuman speed from the kitchen, blocked his path and snatched up his motorcycle keys from the bowl on the sideboard. "No ya ain't. We don't know what she knows and you may be the last thing she wants to see right now."

What if Katey suspects what they are? Logan went cold and every ounce of blood felt like it had drained from his face. This wasn't the way he wanted her to find out. Somehow, he imagined it'd be more informal and thorough. He'd break it to her gently and she might have the obvious questions. Had he killed anyone? Did he change with the full moon? But now, who knows what she thought of him and the pack. She may have answered those questions herself and decided she wanted nothing to do with him anymore.

His knees threatened to buckle beneath him, so he locked them in place and tried to breathe. Dustin came up and guided him to the sofa, as if sensing his weakness. With a harsh shove, Logan pushed him off and forced strength back into his body. He wasn't some flimsy pup. He could handle this.

"Hey, cool it, kid. We're all a little scared here."

"What do you have to be scared about?" Logan snapped. "You have nothing to lose. She's just some girl to you. Just another student."

Darren rose and joined them. "You forget that this isn't just about you or our pack. If Katey knows something and then tells someone else, the wrong person may suspect something and then more lives will be endangered."

Logan wasn't so selfish to not consider that possibility. Both he and Darren knew, firsthand, the kind of damage humans could do when they found out about their kind.

"Someone needs to keep an eye and ear on her," Dustin said. "At least until we can get this straightened out."

"Do I take that as you volunteering?"

Dustin looked at his alpha as if he were going to complain, but then gave in and nodded. "Yeah, fine. I'll go. I wanted to pull another all-nighter anyway." He grabbed his truck keys from the table and made toward the door. "I'll call if anything interesting happens."

Logan let himself drop onto the sofa and ran his hands across his pulled-back hair.

"You said she's friends with Lily," Darren said. "Call Forrest and make sure he's informed of what might have happened. He can run interference, so she isn't blindsided in case Katey decides to confide in her."

"What about that other girl?" Ben asked. "That goth kid."

"Beth," Logan corrected.

"She has no affiliation with us or Jacob's pack," Darren replied. "I'm unsure what to do about her, if it should come to that." The alpha placed a firm hand on Logan's shoulder. "I think it's time to come up with that plan. We'll need to sit with Katey tomorrow.

There may still be a chance she wasn't listening and doesn't suspect anything, but in the event that she did and she does, we need to set the record straight."

"What about durin' our classes? What're we supposed to do?"

"We will let her take the lead and act accordingly." Darren turned back to Logan. "I'm relying on you to make sure she doesn't leave school grounds before we talk to her." The alpha let out a long breath. "With any luck, this whole affair won't turn into a disaster."

Logan gritted his teeth. This was all his fault, and they all knew it. His problem of getting closer to Katey was suddenly their problem. If he hadn't been so eager, or if he had waited to talk to the pack when they were far away from humans, none of this would have happened, and his world wouldn't be spiraling out of control.

CHAPTER 10

Feet and paws beat against the forest floor. Low lying branches and tall ferns slashed at Katey's arms as she ran, adrenaline pulsing through her veins, urging her faster. They were gaining on her, closer now. She could almost feel their hot breath on the backs of her legs, hear their heavy doglike pants and yips as they pursued her.

Moonlight illuminated a clearing ahead. Headstones littered the space. Once past the trees, Katey finally glanced over her shoulder, but saw nothing. Stone collided with her knee and she fell forward over a headstone, sending her rolling across the grass.

When she managed to push herself up, they were there. Four wolves circled her, eyes an iridescent gold. In the dim light, she could make out the distinct shades and patterns of their pelts. One silver and black, another brown and beige almost like a German Shepherd, a third mostly black with gray streaks, and the last as ebony as a moonless sky. They didn't growl or snarl, but watched her with such intensity that Katey couldn't help but be afraid.

Their light walk quickened to a run, circling her faster and faster. The ground beneath her softened and churned, as if the wolves were creating their own whirlpool in the earth. Katey sank in the middle, arms flailing for anything to keep herself aloft, but the grass and dirt slipped through her fingers.

Just when her head became submerged in the earth, it released her and she dropped into a field of pristine snow. Katey had never seen snow, but felt its biting cold deep in her bones. In front of her stood the woman in white from her dreams, golden hair fluttering in the icy wind. Katey struggled to stand, but went still as the woman approached her.

She smiled and cradled Katey's face in her hands. "Do not worry, sweet girl. It'll all be all right."

Katey reached out, but the woman's image shimmered into snow flurries that began to swirl in big gusts around her. That, however, wasn't the most distressing. The back of her hand began to sprout fur as white as the snow, her palms grew rough pads, and fingernails extended into claws. She tried to scream, but the sound came out in a yowl as the rest of her body morphed. In seconds, she was no longer a human, but a pure white wolf.

The four wolves materialized from the blizzard and fell in beside her. The black one, so different from her own pelt, gave her an affectionate nudge. Her actions, as she understood them, were not her own and she nudged back, burying her muzzle in the thick fur around his neck. It was comforting and intimate to feel his heat against her.

More wolves lopped into the field. Yips and grunts and all manner of canine sounds filled the air. They were of all shades from blonde to red to silver, but she was the only white one among them. Several approached her, and Katey had the sense that she should have known them, though, how could she?

All at once, they began to run. Katey and the black wolf took the lead, flanked by the original three. They ran with no destination toward the horizon, breaths steaming from their open muzzles. Complete and total freedom in this arctic wasteland.

However, in an instant, something was wrong again. The black wolf stopped and began to writhe upon the ground, whining and whimpering as if in pain. Katey padded to him, but soon skittered back as he changed forms. He grew massive, body shifting from wolf to a man-wolf hybrid, eyes glowing a sinister red. Behind him, in the *empty void above the snow, shadows appeared. Formless shapes that only conveyed scenes and ideas. Guns. Fire. Crossing blades. Castles and towers. Noises that matched the scenes overlapped one another in a chaotic symphony that sent Katey cowering toward the rest of the wolves. But, all that remained were the three wolves from the graveyard. They gathered about her, tails erect and lips curled back into vicious snarls at the black beast.*

The monster roared and struck at them with razor sharp talons.

Katey screamed and fell off the edge of her bed, sheets and blankets tangled in her legs. Her elbow hit the floor and she groaned. She laid there for a while, forehead against the carpet and heart pounding painfully against her ribcage. Her face was damp with sweat and body exhausted from the vivid dream.

The night before, she had tried her best not to let her thoughts dwell on the impossible. Werewolves didn't exist, but her need for some explanation took her to the internet. Of course, there were crackpot blogs and web pages that claimed preternatural monsters walked among humans. She blamed them for the crazy dream.

Her mind played back the details of that dream and how each moment made her feel. Terrified, confused, utter peace. None of it made sense, though she could see some bits of her reality slipped in. The black wolf must have been Logan. Why else should she have nuzzled so intimately with him and no other? Then the other three had to be the teachers. But what about the rest? The shadowed images, how she became a wolf, the appearance of the woman in white.

Katey pushed herself off the floor and unknotted herself from the bed linens. She didn't feel like going to school at all, knowing who would be there waiting for her. How could she face them after what she had heard yesterday. She tried to tell herself that she still knew nothing for sure. It could all be some weird misunderstanding, and the only way to straighten it out would be to talk to them directly. No games, no secrets, no vague brushoffs. But could she muster one last push of bravery to demand the answers she needed, or would she run away like in her dream?

Darren stood watch outside his classroom door, arms folded but his stance intentionally casual. Across from him, his neighboring teachers chatted about some reality television show as students passed in the hall like a river of bodies running in both directions. As every morning, he kept an eye and ear out for the usual trouble. A boy wearing prohibited headphones, couples sneaking a kiss before the bell rang, arguments or general rowdiness that could dissolve into a fight.

This morning, he kept his senses vigilant for one signature presence.

A gust of morning air from the bus ramp doors carried Katey's scent to him and he honed in on her movements.

Dustin had returned to the house just after midnight when Katey had finally cried herself to sleep. That fact injured Logan most of all, but the pack lamented her anguish. Though Dustin reported nothing of interest, that alone seemed to add credence to their suspicion that she had been listening to their meeting. Dustin said she barely made a sound besides the occasional reproving murmur to herself, which he heard from his truck parked a couple of houses away. She never left, never called anyone. That should have given them some hope. Ben took the next shift at dawn. It wasn't long before he sent a text to tell them she awoke from some nightmare, indicative of a scream and the potent stench of fear coming from her bedroom. Ben later told Darren that he ventured closer than

Dustin had dared, hiding near her back door. He wouldn't have approved of that decision, but Darren might have done something similar if he heard the poor child scream.

So far, nothing led them to think Katey was a threat to their secret, but the day was still young.

When Katey entered the hall, Darren did not look her way. She reeked of fear and stale saline tears. He waited until she was close, then gave into his curiosity. Fatigue rimmed her eyes, but nothing else in her posture or expression suggested what he sensed beneath the surface. Logan's words came back to him. She was strong and seemed to understand the importance of hiding her weakness in front of others. It reminded him of young alphas and betas who were desperate to prove themselves. She had nothing to prove, not to him or any of the pack, but she wouldn't know that. Not yet.

"Good morning, Miss Katey."

She looked up and her toughness softened, but didn't yield. "Good morning."

It wasn't until she stood in front of the open classroom door that her mask dropped and shattered. Logan was already in his seat and Darren wondered if he was the cause.

He angled to face her, alert to the change. Her eyes widened, heart rate rose into a gallop, and the peppery odor of fear rolled off her like billowing smoke. Katey took one shaky step back, and then another, as if she were debating whether to run.

Only prey run, he thought. *You're not prey and never will be.*

Unsure what inspired him, Darren approached, slow and calm as if she were a skittish horse. He touched her elbow, and she broke away from her fixation on Logan to stare at him.

"You're safe. It's all right."

He knew saying as much might have acknowledged that he knew that she knew, but such a charade was bound to crumble soon anyway. Katey let out a thin breath and her fear lessened.

Whatever she believed, she did not perceive him as dangerous. Logan was a different story.

"Can you ask Logan to sit somewhere else?" she whispered.

It was unlikely Logan missed that request and Darren felt sorry for it. His ward barely slept the night before, so torn up over Katey's silence. Darren wished he could have advocated for Logan and make her realize how much her neglect hurt him, but it wasn't his place. His duty was to protect the pack, not play matchmaker. And in order to protect the pack, he had to keep the peace, even at Logan's detriment.

He nodded to her. "I will. Go on in."

Darren stayed by her side several feet inside the door for moral support. Logan looked over his shoulder to her, then to Darren. He motioned for Logan to come out and he obeyed. Not wholly ignorant of her discomfort, Logan gave her a wide berth as they passed in the aisle between tables. That didn't keep them from locking eyes. An energy shimmered between them, tense and pulsing with all the unspoken emotions they hid from one another. He knew that feeling, once upon a time, but he didn't want to admit that such a thing could happen for Logan and Katey, not so soon after getting to know one another.

When they broke contact, the energy abated. Logan joined Darren outside and they lowered their voices in conference.

"I heard," Logan began. "Back row?"

"That would be best."

"Does that confirm it?"

"She undoubtedly heard something yesterday. Her reaction to you and her behavior last night makes that obvious, but she doesn't seem to be worried about me."

Logan hardened to conceal the true distress beneath. "Should I go home?"

If they weren't around students or teachers, he would have shaken the pup's shoulder to snap him out of this self-pity. "You stay. Instead, give her space today. As I said last night, let her lead the way. Only speak to her when she begins the conversation. Say nothing of yesterday. Don't even text her. But after school, we need her to stay so we can have the talk."

Logan cast his eyes to the floor and nodded. It wasn't ideal, but if Logan pushed too hard, she was liable to push back or bolt. If Logan showed himself harmless, that may help their case.

"I'll let the others know what we've seen and direct them accordingly." Darren tilted his head to meet Logan's eyes. "We will get past this, but you need to accept whichever way this may go."

"I haven't stopped thinking about that... What if she rejects me?"

Logan may have been much older than he appeared, but he sounded like a lovestruck adolescent with his first crush. Darren gave him a sympathetic smile. "It won't be the end of the world. I promise."

That wasn't enough to cheer him up, but it wasn't meant to. It was only a bit of wisdom from hard-earned experience.

It took a moment for Logan to gird himself with the courage to go back into the classroom, grab his bag and throw it next to the empty seat at the back of the room. Darren watched the change in Katey and became more confused. She wasn't as scared as before, but looked after Logan like a child whose favorite toy had been taken away from her. She wanted distance between them, so why so regretful? He may have been centuries old, but the mind of a woman was just as mysterious as it had always been. He stepped outside to send a mass text to the pack to let them know what happened. It would be a long day, waiting for the final bell.

"Are you all right?" Lily asked. "You haven't eaten anything."

Katey looked up from her lunch tray. Some time had passed since she, Lily, and Beth sat down at a table in the lunchroom, but she didn't know how much time. Lily was right, though. She hadn't touched her chicken nuggets, green beans, or mashed potatoes. She only pushed the bits of food around with her fork, too numb to even try to eat.

Logan didn't speak a word to her all day. She caught the occasional aggrieved glance, but nothing more. Yet, Katey couldn't bring herself to encourage him. She was thankful to finally be in a room without him. Yesterday still burned hot in her memory. The hurt, the rage, all of it made her both glad and yet his silence nearly destroyed her now. He didn't even try to fix what he'd unwittingly broken, but neither did she dare to confront him. Part of her wanted the truth, but the other part wanted to hide in a hole until graduation. She hated to feel so conflicted, torn in two drastically different directions.

"Is it about Logan?" Lily asked.

Katey resisted the tears that pushed at the edges of her eyes. She hadn't cried this much in years. "Yeah... It didn't work out."

Beth leaned closer. "That was quick. What happened?"

The callous way she said that made Katey ache. "He just... wasn't the kind of guy I expected him to be."

Lily dropped her fork. "What do you mean?"

If her insane theory was right, Katey knew she couldn't say a word about it. She didn't know much, but if the world didn't act like werewolves existed, then it was likely supposed to be that way. Logan betrayed and lied to her, but she wouldn't be so vindictive to give away what he might have been.

"I just heard him say some things yesterday. He doesn't like me as much as I thought he did. I feel so stupid." Katey folded her arms and pushed away her food. She had no appetite.

Lily appeared anxious, but she couldn't begin to know why. "Maybe you misunderstood him. Have you tried to talk to him?"

"No, and I'm not sure I want to."

Beth shrugged. "Maybe you dodged a bullet. If he seems two-faced, you don't need that kind of torture. I had a boyfriend that was so unpredictable. One day, he loved me, the next he yelled at me over something stupid. You're better off without a guy like that."

Lily passed Beth an indignant look as if she didn't agree. "I think you should talk to him before you drop him. If nothing else, it'll give you some closure."

Katey shook her head. "I don't know... The worst part is despite everything, I still... I guess I still want to be with him. I wish I had never heard what I did. Then I'd still be blissfully ignorant of... of something I wasn't meant to hear."

Beth's eyes went wide. "Did he commit some crime or something? You're making it sound so serious."

"No, nothing like that. I don't think so anyway."

Lily reached out to put her hand on Katey's arm. "If you still have feelings for Logan, talk to him. I saw the way he was looking at you in second period. I'm not saying you're lying, but I think he still cares about you a lot."

Katey winced and looked away. They couldn't understand, and she wouldn't give them more details to help. She was sure his words couldn't have been misinterpreted, but Lily was right. Either Logan was great at pretending, or he still cared about her, even a little. But if he did, where was he? Why didn't he try to talk to her between classes or drag her out of the lunchroom to clear the air? If it mattered to him at all, why didn't he make some attempt?

Mulishness and old pride made Katey determined not to be the first to break the silence. Hope and insanity told her that things wouldn't get better until she sought him out and asked him plainly if he was a werewolf and if he was willing to kill her to make her into one too.

Katey shivered as the wolves of her dreams raced through her mind, howling and baying as if to say, "Come on, it wouldn't be so bad."

From what little she saw on the internet, she wasn't so sure. She still fought the ridiculous idea with every bit of sense she had left, bashing down the impulse to consider it as if she were playing a game of whack-a-mole at the arcade. Every time the errant thought came to mind, she beat it down again until it stubbornly resurfaced moments later. The only way she would get rest, would be to let the thoughts take root and become just as crazy as those blog writers. She wasn't too weak for that, but she might have been just weak enough to give Logan a bone and try one more time to forge a relationship.

By the end of the day, Katey had drafted a text to Logan. Just a simple, "We need to talk." She hadn't decided whether to send it or not before leaving her sixth period study hall in the auditorium.

Katey caught herself on the lookout for Logan, but hadn't found a trace of him. Neither did she see the three teachers who had been nothing but kind and courteous to her all day. It only confirmed what she felt that morning before first period with Darren. The teachers could be trusted, even if she was still unsure of Logan.

She stepped onto the bus ramp and passed by the throngs of students waiting for their cue to load up into the endless line of yellow buses. There was safety in crowds, she convinced herself.

Even if Logan showed up, he couldn't do anything to her with so many witnesses. In the senior parking lot, there were fewer students loitering while cars backed out of stalls and drove away. She had been too busy searching for her keys at the bottom of her bag and noticed too late that Logan leaned against her jeep, arms folded, and eyes fixed on her.

Her body froze, still several yards from him. He stiffened too, and she had the crazy thought that maybe he could smell her fear. A quick glance around told Katey that they were suddenly alone. No students, no faculty or staff. Not safe.

The thrumming of her heartbeat in her ears drowned out the rumble of so many engines. Blood surged beneath her skin and despite the cold air, a sweat broke out on the back of her neck. Like a rabbit caught in a wolf's gaze, she couldn't will herself to move or even breathe. Her limbs tingled with the need to run, but the command stalled somewhere along the way.

Logan made the first move and took a step closer. In a moment of blind instinct, Katey was released from his spell, turned and ran back in the direction she came. She may have gotten in trouble with the teachers who maintained order on the bus ramp, but getting detention was preferred over a premature confrontation with Logan. She wasn't ready for this, for whatever he had to say to her, and she hadn't decided what she'd say to him. Running was easier.

"Katey, stop!"

Logan's pleas only pushed her harder.

Katey ducked and weaved through the crowd, gripping her bag so it wouldn't bang against her back or hip. The shouts of faculty telling them to slow down blurred with the noises of the bus ramp.

Thinking quickly, she tried to think where she could hide. If the internet didn't lie, it wouldn't take long for Logan to catch up with her, and he could follow her scent no matter where she fled. She had to stay in a crowd or seek shelter in a place where he couldn't hurt her.

Dustin's classroom was the closest to the bus ramp and had fewer obstacles in her path to slow her down. Muscles aching from the exertion, she pressed on toward the senior hallway. She crashed into the level to open the doors and found the hallway empty of students. She tried to tug on the door behind her to make it close faster, but snatched at the edge and thrust it open. Only a few bounding steps across the tile floor and his arms were around her, trapping her against him.

Instinctively, Katey screamed and thrashed wildly against him, twisting and kicking backward against his shins. Logan was as solid as stone, undaunted by her struggling.

"Let me go!"

"Katey, calm down!" he begged. "I'm not going to hurt you."

His breath felt hot on her neck and she flung her head backward, hoping to knock into something hard enough to break his hold. She heard a slight crunch and Logan grunted in pain, but his arms never slackened.

"Logan, drop her!" Dustin's voice bellowed from down the hall, his tone firm as if he were commanding an unruly dog.

He released Katey instantly and she fell to her hands and knees on the floor. Looking up, a couple of other teachers had poked their heads out of their doors to see what the commotion was about. Dustin gave them hasty assurances that he'd take care of it.

Katey tried to scramble up, heaving for air and still desperate to find some safety away from Logan.

"Don't you move, Katey," their teacher ordered, a finger pointed at her. He had pulled out his phone and looked to be calling someone.

Her muscles gave out and she fell again, never rising to her feet. Behind her, Logan's hand covered his nose and mouth, some blood seeped through his fingers, eyes rimmed with moisture closed tight. Maybe she broke his nose. A pang of regret countered her fear of what he'd do when he recovered.

Despite his command, Katey scooted herself a couple of feet in the direction of Dustin's classroom. Logan groaned and shook his head briskly before wiping his sleeve across his face. Blood smeared across his cheek. "Damn it, why did you run?"

Katey gulped for air. "Why did you chase me?"

"Would it be so hard to believe that I wanted to talk to you?"

Fury boiled up to consume her anxiety. "You had plenty of chances to talk to me today and you didn't say a fucking word!"

Logan opened his eyes and she could have sworn she saw a flash of some other color besides blue. "I was under orders. Besides, you looked like you could have cared less if I was even around."

Too befuddled by what he said, she tightened her lips and forced a scowl to fully communicate that she still wasn't happy with him.

The doors of the senior hallway opened and Darren and Ben appeared. They looked between Logan, Katey, then to Dustin who stayed by his classroom door.

"What the hell, Logan?" Ben muttered and gestured to Katey still sitting on the floor.

Logan started. "Me? She's the one who broke my nose."

"Looks like ya might've deserved it." Ben walked past them to join Dustin.

Darren shook his head at both of them, but offered his hand out to Katey to help her up. "I apologize for his behavior." He shot a pointed glance at Logan. "Excessive force is never necessary."

Logan rolled his eyes and continued to poke at the bridge of his nose and scrub at the drying blood on his face.

"Go get cleaned up and meet us in the classroom," Darren told him.

He nodded and ducked into the nearby bathroom. Katey accepted Darren's help and stood.

"Is... Is his nose really broken? It didn't look crooked."

Darren gave her a sympathetic look and directed her down the hall. "Let's hold all questions for now. We need to have a talk with you."

Katey shook her head and edged back toward the door. "I can't stay. I—"

"Miss Katey... I insist. This is very important, and I think we both know that you deserve some explanations. We're willing to give them, but I ask that you cooperate."

Did they know she listened in on their conversation yesterday? A little off-put by his choice of words, Katey warred between running again and giving in. He was right. She wanted answers. Under the gaze of all three teachers, she consented and took one uncertain step after another toward Dustin's classroom, not entirely sure what she'd learn behind its closed door.

CHAPTER 11

Katey got the feeling she was on trial, though their relaxed postures didn't suggest as much. Dustin sat on the corner of his desk, Ben near him in one of the student's desks. Darren stood in the open space in front of the marker board, hands on his hips in that authoritative way he often did in his own classroom. Logan was the only one who couldn't stay still. Now cleaned up and looking as if he had never been knocked in the nose, he paced in long, languid circles with hands in his jean pockets, the furthest away from the group. The sight of her teachers all in the same room was definitely odd.

Katey sat atop one of the desks and swiveled to plant her feet in the chair, subconsciously hoping to gain some height on them. Didn't wolves perceive dominance in size and posture? Was it wise to try to assert her own or should she have been sitting on the floor?

"Before we go any further," Darren began, "did you eavesdrop on our meeting yesterday afternoon?"

Though she was tempted to lie to save her own skin, she saw little point in trying to hide anything now, and nodded. The reactions in all four were thinly palatable, and it was not relief, but something like nervousness.

"Then I'm going to ask you to set aside what you heard, or what you thought you heard, and listen to what we have to say now. Reserve your final judgment until we have finished."

Katey wrapped her arms about her stomach and waited, nerves knotted in a ball in her gut. Darren seemed hesitant to begin, as if this wasn't easy for him to say. She imagined it couldn't be easy for any of them, if she guessed the truth correctly.

"All over the world, and throughout time, myths have been told and retold to help explain the world and how it works. Many have evolved into folktales designed to frighten children or teach some moral lesson. But, at the heart of these legends, lay a hint of truth, though few would recognize it."

Darren began to talk with his hands, taking a few steps this way and that, as he did when giving a lecture. "One such theme amongst these tales is the ability for a man to transform into some-thing else. The most common is a wolf, though different countries feature other animals specific to their culture and environment. Tales of this nature date back to Roman times and have cropped up in nearly every country in every century. The majority of the time, these shapeshifters are associated with evil, with magic, and are the villains of the story."

At this brief pause, Dustin chimed in. "In other cultures, they were the heroes and represented the merge between mankind and nature. The Faoladh in Irish folklore is one great example."

Something in the way Dustin spoke that Gaelic word suggested that he was personally familiar with the language, his voice lilting with the pronunciation.

Darren took up the speech again. "However, those tales are buried underneath the nightmarish stories of wild beasts that eat babies or kill entire families. These tales were believed so... so ardently that innocent men and women became the targets of prejudice and speculation. The days of hanging witches were not exclusive to old hags or wise women, but hermits and outsiders suspected of being these half-man, half-wolf creatures."

Darren took a breath to regain a measure of composure he had lost in that last part. "Over time, science and technology pushed aside these stories as nothing more than fantasies. The world, for the most part, stopped believing in shapeshifters. They still capture the imagination, but are relegated to movies, books, and television shows. They're creatures for entertainment and everyone has their own interpretation of what they are and how they should be seen."

Katey held her breath as she waited for the final shoe to drop. The deafening silence in the classroom seemed to ring just seconds before Darren took the last plunge.

"What we brought here to tell you, is that these creatures... do exist."

Against her will, her face scrunched as if in discomfort. Yet, Katey remained quiet.

"They're not entirely as the legends and movies suggest. There are some fragments of truth, but not many. The full moon, for instance, has nothing to do with the shift. It takes place once a month, but it's different for everyone... We can shift at will, but it's painful."

Katey caught the shift in tense. Her intuition had been right.

Somehow, that final, subtle admittance didn't explode like the bomb she expected. Perhaps it was the fact that she had already stewed over the idea that Logan and her teachers might have been werewolves since the day before. Or maybe it was the strange feeling that, despite what they claimed to be, she didn't regard them with any less respect or admiration. It wasn't as if they had just become werewolves. They were werewolves last week, last month, and since the beginning of the year. They were still the same guys, only more interesting now.

"Of course, attributing our many unnatural abilities to some pact with the devil is purely false. Loups-garous, as we prefer to be called, are either born this way, inheriting that nature from their father, or bitten and purposefully turned. Our preternatural nature takes hold at different times. Some turn when they reach puberty, and others a little later in their teen years." Darren gestured to himself, Dustin, and Logan. "Three of us were born loups-garous. Ben was bitten."

Dustin raised a hand, reluctantly stating guilt. "By me, if I can add."

Katey wanted the story behind that, but kept her teeth clamped shut.

"I also want to stress the point," Darren continued, "that horror movies exaggerate. We do not make a habit of killing and eating people. The days of rampant, uncontrollable monsters are over. Loups-garous belong in packs and are guided in a similar way as wolf packs are. There is an alpha, and if the pack is large enough, a beta or two. They keep order and ensure that newly turned loups-garous do not become feral."

Dustin said, "Now, there are some who do eat human flesh, but there are very few and they're not right in the head." He tapped his temple with his finger.

"That is a story for another day." Darren crossed his arms, though Katey could tell they all became a little more relaxed the more he shared. "Our abilities include inhuman strength and speed, heightened sense of smell and hearing, and accelerated healing." Darren nodded to Logan. "Hence, why his nose is perfect-ly fine now."

Katey hardly passed a look at Logan since the speech began, but she turned to him now. He wouldn't meet her stare, but continued to pace in the restless pattern. It was possible that, despite every-thing, he was the most nervous of them all. But why?

"Our healing ability also inhibits a natural course of aging," Dar-ren said. "I'm the eldest at around four hundred years old. After some time, it hardly seems worth it to keep track."

"I'm about 250, give or take a handful of years," Dustin said.

"I was born in 1840. Bitten in 1862," Ben said.

"And Logan will be 127 by the end of this month."

At these figures, Katey's eyes widened and mind swam with the implications of it. How much history they lived through, how many of those painful shifts they endured. That was definitely not something the internet or Hollywood movies covered.

"We aren't quite sure how slow the aging is, as far as the ratio."

"It's like dog years, but in reverse," Dustin explained.

After a bit of thought, Darren looked to the other loups-garous in the room. "Have I left anything out?"

"Diet," Ben offered. "We can't eat much outside of meat and fruits, just like wolves. If we try eatin' stuff like vegetables or breads, we get sick."

Dustin pointed to Darren. "And just to set it straight, he is the alpha." Then pointed to himself. "I'm the beta."

The alpha nodded. "Yes. Alphas, of course, are the leaders of a pack. Betas are in charge of enforcing and protecting the pack from both internal and external threats, and serve as a second in command to alphas. Rank has less to do with size, age, or experience, but something we call dominance. It's innate, not something learned or granted. Some are born leaders or protectors. Others aren't born with even a little dominance, and are destined to be submissive to all other loups-garous. You may have felt a little of this dominance in the classroom whenever we've tried to establish order. Dominance can serve a dual purpose, as well. It can be used to discipline, but it can be used to comfort and bring a sense of security to a pack."

By now, Katey had propped her elbow on her knee, hand covering her chin and mouth, fascinated by the complexity of this world she never knew. The internet couldn't touch the depths to what werewolves, loups-garous, really were like. It wasn't so simple as turning into monsters by moonlight. This was so much cooler, so much more fascinating.

A few beats of silence passed before Darren said, "Now, we may have unintentionally skipped over some things. We have never had to explain this to someone who knows nothing of our existence. Do you have any questions?"

Katey felt their eyes, even Logan's, fasten upon her, anxious for any word. What could she say? What could she ask first? She asked the only thing that easily came to mind. "Why me?" she whispered. "Why are you telling me all of this?"

Darren blinked, as if that was the last thing he expected her to say. The three teachers looked to one another, waiting for one of them to take the initiative.

"Since the first day we met you," Dustin began, "all of us felt like... Man, it sounds weird to say it out loud, but we all knew there was something special about you."

"Almost like ya were already part of the pack," Ben added. "Or that you were supposed to be."

"Which is what you partially overheard yesterday." Darren nodded toward Logan again. "Logan feels the same as we all do, but he was the first to propose that it be made official."

Katey felt a cold chill run down her spine. Yes, she remembered that bit all too well. "But... I'm not one of you. I heard you say there can't be a female... loup-garou?" The words sounded strange rolling off her tongue.

The alpha nodded. "That is correct. To our understanding, there has never been a female of our kind. Only sons begotten by loup-garou fathers carry on the gift, and only men can be turned by the bite. No one is sure why. Older theories alleged that the female anatomy was too frail to accept the change. While I don't agree with that, I do think there is a biological aspect involved."

"And if a female is bitten, she dies." Katey tried to keep her tone neutral and cold, but there was nothing calm about the way she felt about the matter.

"That is also true." Darren struggled with his next words. "Though, there is a... rather persistent feeling amongst some of us that if you were bitten, you would not die." She knew he spoke of Logan, but wouldn't look at him. "I can personally assure you, Katey, that nothing of the kind will be attempted. You are safe with us."

"Probably the safest kid in the whole damn school right now," Dustin muttered.

Safe, but in a room of monsters, was what she wanted to say, but wouldn't. How sensitive were they to being accused of resembling the hellish beasts of nightmares?

"But the point is that we feel we can trust you with our secret." Darren cautioned a few steps closer to her. "It is very, very important that you tell absolutely no one about what we are."

Feeling a little bold, Katey said, "How do I know this isn't some elaborate joke? Can you give me any proof?"

"Unless ya wanna see us naked as a jaybird, we ain't gonna shift in front of you," Ben retorted.

"There are easier ways than that, ya idjit," Dustin snapped.

Darren took a breath and turned to Katey. "We can show you in one way, but you have to remain calm." He waited for Katey to nod in agreement.

Then, his eyes began to change. From the edges of his pupils, a wolfish gold hue spun to consume his usual brown irises, rimmed in a thick band of black.

A breath escaped through her parted lips, dazzled by the gold depths of the wolf eyes that stared at her with a calm intensity. They were beautiful, and yet so out of place on a human face.

She looked to Dustin and Ben, their eyes the same shade. Now she knew what she had seen on Friday during math class wasn't a trick of the light. Ben's eyes had really turned gold, just as they were now.

When she swung to see Logan's wolf eyes, his back was turned to her.

"Logan, show her." Darren's voice came out in a slight growl, but it didn't scare her as she thought it might.

Slowly, Logan turned and did as his alpha said. To see any-thing but blue in his eyes was strange, but by the way her body responded to such a fierce change, she wondered if she preferred the gold.

"How can you do that?" she asked, voice breathy with aston-ishment.

"The wolf shows itself in moments of stress or heightened emotion," Darren explained. "But all of us can control it."

One by one, their golden eyes receded, and they looked fully human again.

"That's so cool." Katey felt like laughing, but she could read the room well enough that laughing would not be received well. "You said, 'the wolf shows itself.' What do you mean by that?"

Darren made a sign of reluctance. "That may be beyond the scope of what we wanted to discuss today. You have a lot to process."

Katey shifted on the desk. "I didn't stick around to listen to the whole thing yesterday... Was anything decided?" She couldn't put her true question into words. Would they welcome her into their pack?

"Telling you what we are is the extent of our decision," Darren replied. "It's more than we have ever done for any human."

Disconcerted, Katey slumped a bit. "And what now?"

Logan finally stepped forward. "I'd still like to talk with her, Darren... with your permission."

Katey wasn't sure how to feel about that, or about Logan in general. How determined was he to try and turn her? Darren assured that she'd be safe, but if they were alone, only another loup-garou could fight off Logan. Or had too much changed in twenty-four hours to let him even consider trying it? Maybe that's why he wanted to talk. A need to know more about what he was and how to make sense of the last week overwhelmed any former apprehension.

Dustin must have seen the indecision in Darren. "He's been through hell today. Give him a little leash."

The analogy sounded humorous, but Katey must have been the only one who thought so.

With a sigh, Darren gave his consent. "Fine. But stay on campus. Use your best judgment on where to talk away from listening ears."

Logan nodded, then deferred to Katey. "Only if you want to. I won't force you."

If he really had been suffering through the day, or even half as much as she did, then perhaps they were both entitled to a few moments to get their feet back on solid ground. She remembered what he said in the hall, that she acted like he didn't matter. That wounded her more than she'd ever tell him. How, even after everything, could she have not cared whether he was there or not?

Finally, she nodded. Logan lifted his hand to offer it to her, but withdrew before it reached halfway, the sentiment spoiled by some admonishing thought. It didn't go unnoticed, and it convicted Katey for her earlier behavior toward him. She was justified, and there was nothing to suggest that she would have done anything differently, but she still regretted it. If he offered his hand, she'd take it again in a heartbeat, loup-garou or not.

She slipped from the desk and passed by the loups-garous to fall in beside Logan toward the door.

"Logan," Darren began, "come back here after you two are done. If we don't see you before we're ready to leave for home, we will come to get you."

It sounded more like a threat than a request. Logan nodded and opened the door for her.

"How about the football field?" he asked. "Or would you prefer a place with more... witnesses?"

His tone cut her. "The football field is fine."

They walked in silence, but Katey permitted herself to study him. She marveled at just how human and normal he could look for a 127-year-old shapeshifter. There was nothing about him that would ever give him away. She would never have known the truth if she hadn't been told.

The gate to the field was unlocked and they climbed the stadium seats to the very top near the announcer box. The metal benches were icy cold and the wind tossed her hair over her shoulders to chill the nap of her neck. Logan kept his focus across the stadium, elbows on knees and fingers laced together. The space between them felt more like an insurmountable chasm than a mere several inches.

"So, let me see if I can connect the dots," Katey said as she wrapped her arms around her stomach and drew up her knees to keep warm. "Every time you talked about your family, you really meant your pack."

"That's right."

"Darren is your alpha, so he's the one that's been knuckling down on your freedom?"

"Over the last couple of days, yes. I had lied about where I was on Friday, because I didn't want them to know I had met you at the cemetery, though Dustin knew. He could smell you on me. When you came to school in my jacket, I was busted."

Katey winced. "And that's why Darren was so mad."

"Yep. I got chewed out later that day, making my disappearance on Monday night even worse. On top of that, Darren shifted that night and I was supposed to be home. They were thoroughly pissed when I ghosted them in exchange for spending time with you."

Her mind jumped from the fact that, once again, she was at fault for getting Logan into trouble, then to the idea of Darren shifting just a couple of nights ago. He said the shift was painful, but the next morning he looked totally fine. The accelerated healing made complete sense. If every loup-garou had to take a sick day or two every month just to recover from the transformation, it'd raise questions.

"So, you were put on lockdown because they didn't want you to spend time with me?" she asked once she could grab hold of a single train of thought.

"For the most part. I shouldn't have been so careless and defiant toward Darren. Even if my disobedience didn't involve you, I would have been punished in a similar way."

That eased a bit of weight off Katey's conscience. "Then the deer meat, your ability to sneak around, that's the loup-garou side of you?"

"It is."

"Was anything you told me true?"

Logan turned to her. "Yes, the majority of it was. You have to understand why I couldn't be completely honest with you."

"Oh, I get it. I'm not mad... not anymore. Something in the back of my head told me you were hiding something, but I couldn't have imagined it was this."

"Few would. No one believes in us anymore. It makes it easier to hide."

Katey took a deep breath. "How many of you are there left?"

"In the world, thousands, if not a couple million. In Crestucky, there are just two packs. One belongs to Darren. The other we call the Deviants. They're a very large, old pack with a history." Logan gestured to the north. "They made their home in that town we visited on Monday. I spent my first few months as a loup-garou there. It's where I met Darren. Hunters struck the town and the Deviants scattered. It's only been in the last few decades that they've reunited and settled in Crestucky. There's probably a couple hundred of them, if you count the women and children."

Katey's jaw dropped somewhere in his long answer, and the look made him smirk. That was the first hint of humor he allowed all day.

"When you say hunters, you mean werewolf hunters?"

Logan nodded and eyes dulled with some dark thought. "They killed many. Hunters are a very serious thing, which is why it's so crucial that you tell no one. If word gets to the wrong person, we could be in a lot of danger."

"There are still hunters around? I get hunters over a century ago, but not in this day and age."

"As long as there have been loups-garous, there have been loup-garou hunters. Whole family lines keep up the tradition of tracking down and exterminating us. Technology has helped them become more efficient, which means just one slip-up can mean disaster."

Katey's flesh chilled and she rubbed at her arms. As he had on Friday, Logan slipped off his jacket and draped it over her shoulders without even asking. His fingertips brushed her upper arms and that warmed Katey more than the heavy leather. She gripped the flaps and drew them closed across her core before passing him a silent thanks for the gesture. Now, just like on Friday, he was left in only a brown shirt, the sleeves hugging his muscled arms in a way that made her pulse quicken.

"I promise never to tell a soul. I couldn't stand the thought of any of you being killed." She straightened, remembering her many questions and finding it much easier to ask them now. "I want to know everything."

Logan quirked a brow at her. "Everything? Are you sure?"

"Uh, yeah! Darren has been around for four hundred years? He's older than the United States! And Dustin bit Ben? How did that happen? If three of you were born this way, where are your fathers? What about your mothers? Why do you call yourselves loups-garous instead of werewolves? How have you managed to fly under the radar if you don't age? How many times have you gone through high school? College? Have you ever even been to school?"

Logan began to laugh and held up a hand to stop the flood of questions. "Okay, okay. Slow down. Let's start with the easy questions.... Ummm..." Now Logan laughed at himself. "Well, I guess none of those questions are easy to answer."

"Start with Dustin and Ben," she suggested greedily.

"It may be better to start from the beginning and maybe the answers will fall into place from there."

For a moment, Katey realized just how much she had missed his company and the sound of his voice. He had a crazy way of making her forget her fear and her anger, and it didn't seem fair. By the way he seemed to have loosened up since they left the classroom, she must have had the same effect on him. The worry he showed so plainly less than an hour ago was gone, leaving the Logan she knew before her.

"Darren was born and raised in England without a father. His mother was French from what he's told me. When he turned, he didn't know what to do. On a tip, he went to France to find an alpha who took in orphaned loups-garous and trained them to control their wolf side. That's why we prefer to call ourselves loups-garous. It's what Darren knew best, and it sounds better than werewolves.

"Dustin is from Ireland and didn't have a father either. He turned and... Well, it wasn't under the best circumstances. I'm not at liberty to tell his story, but it didn't take him long to make it to France. He and Darren made a pack, with Darren having more inherent dominance of the two to become alpha. They came to the states in the nineteenth century to help settle the community with the Deviants. Dustin didn't want to stick around, so they agreed Dustin could go off on his own. Packs form and break apart all the time so it wasn't uncommon.

"Anyway, Dustin joined the Confederate army during the Civil War to find a way out of the South and through the blockade. I don't get his logic, but I wasn't there, so what would I know? In the army, he met Ben, who was human at the time. At the battle of Antietam, Ben was shot and would have died, but Dustin turned him to save his life. They don't talk about it much, but they didn't get along during his training. A bunch of stuff went wrong and they separated. Ben went off to do his own thing for a few decades, and Dustin went to Europe, but not before shaking up with my maternal grandmother."

Katey gasped. "What?"

"Yeah, Dustin is my grandfather."

She reeled in her seat from the shock. "No way!"

"I know," he chuckled. "If anyone ever saw the resemblance, we had to play it off like we were cousins, but we're not alike at all. So, back to the story. Dustin ran off to Europe, and my grandmother had his daughter, who was my mother."

"So, the loup-garou gene can skip a generation?"

Logan grimaced. "Not really. Everyone we have talked to says I'm an anomaly." He took a breath as if he didn't want to tell the next part. "My father was human. He didn't take care of us very well. He drank away his earnings, meaning I had to find work wherever I could to keep food on the table. He wasn't... wasn't a good man when he had too much to drink. My mother couldn't hide the bruises from the other townsfolk, and they took pity on us, which I hated... I also hated that I was never strong enough to fight him back... until the night I turned."

Katey braced for what she suspected.

"I killed him and... I hurt my mother badly. When I turned back to my human form in the morning, she was still hanging onto life. She told me about a journal my grandmother had written about Dustin and all she could find out about loups-garous. She didn't know for sure if I would turn, but kept it just in case. She forgave me for what I did... The next moment, she died in my arms."

Katey did not know how to stop the hemorrhage of his sudden grief. What he said Monday came back to her, about how someone never stopped mourning for the dead, but it could sneak up every now and again with the same power it had before. For Logan, over a century wasn't enough to lessen the guilt.

"It took me a long... long time to stop hating myself for what I did. Everyone tried to explain to me that nothing could have been done. A freshly turned loup-garou without an alpha is uncontrollable. They are the stuff of the myths and legends Darren mentioned. I kept thinking if Dustin had stuck around, if my mother gave me the journal sooner, if somehow I could have done the impossible and controlled myself during the shift... But nothing can change what I did."

Katey couldn't let his grief go unaddressed. She couldn't just let him fester in that pain and not say anything. Yet, she knew there were no words she could give to a man haunted by mistakes that were totally outside of his control. Instead, she reached out and placed a hand on his forearm. His muscles tightened beneath her fingers and Katey admired the power his loup-garou nature gave him. That touch of skin to skin seemed to bring him back into this century and he covered her hand with his own, accepting her comfort.

"The journal mentioned the Deviants, so I traveled from South Carolina to Alabama looking for Dustin. Instead, I found Darren teaching school for the Deviants."

Katey could somehow picture Darren in a turn-of-the-century, one-room schoolhouse, complete with an old chalkboard and reading primers.

"After the hunters destroyed the community, we went to Europe to find Dustin. It took several years and a lot of roaming, but we tracked him down in Italy. Then, he told us about Ben and we knew we had to find him, too. His training wasn't complete, and Darren didn't feel right about the way Dustin abandoned him. We got back to America and... Oh, on that note, don't ever go on the maiden voyage of a ship." Logan shuddered. "Bad luck... They dropped me off with friends in Chicago and Darren and Dustin went to find Ben living on his own in the mountains of Idaho. We've been a pack of four ever since. That's the Reader's Digest version, of course. There was a lot of shit in between that I'm sure you'll hear about eventually. They're always telling old stories. Some are even new to me on occasion."

He didn't spin the details as artfully as Darren, but Katey still found herself enraptured, and longing to hear more about their adventures.

"Wow... You've really been everywhere."

"Now you know why I couldn't give you a straight answer about where I'm from. Over the last eighty years, we've lived in many places, remaking ourselves every time with the help of forged documents. I've never had a formal education, to answer your other question. Darren has always been a teacher and the other two have worked just about every trade. I've never found much to interest me. I'd work a few places, but I get bored easily."

Katey tried not to let her wonder invade her voice. "For eighty years, you've stayed together."

Logan gave her a soft smile. "We're a pack... That's what I wanted for you when I told the guys I wanted to meet with them yesterday. I... After you told me about your past, asking for you to join the fold just seemed right."

The hand that remained on his arm withdrew, slipping from his hold. "Logan... I just don't get it." All the angry words she had bottled up since the day before returned. "You've been so amazing and kind to me over the last few days, and... and then I overhear that you're okay with killing me? How was I supposed to react to that?"

Logan sighed. "You weren't supposed to hear any of it to begin with. I don't know exactly what you heard, but it must have been out of context. I don't want to kill you, but like Darren said, I also think the bite would work."

"But you're willing to take that chance."

"So that you can have a family, yes."

A ball of emotion rose in Katey's throat and she swallowed it back down. "It's not your job to make a family for me."

"I know it's not, but I hate seeing you alone." Before she could pull back, Logan grabbed her hand again and cupped them between his own. "I would never do anything to intentionally hurt you, Katey. I... I care about you too much."

No one had ever held her hand that way, no one that mattered. The warmth from his palms reached through and threatened to set her on fire, his words the perfect kindling to get it started. Logan's complete, candid sincerity was enough to make her forgive him for everything, but she white-knuckled every last shred of resolve. He couldn't make her cave so easily every damn time he did or said something sweet.

"But why?" Katey pleaded. "I also don't get why you and the teachers think I'm something special. I'm not. There are plenty of charity cases out there that would deserve your attention more."

His grip tightened. "You are not a charity case, and I'm just as clueless as the rest of the pack as to why we all want... need to make sure you're safe. If I had a better answer for you, I'd give it." His tone turned more serious. "Promise me one thing. Please consider taking the bite. Being loup-garou can be an absolute living hell, but you'll never be alone."

Katey cocked an eyebrow at him. "You sell it so well."

"I'm just being honest. There are a lot of challenges and dangers that come with both being a loup-garou and being around them. It's something to consider, even if you never turn, but especially if you do. Nothing would ever be the same, for better or worse. I don't know if I could ever fully express all its complications, but if you hang around with us long enough, you'll see what I mean."

Katey remembered how she thought she could never deny Logan anything he asked for. In that moment, he asked her to consider potentially forfeiting her life for the chance to spend a near eternity with him and his pack. She'd have to be desperate. She'd have to be insane. She'd have to be totally, madly, and completely in love. Could she ever reach that point?

"I'll think about it, but don't get your hopes up."

Logan's smile returned and he nodded. "That's all I ask."

Katey bit her lips. "Can I ask for one thing, though?" When he nodded, she said, "Can I see the wolf again?"

Almost taken aback, Logan leaned away. "Why?"

She shrugged shyly. "I don't know. It looked cool."

Logan gave her a wry look and in an instant, blue changed to gold. Katey grinned, still in disbelief how beautiful they were.

"Yeah, it still looks cool." She reached out and touched his cheekbone just below his eye, as if testing if she could chase the wolf away somehow. Instead, she discovered what depths of emotion the wolf could convey from just a simple gesture.

"Try saying that when the rest of the package is standing over you licking its lips."

Katey gave him a playful shove. "Not funny."

"It wasn't meant to be funny." The gold dissolved. "These eyes may look cool, but only because I'm in control of them right now. When they come out when I don't want them to, you better be prepared for whatever happens."

"Those moments of intense stress and emotion?"

"Emotions like anger and fear." Logan glanced toward the main school building. "I just hope you'll never be on the receiving end of that, but it's bound to happen."

Katey remembered when his eyes seemed to change color in the hall after he dropped her. He had been in pain, and he seemed a little angry, but not so angry that he'd hurt her. Perhaps he was only exaggerating to make her cautious.

"Dustin's waiting for me."

She turned to follow his gaze, but saw no one and heard nothing. "I don't see him."

"You wouldn't. He's by his truck now. I can smell him and heard him say my name to get my attention."

He stood to begin the trek down the concrete stadium stairs and Katey hastened after him. "What's the range of your senses? That seems impossibly far away."

"I've never tested it, but being this high up increases the range. The wind picks up more scents and carries voices further. That's one reason I suggested coming here."

She shook her head in amazement. "I am going to really look forward to getting to know you guys. I'll admit I was pretty freaked out before, but all of this is..."

Logan stopped and turned to wait for her to find the right words.

"I don't know. It's like this just seems right, to know that loups-garous exist."

"You weren't the least bit afraid?"

Katey realized she still had his jacket and slid it from her shoulders. She wasn't so blind not to see the incongruity of her situation. Any other sane person would have screamed or rejected what they said as lies. Her calm acceptance of what they were and everything that came with it wasn't natural, and she knew that, but she couldn't begin to understand it.

"I mean, maybe a little, but the more we've talked, it just feels natural and all I know is I've got to know more and hear all those stories. Maybe it's the same thing that makes you guys care about me."

Logan took the jacket from her and slid it on. The way he moved elicited now familiar aches and thrills in places she wouldn't name. "Maybe it is... I'm just glad you didn't faint or scream."

Katey propped her fists on her hips. "I am not some damsel in a fairytale that swoons at the first sign of trouble."

He gave her a toothy grin. "No, I suppose you're not."

CHAPTER 12

Logan lounged across the sofa in the living room, sketch-book rested against his propped knees. He hadn't picked up his pencil since last Friday afternoon. That project, a flip book depicting a wolf fight, didn't spark his interest as much as this new inspiration.

With quick, careful strokes of the lead, the figure of a woman took form over the course of an hour. Around her legs crowded three wolves, wolves he knew well. He didn't have the courage to put himself in the portrait in the same way. It'd be wishful thinking.

As Logan tried time and again to do justice to her features, drawing her eyes only to furiously erase the lines, Darren prepared their evening meal in the kitchen. The pack had been uncharacteristically quiet since they arrived home. Logan imagined it was for the same reason he chose to take up his sketchbook. Their thoughts were too absorbed in processing what happened that day.

Katey knew their secret, and she didn't run. Seemingly, she accepted the truth. She even seemed eager, if she spoke honestly as they parted ways at the football field. It was the best outcome they could have hoped for, almost too good to be real. Logan didn't want to look a gift horse in the mouth, but the nagging question was shared by the rest. Why was she so calm after learning that werewolves existed? Maybe she was right, that the same inner prodding among the pack to care for her was what whispered reassurances to her now.

Ben aimed to cast doubt by suggesting she was already associated with hunters, an undercover operative trained to gain their trust in order to gather information. That theory didn't sit well with them. There was nothing to validate it, and they forgot it as casualty as it was mentioned.

More than anything else, Logan wondered what it all meant, and how the future would unfold. They had never let a female into their circle. Dustin had his occasional romantic trysts that led nowhere, and neither Ben nor Darren ever entertained the idea of such an attachment, the ghosts of their former mates still shackled to their feet. They had been a house of bachelors for so long. How would Katey change that?

Of greater concern than how she would influence the pack, Logan pondered his own fate with Katey. She didn't reject him, and with a touch of her hand, hope revived. Could they be together? Could he, after so long of never knowing the abiding love and affection of a woman, find the missing piece of himself in Katey?

He might, but for how long? If Katey remained a human, he would have several decades at best, as she withered with age while he appeared the same. They wouldn't look like lovers in those final years, as any outsider would assume her to be his mother or grandmother, and intimacy would become impossible. The hope of love for *her* lifetime was poisoned by the inevitable end.

Yet, if she could be like him, become a loup-garou... His pencil stilled on the paper, lead tip touching the corner of the woman's eye. It was the only way they could be together, but they couldn't ignore the dangers of it. Divided between settling for a complicated future with a human mate and the risk of killing Katey for the chance to have centuries more with her, Logan tried not to think of it. Better to enjoy the next few months or years, than to agonize over a future that was not guaranteed.

He sighed and inspected his work. Logan was almost ready to give up getting her face just right. Not even his talented hand could replicate her beauty.

Dustin came thundering down the stairs. "Dinner ready yet?" Then he looked at Logan. "You still working on that?"

He muttered an affirmative and made a couple of extra strokes, testing if they belonged there. Dustin came over to glance at the portrait and gave some sound of approval before going to the kitchen.

"Supper will be ready momentarily," Darren replied over the sizzle of deer sausage in the hot cast iron skillet.

Logan heard the refrigerator door open and close, and the sound of glasses being brought out from the cupboards. He set the sketchbook aside when his pocket vibrated just a second before a muffled guitar rift sounded from his phone. He pulled it out and couldn't answer the call fast enough.

"Katey?"

All motioned came to a dead stop in the kitchen and Logan knew the alpha and beta stared at him, waiting.

"Hey, Logan," Katey said on the other side of the line. "Is this a bad time?"

He looked over his shoulder to his pack. Darren and Dustin mutedly counseled, probably forgetting that Katey didn't have the kind of hearing to know what they said. He was still on lockdown, but they never considered any restrictions on phone calls. With dinner almost ready, getting wrapped up in a phone call was ill advised, though Darren was the only one who thought so. Dustin was more amiable and didn't see the harm. Neither did Logan and he seized upon their indecision.

"No, now is okay." Logan jumped from the sofa and fled upstairs to his room before the pack could stop him. "Are you all right?"

"Yeah, I'm fine. Just wanted to talk."

Logan shut the door behind him, though he knew that wouldn't keep the pack from hearing his side of the conversation. "About what?"

He heard a few mechanical beeps in the background of her end. "Just... to talk. You never just got on the phone to talk to someone?"

"I guess not. Phone calls are a little utilitarian around here." He flopped on top of his comforter, pillowing his head with one arm as he lay on his back. "How do these sort of phone calls usually go?"

A metallic crinkling preceded a sharp shredding sound. "We ask how the other is doing and just let the topics roll from there. It's not any different from an in-person conversation."

"Except that I have to ask what you're doing."

Katey giggled. "That's part of it too. I'm about to put a frozen pizza in the oven for dinner... Can you eat pizza or is the crust too much bread?"

Logan frowned at the ceiling. "The bread, the sauce, the cheese, the vegetable toppings..."

"So, that's a no."

"If I had just two bites, I'd be sick for the rest of the day."

The rustling of snapping lightweight cardboard and ripping of a plastic wrapping completed the picture of Katey in her kitchen in front of the oven. "Yikes. That sucks... so you can't have French fries either, right? No potatoes."

"No potatoes."

"Well, that's something to add to the list."

Logan's brow furrowed. "What list?"

"The pros and cons list I've been making to help me decide. If I were to be loup-garou, I couldn't have French fries ever again."

"I don't know whether to be glad you're thinking about it or disappointed that the cons list is getting longer."

Katey sighed. "Well, I still have a long way to go before I make a decision, so don't pick a way to feel about it just yet... What are you having for dinner?"

"Darren is cooking deer sausage."

There was a pause. "You live with Darren? I thought you'd live with Dustin since you left with him today and he's your grandfather."

Logan realized they had left out a rather crucial detail regarding their lifestyle. Their living situation may not have been so strange from what he knew, since single men became roommates all the time. But, how would she take it? "We all live together."

"Oh... kind of like a group home."

"In a way, I guess it is, but it's a very permanent arrangement. I've never lived on my own. I think the quiet would drive me nuts."

He wasn't sure what made him add that last comment, but it was true. He never knew what it was like not to have another loup-garou in the house. Even those nights when the pack shifted and ran in the woods on their property, he hated the silence of the empty house.

"And that deer sausage," Katey said, "is that something you hunted like you told me before?"

"If you mean hunted as wolves, then no. If we eat it as humans, we hunt it as humans. Anything we hunt down as wolves, there's usually nothing left... If I'm grossing you out, stop me."

"No, no. It's... Okay, it may be a tad gross but I guess it's completely natural for you... I will say it's hard for me to imagine the four of you seated at a dining table eating dinner... It's just such a human thing."

"Yeah, we sit at a dining table, but don't use utensils and eat face-first into our plates. Then we take baths in tin tubs in the backyard and go to sleep in dog beds by the fireplace."

A boisterous laughter, one he recognized as belonging to Dustin, detonated from downstairs. Katey echoed with her own giggles and Logan smiled.

"I guess I deserved that," she said after composing herself.

"It's good to hear you laugh though."

"I don't often have a reason to."

Logan had to make a point of changing that. "I can tell when you fake it, though. It doesn't quite sound the same." More silence told him he might have said too much. "And this is why I'm not very good with phone calls. I can't tell what you're feeling right now."

"Sometimes that can be an advantage, to not be so transparent to the other person on the line."

Logan crossed his ankles at the foot of his bed. "I rely pretty heavily on those little changes. A shift in someone's scent can tell you a lot."

Something like the stiff impact of a body onto a seat cushion told him Katey may be in the living room now. "You can tell that from scent? Like a dog does?"

"Sure. I can tell when you're happy, when you've been crying, when you're afraid... fear has this spicy odor that can be pretty overpowering."

"So... you've known all the times I've been afraid?"

Logan nodded, then remembered that she couldn't see him. "Yeah... there's not much you'll be able to hide from us."

Katey huffed. "And here I thought I was being clever."

"I'm sure we are the only ones who knew about your mask."

"The guys knew?"

By the tight pitch of her voice, Logan knew for sure that time he had said too much. "Yeah. They talked about it sometimes. Dustin knew you had a panic attack in his class on Friday."

Katey groaned, likely from embarrassment. "And I bet he used that dominance trick to calm me down. That makes so much more sense now."

Logan smirked. "I'm glad he could help, even a little bit."

"Do you think it's your dominance that chased away the depression?"

Logan shifted on the mattress. "Nah. Dominance isn't constant like that. It's intentional, like forcing your will into the room for a few seconds or a few minutes." On the other end of the line, he heard the oven chime. "Pizza's done?"

"That was just to preheat the oven. I've got a little more time." He listened to Katey rise from the couch and slide the pizza pan in the oven, tin grating against the metal rack. "What were you up to when I called?"

"Sketching."

Katey made an intrigued sound. "Sketching? Is the big tough cage fighter an artist?"

"There's plenty more about me that I haven't told you yet."

"Trying to keep a bit of mystery in the relationship, huh?"

Logan went quiet and tilted his head, picking apart her choice of words.

"Oh, I didn't mean it like... you know, that we're in a relationship... Unless you want that. Is that even allowed? Well, of course it's allowed. Otherwise there wouldn't be any loups-garous born at all. You said before that it was complicated, though, so... Oh God, just forget I said anything."

Now it was Logan's turn to laugh. "If you insist, I'll forget. Being with a loup-garou is complicated. It's more than just dating or going to a church. It's... it's more involved. Nothing you need to worry about."

"Oh, good," she said with a sigh of relief. "But, we're still friends, right?"

Logan would have given her a consolatory smile, but in the privacy of his room, he didn't bother. "Sure... What else did you have planned for your evening?"

"Watching a movie I rented over the weekend. It's going to be overdue soon, so I thought I'd watch it and return it tomorrow."

Logan wondered if he could grow to enjoy this kind of casual conversation. "What movie?"

"*The Tower Heist.*"

He made a disgruntled sound and shook his head. "That one with Rodney Bator?"

"Yeah, have you seen it?"

"Nope. Darren has a ban on all of his movies."

"Why?" A few beats, and Katey gasped. "Is Rodney a—"

"Yep. He's a big point of controversy in our world. Some think he's doing a great job of proving that we can integrate into society without discovery, but most everyone else, including Darren, thinks he's going to screw up any day now. A loup-garou shouldn't be a celebrity. Too much attention."

"That makes sense... Are all loups-garous buff and hot?"

Logan barked a laugh. "I won't tell the guys you said that."

"Oh, no! Not them. I'm just looking at Rodney on the case cover and I'm just seeing some similarities. Big muscles, handsome features, that sort of thing."

He wasn't sure whether to take that as a compliment, but a knot of jealousy churned in his stomach to think that Katey would find Rodeny attractive. "Not all loups-garous look the same, but the obvious appearance of strength is pretty typical, though some are leaner than others."

At that moment, Ben gave a light tap of his knuckles on the bedroom door. He opened without permission and from the hall, gave the universal sign that Logan needed to wrap up the phone call.

He waited until Ben was down the hall again before mumbling, "I've got to go. Dinner's ready."

"My pizza's almost done too."

"I'll see you tomorrow? You won't skip town on us?"

Katey gave a breathy laugh. "Even if I did, I have a feeling I wouldn't get far with four loups-garous on my tail."

Logan smirked. "Probably not."

"I'll see you tomorrow in class."

How was he supposed to end the call? He always simply hung up on the pack, but Katey deserved more than that. "Sleep well."

"Yeah... You too."

Several seconds of silence stretched before the line disconnected. Logan laid there for a few moments longer, replaying the phone call in his head. He closed his eyes and tried to imagine Katey moving about the house, the way her face would have lit up with every smile and bout of laughter.

He placed himself there in her kitchen surrounded by the aroma of pizza he could never eat, and the scent of the woman he couldn't get enough of. If he had been there, he would have shown her that they couldn't just be friends. Not anymore. He would have taken full advantage of their aloneness, as he couldn't have done on Monday night, and held her tight. He'd feel her body against his, taut muscles melting into him in sweet submission. His hands would weave through her hair and he'd drink in her scent until he became dizzy with it. Holding would turn into caresses, then into...

"Logan!"

His alpha's voice snapped him out of the fantasy and he jumped from the bed to hurry downstairs. He didn't need to be on the receiving end of Darren's dominance again. He learned his lesson... for now.

All night, Katey's imagination created both mundane and super-natural scenes with Logan and his pack as the star players. Based on all she knew, she pictured how they lived together. Everything from mealtimes, morning routines, grocery shopping, if they did such a thing, and all the little ways that the wolf emerged in their personalities and relations.

In some attempt to educate herself, Katey did some cursory research on wolf behavior. Loups-garous may not exactly imitate wolves in everything, but something must bleed through every now and then. If she could learn more about wolves, then per-haps she could understand the loups-garous better, and add more items to her pros and cons list on whether she wanted to become one or not.

She kept all she imagined in mind as she made her way to first period. Darren was neither in the hall nor at his desk, but Logan was already there, seated at the back of the room and fidgeting with a pen as he usually did. He wore the same leather jacket as the day before, but a pair of jeans without tears and a dark navy shirt that hugged his powerful frame. The moment she stepped into the classroom, his gaze fixed on her, and she couldn't help but grin.

As awkward as their phone call had been, his voice was welcome company for as long as it lasted. She also hoped that taking the initiative to call him would give him some measure of hope that she was taking all of this new information well, and that she still wanted to have a connection with him. They may have only been friends, but there was no reason they couldn't be on the path to something more.

She immediately gravitated to him. "Where's Mr. Dubose?" She was mindful to put on the right pretenses in case any other stu-dent listened.

"Off making copies of the semester exam reviews."

"I forgot semester exams are next week," Katey grumbled. "Why are you still back here?"

Logan shot her a mildly condemnatory look. "You were afraid of me yesterday, remember? Darren hasn't rescinded his order, so here I stay."

Yesterday morning seemed like a lifetime ago and so much had changed. He was right that she had been afraid of him then, but all of that was behind them, she hoped.

Katey pondered for a moment, looking between the open seat next to Logan at the end of the desk and her usual seat at the front of the room. If Logan moved, he might get in trouble with Darren. She didn't know the alpha's limits as well as Logan did, but didn't want to push him either.

Instead, Katey put herself in the line of fire and claimed the seat by Logan.

"He won't like that," Logan advised and leaned closer so their conversation was more private.

"Any way I can make him okay with it? I read a little about wolf behavior. How do I... appeal to his better nature?" She wasn't exactly sure how to put it without sounding weird, but she wanted to do whatever it took to make the more dominant alpha give her what she wanted.

An amused glint shone in Logan's eyes. "Submission does not become you. I wouldn't want to teach you such a thing."

"But is that how it works?"

He shrugged. "In a way. It's not what I do."

"What do you do?" Katey propped her chin in her hand like a child ready for a story.

"I hold onto my pride for dear life, even when his dominance tries to break me down to my knees."

"I bet he doesn't like that."

"Not at all. So, I try not to ask for much anymore. I've made more supplications to Darren just this last week than in the last year."

She guessed that had something to do with her, but wouldn't ask.

"On a better note," Logan said a little louder, "I've got good news. They let me drive to school by myself this morning."

Katey's smile widened. "Does that mean your lockdown is lifted?"

He scowled. "Not quite, but it's a step in the right direction."

"How long do you think this will last?"

Logan looked away and exhaled. "Hard to say. It depends on if they think I've suffered enough."

Katey also wondered if something about Logan's desire to turn her played a role in his lockdown. If they kept Logan close, they could make sure he didn't act upon any reckless impulses. She remembered what Dustin said about Logan being impatient. "Anything I can do to help convince them?"

"It'll just take time." He suddenly looked toward the door.

Katey followed his gaze, and within the same moment, Logan scooted his chair closer and bent close to whisper in her ear, "He's coming."

Pleasant tingles gushed down her spine and through her limbs to the feel of his breath on her skin. Distracted by these sensations, Katey hardly noticed when Logan's hand slipped to her lower back and gently pushed her hips forward. The gesture was firm and direct, like from a leading partner in a dance. The result was Katey's body slumping in her chair until her head was a great deal lower than Logan's. Then, he settled his forearms and elbows on the tabletop in front of her, his upper body angled in such a way that he practically hovered over her torso. All the while, his attention stayed on the doorway.

The position reminded her of something she saw last time in her research. One wolf stood over another, the weaker wolf tucked beneath its protector in front of an aggressive packmate. Was that what Logan tried to communicate? That he would protect Katey from Darren's discipline? That wasn't what she intended by sitting next to him, but this dominating gesture inspired a sense of both safety and intimacy. Because of that, she remained perfectly still and endeavored to enjoy the view of Logan's powerful body so near to hers.

The alpha entered the classroom, a thick folder of papers in one hand and a steaming mug of tea in the other. He looked from Logan and then to Katey. Nostrils flared and his stare hardened with indignation.

"We are not playing musical chairs today. Miss Katey, please return to your seat."

A heaviness of atmosphere dropped around Katey that made her suddenly uncomfortable. Was loup-garou dominance? If so, who did it come from? Logan or Darren?

Logan's chin dipped by the slightest degree and the energy thickened. Yep, that was Logan.

Irritation sharpened Darren's voice. "I don't have time for this."

Katey could barely breathe as another wave, more intense than whatever Logan put out, swept over them. That had to be Darren. She squirmed out from under Logan, her chair legs groaning against the tile as she scrambled to move as quickly as possible out of the war zone.

The moment she did, the air thinned and the tightness in her chest released. At the same time, Logan lost his reason to battle with the alpha and stayed in his seat. Darren sighed and motioned for Katey to proceed ahead of him toward the front. She did, giving Logan an apologetic glance along the way. He, however, didn't seem so regretful about what happened. There was an almost sly look on his face that told her he might have enjoyed the little clashing of wills. She didn't. If that was what alpha dominance felt like, she had no interest in being on the receiving end again.

Katey sat beside Beth at their table as the bell rang.

"I guess you two made up?" her friend asked.

She had almost forgotten how much she told Beth and Lily about the drama between her and Logan during lunch the previous day. "Yeah. I took Lily's advice, and we had a long talk after school."

Beth gave her a dubious look. "I really hope he isn't playing you. Guys like that can really mess with your head."

Within hearing range of the alpha loup-garou at the front of the class and Logan at the back, it dawned on Katey that she would need to be mindful of everything she said in their presence, even if it was in a whisper.

"It was a big misunderstanding. Everything is all right now."

She hoped Beth was convinced, because she needed to convince herself of the same. Maybe it was too soon to tell just how much knowing about loups-garous would change everything. She still had no solid plans and just the next few weeks would be a whirlwind of chaos as she continued searching for a place to stay, but something told her that Logan and his pack would be a new permanent fixture in her life.

That thought made her smile a little. Something constant, something reliable. Were these loups-garous that safety net she needed? She may not have been part of their pack, but they admitted that they cared for her. Such a revelation escaped her before, too immersed in all the details and the stories. Her heart warmed at the thought that if she was in trouble, she could call, and they would be there. She had some idea of it before, but now it was confirmed.

Overcome, Katey looked to Darren, seeing him and all he represented in a new light. Their eyes met for a second as he took attendance on his laptop. The alpha did a double take, something catching his notice. Pending tears of happiness blurred Katey's vision. To assure Darren that she was fine, she smiled and casually rubbed at her eyes to rid herself of the evidence of this comforting epiphany.

"I thought you had to eat with the guys?" Katey asked as they made their way to the lunchroom.

Logan gripped his lunch box instead of reaching for Katey's hand. "Darren said I could spend lunch with you as long as I stayed in the building."

"Another good sign that lockdown may be over soon?"

"If only," Logan grumbled. "Dustin said they're going to re-assess the lockdown and wanted me out of the way while they do it."

"Does it have anything to do with this morning? We behaved in all the other classes."

Renewed satisfaction washed through Logan at the recollec-tion. It had been a gamble to make a show of claiming Katey the way he did. The gesture wouldn't have gone unnoticed by Darren, and that flood of dominance proved it. Katey diffused the tension by jumping away, but the damage was done. It wasn't as blatant as some may have seen it, but Logan made his intentions clear to his alpha. Of course, he wouldn't tell Katey what all of that meant, not even if she asked.

"Probably not. It'll likely turn out for the better, but I won't know until after school."

They entered the lunchroom and Logan had to take a mo-ment. Hallways and classrooms were one thing. A packed lunch room of loud teenagers was another. Smells both sweet and odorous made his head ache along with the racket.

"You okay?"

Logan shook his head to acclimate his senses. "Yeah, it's just a lot."

"Katey!"

Logan looked across the room and saw Lily waving them over. Katey didn't seem to notice, the little blonde's voice lost in the noise, so he drew her attention that way.

"Are you okay if we sit with Lily?"

Logan gave a nod and they joined her at the table, just the three of them. Forsaking propriety, he settled himself so close to Katey on the bench that he could feel the warmth of her body. Just inches apart, arousal bloomed from Katey, and he secretly basked in her scent. She reacted the same when he guided her into submission in first period. Perhaps that was why he did it. Ever since he first sampled such an erotic aroma, he purposefully did certain things, knowing exactly how it would affect her. It might have been cruel, but he held out hope that one day, it wouldn't be such a forbidden feeling for either of them.

"I'm so glad to see you two made up!" Lily cried, giddy as always.

"Me too," Katey replied with a furtive grin.

"Are you going with Katey to the party at the studio this week-end?"

By the exchange of looks between Katey and Lily, Logan knew they both had very different feelings about that question.

"She didn't tell me about a party."

Katey tried to laugh it off. "Well, a lot has been going on this week. It never came up. I'm still going though."

Lily was undaunted. "You should be her date, Logan."

Katey's eyes widened and she paled. Fear displaced arousal and Logan was denied his fun.

"We're not dating," Logan corrected. He didn't dare check with Katey to see if that was all right to say. It wasn't the complete truth, but it was close enough. He knew anything he told Lily would get back to Forrest, and then somehow make it through the loup-garou grapevine to Darren.

Lily couldn't have looked more confused if he had sprouted a second head. "But... I thought..."

"Let's change the subject," Katey quickly interjected. "You ready for semester exams next week?"

Lily pouted. "I am not changing the subject."

"I think it's best we do," Logan asserted, pinning Lily with a look that said she should know better than to argue with him.

Not happy, but unwilling to garner Logan's ire, she sighed. "Fine. But I'm not talking about exams. I'm freaked out enough as it is." She turned to Katey. "Forrest wanted me to tell you that he might have found a place for you to stay until summer. He wants to talk with you about it this weekend."

So, that was who she had recruited to help. Logan couldn't be too disappointed. Forrest knew plenty of reliable families within his pack that would be more than willing to take in a refugee. They knew what it was like.

"That's great." The note in Katey's voice was comparable to sincere, but she was good at faking enthusiasm.

"Who is it?" Logan asked.

Lily's lashes fluttered in bewilderment. "No one you'd know." She gave a pointed look to Katey.

He understood her. But didn't care. Part of him wanted to test if Lily was trustworthy of keeping a level head in front of her friends. "Try me."

The feisty girl straightened. "The Matthews family."

Logan snorted a laugh. "She can't stay with them. They already have three kids under ten years old. It'd be a madhouse."

Inspired to spar, Lily fired back. "They would be better than the Jenkins family. They have two boys about to go into puberty and you know how bad that'll turn out."

"I wouldn't think them to be a good host family either. Did Forrest check with Jacob?"

"Of course he did, but Jacob is a bachelor and he said it would look wrong. He doesn't want to lose his job with the police."

"No, I mean if Forrest has tried to get Jacob's opinion on who would be the best fit."

Color rose up in Lily's face, but it was not in embarrassment. "Forrest has just about as much pull as Jacob does. He's Robert's son for God's sake."

Now she crossed a line. "Not even half of them knew Robert and everyone else is given to worshiping him as some hero, so of course they're going to think Forrest is some prince. Jacob deserves their loyalty more than he does."

Katey finally exclaimed, "What the hell are you two talking about?"

The red rage in Lily's cheeks drained away as she regarded her friend with mixed horror and humiliation.

While he enjoyed getting Lily's dander up, Logan decided to deliver her from her suffering. "We know each other through Forrest."

It took a second before Katey gasped aloud. "Forrest? Is he...?"

"Yep."

"And you..."

Lily gave her a sheepish grin. "Yeah, I've known for years."

Instead of lashing at her friend, Katey smacked Logan's arm. "Why didn't you tell me sooner?"

"It hasn't even been a whole day."

Then, Katey turned on her best friend. "Did you know that I knew?"

Lily gave her a pleading look, as if asking for forgiveness. "I didn't know that you knew for sure. They sent out a sort of 'red alert' that you might have known a couple of days ago, but I haven't told a soul ever since Forrest and I became serious, so I wasn't about to go blabbing now."

Katey was silent, mouth agape. He could see the gears turning behind her shifty eyes as she put the pieces together. "Oh, my god... I've been friends with a loup-garou for years and I never knew it."

Lily reached out to put her hand on Katey's. "If it helps, Forrest thought about telling you several times, but with everything you were going through with the foster families and all, we didn't think it was a great idea." She shot daggers at Logan. "Why this asshole decided to tell you after only a few days is beyond me."

"Wait, so when I was talking about Logan last Saturday, you knew who I was talking about and you didn't say anything?"

Logan sat back, enjoying the banter.

"Yeah, we did, but it would have made everything super complicated. Please understand that we never meant to hurt you by keeping secrets."

Katey took a breath and seemed to bring herself back to reason. "I know you didn't, and I'm not hurt. I guess I'm still trying to get a handle on all of this. I mean, learning about the teachers and Logan was one thing, but now I wonder how many I've met in the past and I never knew."

"Does it matter?" Logan asked. "We try to live like anybody else, and even if you've met hundreds like us, then that means we've succeeded."

"I guess you're right... So, if the Matthews, Jenkins, and this Jacob guy aren't good options, then who would you recommend?"

Logan tried to swallow back the lump in his throat. He knew exactly who he would prefer she stayed with, but he already knew that was out of the question. "I'm not sure... And Jacob is the alpha of the Deviants."

Katey propped her chin in her hand. "Is it safe for you to tell me what this whole Jacob versus Forrest rivalry is about?"

"It's not a rivalry," Lily said. "Just a difference of opinion on the past. Nothing more."

"I'll tell you the story later," Logan assured.

"Oh, he's got a ton of stories, don't you?"

He didn't appreciate the saucy way she said that and bared his teeth in a mock growl. He knew exactly what she meant by that, and Katey didn't need to hear any of those stories. Not yet. It was too soon to tarnish the image of who she thought he was. She was right about one thing in their phone call. He preferred to keep some things a mystery.

CHAPTER 13

Ben listened to the heated back and forth between his alpha and beta.

"Logan will not learn to listen and obey if we continue to be flexible in his discipline," Darren said.

"The boy hasn't listened to you for over a century. If he hasn't learned by now to take you seriously, then he never will," Dustin replied.

"Each and every time in the past, we've set restrictions in place for a short time, only to lift them days or weeks later. That's why he doesn't take us seriously. He knows that no punishment will last."

"Of course it won't last. We can't keep him on lockdown forever. He's too restless. He always has been."

Darren pointed a finger at the beta. "Because you've encouraged him. Look at this mess with Katey. If you hadn't kept information from me, we could have addressed this much sooner."

"Don't go blamin' me for all that shite." In his anger, Dustin slipped into his old Irish brogue. "The lad chose to lie to you. That's not my fault."

"But if you had told me that he met with Katey, we could have put two and two together to realize that he wanted to enroll in school early to be close to her."

"The boy has a crush. What's the harm?"

Darren's eyes went gold, likely without his consent. "Logan threw down the gauntlet at me this morning, hovering over Katey like she belonged to him. Whatever is developing between them is dangerous and has to be stopped."

Dustin scoffed. "Logan knows better than to do something so barmy like put a mating bond on her."

"I'm worried he'll do much worse than that. If we don't limit their interactions, we could end up with a dead student on our hands."

"I'm just as concerned as you are about that likelihood, but hear me out. If we continue to tighten Logan's collar, he's bound to break out of it eventually and then he'll be completely unmanageable. Making more rules just means he's more likely to sneak behind our backs."

"But if we set no boundaries, he'll do something reckless. He's done it before and he can just as easily do it again. We can't permit another scenario like what happened in Chicago happen in Crestucky."

Dustin held up a cautionary hand. "That was a very different situation in a very different era. It won't happen again."

"You are in no position to make promises like that."

"I'm the fucking beta, aren't I? This pack's safety is my responsibility too."

He hadn't uttered a word since the meeting began, but chose now to speak up. "Why are we even talkin' about this? No matter what we do, Logan is gonna find a way to do what he wants, whether we like it or not. Nothin's gonna keep him from seeing Katey, and there ain't nothin' we can do about it. If he feels that strongly about her, when he won't kill her neither."

Alpha and beta looked to him, and he hoped somehow he had broken the cyclic argument. Darren wanted to shorten the leash, and Dustin wanted to lengthen it, but Ben suggested letting go completely. There may have been no safe option, not when Logan was clearly smitten with Katey enough to lie and disobey his alpha. And he knew all too well from his own experience that wild horses couldn't keep a man from his mate for long.

Darren ran his fingers through his hair and the wolfish gold withdrew. "I don't know if I could stand to put Katey's life in Logan's hands that way."

Dustin gave him a sympathetic look. "I know trusting Logan is hard. He hasn't proven himself the most reliable in the past, but maybe Katey is enough to change him for the better?"

The alpha sniffed. "Yes, and the last week has been a wonderful precursor to the kind of changes we can expect out of him."

"All I'm sayin'," Ben chimed in again, "is give him a chance. He might surprise you."

The alpha slowly paced, his arms folded in deliberation. None of them wanted to see Katey dead, and none of them wanted a packmate foaming at the mouth to get to her. In truth, they all needed to know if Katey could truly belong with them, whether as a human mate for Logan or as a loup-garou pack member. It was a risk, either way, but they would never know unless they let fate take its course.

Darren finally stopped and then nodded. "Fine. I'll lift his lockdown. He can go where he pleases with whomever he pleases, but my only request is that he inform one of us of where he is."

"Which will be wherever Katey is," Dustin teased.

The alpha grimaced and rubbed at his face. "If she turns up pregnant before next spring, I'll kill Logan."

"You'll have to get in line," the beta quipped.

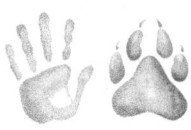

There was no way Katey could focus on studying for the semester exams. Her mind continually jumped to Logan, the teachers, Lily and Forrest, and the refreshed crisis of finding a place to stay before Mary came back from her trip. In just one week, it seemed as if her life had completely changed, and the reality of it finally caught up with her.

More than that, Logan's words bounced around in her brain like a wrecking ball.

We're not dating.

She knew they agreed to be friends. She knew anything more was too complicated, according to Logan. But what about the cemetery visit? What about when he crashed on her couch for the night? What about that moment in the wrestling gym when they shared the same air and time stood still? Did all of that mean nothing? Were they just hanging out? Was he just acting the part of a concerned protector this whole time? The idea that they could be more dissolved like salt in warm water, little more than a distant fantasy. It seemed simpler when she thought he was a mere man and not a loup-garou.

Katey didn't know what to do or how to feel anymore. Perhaps she had been fooling herself this whole time, thinking that Logan cared for her as more than someone to shelter and protect from a harsh world. Maybe all of those little signs meant something completely different in loup-garou culture. Wolves were, after all, very physical creatures. Besides vocalizations, touch and body language was their only other way of communicating. Maybe Katey had been reading him wrong.

The phantom voices taunted her with doubts.

Why would he want you anyway? He had his choice of girls and they would fall over themselves to spend an evening with him. He's probably comparing you to old girlfriends from the last century. You could never measure up, that's why he just wants to be friends. Not pretty enough. Too damaged. Why even bother?

While these thoughts didn't bring back the darkness in its full vigor as before, Katey's world became a little more dull, less vibrant, less stable than it had even the day before in Dustin's classroom. How could the knowledge that loups-garous existed be almost nothing in comparison to this dilemma with Logan and what they meant to one another?

The final bell rang and Katey left the auditorium, heart heavy and mind laden with all the thoughts she couldn't push aside. Before she could get far into the hall, an arm wrapped around her waist and hand latched over hers. She let out a shriek a second before she realized who had grabbed her.

Her cry trembled into an involuntary laugh and she let Logan swing her in two or three circles. He set her back on her feet, breathless and dizzy.

"Let's get out of here." Logan's voice was husky with some flavor of excitement.

"What?" she asked once she caught her breath.

She had never seen Logan this ecstatic before. "Let's go somewhere. Where do you want to go? Mobile? Tallahassee? The beach? Just name the place and we'll go. Right now."

Katey glanced around at the other students watching them and she realized Logan still held her as if he were prepared to whisk her away.

"But, you're on—"

"Nope. Darren lifted it. We can go anywhere. I just have to tell him where I'm going. Not even a mention of a curfew."

It took a long moment before Katey could bring herself back to earth, too distracted by the way her body pressed against his. Logan must have come to his senses too and loosened his hold just long enough for her to put some distance between them

"Those places are pretty far away."

"So? Just a few hours of travel and we can have a little mid-week adventure."

Katey giggled and shook her head. "You're nuts, you know that?"

"Fine. Where do you want to go?'

If Katey hadn't been so torn up over the last couple of hours, she would have asked to escape to some faraway place where no one knew them and they could do anything they wanted. Instead she answered, "The library."

Logan's countenance fell. "You're joking. We've just been given a pass and you want to go to the library?"

Coolness rushed in as Logan's arm dropped away from her, but their hands stayed clasped between them, her fingers safely secured between his.

"I'm not ready for the semester exams and I really should study."

Logan rolled his eyes and gave a short, even-tempered growl of frustration. "All right. I guess I can settle for that."

She couldn't account for why Logan would have been so eager to spirit her away like that. Not until she remembered how Beth talked on and on about a long weekend she spent with a few of her friends in New Orleans under the supervision of an older sibling. Friends sometimes went on those sorts of adventures. Logan's offer had nothing to do with any deeper affection, she tried to tell herself. It meant nothing, just like everything else.

That realization broke the last seal of the spell and she easily wrenched her hand from Logan's. A flash of confusion in his eyes made her want to revisit that assumption, but she wouldn't allow herself to hope again. Better not to hope so she wouldn't be hurt. Of course, it wasn't Logan's fault. She broke her own heart by reading past his words to focus too much on his actions. She didn't know which held more weight anymore.

Katey readjusted her backpack strap and mustered some measure of poise again. "How do I know you're not just saying that and you're trying to get yourself in trouble again?"

"Fair assumption, but I assure you I'm not lying." Logan pulled out his phone and showed her the short text from Darren.

She read the text and nodded in approval. "Very cool. I think you're fibbing about how harsh they are. It's only been a few days and you're already free."

They began to walk down the hall, joining the flow of students as if they hadn't just embraced and acted like lovestruck teenagers.

"Oh, this is odd for them. Some punishments have lasted much longer. Back in the twenties, they never let me out of their sight for at least half a year."

Katey tried to hide her shock. "You must have done something really bad."

Logan's eyes went dark and he looked away. He only did that when the conversation took a turn he didn't like, but he was the one that brought it up this time. "Yeah, it was really bad."

"I won't ask."

"Thank you... My bike is parked on this side of the school." Logan guided her toward a set of doors that led to an outside picnic area near the auditorium.

Katey made some attempt to plant her feet to resist. "My jeep is in the senior parking lot."

"We can take my bike. It'll be faster than driving separately."

A touch of nervous nausea made Katey shake her head. "I've never ridden on a motorcycle."

His cunning smile didn't make her feel any less sick at the idea. "You're not the one driving. You just hang on."

Katey had seen plenty of couples on motorcycles around town and on television, but she never imagined she'd ever ride one. Lily would have thought the idea totally romantic, but Katey had been subjected to too many gory pictures of motorcycle accidents during her driving lessons.

Logan could likely sense her fear as they stepped outside. "Don't worry. I've never crashed."

That day's weather was unusual for December, the bright sun combating with the frigid winds.

"Yeah, but if you do, you'll walk away with only a few bumps and bruises. I might not be so lucky."

Logan chuckled. "I promise I'll be extra careful."

They approached his motorcycle and she only saw one helmet. She should have immediately refused and marched back inside, but she knew Logan wouldn't let her.

He mounted the bike, slid on his helmet and started up the engine, the noise drowning out all others in the parking lot. If Logan struggled with the lunchroom with sensory overload, how could he tolerate the motorcycle?

Katey stood there, unsure how best to tackle the task. There was something erotic about the combination of Logan atop his bike, face concealed behind a black visor, sporting his leather jacket. Yeah, any girl with even half a brain would have sold their soul for this opportunity. Why was he so determined to screw with her?

Slowly and carefully, Katey swung onto the seat behind him, finding the effort awkward as her feet searched for a place to perch. Her body slid forward by itself, dangerously close to Logan's back, though she continued to sit as upright as possible to avoid contact. Heart pounding, she forgot exactly how she was supposed to hang on. Logan had the handlebars, but what did she have?

Likely assuming she needed guidance, Logan reached behind him, took her hand and pulled her forward. She fell into him with a squeak of surprise, and she could feel the purr of his chuckle against her chest. Her arms hugged his middle and for an instant, her fingers brushed the ridges of his torso, sending flutters through her already roiling stomach. His muscles tensed for only a second, then relaxed as she did.

Katey pushed back the torrent of feeling and held on to her own wrists to avoid touching Logan so intimately again. With eyes squeezed shut, she toughened herself for the short ride to the public library and willed herself not to whine in panic at every turn and acceleration.

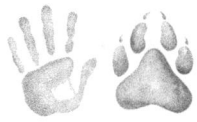

Libraries were supposed to be quiet places, but for Logan, he might as well have been riding down the highway next to semi-trucks. He could hear every conversation across the building, even the children's story time session in the semi-sound-proof room. Page turns, keyboard tapping, the low hum of the fluorescent lights, the variety of vehicle noises in the parking lot, and Katey's heartbeat across the table. They had found a spot toward the back of the library, wide windows to their right overlooked the woods behind the property, and a clear shot down a row of nonfiction books on history to their left.

He had no reason to study. Darren already told him that the exams wouldn't count for anything since he wasn't truly enrolled. For appearance's sake, he had their human geography textbook open in front of him, but that was the only semblance to studying he could maintain. He had already ripped out several pieces of paper from his notebook and folded them into all manner of shapes to distract Katey. After a curt word from her, he stopped, but grew bored again as he reclined in the plain wooden chair.

If he let his thoughts wander, they often entered dangerous territory, such as remembering the way Katey held onto him during the ride to the library. It was the longest they had been that close to one another, and it wouldn't be the last time. He'd make sure of it.

After he attempted an origami dog and failed to get the right fold due to the dimensions of the paper, he wadded it up and looked to Katey. Lips tight together, brows pinched in concentration, and green eyes darting across the environmental science review, she looked adorable.

He held perfectly still as he took his aim and waited for her to notice. When she didn't, he let the paper ball fly in a lazy arch toward the crown of her head. It bounced off and she perked up to glare at him. Logan quickly looked away, feigning innocence.

Katey snatched up the ball from the table and chucked it at him with greater force. He reflexively dodged and it missed the tip of his nose by nearly an inch. They both suppressed a laugh, the bit of play breaking the tension.

"You're supposed to be studying," Logan teased in a whisper as he tapped the review. "Not playing."

"Look who's talking. You haven't turned a page since we got here."

Logan sat up straighter and leaned over the open textbook. "I probably should confess... I'm not actually enrolled."

The whites of Katey's eyes grew more prominent. "What?"

"I'll start from the beginning. I told you before that I've never had a formal education. That was true, but when the rest of the pack got jobs this past fall, that left me at home. I made a deal with Darren that I could try high school for one year and if I liked it, I'd continue on to college. I wasn't supposed to start until next year because enrolling someone like me takes time. We have to have documents and past records forged, after all."

Katey leaned forward to join him in their hushed conversation. "What changed the plan?"

"You. After I met you on Friday, I wanted to start school immediately."

Katey's eyes narrowed and her pulse quickened. "Why?"

Logan tilted his head, expecting her to understand the obvious. Either she didn't, or she wanted him to openly admit it. "You intrigued me. The guys talked about you all the time, but I didn't know what all the fuss was until I finally met you. After that, I knew I had to get to know you more."

A blush rose to her cheeks, such a complimenting color to her complexion. She averted her eyes and leaned away in silence. By the delicate change in the aura around her, he knew he had upset her.

"I liked the other explanation better."

Logan blinked. "But it was a lie."

From the end of the aisle, an elderly woman passed by with a cart of books and shushed them. He waited until the hag was out of sight before turning back to Katey, but she beat him to it.

"If you're not going to study, go find a book to read or something."

Logan fought the buildup of indignation in his chest. "You're mad at me."

"No, I'm not."

"That little scowl on your face says differently."

"I just need to study and you're distracting me."

"What did I do?"

Katey snapped at him. "Bother me while I'm studying."

Logan gave as good as he got. "No, I upset you before that, didn't I?"

"No, you didn't. Shut up before we get in trouble."

"You mean that old bat in the glasses?" Logan purposefully raised his voice to just above normal conversation level. "Don't worry about her. Tell me what I did."

"We're going to get thrown out," Katey hissed vehemently.

"I really don't care."

"Don't be an ass, Logan."

"Then tell me why you're mad."

The heat and sudden fury in her eyes almost startled Logan into surrender. A long, edgy minute passed, wills locked with neither giving any ground. Katey was the first to break and began to furiously pack up her things.

"Where are you going?"

"What, are you my alpha now?"

Struck by that retort, Logan lingered in his seat while Katey stood and stormed toward the back door. What the hell had gotten into her? What had he said or done to deserve this? He told her the honest truth, admitted that she was the reason he nearly got his head bit off by Darren that Friday night, and she acted as if he had insulted her instead. Shouldn't that have been a complement?

He belatedly followed her outside to the grassy lawn that sloped from the back of the library to the edge of the woods. She whipped around to face him, the edge of her rage as sharp as before.

"You wanna know why I'm mad? I'm mad because I don't understand you. What are we doing here? What are *you* doing here? What's the point of all this? Is it a game? Are you that bored that you thought barging into my life, making me question everything I know and feel, would be a good bit of fun?"

Logan stared dumbly, unsure how to fight back, or if he even should. If this were Darren or Dustin, he'd heap plenty of abuse on them, knowing they could take it. But this was Katey in front of him, figuratively baring her teeth and fur bristling, and challenging him.

"No, this isn't a game," he replied. He made every effort to keep his cool even when her rage could prove infectious.

"Then why, Logan?" Katey begged. "Why are you telling me all these things and doing stuff that, in any other circumstance, would mean you cared for me as more than just a friend? Is this what loups-garous do with their friends?"

"No."

"Then explain it to me. Ever since yesterday, any time we get to a topic you don't want to talk about, you give me some bullshit excuse like, 'it's complicated' or 'I'll tell you about it later'. You'll tell me that you killed your parents, but you can't explain how you feel or why we can't date?"

Logan's breath froze in his lungs and it took him too long to find the words. Katey turned as if she'd leave and he grabbed for her arm to hold her back. At the risk of losing her, he let out the first thing that came to mind. "I can't tell you what I don't understand."

"Try... For me."

Fear tore through Logan, but he didn't know why. Telling her what he was had been easy, mostly because he let Darren do all the talking. Telling her about his parents had been difficult, but he had told so many people by now that it came out almost mechanically, though it brought back feelings he didn't care to sit with. As he looked into her eyes, sparkling with unshed tears and pleading with him to put her warring mind to rest, he couldn't find the words.

"All I know is that after yesterday, I have no filter." Logan stretched out his arms as if to show her. "When it comes to you, I say what I mean and I do what feels right. How you interpret the meaning isn't my problem."

That was a mistake. Katey trembled and lips tightened as if she were trying to bottle up renewed wrath. It didn't work.

"Not your problem? It is when it can give people the wrong idea... When it can give *me* the wrong idea. Don't you get it?"

"What do you want me to tell you? You act like I should know all of this."

"Don't you? You've been alive for over a century. You should have figured these things out by now."

Her rage became infectious. "Well, I haven't. Sorry to disappoint. I'm just as oblivious as the next guy."

"Then I feel sorry for the dozens of girlfriends and wives you must have had by now, to have to put up with someone who doesn't even know how to express himself."

Logan could have laughed if she weren't still fuming mad. "Girlfriends? Wives? You think I've done this before?"

Katey softened. "Haven't you?"

"No." Logan couldn't repress a little chuckle. "You've likely had more lovers than anyone in the pack... Well, save for Dustin."

Now it was Katey's turn to bust a seam. Logan grew a little aggravated with just how humorous she found the concept that he was so inept at lovemaking in the traditional sense of the word.

When she regained some calm, she said, "I've never had a boyfriend. You think anyone would actually want this?" she gestured to her body as if there were some glaring flaw with it. He saw none.

Logan stared, finally comprehending that they were both new to this and didn't have a clue what they were doing. At least, not completely. Did she know her own mind better than he did? Was he telegraphing signs that he wasn't even aware of?

Logan put his palms together as if in prayer. "Okay... Can we start over? You're mad because..."

Katey groaned and tossed her head back like a toddler in the midst of a tantrum. "You're acting like you like me."

"I do like you. I enjoy spending time with you."

"No, I mean not 'like' as an okay person, but 'like' as in something more than a friend. You said we were just friends, that we weren't dating, but the way you talk to me, the way you treat me, none of that is 'friend zone' behavior." Katey graciously provided her own air quotes to emphasize her point.

The pack had always kept him accountable for his actions, when it came to manners and safety, but never in matters of the heart. His only frame of reference was what he observed in others. Dustin was not the ideal role model, chasing skirts for the better part of the century. He was never permitted to see the budding stages of relationships amongst the Deviants. Was this transition from nothing to friends to lovers supposed to be so difficult? Wasn't it just supposed to happen as naturally as lightning?

"Would it be better not to give this a name?" he asked. "You seem hung up on the label."

"No, I need a word for it. That helps me know how I need to act and what to expect."

Expectations. Like roles within a pack. Alphas, betas, and omegas all had their responsibilities specific to them. She needed to know her place in his life. Finally, something he could translate.

"I don't have a word for it. We're not mates. According to you, we're not friends, and we certainly aren't strangers... We aren't dating, because there isn't such a thing for us, for loups-garous."

Katey folded her arms. "Lily and Forrest have been dating for years."

He suspected that they would be dragged into the discussion. "No, they're not. It may look like it, but they're only on track to being mated. They're only waiting for Lily to graduate."

"So... They're engaged?"

"Again with your labels. Mating and marriage aren't the same. Their processes and endgames are different. You can be mated but not married, and vice-versa."

"That makes no sense."

Logan put his hands on his hips, glad his point had been proven. "And that's why I told you it was complicated."

"Then what weird, nameless level of relationship are we stuck at?" Frustration gripped her words.

Logan had no answer. Just as she said, they were stuck. Human relationships were so broken apart in a dozen stages that flowed imperfectly. For loups-garous, it was much more straightforward and less fussy. They were free with their affections, if they existed, and less pretentious when they didn't. Their commitments weren't based on a piece of paper or a ring, but by loyalty, respect, and passion. He couldn't expect her to understand, immersed in a society that needed those legal and outward proofs of connection to link one human to another.

Logan took a long breath to buy him time before some answer came out in a grating, forced way. "Can it be enough for us to just enjoy how we feel in the moment, and not overthink it?"

Katey turned thoughtful and cast her gaze to the woods. He couldn't imagine how hard this was for her, to just let go and let life happen. Perhaps he had come on too strong, too forward, just like the first night they met. He relied so heavily upon his senses and observations, and let what was hidden within her encourage him instead of what she allowed him to see. He took for granted that her actions had little to do with any notion of self-control.

"What if things go too far?" she asked, voice smothered in some emotion he couldn't place.

"There's no such thing. Not as long as we both feel the same."

Katey looked back to him, much more resigned. "Do we? Feel the same?"

"Only you can tell me that. My actions match my feelings... Do they match yours?"

More agonizing silence as he waited for her to finally join him in some mutual understanding.

"I think they do."

Logan stepped closer. "And is that enough?"

He didn't mean for it to come out as a challenge, but he knew it could have been mistaken that way, so he dulled his inquiry by reaching for her hand. She didn't snatch it away, and he tenderly stroked his thumb over her fingers as if that would soothe away any last vestiges of doubt.

He sensed the swell of feeling in her and saw her throat work past the words that wouldn't come. She only nodded and shyly dropped her stare, all the fight gone out of her. Logan wasn't sure he liked that. He didn't lie that morning when he said that submission wouldn't suit her.

"By the way, please don't mention to the guys that we had this conversation."

Katey found the remnants of her voice in a whisper. "Why?"

Logan gave her a suggestive smirk. "They might put us both on lockdown."

She snorted a laugh and glanced toward the library.

"You still need to study," he said. "Better get back inside."

She resisted the tug of his hand. "It's a pretty day. Can we stay out here?"

Logan inspected the clear sky and nodded. "Sure, but let me know if you get too cold."

"I'll just take your jacket again if I do."

And with her smile, all sins seemed forgiven for the time being. Logan made a mental note to temper his actions going forward. He would maintain his candidness and give her affection as freely as he pleased, but he would take her heart into consideration. He dared not play with it as so many others might. She deserved better, much better than he could give her.

CHAPTER 14

He wanted casual. No labels, no strings, or commitments. It wasn't ideal, but Katey had seen it before. They could hang out, mess around if they wanted, and even see other people on the side or decide to abandon what they had when it ceased to satisfy them. They would live like tomorrow and yesterday didn't matter, even though it did. There was only the present moment.

She'd never let him see how much it crushed her not to be exclusively his and only his. Though she was no romantic by any stretch of the imagination, Katey wanted to be someone's girlfriend, or mate, or whatever it was loups-garous had in the way of female companionship. She wanted to be that to Logan, and he didn't seem interested in anything that serious.

"How do you manage to win a fight without hurting anyone?"

Katey leaned her elbow on the open textbook in her lap, one hand holding Logan's paused mp3 player. She had barely given any attention to studying since they decided to sit outside. They spent the majority of the time talking and listening to music. One earbud was lodged in her ear, but Logan didn't need his half in order to listen.

Logan laid stretched out across the turf, arms folded behind his head to display all of his gloriously ripped loup-garou body. Katey's mouth watered as she thought about what his clothes concealed. If pace no longer mattered, she might find out sooner rather than later. That idea made the moment of discovery feel cheap. It made *her* feel cheap.

"I mostly fight other loups-garous so I don't have to hold back the punches. It's easier that way, but hurts a hell of a lot more because they don't hold back either."

"And the rest of the pack doesn't care that you fight?"

"Oh, they definitely care, but they know it's the only way for me to blow off some steam."

"Seems like a pretty violent way to blow off steam."

"Better than corking it up until it explodes on someone who doesn't deserve it."

Katey shrugged. "I guess so. But what about sketching?"

Logan screwed up his face. "Not the same. Sketching is for when I'm bored or don't want to think."

"Which was it when I called yesterday?"

Their eyes met and that familiar shock zipped through her core.

"My brain wouldn't shut up."

Katey could guess why so she didn't ask. "Did it help?"

"For a little while. I have to go to sleep at some point."

Katey's imagination spun scenes of Logan lying in bed, a comforter covering his lower body. Did he wear pajamas or sleep in the nude as she heard some men did? Did he have a nighttime routine? What about the rest of his pack?

"What's that faraway look for?" he asked.

Her lips curled in a whimsical smile. "I've been imagining what it's like to live in a pack... your pack. All the little things you all do on a daily basis. I've been in group homes before, but there was never any real fellowship among them. Everyone did their own thing and didn't care about anyone else. It was easier, because making friends always meant losing them. But with a pack—"

"Being in a pack doesn't make you immune to loss, if that's what you were thinking."

The lovely, unspoken fiction cracked under Logan's interruption. "You four have been together for the better part of a century, though."

Logan's expression turned somber. "Yes, but we are loup-garou. Not everyone we make connections with is like us... We make friends, we take human mates, we have children, but not all of them are destined to stay with us. Death and loss are just as real to us as anyone else."

There was that touch of grief again. Before, it had been for his parents. Who did he mourn now?

"Immortality isn't all it's hyped up to be?" She hoped the flippant note of her voice tempted him out of his morbid thoughts, but it didn't appear to work.

"Not at all."

Katey looked away and turned over the mp3 player in her hands. She didn't want to speak her thoughts in the open. It would sound ridiculous and childish. Why would she or anyone in his pack think that she could have been a permanent fixture in each other's lives and still remain human? The only way to keep them was to become like them. Their secret would become hers and she could live for centuries, hearing their stories and making memories with people she could rely on, with people who would always be there for her.

One more to add to the pro side of her list. That one would be weighted heavily.

The lights that streamed from the library windows dimmed, plunging the lawn into twilight darkness. Only street lamps from the parking lot cast an amber glow across the lawn. Katey looked around as if she forgot where she was.

"How late is it?"

Logan pulled out his phone. A bright, bluish white lit up his features. "About a quarter till five." Almost in the same breath, the light on his face changed to a brownish, yellow hue, and the phone vibrated with a call.

He answered as Katey gathered up her study materials. "Yeah?"

Katey heard some low voice on the other end of the line but couldn't make out the words.

"We're still at the library... Hadn't made any plans yet... Hold on, I'll ask." Logan turned to Katey. "How do you feel about barbecue?"

She thought she knew where this was going, and two desires warred in her. Should she lie and say she hated it so she wouldn't have to turn down dinner with the pack directly, or go with the flow of the evening? It wasn't as if anyone was waiting on her back home.

"I like it."

"You heard?... Yeah, we can be there in fifteen minutes... What do you want to drink?"

Katey knew that last question was for her, and she gave him a simpering look. "It's polite to ask if I even want to go out for dinner before assuming I will."

On the phone, she thought she could hear laughter in the background.

Logan sighed and sat up to take her free hand as if he were about to ask something utterly serious, though the devilish smile gave him away. "Katey, would you do me and the pack the honor of your presence for dinner at Johnny's Barbecue Shack this fine evening?"

More laughter and Katey grinned. "Why, yes, good sir. I'd be delighted."

"And what would madam care to drink?"

She couldn't keep up the act and giggled. "Coke is fine."

Now with the phone closer, she could make out some words and knew Darren was the one who had called.

"We'll see you there," Logan told him. "Usual spot?"

"Yes," Darren replied. "Make sure Katey understands the protocol."

Logan ended the call and brought the back of her hand to his lips for a quick kiss. Katey felt heat creep up her neck and mentally bashed at the butterflies in her tummy.

"I didn't mean to assume you were eating with us." Logan took on an apologetic face. "That was rude of me."

"It's okay. Who was laughing?"

"Dustin. That's another thing, phone calls are never that private among us. Might as well be on speaker phone the whole time, so be careful how much you say."

"Noted. And the protocol for dinner?"

Logan rose to his feet and helped Katey to hers with one smooth, powerful pull on her hand. "No mention of loups-garous or anything even remotely close. We don't go out much, but when we do we pretend as if we're friends just meeting up for dinner or lunch. It's been a little more difficult since they all work with each other now, but we haven't encountered too many weird looks yet."

They made their way up the hill toward the library parking lot. The only vehicles that remained were Logan's bike and a couple of cars that belonged to employees.

"What's my excuse for going out to dinner with three of my teachers?"

Logan paused and seemed thoughtful. "Well, I'm supposed to be Dustin's cousin instead of grandson, and to anyone else, we may look like we're a couple, so you're there because of me, and I'm there because of Dustin, and he's the one who is friends with Darren and Ben."

"Doesn't it get confusing having to keep up appearances like that?"

He shrugged and picked up his helmet. "Sometimes. It's much easier just to pick up food and take it back to the house. After dinner we can go back and get your jeep."

"Unless we want to do something after dinner," Katey offered.

By the way Logan paused before slipping on his helmet, she knew he caught onto the suggestive lilt in her words.

"Oh? Like what?"

Katey swayed closer and played the part of the casual lover like he wanted. "We could go back to my place. No pack there to watch us."

A new energy hummed between them as Logan's face split in a mischievous grin. "Why, Miss Katey, it's a school night."

"That didn't seem to matter to you on Monday, or when you offered to whisk me away to Mobile earlier today."

"What might you have in mind? Movie?"

Katey matched his grin. "Maybe."

He chuckled and slid his helmet on. "Sounds like a plan to me."

With his back turned as he mounted his bike, Katey let her mask drop. This wasn't her, but this seemed to be what he wanted. Have some fun and don't get caught up in semantics about what they could or couldn't do. Enjoy it while it lasted. Go with the flow. No ties, no regrets. She hoped.

***

The inside of Johnny's Barbecue Shack was warm, the air saturated with the scents of roasting and smoked meats, tangy sauces, and all manner of spices. The decor reminded Katey of the inside of a barn, complete with old farming equipment mounted on the walls. Tables were covered in generic red and white checkered tablecloths, each supplied with half a dozen bottles of sauces and condiments. Country music filled the air, along with the general bangs and sizzles of kitchen activity out of sight from the public.

For a Thursday dinner hour, they were not as packed as Katey expected, but enough eyes turned to her to make her squirm and edge closer to Logan.

With Logan leading the way, they walked past the dining families and couples to come to a back room. Only a few tables lined the walls with four tables in the center. Two of them were pushed together, occupied by the pack. No others had been seated in the room, giving a sense of privacy to the pack. Drinks had already been served with two baskets of some appetizer between them. At the end of the table were two lone glasses at empty place settings, one water and one soda.

Suddenly shy again, Katey avoided their stares and pinched the edge of Logan's jacket as she trailed behind him.

"Glad you could 'honor us with your presence,' Katey Kat." Dustin's humor made her feel a little more comfortable, though she would have never imagined that she'd ever sit down to a meal with any of these men in her life.

Ben snickered, but Darren was all seriousness.

"Did you two have a productive time studying?" the alpha asked as they took the empty seats.

"Not really," Logan replied. "We talked most of the time until they closed."

Katey would have lied, and Darren's disapproving look justified her.

"You don't have much time until the exams." That comment was reserved for Katey alone.

She took hold of her glass, but didn't lift it from the table, afraid that it would shake with her hands if she took a sip too soon. "I know. I'll do more studying over the weekend."

"In that case, you better make yourself scarce, Logan." Dustin picked up one of the appetizers, what she now recognized as chicken wings slathered in a thick red sauce.

"That's a good idea," Darren affirmed before picking up a wing for himself. "The less distractions, the better."

Katey waited until her suspicion was confirmed, and then remarked, "You just let Dustin eat first."

The loups-garous froze and looked at her in confusion. She had almost forgotten the protocol not to mention their secret, but the way she said it didn't obviously imply anything that an outsider might catch.

Darren seemed to catch her meaning first and nodded. "Yes, I did. There's no reason we can't be egalitarian in our table manners."

That was her answer. In the wild, wolves ate according to rank. Alphas had first pick of the choice organs, while lesser wolves had less. She thought she read somewhere that their diets also determined the variation in their fur color, and Katey wanted to ask if that was true among loups-garous as well, but this was not the time or the place. She simply gave Darren an appreciative and contrite smile and steadied her nerves long enough to take the first sip of her soda.

"She's a little more observant than we thought," Ben muttered behind his own glass.

"Makes me wonder what else you've noticed," Dustin added pointedly. "Getting a little careless, Ben."

She saw Dustin jerk and heard a thud from underneath the table. Ben jumped and nearly spilled his water in response to being kicked. The two glared at one another before Ben good humoredly picked up a pre-packaged set of silverware and tossed it at Dustin. The beta caught it and chuckled.

Katey would have remarked on how a tense moment was just broken up by a bit of fun, just as Logan had done with her in the library. Another wolf behavior, though usually reserved for the omega of the pack. Was Ben or Logan the omega? They didn't mention that during their grand reveal the day before.

Logan nudged her and tapped the menu in front of her. "Have you been here before?"

She turned her attention to the list of the usual barbecue faire and shook her head. "No, but I've heard good things."

"Get whatever you'd like," Darren said at the head of the table. "My treat."

"I can pay for my own meal, it's no problem."

Darren leveled an alpha stare on her. "I insist."

"Let him," Dustin advised. "There's no point arguing with the old man."

"Old man?" Darren exclaimed.

Ben leaned back in his chair. "Sure. You've had those silver highlights for some time now."

The alpha gave a scathing look to his subordinate, but only sighed. "I accept aging gracefully, unlike some."

Dustin thumped his hand on the tabletop. "Oh, what was the name of that one guy in Minnesota that kept dying his head hair black, but let his beard turn gray."

"Mark Thompson," Logan answered.

The beta dramatically pointed to his grandson. "Mark Thompson! He ran the car lot, remember?"

Ben laughed. "I remember. He sold ya that lemon of a VW, too."

Dustin groaned at the memory. "Feckin' swindler if there ever was one."

Katey listened and caught herself smiling in the exchange. These were the stories Logan mentioned, the ones that made them more human than monster. Back and forth they went, talking about places and people she would never know. Only little details gave away that some of these stories didn't take place in this decade, but no one else would have known it. They hid the truth buried beneath vague elements.

Soon, a waitress arrived with a notepad and pen. "Have you bunch decided what you want to order?"

They went in clockwise order around the table, but Katey noticed they all ordered one of two things, either the three-meat combo of different variations, or a full rack of ribs. The sides were all vegetables of some sort, but since they came with the meal, the guys included it with their orders. Katey had been so absorbed in paying attention to their orders that when the waitress came to her, she hurriedly picked the beef brisket sandwich with a side of fries.

When the waitress left to put their order in, Katey looked to Logan and bit her lips together. She so badly wanted to state the obvious about their orders, but didn't want to speak out of turn.

He smiled and rested his arm over the back of her chair. "Yes?"

She kept her voice low, even though they were the only ones in that dining room. "You all ordered the meatiest stuff on the menu and I bet you're not even going to eat the sides."

"Why do you think I got fries? I'm only going to give them to you."

"This place is a favorite of ours," Dustin said. "We know someone who smokes the meat here."

Katey assumed that when he said they knew someone, that the someone was also a loup-garou. They really were everywhere.

Darren steepled his fingers on the tabletop. "I presume you're adjusting well?"

She gave him a slow, meaningful nod. "I believe I am."

"Logan told me that you have some urgent need to move out of your foster mother's house. Do you need any help with that?"

The crazy, impetuous part of her wanted the next words to come out of his mouth to be some invitation to stay with them. It was insane and totally impractical, but she would have agreed in a heartbeat.

"I don't think so. Forrest has been helping me find a place."

She expected dropping that name would spark a reaction, but it didn't. The fact that she knew him wasn't news to them.

"Forrest knows a lot of people," Dustin remarked as he gnawed into a chicken wing. "He should be able to find someone for you."

"He suggested the Matthews family," Logan said, a flavor of contempt in the statement.

Darren made a show of approval. "The Matthews family are nice people. It's very gracious of them to open up their home to Katey."

"They've got a bunch of youngins runnin' around, don't they?" Ben asked.

Logan nodded. "That's what I said."

"It's only for a few months, right?" Dustin asked. "You can put up with a passel of rugrats, right Katey?"

She made a sullen face. "Maybe, but it wouldn't be my first choice."

"You haven't even met them yet," Darren pointed out.

Logan edged his way into the conversation, likely knowing that Katey had backed herself into a corner. "I suggested some other families, and that Forrest consult with Jacob."

"Jacob knows a lot of people too," Dustin commented. "Last year in Alaska, he could barely walk ten feet without bumping into someone he knew."

The mention of Alaska reminded Katey of what Logan had said to her earlier that week. They were going away for winter break. Panic loomed over her, ready to seize an opportunity. She looked to Logan, who was staring at her with alarm.

"You okay?" he asked.

A quick assessment of the table saw that the rest of them were equally concerned. It must have been their wolfish senses picking up on her anxiety.

"That thing about Alaska wasn't a lie? You're really going?"

"We go every year," Darren answered, though the question was directed at Logan. "It's a kind of family reunion."

"That's what Logan said... I guess I just assumed it was part of... you know." She wanted to say that it was part of the charade he put on for her, but that was revealing too much in public.

"He might have told you too much too soon." Darren shot Logan a reprimanding look.

"We fly out the weekend after next," Dustin picked up another wing, his fourth since Katey arrived.

Her throat closed up. They would leave around the time Katey would need to find a new home. She connected the dots, and understood what the trip was. It wasn't exactly a family reunion, but a meeting of other loups-garous. Logan's pack, Forrest's from the sound of it, and perhaps other packs would be there. If Jacob received attention from others outside of his pack, then how many would gather in Alaska, and why? But, oh, the very thought of such fellowship, to be amongst a ton of people who knew one another, accepted one another, could laugh and talk like old friends. To her, it sounded magical.

A wayward thought touched her mind and once more, she felt stupid. Katey wished she could have gone with them, but she dared not ask. She wasn't some child trailing after them like a lost puppy.

You don't belong with them.

The dark voice in her head made her dip her chin and stare at the pattern of the tablecloth. She suddenly felt out of place, an outsider looking in on this picture of what it could be like to have a family. It was as if they were perfectly sculpted masterpieces, and she was a toddler's finger painting. They didn't even deserve to be in the same building together. She didn't deserve to have anything to do with him. She never had, but she let herself believe that she could somewhere between yesterday and today.

"Katey?" Ben's firm but gentle voice beside her drew her out of her own eddying thoughts. It might have been the closest she had come to the darkness since last Friday and she couldn't fight it.

She realized not a word had been spoken since she shut down. Embarrassment swallowed her up.

"I'm sorry. Logan, can you take me home?" She hated how the darkness made her voice nearly inaudible and shaky.

"The food's not even here yet," Dustin argued.

"What's wrong?" Logan's hand fell on her shoulder and she could hardly stand it.

Katey abruptly stood, grabbed her bag, and stormed toward the exit. Predictably, Logan followed.

Once they were out in the cold night air and in the dirt parking lot by the side of the restaurant, Logan blocked her path and took her by the arms. He didn't hold her tight, but enough for her to reclaim some sense of herself.

"What happened? What did we say?"

They all must have sensed the anxiety drop upon her, but she wouldn't explain herself for anything. It would sound silly, and they would just laugh at her. She knew Logan wouldn't leave well enough alone. Like at the library, he would hound her for an explanation until she gave it.

"I just... Going to dinner with the pack was a mistake. It's not right for me to intrude on your time together. Just take me home and you can come back."

It was a half-truth, but Logan seemed to buy it. The flood light beaming from the eaves of the roofline outlined his sympathetic expression. "We invited you. You didn't invite yourself. We want you here."

"Maybe I don't want to be here," she snapped, sudden anger spilling out. "Take me back to my jeep."

She didn't want to hear any white lies. Not from him. They sounded too much like those thoughtless platitudes her former foster families fed her in those first few days in a new home.

Logan jerked back as if he had been slapped. She wouldn't meet his stare and they didn't speak for a long, heavy moment. Only the rush of cars along Main Street and the muffled sounds of the grill and smoker toward the back of the building filled the silence between them.

"All right," Logan quietly conceded.

Katey mechanically mounted the bike with him, and they sped out of the parking lot. When he pulled up alongside her jeep, the only car left on the campus, Katey didn't wait for him to shut off the engine before hopping off. She dug around for her keys in her bag, irritation and hurt prodding her to find them quickly so she could flee. Logan was too fast, and he snatched at her wrist before she could get too far.

"I'm following you home and staying."

Katey just barely heard him over the roar of the bike and glared at the black visor that covered his face. "I don't need a bodyguard."

"The way you're acting right now, I think you do. Don't argue with me."

The command only made her more furious, but she knew it would do no good to fight. Maybe Logan was more perceptive. If she allowed herself to wallow in the darkness tonight, there was every likelihood she'd do something she would regret. It had happened before.

Katey wrung herself free and went to her jeep. All the way home, Logan never left her rearview mirror. A little distance to cool down and she had trouble holding onto the full force of her despair. By the time she threw the car into park in the driveway, her thoughts didn't seem so overwhelming. She had gone through similar spirals and recovered, though usually not as quickly. The memory of every foster home had been corrupted by the realization that she didn't fit in, that the people who took her in were not her family, and that the happiness of belonging would never be hers. She didn't belong to the loups-garous, the pack, or to Logan. She didn't belong among humans or nonhumans. Nothing had changed, and there was little use being so heartbroken over it. She had to harden herself to it before it devoured her.

She slid out of her jeep and didn't even jump when Logan was suddenly beside her on the path to the front door.

"I'll text Darren to let him know I'm with you."

She didn't reply. She didn't feel the need to as she unlocked the door and turned on the lights.

"I'll sleep on the couch again."

Katey looked back at him and remembered all the little secret things she had planned to do with him before dinner. Was it worth it now? She swallowed hard and felt her insides tingle as she watched him set down his helmet in the same place he had Monday night. Back then, she had entertained the thought of Logan breaking his promise to keep his distance. But now, there were no promises, no commitments, no lines that didn't need to be crossed. She was nothing but a plaything to him. He hadn't said it in so many words, but if she wasn't something precious and worthy of a title, then she might as well be nothing. She was used to that too. Perhaps something good could come out of this evening. Good for a short while, anyway.

"You don't have to."

Logan looked up and his face pinched with a blend of confusion and intrigue.

She strode forward, trembling all over as she slipped her hands beneath his jacket atop his shoulders and peeled the garment down his arms in that languid, sensuous way she had seen in the movies. It dropped to the floor in a pool of leather and she let her fingers skim over the curves of his rock-hard chest and abs through his shirt fabric.

A shuddering gasp escaped from Logan's lips, and he murmured her name. She ignored him, much easier than she could ignore the surge of fear and heat rush through her. Her breathing quickened and came out shaky through her nose, a hint that she wasn't so experienced as he deserved.

Her roaming hands found the bottom hem of his shirt. Before she could finally feel the skin she had fantasized about, he grabbed her wrists and tugged her away.

"You're not yourself. Let's just take a breath." His voice was husky with the need she also felt, though her rattled nerves wouldn't let her enjoy it.

"Isn't this what you wanted?" Katey wouldn't look up, wouldn't let him see her eyes lest they betrayed the tiny fragment of shame in their depths.

"Not this way. You're upset. It wouldn't be right."

In some effort to prove him wrong, she tried to break free so she could steal their first kiss in a rough, demanding way so he couldn't mistake her resolve. But his fingers were locked in a vice grip, and she knew she'd break something if she struggled too hard.

He doesn't want you.

Humiliated, tears brimmed at the corners of her eyes. Giving herself to Logan might have allowed her some consolation for breaking her own heart over not being part of his pack. She didn't belong with them, and he didn't even want her. Every starry-eyed notion lay shattered in a million pieces at her feet. Couldn't she just get one thing right?

It wasn't until her face was pressed into Logan's shoulder that she realized she had begun to sob. Fat tears wetted his shirt and his arms cocooned her in a warm and comforting embrace that chased away some of the pain. But she didn't want to lose her grip on this. She needed this pain to ground her, to keep her from making any more assumptions about him and the pack and what she was to them. She was nothing and she could never forget it, but in his arms, she almost did.

Logan stroked her hair as he continued to hold and shush her like a tiny, inconsolable child. Against her conscious knowing, her arms wrapped around his torso and held fast as if he were the only thing keeping her from sinking below the surface of her grief and drowning.

He never asked for an explanation, never demanded she calm down. There was nothing she could say, nothing she could do to make him understand, so she didn't even try.

For an indeterminate amount of time, she cried out years' worth of heartache and he waited until her sobs dissolved into sniffles, and then into a calm silence in one another's arms.

Logan gingerly pulled her back to force her look up into his face, so full of compassion that it almost made her want to weep again. He brushed away a bit of the moisture from her cheeks and his mouth twitched as if he wanted to muster up a smile, but couldn't.

"You should go get cleaned up."

She nodded and let him guide her toward the hall bathroom. Numbly, she splashed her face to wash off the remnants of her weakness.

When she left the bathroom, Logan was there, his back to the wall and expression spoiled by self-loathing that he must have collected since she went into the bathroom.

"Katey... if I ever gave you the impression that I wanted... only wanted that from you, please forgive me. That was never my intention."

The brokenhearted look in his eyes had Katey wondering if it was her turn to comfort him. That was laughable, to think a big bad loup-garou needed her shoulder to cry on. Part of her wanted him to suffer for letting her think such a thing, but perhaps she had understood wrongly. He implied that he wanted a casual relationship without boundaries, but maybe their definitions of what that looked like were different. He said they would never go too far as long as they felt the same. Did he mean something different? Or did he have his own expectations of when to take those bold steps? They were born in different centuries, after all. They may have not been on the same page, in the same book, or even in the same library when it came to matters of romantic relationships. Once more, she felt lost, but there would be time to figure it all out again.

She didn't trust her voice to say the words he needed, so she let her actions impart her forgiveness. Wolves did it all the time. With deliberate slowness, Katey leaned her forehead against his jaw and nudged. His fingers tangled in the hair at the base of her skull as he angled his own head, brows bent together as they did in the wrestling gym. He closed his eyes and she closed hers.

The act wasn't so intimate as what she had been tempted to do before, but Katey thought this a hundred times better, more personal, as if their souls touched through their skin. She blew out a breath of relief and let the last of her pain seep away, through her feet and into the ground. She might have royally screwed things up, but Logan didn't seem to mind. Any other guy would have called her crazy and ran out by now. Yet, he stayed. For whatever godforsaken reason, he stayed with her.

The bubble of serenity around them burst when Logan snapped away. Every line of his body tensed as if ready to pounce at some unseen danger toward the front of the house.

Then, Katey heard the familiar sputter of Mary's old car roll up the driveway. Ice swept through her veins.

"I thought you said she'd be gone for a while?" Like her, Logan didn't move from their place in the hall.

"She's back early."

Katey's mind clambered for a plan. There was no point in hiding Logan or ushering him out her bedroom window. His bike in the driveway gave him away. No plausible excuse for his presence came to her immediately, and it was unlikely that Mary would accept anything she said. They were in for hell, and Katey knew how this would end.

CHAPTER 15

Mary struggled through the front door, a hefty bag hanging from one shoulder and dragging a suitcase behind her, one of the wheels catching on the threshold. By the way the woman staggered, Katey knew she had a few drinks, perhaps on the plane on her way back to Florida.

Katey and Logan stood in the living room when Mary finally looked up. Her bloodshot eyes flitted between the two, bafflement gradually giving way to anger.

"Who are you?" she slurred. "What are you doing in my house?"

Katey stepped forward, putting herself between her foster mother and the loup-garou. "This is Logan. He's a friend from school. He came over to help me study for semester exams."

Mary let the bag drop to the floor and she almost lost her footing after shedding the weight. "I didn't tell you that you could have friends over while I'm away." She sneered at Logan. "Especially boys."

"We were just studying. I didn't think it would be a problem."

"Well, you thought wrong! I've had it with you doing whatever the fuck you want around here. If you want to make your own rules so fucking badly, you can." Mary pointed toward her room. "Pack your shit and get the fuck out of my house!"

Katey's mouth fell open, but she didn't move. This wasn't unexpected, but somehow the demand still shocked her. "I don't have anywhere to go."

"I don't give a shit. Get out!"

Behind her, she heard Logan edge forward.

"Ma'am, if I can explain—"

"You shut the fuck up! I know your type. Only one thing on your mind. You go after those ugly, sad girls and make them think you care, only to toss her aside when you're done with her."

Some key of pain in Mary's voice hinted at why she was home early. Something must have happened between her and her boyfriend. Her drunken accusation was still no excuse and Katey rushed toward her.

"You don't know anything about him!"

She made the mistake of coming within striking range. Despite her inebriated state, Mary slapped Katey hard enough to make her sway sideways.

"Didn't I tell you to pack your shit? Get out, you dirty slut!"

An inhuman growl erupted behind her. Cheek raw and vision crossed, she looked around to see Logan take a bounding step toward them. His eyes were washed with gold, but not the same gold she thought was so beautiful before. This gold was brighter, more menacing, the whites of his eyes consumed by black and backlit by animalistic rage. His lips curled to reveal a mouthful of fangs, face twisted with fury so much that she barely recognized him, and body hunched like he was ready to spring at them.

Mary screamed and seized Katey. Still reeling, she allowed herself to be led to the front door.

"Stay back!" Mary shrieked.

"Let her go." Logan's demand came out harsh and guttural, as if he and the wolf spoke with one voice.

Katey became aware of the cold as Mary dragged her onto the front porch. Logan continued to stalk closer. She had enough clarity in the heat of the moment to know he shouldn't leave the house. He couldn't afford anyone in the neighborhood to see him like this.

She stumbled, her arm trapped in Mary's grip, but she held up her free hand as a sign for Logan to stop. He either didn't notice or he didn't care, because he never paused in his pursuit of them. What had come over him? This paroxysm of bestial rage made no sense, unless Mary's treatment of her had triggered something deep in his subconscious.

Transfixed by the change in Logan, she hardly noticed that Mary had stooped down to pick up a rock from the sidewalk landscaping and hurled it at him. Logan lurched backward and his hand flew up to cover a bleeding gash at his temple. His head bent low to hide his beastly features. It was then she noticed razor sharp talons tipped the ends of his fingers. The wolf's snarl grew louder, and she thought she saw Logan's frame broaden and shiver violently. Was he about to shift? He had never explained the process, so she didn't have the first clue what to look out for.

Katey didn't have time to watch as Mary tugged on her even harder toward her car, crying out for them to hurry and escape while the monster was distracted. She fought the woman every step of the way, but couldn't resist being pushed into the passenger seat. Mary's terror somehow made her twice as strong.

She peered out the window to see Logan still on the porch, chest heaving like a bellows, the back of his hand darkened by blood.

What had come over him in those few chaotic moments? He should have known better than to go berserk like that. Did he not have control over his wolf when he became that angry? Was this why Darren kept a tighter hold over him more than the others?

Katey knew she should have been terrified. If Logan didn't even respond to her, it was completely possible that he had lost all human sense of himself, and the wolf was just one push away from the surface.

Logan's hand lowered and even in the dark, she could tell he had partially recovered from his madness. Gold eyes watched her, but not with that same murderous commitment as before.

That was the last she saw of him before Mary peeled out of the driveway, burning rubber as she sped away down the street.

He could have killed Mary. He certainly thought about it. Flashbacks of his childhood, of a cold January night, of weeping and shouting, clouded his mind until all he could see was red. Just like that night, the wolf surged forth to take control and do what needed to be done. He thought he was over such episodes. He hadn't had one in decades, not since Chicago. A piece of the beast from eighty years ago chose now, of all times, to emerge from the black corners of his soul. If Mary hadn't thrown that rock, he might have done more than scare. It had already happened before.

A moment of steady breaths expelled the beastly temper, and he pulled out his phone. Darren answered on the first ring and Logan refused to waste time.

"Mary took Katey."

"We're just now leaving the restaurant. Where are you?"

"Mary's house... I was... I almost..."

"We felt it," Dustin said in the background. "Stay cool and stay put."

Oftentimes, he hated the pack bond and its lack of privacy. Other times, like now, he was thankful. They would have sensed his near shift and the tremor of unmitigated rage that brought him to the edge of insanity. They didn't know the details or context, but they knew it happened anyway.

Logan shook his head. "No, I have to go after her. Mary drove off and she's drunk. I'll call when I've got Katey back."

"You've done enough," his alpha snapped. "Stay out of sight and—"

Logan disconnected the call, grabbed his helmet and jacket from inside the front door and dashed to his bike. If he hurried, he might be able to catch up. He had no plan for what to do when he did, but the wolf would have nothing to do with it this time.

"What the fuck was that?" Mary shouted, quite a bit more sober than she had been ten minutes ago.

Katey's eyes were riveted upon the side and rearview mirrors, watching for Logan's bike, begging it to come speeding up on their bumper any minute now. What would happen if he did, she couldn't guess, but she knew she didn't want to be in this car with Mary, driving a couple dozen miles over the highway speed limit.

"Where are you going?" she asked, so devoid of the panic so prevalent in her foster mother. Her cheek and jaw were not as sore as they had been, but she couldn't stop rubbing the skin, wondering if she would go to school tomorrow with a bruise.

"I... I don't know. Do you know what he was?"

Was there any point in denying it now? Mary saw Logan and a glimpse of his wolf. What would the pack do to her? Would they even be able to find her, wherever Mary was kidnapping her to? The woman may have thought she had done Katey a favor by carting her away from the half-crazed beast in her living room.

"No."

"Why... Why are you not freaking out?"

Katey shook her head, unable and unwilling to answer.

Mary swerved too far to the right and nearly careened off the edge of the blacktop.

"Will you watch where you're going!" Katey gripped her seat and the passenger side door for stability.

"I've got to go to the police... the news... somebody."

Katey's eyes went wide. "No! You can't!"

"That thing almost killed us!"

Katey wished she could have corrected that Logan would have only killed Mary, not her, but she wasn't all too sure of that just yet. She'd never forget that version of his golden eyes.

Once more, the car drifted into the opposite lane and Katey banged her hand on the console between them. "Hey! Either stay between the lines or let me out!" At this hour of the night, there weren't many cars out, but they had already passed a couple of semi-trucks. Katey could see the headlights of one coming up the road in their direction.

Mary was too engrossed in her panic and hyperventilating to listen. "What was he? Some monster? Some demon?"

That semi-truck was coming up fast and their car began to drift again, the driver's stare growing more and more vacant as if she were in some trance.

"Mary, stay on the road... Mary... Mary!"

Katey grabbed the steering wheel to get the car out of the way of the oncoming truck, but it was too late. The truck headlights shined brightly through her window and the sound of the horn blared in her ears.

Katey ducked below the window, covering her neck with her hands as the full force of the semi crashed into the back passenger side of the car. Shattering glass, the crunch of metal, and her own screams faded into black.

Logan's sped onto the scene just moments after the wreck. He jumped off his bike and raced to Mary's crumpled car. The semi was hardly dented, but the sedan was totaled. Logan could hardly recognize the tangled mess of blue metal and jagged, shattered glass.

He was tempted to crumble to the blacktop and weep, knowing that no human could have possibly survived this. The stench of death wrapped its ugly claws around his heart, squeezing so tight that he could barely breathe. It was an odor he knew too well.

There was no time for sorrow. He had to hope, had to have confirmation that the one thing he had come to care about in this world was not yet gone.

His heart hammered within his chest as his eyes probed the wreckage for Katey's body. He looked through the fragmented windshield and saw Mary first, hunched over the steering wheel with a piece of metal impaled through her neck. Blood drenched her side of the vehicle. He closed his eyes and listened hard. Mary had no heartbeat.

He could hear Katey's.

The faint, but steady pulse brought a flood of relief. She was alive, but for how much longer? Logan's keen eyes probed the darkness and found Katey leaning back in her seat with a multitude of cuts and darkening bruises upon her face and neck. She was unconscious, but still breathing.

He quickly jumped onto the mangled hood of the car and sent his fist flying through what was left of the windshield. Shards sliced into his knuckles and wrist, but the cuts healed quickly by the time he yanked the jagged wedges out of his path.

Logan grabbed the bent frame of the car between his power-ful hands. Calling on his inhuman strength, he pried the steel apart, just wide enough for a body to slip through. His eyes faded to gold as he reached in and tried to pull Katey from her seat. She wouldn't budge against her seatbelt, so he extended one of his claws. A gnarly, tawny, razor-sharp nail grew from his fingernail and sliced through the coarse bands that kept her strapped in.

Once Katey was free from the twisted car, he cradled her in his arms and carried her far from the vehicle onto the grassy shoulder of the road. Her head fell upon his chest, and he held her tighter, grateful that she was alive despite the odds.

Humans were such fragile creatures. A loup-garou could have easily walked away from the accident, but Mary's corpse was the handiwork of the hateful muses that held the thin threads of the lives of mortals. If Katey remained in the car much longer without aid, she might have fallen prey to the reaper as well.

She wasn't a true member of their pack and not part of his family, but Katey had latched onto his soul. Losing her would have been to lose his own life, too. A small tear seeped from his eye, the first he had cried in decades, and wetted the bloodied skin on her forehead.

Just then, he caught a trace of danger that sent his nostrils flaring. He glanced over his shoulder. A black puddle formed under the car as oil and gasoline leaked onto the highway. He could also detect the faint scent of smoke from sparks emitting from shredded wires somewhere in the engine.

The truck driver jumped down from the cab, holding his forehead. He had just come to after hitting his head during the collision. He was fortunate that such a massive truck couldn't be fazed by Mary's tiny sedan.

"Get back!" Logan shouted to the driver as he carried Katey closer to the tree line and well away from the blacktop.

Logan dropped to the ground just as the gas and oil ignited underneath the car, engulfing the wreckage and the fuel around it in a giant burst of flames. Katey lay curled beneath Logan's body as he acted as a fleshy barrier against the intense heat. They were too far for the fire to do any damage, but he took no chances. Not anymore. Not with her.

***

From the black, formless void, came a sound. A rhythmic beep of some machine. Katey listened to its steady, comforting cadence. Steadily, more senses came into focus. A heaviness of body, fatigue and aches in her limbs. She couldn't move, though sleep paralysis pinned her to the firm mattress. She wasn't completely prone, her upper body at an easy incline. Something scratchy encircled her wrist, her finger lightly pinched by some plastic. The weight of a blanket or sheet covered her lap and legs, but the skin on her arms and neck were chilled.

A sense of light beyond the blackness behind her eyelids made her think sunlight was somewhere close. More sounds, muffled by distance and walls joined the beeping. Voices, wheels on tile, plastic tapping, and shuffling feet.

A hospital.

Katey's mouth and throat were bone dry, and it hurt to swallow. Progressively, her muscles obeyed and her toes twitched against the rough blanket. Then her fingers curled on the sheets at her sides. Something in her forearm tugged and pinched. An IV. The thought that she had been pricked by a needle made her want to squirm, but she hurt too much for that.

Movement in the room prompted her to open her eyes, but it took more effort than she expected. The bright white light from a wide window nearly blinded her and she closed her eyes again. She turned her head away too quickly and pain shot down her spine. A groan escaped her chest, and she sensed someone by her bedside.

"Stay still."

She didn't know whether or not to be disappointed that the voice belonged to Darren and not Logan. The familiar accent and scent of whatever cologne or body wash he used mixed with the sterile atmosphere of the hospital room.

She crimped her eyes shut and focused on each breath until the pain subsided. Darren picked something up from the mattress and she heard another beep of a deeper tone. Less than a moment later, a door opened. The noise from the hall grew louder, then died away.

"Is she awake?" a feminine voice whispered.

"I believe so."

Katey proved the alpha right by lifting her shaky, unburdened hand to tell them she was awake, but weak.

Some more movement, and Katey tried to open her eyes again. This time was more successful. After a few clearing blinks, she saw Darren standing close by with his arms folded and the nurse attending to the machines around her bedside.

The alpha gave her a soft smile. "Good morning, Miss Katey."

It was a heartening greeting, a piece of familiarity as her memory struggled to catch up.

"Not quite morning," the nurse said. "It's just after lunch time." The nurse pulled out a blood pressure cuff and slipped it over Katey's arm. "Stay still for just a minute."

The inflated cuff strangled her arm, then pumped loose as it got a reading. The whole time, she watched Darren, mutedly asking that burning question. His eyes wouldn't convey a definite answer, but promised more once the nurse was gone.

"You're looking good, young lady," the nurse said. "I'll have the doctor come in and give you a final checkup and the results of some tests we ran while you were asleep. Now that you're awake, we may have to do a couple more. Depending on how they turn out, we may be able to send you home this evening."

"Any prescriptions for the pain?" Darren asked.

"Probably, but that will be up to the doctor."

The nurse conducted a few more brief tests, such as her eye dilation and reflexes. When she made her notes, she reminded them that the doctor would be around shortly and left the room.

Darren pulled a chair from the other side of the room to her bedside. "Do you remember what happened?"

Katey licked her parched lips as her mind groped for the memory. "Where's Logan?'

"In the waiting room. I would rather he be at school, but he hasn't listened to me since yesterday."

She closed her eyes as the previous evening came rushing back all at once. Running out of the restaurant, nearly pushing Logan for sex, Mary trying to kick her out... and then Logan and his wolf. Mary was still drunk but hysterical when they pulled onto the highway

"Your foster mother... She didn't make it, Katey."

Darren's voice, laden with sorrow, helped to complete the rest of the night. The semi-truck, horn blaring, shattering glass. It didn't surprise her that the accident killed Mary, but it made no sense that Katey was alive. The truck practically plowed right into her side of the car, though at an indirect angle. Yet, the nurse implied that she was barely hurt. If she was more seriously hurt, there was no way she would go home within twenty-four hours of being admitted. She saw no casts, so she had no broken bones, and she thought she could feel a bandage on her forehead, but nothing more.

She felt numb to the news, unsure of what to feel. Angry that the drunk bitch nearly killed her, relieved that she was alive, or sad that the woman who only saw her as a benefit check was dead because Katey didn't fight harder to get her to pull over before it was too late.

"Katey... did you hear me?"

"Water?" The request came out hushed and hollow. She needed a minute, and she needed to get Darren out of the room long enough for it.

"I'll go to the nurses station. I'll be right back."

Her ears tracked him across the room, to the door, and she waited until she was perfectly alone to take one deep, shuddering breath. Then, she allowed herself to feel it all in one sweeping release. She was alive, Mary was dead, and she officially had no home to go back to.

Logan's leg bounced as he waited impatiently for any word. The seconds felt like hours, minutes like days. He repeated the previous night over and over again in his head, working through the thousands of different ways things could have gone a hell of a lot better than how they did. Each and every time, he came to the conclusion that this was all his fault. If he hadn't stayed with Katey, if he hadn't nearly let his wolf out in front of her foster mother, if he had forced them to stay instead of driving away, if he hadn't waited so long to follow... then Mary wouldn't be dead, and Katey wouldn't be unconscious in a hospital bed.

The ambulance crew and police that showed up on the scene had said he was a hero for pulling her from the wrecked car before it caught fire, but he felt nothing like a hero.

Katey had been admitted outside of visiting hours, so they couldn't stay, no matter what lies he told the paramedics and nursing staff. Darren had to forcibly remove him from the hospital grounds before he made a scene. There was nothing he could do, but leaving her side felt like a betrayal after everything they had been through.

After a lot of shouting, golden staring matches, and even some half-serious threats, Darren agreed that Logan could skip school to stay in the hospital, but on the condition that the alpha accompany him, and he had to stay in the waiting room until Katey woke up. It was better than sitting through hours of pointless lectures while he could have been by Katey's side. He didn't tell them that Mary saw what he was. As far as they knew, Logan was able to hide his near shift and preserve their secret. They were more upset that he nearly lost control anywhere near Katey and Mary. If they knew the truth, he'd be put on lockdown and yanked out of school for the foreseeable future.

For several hours, families and guests came and went from the waiting room. Logan passed a few of those hours pacing, and a few more catching some fitful bits of sleep. Darren was permitted to pop into her room every now and again, mostly to check for himself if she was stabilizing. The nurses, too, kept them informed, though they were reluctant at first. According to their records, they knew she had no family, so Darren passed himself off as a concerned friend with whom she'd be staying.

Logan checked the clock for the millionth time. Darren had been gone for half an hour, much longer than usual. Finally, he stood, resolved to go back there himself when his alpha appeared around the corner.

"She's awake," Darren told him. He brought up a hand and caught Logan by the shoulder before he could rush past him. "They have to do a few more tests, but she's showing very good signs that there is no permanent damage. By all accounts, it's a miracle she's come out with hardly a fractured bone or pulled muscle."

He let out the breath he felt he had been holding since the moment he pulled her from the car. "Are you going to let me see her?"

"In a little while. The police are with her right now getting her statement for the accident report... Logan, one of the tests they need to do is a psychological evaluation. When they were removing her soiled clothes to put her in the hospital gown, they found scars on her thighs. They weren't old."

Logan closed his eyes. Katey had mentioned her depression, but self-harm hadn't been brought up in any of their conversations. He had thought it a possibility, but didn't want to accept it. Being loup-garou, he could take out his anger and grief on himself all he wanted and there would never be a single shred of evidence. Each of Katey's scars told a story that she was unwilling to share with anyone, not even him.

"They may prescribe her medication or suggest that she see a therapist."

Logan nodded and pushed back the wave of unwarranted guilt. She had the pack now. She would be all right.

"Have you had a chance to talk to her?"

Darren smirked. "The first words out of her mouth was to ask where you were."

That almost made up for the sleepless night and calling Darren all sorts of vile names in order to be here in this moment.

"Apart from that," Darren continued, "she hasn't said much. I'm sure she's still processing what happened. I know she wasn't close to Mary, but she may be feeling a lot right now."

Logan nodded again, understanding what his alpha meant. Be gentle. Don't ask too many questions. Treat her like a newly turned loup-garou that had just been to hell and back after their first shift.

"Have you eaten?"

Logan shook his head.

"Let's get something to eat, and then we'll go see her."

Begrudgingly, Logan agreed. He may not have had an appetite, but his stomach was so empty it felt as if it were caving in on itself.

The thought of facing Katey had once been the hope that kept him going, but now he dreaded it. What would she say to him? Would she heap hot coals of blame over his head, as he had been doing since last night? Would she be afraid of him? She saw the worst side of him while still wearing his human skin, yet she asked for him the moment she awoke. In that moment, he seemed to lose his courage, but the need to see for himself that she was whole and well overpowered his cowardice. One look in her green eyes, one touch of her hand, and he felt he could conquer his wolf again and be the man he was always meant to be.

CHAPTER 16

K atey stared out the hospital room window from her place on the bed. The view was unimpressive, racing wisps of clouds against a sheet of pale blue. On the third story and at this angle, she couldn't expect much, but it was a better focus than any other random spot on the wall.

She let her thoughts drift, but occasionally directed them just enough to avoid the things she didn't want to acknowledge. She thought of what she would need to pack, how she might beg Lily to get her parents to agree to take her in, at least for a little while. She wondered what she'd missed from school that day that she would have to make up next week. She thought of a long-ago conversation with a social worker who told her about what options she had for health insurance after she aged out of the system.

What she wouldn't think of was anything pertaining to Logan or the pack. She even let herself mourn for Mary, but thinking about the loups-garous was too much. If she did, she knew she would imagine herself eating dinner with them, hanging out with them over the weekend, the hard conversation with Logan about what happened in Mary's living room. Those thoughts would make her fantasize about a life in the pack, reconciliation with Logan, and happiness that she didn't deserve.

A knock at the door, like an explosion of cannon fire, made her jump and the beeping machine picked up its pace to match her heartbeat. How was she supposed to answer? This wasn't her room, not her domain, so why claim privacy.

"It's open."

Darren stepped through, followed shortly by Logan. He looked worse than she felt. A pang of sympathy made her want to jump out of the bed and run into his arms and say all was forgiven and forgotten, anything to wipe away that terrible look of despair and timidity in his eyes.

"How are you feeling?" the alpha asked as he closed the door.

"Like I was hit by a truck."

Apparently, it was too soon for jokes because neither of them smiled. Logan dropped into the chair on the other side of the room next to a small round table. Darren decided to stand, his thumbs hooked in his jean belt loops. Katey had never seen him in jeans, but he wore them well.

"The doctor and nurses are all amazed at how well you've come out of such an accident."

Katey shrugged, feeling less sore and tender as earlier. "Just lucky, I guess."

"It was lucky Logan disobeyed me and followed you and Mary so he could pull you from the car before it caught fire."

Katey wondered if he said that for Logan's benefit, because she already knew that he saved her life, even if he was the reason she and Mary took to the road in the first place.

She willed her lips to pull into a heartening smile just for Logan. "Thank you for that."

It did nothing to brighten his mood. Despite being hooked up to an IV and machines, she would have done anything to see his smile again.

"We know you may have a lot on your mind," Darren began, "but I want to assure you that this hospital bill will not be one of them."

"What do you mean?"

"I'm taking care of it. Before you argue, it's no trouble. We have emergency funds, perhaps not for these sorts of situations, but enough. Better to tie up loose ends than walk around with massive debt so young."

One burden lifted from her heavy gut, but Katey didn't feel right about letting him pay for all those expensive tests and lab work. She hardly felt right about letting them pay for the dinner she never ate the night before. She promised herself that she'd pay him back one day, even if it took fifteen years.

It took all her strength to set aside her pride and work out another, "Thank you."

"Also, the doctor advised that you not be left alone for the next few days in case some latent injuries decide to show themselves. Since you haven't been able to confirm any living arrangements... you'll come stay with us until you can find a more permanent host."

Katey felt as if she had been struck by a bomb. Her silent, puerile wish had manifested. But could she accept it? Would she bow to the circumstances? Darren didn't word it as a question, so this may not have been up for discussion. She didn't think she had enough strength to fight him, and deep down, she didn't want to. She wanted to be part of their world more than anything, especially now when her own decided to crumble around her so suddenly.

Her gaze shifted to Logan and he looked just as surprised, but even less willing to contradict the alpha. Katey decided to follow his lead and remained quiet.

"Logan will go home to get Dustin's truck and we will take you to Mary's to pack up your things."

Katey shook her head, reviewing what she had thought about before they came into the room. "I only need two suitcases. I don't have much."

Darren tilted his head. "No furniture? Books?"

"Just clothes. Foster kids travel light."

The alpha dipped his chin in understanding. "I see..." Darren thought quickly. "Once you're discharged, I'll take you to Mary's and Logan will follow. I don't want you to ride on a motorcycle so soon. From there, you can follow us to the house. I'll have Ben and Dustin prepare the guest room."

Perhaps that was better, Katey reasoned. She wasn't sure about being alone with Logan, in her bedroom. The fact that Darren would allow Logan to come along was a mystery. Packing up her few belongings wasn't a three-person job. Maybe it has less to do with usefulness and more with emotional support. Or maybe Darren knew by now that Logan wouldn't dare be ordered away from her.

"I promise I won't stay long," Katey finally said. There was no way she'd impose on the alpha's hospitality. The minute she knew she overstayed her welcome, she'd have her bags packed and be out before they could kick her out. At least she had the complete freedom to do that now, rather than waiting for a social worker to do the paperwork. Maybe she'd just live out of her suitcase for a week or so to be on the safe side.

"You will stay as long as you need to. You are welcome in our home. You will be safe and anything you need, we will take care of."

It wasn't quite the same thing her foster families had told her. It held more meaning, more promise, more sincerity. She was ready to believe him, but fought it. No need to get too excited for something that may not work out. Katey didn't know how long she would last under the same roof with four loups-garous, but however long it was, she wanted to create some good memories.

Darren turned to Logan. "You'll catch flies with your mouth hanging open like that."

Logan's teeth clicked back together, and Katey held in a tiny laugh. That verified her suspicion that Logan knew nothing of his alpha's decision. She hoped it would make him happy, even if it also meant that alone time would be next to impossible in a house of men who could hear a pin drop from the backyard.

As if he read her thoughts, Logan asked his alpha, "Can we have a moment alone?"

Some subliminal communication was exchanged before Darren nodded and moved toward the door. "I'll call Dustin and give him an update."

The click of the latch on the door echoed like a gunshot in Katey's heart. He'd be able to smell her fear just as keenly as she felt it. Too bad he wouldn't be able to understand just why she was so fearful without spoken words. She knew she was safe, at least in body. Her heart, not so much. They had left so much unresolved since the night before, and now seemed hardly the time to work through it all, but it had to be eventually.

"Katey... I'm so sorry... I can't begin to imagine what you must think of me after... after what happened."

She couldn't hide her confusion. "You're sorry?"

"I lost control."

The image of his wolfish eyes made her stomach so somersaults. "I'm sure it happens all the time. I can't blame you for that."

"It shouldn't happen."

The tenseness in his statement made her stare. Self-loathing mingled with the look of regret in his eyes and a tight muscle jumped in his jaw.

"When she hit you, I lost it. You never told me that she abused you like that."

Katey snorted. He didn't understand how the system worked. It didn't matter if anyone knew. "No one would believe me. She was a perfect angel around the social workers."

Logan burst to his feet, his anger now turned on her. "You could have told the guys. You could have told me. We would have believed you. We could have done something."

Dumbstruck, Katey went still and braced for the wolf to come out, but it didn't. It was then she remembered what Logan had said about his mother, about how his father beat them. Mary's treatment of her must have brought back painful, unresolved memories. This wasn't just a friend acting out of concern. This was a man who still tried to work through the trauma of his past. Maybe he wasn't as over it as he made her believe.

Logan softened, as if he realized his temper had gotten the better of him. Cautiously, he went to the chair by her bedside and sat down, each moment waiting for her to deny him closer access. He should have known that she would never do that. His presence was all she wanted, even if it was difficult on days like today.

"Why... why didn't you tell me about the cuts?"

It seemed completely out of left field and heat radiated down her back. "What cuts?"

Logan gave her a look. "You know what cuts... Darren told me they're going to send someone to do a psych evaluation."

Katey hadn't been told that and she felt that familiar panic like when she used to be told that a social worker would be coming to visit soon. She mentally prepared her lies and the mask that would convince them all that she was perfectly fine now and totally over her random "emo phase."

She bit her lips and looked to her lap. If anyone looked beneath the blankets and hospital gown, the cuts would have been impossible to miss. "It was part of the darkness I told you about... I didn't think it important to mention since I don't do it anymore."

Logan reached out and took her hand. She allowed herself the thrill of his skin touching hers again. "I won't bother asking why you did it... I've been there before, so I already know what goes through your mind in those moments... Did you try to—"

Startled by his admission, Katey needed to interrupt. "You used to cut?"

"Cuts, broken bones, gunshot wounds... It was more from purposeful neglect than anything else, but still with a similar intent... Please answer my question."

Logan had lived for so long and had a great setup with the pack. What reason did he have to damage his body like that? Of course, he could afford it. Hardly anything would hurt him for long. For that confession, he deserved equal honesty. She blinked back her million questions and nodded, knowing what he asked without speaking the specific words.

"Once. I found Mary's sleeping pills and took a handful. I chickened out and made myself throw up five minutes afterward."

A breathy, canine whine whistled from Logan's throat. Apparently loups-garous could make all lupine noises.

Logan squeezed her hand tight. "I wouldn't call it 'chickening out' but coming to your senses."

"That's not how I felt at the time."

Bolder now than he had been a few minutes ago, Logan kissed the back of her fingers. The warmth and smoothness of his lips was like a balm to her prickly nerves, trimming back the sharp barbs that might have made them both bleed if they clashed just the right way. It made her think back to the night before, how she was ready to give herself completely to him. She'd do it now, her own stupid neurosis aside.

"I'll forgive you for wolfing out," she said, "if you forgive me for pushing you to... you know."

Logan lifted his head, but it took him a moment to understand what she meant. "Only if you tell me why you tried. What had upset you so badly at the restaurant?"

Katey took a deep breath and her ribs ached in protest. Again, he deserved a clear, straightforward answer. "I just felt so out of place. I'm not loup-garou, so I thought, 'What the hell am I doing here? Why would I have any right to be here?' It... it messed with my head, and I needed to get out of there... At the house, I guess I wanted to make up for being crazy and I thought that's where you wanted this whole thing to go anyway, so..." Katey meekly lifted her shoulders, her gaze cast to the wall halfway through her story.

Logan never let go of her hand, his grip steady, but not crushing. When she finished, she could almost feel the mass of words Logan wanted to unleash. Instead of trying to tell her with words that she had been all wrong or that she wasn't crazy, his eyes conveyed it in a sweet, caring way that almost had her believing it too. Not an ounce of condescension.

"I forgive you... for all of it."

Katey gave him a tight-lipped smile. "Therefore, I forgive you... Do you forgive yourself?"

He cocked a brow. "That wasn't part of the deal."

"No, but I think it's necessary if we are ever going to get past this."

She was right, and he knew it. They didn't need this whole affair hanging over their heads while Katey tried to set herself back on her feet again. If they were going to be around each other day and night, sleeping and eating in the same house, they needed to make amends and try to get back to the way things were before.

Though, it seemed almost inconceivable to reverse all the damage that had been done. She knew what his wolf side looked like when he lost control, and he knew just how disturbed she could become when triggered the right way. They were both a little damaged, both in need of healing. It wasn't healthy at all to assume that they could fix each other, but hadn't they already? Wasn't that what happened a week ago in the cemetery? Maybe they were good for each other all along, but they hit a snag along the way, as couples often did.

Logan sighed. "I can try."

As she predicted, packing didn't take long at all. Darren watched from outside her room as she pulled out her two battered suitcases from the closet. It was easy to forget he was close to four hundred years old, especially when he leaned against her door frame and frowned at her chaotic mess of a bedroom, as casually as anyone else. Old school papers were strewn across the floor, dirty clothes hung over her footboard, and dishes and empty glasses littered nearly every surface.

"You live like this?"

Katey hefted her suitcases on the unmade bed. "Never seen a teenager's room before?"

"Not one this filthy."

"Are you going to inspect the guest room a couple of times a week while I'm there?"

She had a foster mother that did that. After Katey left that home, perhaps she stopped caring about the clutter and untidiness. She hoped Darren caught that she didn't claim the new room as her own. It would be "the guest room" not *her* room.

"No, but I'll ask that you not let it get this bad."

"Fair enough." Katey pulled out bundles of clothes from her drawers and set them in the suitcase in some vaguely organized manner. "Any other rules? Curfew? Rooms I can't go in?" She knew what to ask when coming to a new home.

"You're an adult. Use your best judgment and give the same respect you'd want to be shown."

"How come she gets off so easy?" Logan called from where he waited in the living room.

"Well, there is more I'll go over later, but that is the core of what we would expect of you."

Katey slowed, thinking just how much freedom she'd be granted with the loups-garous. Certainly, there was more to it than
just respect.

She made quick work of emptying her dresser and closet, then
gathered up the dirty clothes to shove into a black trash bag she
grabbed from the kitchen earlier. Darren and Logan let her do
as she needed, giving her space and quiet. She passed the psych
evaluation and appeared stable in mind and body, but she could
sense a level of alertness in them, as if they were waiting for her
to break apart into a hundred pieces as she should have during
the accident.

They, above anyone else, should have had more faith in her
resilience. Of course, part of that was to let herself forget the
details and put off processing what happened until it became a
problem. That was a habit she'd need to break, but some other day
when she wasn't being tossed around through so much change.

As she picked up the dated schoolwork, she saw the white,
furry tail peeking out from beneath the edge of a blanket draped
across the floor. She snatched it up and crushed the tattered,
stuffed husky toy to her chest. Its hard blue eyes were dull and
scuffed, a few stains crusted its haunches, and its underbelly
fur had been trimmed to its fabric skin, but this toy was her
most precious possession. Eighteen-year-olds weren't supposed
to cling to stuffed toys, but Katey wouldn't be embarrassed for
Captain Jack and how much she loved the old stuffy. It had been
with her since she was a baby, and was all she had left of the
parents she never knew. When a boy in one of the group homes
had taken a pair of scissors to the husky, trying to mimic some
surgical procedure they saw on television, Katey rewarded him
with two black eyes and a bloody nose. She was six and the boy
was nine.

She placed the dog in the suitcase with extra care and stowed
her school papers in her backpack to sift through later. Her bath-

room amenities were dumped into a smaller travel bag, and she was done packing.

"You're sure there's nothing else?" Darren asked as he took up the two suitcases as if they weighed next to nothing. Logan retrieved the dirty clothes bag while she carried her own backpack and bathroom kit.

"Nope. Nothing else in this house belongs to me."

Pity touched his expression before he turned to take the luggage to her jeep. Out the front door, she saw how evening stretched across the sky, pastels fading into a deep purple along the horizon. Katey joined Logan in the living room and spun, giving the house one last look around. She wouldn't miss it. She had no fond memories here, except the ones she had with Logan, but those weren't enough to make her suddenly sentimental.

Logan's hand brushed against the small of her back. "Ready to go home?"

Home. It wouldn't be her home, not in the fullest sense of the word. Maybe it could be for a little while. She nodded, turned, and walked out of Mary's house for the last time.

The caravan headed north to the less developed side of town. Logan passed the city limit sign first, then Darren's car, and then Katey's jeep. They traveled the highway for nearly fifteen minutes, passing isolated mailboxes, dirt roads, and small homes settled in cleared lots surrounded by pine woods.

After a long stretch of unbroken woods, Darren turned on his blinker and slowed. Katey saw no roads or signs of habitation. Up ahead, Logan's bike took a hard turn and disappeared down a hidden path and into the forest. Darren and Katey followed, their cars rocking and dipping down the long sandy drive, unable to avoid the random holes and mounds in the terrain. She wondered if the pack never bothered to fix it because it would slow down any unwanted visitors, or if they just didn't make time for such maintenance. It no longer seemed odd that the tire on Ben's car went as flat as it did. She had to laugh at herself. It was exactly a week ago since she helped him change his tire in the faculty parking lot, and a week since she first met Logan. Her life looked nothing like it used to. Perhaps that was for the better.

It seemed like they had bumped along for a long time before they came upon a few cleared acres. Katey stared at the two-story home, light streaming through the front windows and spilling onto the front lawn as twilight fast approached. Logan and Darren parked beneath the carport alongside the house. Dustin's truck and Ben's car were already there. No empty place for her.

Katey parked on the opposite end of the carport. A blast of fresh air, tinged with all manner of wild scents, met her as soon as she opened the door. So different from the air in town. She breathed it in and smiled. She could understand why the loups-garous chose here to live, so far away from civilization and immersed in the kind of world their wolf sides would have loved.

Before her shoes touched the grass, Darren opened the back door to pull out her bags. "We're I'm the middle of about a hundred acres of land. The drive is a right of way and not exclusively part of our property, but we are completely surrounded by woods owned by various members of the Deviant pack."

"Damn... Total privacy."

"We need it. Don't want to run through someone's backyard when we're... indecent."

Katey understood he meant when they were shifted.

"It's the best setup we've had in a long time." Logan joined them, helmet under his arm. "If you hear something coming from the woods at night, it'll be some of us or the Deviants. No one else lives for miles in any direction." He reached in and took up the trash bag of dirty clothes.

That meant, at any given moment, a shifted loup-garou or pack of loups-garous prowled the forest around the house. Yet, the idea didn't frighten her. It hardly elicited a response in her, as if her spirit already accepted that reality, even when she didn't know what they looked like in their shifted forms.

Darren made his way around the carport. "But don't worry. We never come too close to the house. You'll never see one of us out your bedroom window in that state."

Part of her wished she would.

The three of them walked up the gravel path from the carport area to the front porch, a spacious concrete pad sheltered by an awning supported by two massive brick columns. The exterior of the home, she noticed as she came closer, was of wood siding, painted a dark green color as if to blend in with its surroundings. The thick mahogany front door featured carved floral reliefs, flanked by stained glass sidelights beautifully backlit by the foyer lights.

Darren set down one of Katey's bags and opened the unlocked door to let it swing open. He gestured for her to walk ahead. With timidity, she stepped into the foyer and took a moment to memorize the unique smell of the home. It was the perfect blend of wood, old books, and the spicy traces of their individual scents, all grounded by that aroma of wilderness that flowed from the outside. The floors were paved in dark hardwood, offset by walls painted an orangish brown. A crystal chandelier hung from the ten-foot high ceiling above her, scattering flecks of rainbow in every direction. An antique sideboard to the right housed four plates, half of which held car keys.

To the left was a set of white, windowed French doors, hung with sheer curtains. One door was propped open to give her a glimpse of a sitting room or parlor where the hardwood floors carried through from the foyer. The walls were a bright pale blue wallpaper, complemented by oil paintings of landscapes. A matching sofa and loveseat faced each other, and beyond was the formal dining area. Another chandelier, smaller in scale and grandeur, hung over a long dining table with six ornate chairs pushed underneath.

A cased opening, framed by thin columns and a rounded header, separated the foyer from the massive living room of the same light ochre color. Two identical sofas faced one another in the center, a patterned rug between them, a large leather recliner next to the farthest sofa, and a flatscreen television sat upon a stand against the wall to her right. Behind the farthest sofa was a four-paneled set of sliding glass doors that led out to a back patio. In the waning light, augmented by the interior lights, she saw a metal table and pair of iron lounge chairs. One corner of the living room was taken up by a series of bookcases, each shelf packed with novels and reference books.

To the left of the living room and past the sofas was the kitchen, divided by a counter peninsula. To the left of the counter peninsula was a stairwell, whose first few steps ended at a landing that kicked behind the living room wall to lead upstairs. The raw wood style of the cabinetry went out of style decades ago, and the yellow countertops didn't add to the overall aesthetic, but the size of the kitchen was what struck Katey. It was the biggest she had ever seen in person, and well equipped with a gas range, double oven, and huge side-by-side refrigerator and freezer. On the far wall was a pair of saloon-style doors that opened to the formal dining room she had seen earlier.

Just through the threshold into the kitchen from the living room, was a breakfast nook. She imagined mornings sitting at the round glass table were peaceful while staring out the bay window that looked out over the property.

A hallway stretched on from the right of the nook. Katey spotted one set of folding doors that looked more like tall shutters, a door that may or may not have led to a bathroom, and a stretch of counter space with more windows that must have overlooked the backyard. She remembered while watching home renovation shows that this may have been something like a butler's pantry. A light gleamed at the end of the hall, but the room kicked to the left so she couldn't see what its purpose was.

As she stepped into the kitchen, she heard the voice of Dustin and Ben coming from that room.

"I'm tellin' ya, it ain't gonna work," Ben insisted.

"Shut yer gob. I'm gonna try it." For the first time, Katey heard Dustin's repressed Irish accent and she grinned. It had such a pretty, lyrical cadence.

"Fine, go ahead, but the angle ain't right."

Then came a sharp crack of two solid objects colliding, followed by a series of thuds like something heavy bouncing on a semi-soft surface.

"Told ya."

"How the feckin' hell did ye know any of that?"

"All that stupid math shit I had to learn."

Darren touched her shoulder to get her attention. "You'll have to excuse their language."

"What are they doing?" she whispered, though she was sure they heard everything.

Logan walked past her into the hall with the trash bag of clothes. "Trick shots on the billiard table. Do you play?"

A bit of excitement subdued her shyness. "I did when I was a kid. Or more like I played with the cue ball and sticks at the bowling alley when the table was free. Then I'd watch college kids play some games while I waited for my foster parents to finish a game. They were in a weekly league."

That was likely more information than they wanted, but she couldn't stop herself from sharing, hoping that someone would return the favor.

Logan returned from dropping off the bag in a room off the hall concealed by the shutter-like doors, presumably where they did the laundry. "It gives us something to do and keeps our fine motor skills sharp."

Dustin appeared at the end of the hall, cue stick in one hand. "You're welcome to come play a round. We're just muckin' about."

"Katey needs rest," Darren said sternly. "She can play another time."

When the alpha turned his back to return to the living room, Dustin made a rude face and Katey bit her lips to stifle the giggle.

Logan didn't follow Katey and Darren toward the stairs, but granted her a reassuring smile before going to join Dustin and Ben in the billiard room.

"Thoughts so far?" Darren asked as they went up the stairs.

"I've never been in a house this big before."

He gave a soft chuckle. "Well, something of what Logan said is very true. We haven't been in a place this nice in a long time. We usually stay in more modest homes with fewer rooms, but we suspected that we would be here for a while. The bedrooms are all upstairs, along with the bathroom. There is a half-bath downstairs with the billiard room."

They ascended the stairs, came to the final landing, and doubled back to a long hallway that must have run the width of the house. Darren kicked open the first door on the left to reveal the bathroom. Two more doors to the left, and three to the right. Each door, save for the last at the end of the hall, was marked by engraved initials in the wood, indicating whom they belonged to. Katey noticed Logan's door.

"LK?"

Darren glanced at the door as if he didn't know what she was talking about. "Logan Keith. He took on Dustin's surname. He's told you of their relation, right?"

"He's Logan's grandfather."

"Yes. He used to go by Logan Elster, but for obvious reasons, he dropped his father's family name several decades ago. I think Keith suits him much better. Your room is at the end of the hall."

Darren tapped his foot against the guest room door to open it and she walked through. It was at least twice as spacious as her old room and had every piece of furniture that she would need. The round blue rug in the middle of the wooden floor was a couple of shades darker than the walls and contrasted perfectly with the dark wood trim and furniture. The canopy bed was covered with a dark blue floral bedspread, duvet comforter, and white sheer fabric draped around the posts. A digital alarm clock sat on the nightstand nearest the door and an old-fashioned kerosene lamp sat on the other. She doubted she'd ever be brave enough to use it, but it was a fancy touch that she kind of liked.

On the opposite wall, a desk and simple wooden chair sat beneath the solitary window hung with white curtains. An empty bookcase stood in the corner. The wall shared by the adjacent bedroom held the closet door, and next to it was a dresser with an attached vanity mirror.

Katey stood on the thick rug in the middle of the room and inspected every detail as she always did in a new place. It was certainly nicer than any of her previous homes, like they made it up just for her. All those little things she had secretly wanted in a bedroom, from the canopy bed to the delicate stitch patterns on the curtains. Some may have thought there was far too much blue, but Katey thought it perfect.

Dareen set the luggage at the foot of the bed. "We may be a bunch of bachelors, but we will respect your privacy. No one should come in without knocking and asking permission first."

Katey crossed her arms over her stomach, trying her best not to picture this room in every season, how the sunlight and weather changed the way it looked from day to day, week to week, month to month. She couldn't let herself believe she would be here so long. Just a couple of weeks at the most. Maybe not even until next weekend. If they knew what was good for them, they would find a host family soon and get rid of her. Sadness gushed over her heart and the thrill of finally seeing their home was gone.

"Are you hungry?" Darren asked. "We haven't had time to shop, but we brought home your dinner from last night."

"I figured you would have canceled the order."

"We didn't know if Logan would have convinced you to stay... If we upset you, I sincerely apologize. It was never our intent to make you feel uncomfortable... I won't overstep my bounds and ask what it was, but please, don't be afraid to tell us what is bothering you. In this house, it's better to let it out than let it fester."

Katey blew out a breath and nodded. "I'll try... Can I eat in here?"

Darren seemed to struggle with the idea. "Only this once, because it's your first night. We eat together in the dining room, unless the situation demands otherwise. I'll heat it up for you." He turned to leave the room, then paused at the door. "Please make yourself at home and let us know if there is anything we can do to make settling in easier."

She waited until Darren's footsteps faded down the hall, then sat herself on the edge of the bed. Her eyes wandered, memorizing everything as if she'd be yanked from the home any moment. She didn't believe in God or any higher being that controlled the lives of mortal beings, but she dropped her voice well below a whisper, speaking into the universe as if someone was out there listening and could do anything about her current situation. It wasn't what she deserved, it wasn't likely to come true, but she had to send her wish into the ether, just in case.

"Please... please let me stay... Just this once."

CHAPTER 17

The new rules were undeniably clear. Katey was to be treated like a member of the pack. She'd be shown the same deference and respect as anyone else, perhaps more, given her current situation. Logan couldn't have hoped for a better situation than this. She was so close, just down the hall, and they would see one another outside of school. There was no way the pack could keep them apart now. He didn't care if Darren believed this was a temporary arrangement, Logan knew he would find a way to make it more permanent.

Of course, he'd adhere to his alpha's rules that were set down especially for him. The knocking rule would be enforced, and keen ears would hear if Logan tried to leave his room late at night to go to Katey's. That didn't rankle Logan. After what he and Katey discussed, all thoughts of crossing that line were banished from his plans, if they had ever been there at all. Katey wasn't an object, wasn't a tool to be used for his own physical gratification and never would be. Their first time, if they should ever have one, would be mutual, and the result of clearheaded thinking rather than some mindless, passionate need for one another. Logan hoped that would be the case, anyway.

It was the thought of such things that drove Logan to ask Dustin if they could talk in private after dinner. That meant a trip to the gazebo in the backyard, a place where no loup-garou in the house could pick up their hushed conversation.

Dustin dropped to one of the benches and draped his arms across the back railing. "I bet you're as happy as a clam right about now."

Logan sat beside him, though markedly slower as if he were the one who was hundreds of years older. "Yes... and no."

"Uh oh. Trouble in paradise?"

Logan leaned his elbows on his knees and rubbed at his mouth, searching for the words. "Last night, before Mary came home, Katey and I... We had a moment."

Ever the one to jump at a chance to tease, Dustin pushed at Logan's shoulder and grinned. "You dog! How was it?"

Logan shot him a scathing look. "It's not what you think."

His grandfather jerked back. "Don't tell me you didn't even steal a kiss."

"If I ever kiss her, it won't be stolen."

"So, what do you mean by, 'We had a moment'?"

Logan willed his body not to stir at the remembrance of it. "She was very upset after leaving the restaurant and she made a poor decision. She tried to start something and I didn't let her."

Dustin went silent, as if waiting for him to finish. When he didn't, Dustin asked, "So, what's the problem? You stopped her and everything's still rosy, right?"

"The problem is that part of me didn't want to stop her."

His grandfather gave a big, exaggerated nod. "Gotcha. You're worried if things get too hot again, you may not stop things before they go farther than you want."

Sometimes, Logan took for granted how perceptive Dustin could be, especially in matters like this. Though, the way he became an expert on the subject was less than acceptable. With Logan as evidence enough, a loup-garou who couldn't keep it in his pants could father sons that grew up oblivious to what they were until it was too late. Darren had tried to curb Dustin's wildness, and for the most part had succeeded.

"I don't want to do something that we will both regret... but there's something else about what happened that bothers me." Logan sat back on the bench. "When I stopped her, she accused me of wanting that from her."

"You just admitted that you kind of do."

"Yeah, but I never told her that. I never implied anything of the sort. I don't know where she got it from. When we were at the library, she blew up on me over how to label whatever it is that we're doing, and I thought I had made it clear that there was no way to correctly describe it, so it didn't need a name."

Dustin waved his hand as if he were trying to hold back an overexcited pup. "Hold up, hold up. What are you talking about?"

"We're more than friends. Everything we've been through up to this point suggests as much, and she agrees. We're not dating, because... well, loups-garous just don't date the way humans do. And we're not mated. I haven't explained just how complex such a union is, but I told her we really don't fall within those categories. Therefore, we should just go with the flow, so to speak."

"You idiot." Dustin's insult came out biting and aggravated. "Women want labels. They want a roadmap, a step-by-step expectation of where this is going so they know if it's time to bail or go all-in."

Logan pointed at him. "Expectation. She used that word. I don't expect anything from her."

"She sure as hell is gonna expect something from you, and that's full, honest clarity about what you two are."

"But, we're not mated. Isn't that explanation enough? Why is it so important?"

Dustin put a hand on his grandson's shoulder. "If I understood the 'whys' behind anything that goes on in the feminine mind, I would have written a book and made a fortune by now. Instead, I'm stuck here trying to give you advice." His voice dropped with severity. "Listen, what you basically told Katey is that you two are in a casual relationship, that can be dropped or picked up any-time you please. No strings attached. You two can be intimate, but you're not dating, and there's no commitment to tie you to one another like a mating bond would. So, she probably thought you only wanted someone to fuck around with."

Logan's eyes widened. "How could I have said all of that? That's not what I meant."

"Women have this annoying knack for reading between the lines. That's what Katey may have done, and why she thought you wanted sex when you believed it was too soon."

He bent forward and covered his face with his hands. "Stupid. Stupid. Stupid."

Dustin gave him a hearty slap on the back. "And that's a bit of me coming out in you. Sorry, kid."

Instead of giving Katey comfort and peace of mind about their relationship, he had basically told her that she meant next to nothing to him. She wasn't just a girl to be used up and tossed aside. She meant more, was far more, than anything she could possibly comprehend, which was why he couldn't give her a clear answer. He should have tried harder to explain everything.

"How do I fix this?"

"She's gone through enough in the last couple of days. Maybe give her some time and then try to set the record straight. Darren would flip his lid if he thought you wanted to mate with her, but at least tell her you like her."

Logan looked up. "I don't understand how 'like' can mean so many different things."

Dustin snickered. "And that's another lovely thing about words and labels. They don't always mean what you want them to."

"My point exactly, so why should we confine ourselves to 'dating' when we're not actually 'dating'?" Logan felt silly for using air quotes.

"Think of dating as less of a way to describe what you're doing and more of... that you two are going steady. It's not what the kids are saying these days, but maybe that would suit better?"

He let the words roll around in his head for a minute and liked it better than the blank space left open by his own ignorance. "I'll have to remember that when I talk to her."

"Sure. Dust off some of those old axioms and see if you like any of them. She may not have a clue what they mean, but maybe you'll bring it back in style."

Logan slid a look to Dustin. "Thanks."

"No problem. I'm here to clean up messes. Just do us all a favor and keep your pining to a minimum. It might get a little nauseating." He stood, gave Logan's back one more slap and then made his way back to the house. "Come on. I smell dinner."

He didn't move for a while, mulling over what Dustin had said and all the careless mistakes he seemed incapable of preventing. Having Katey in his life was nothing short of a miracle, and it seemed as if fate was one moment forcing them together, then tearing them apart in the next. Then again, maybe it was his fault that they seemed to take one step forward, then two steps back. If he could just get out of his own way and let things take their natural course, it would work out.

But, even if it did, then what? What was the true end goal? Logan hadn't wanted to think about it too deeply until now. Could he tolerate being mated with a mortal woman who would grow old and die before him? He wondered about the progress of Katey's pros and cons list. Obviously, he wouldn't ask for a few days. Like they all said, she needed time to relax and recover. He sincerely hoped that the pros list would outweigh the cons in the end. She may be treated like one of the pack, but she'd never be a true member of it until she was loup-garou herself, or mated to one. If he couldn't come to terms with mating with her as a human, or this fragile flame of affection between them decided to burn out, there was only one option left to give her the family and home she deserved.

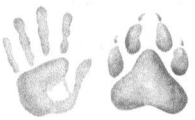

Katey sat in bed, the comforter covering her elevated knees, encircled by her arms as she stared out the window. She watched the dawn leak through the glass and disperse into a beautiful, bright morning. Choruses of birdsongs flitted through the woods. She recognized the repetitive melody of the mourning dove in particular, but not the rest. The pack was sure to know which tune belonged to which bird.

Some time after sunrise, she heard the loups-garous stir down the hall. Katey strained her ears to follow their progress for at least a couple of hours. Floorboards creaked, doors opened and shut, the heavy thump of footsteps on the stairs, the running of water in the bathroom as sinks, toilets, and showers were used. Deep, low voices murmured, but she couldn't make out words. After a while, she heard the clank of pans or skillets from the kitchen. The sizzle of breakfast preceded the greasy, savory smells of sausage and bacon. The noise of their morning routines was occasionally punctuated by laughter or voices raised in jest or some other good-natured conversation. Then came the clatter of plates, the chink of glasses. At one point, she thought she could hear the washing machine hiss and whirl to life as a load of clothes was put through the wash.

It sounded and felt like what she always imagined a true home would be like on any other Saturday morning. No yelling, no stench of cigarette smoke, no ominous dread that kept her shut up in her room, warning her not to come out. This morning, she wanted to go out and see them, to grab a plate and indulge in the meat-based diet as if she were just like them, as if she didn't stick out like a sore thumb.

That desire made her curl up her legs and hug them tighter to her chest. In any other new home, she would have stayed in the bedroom until hunger or a need to relieve herself forced her to sneak out. In those instances, she'd make sure not to be seen or noticed.

Katey wanted so badly for this home to be different, for her stupid brain to shut up and just enjoy this situation while it lasted. But to get used to this place and these people, meant the goodbyes would be that much harder, that much more devastating.

Though, the niggling, unwavering hope taunted her in the back of her mind. If she could have beat it out of her, she would have driven her head through the wall. The switch between hope and jadedness had been worn and abused, becoming stuck in between. *Just make up your damn mind*, she scolded herself.

The smell of breakfast meats lingered long after the sounds of cooking ended, and the house quieted as the pack settled down to eat. Fear and uncertainty kept Katey in bed. That was easier, for now. So, she continued to watch the sky outside her window, tracking the clouds as they inched by.

Time passed and someone began washing dishes in the sink. A loup-garou or two came back upstairs, spent time in the bathroom or their bedroom, then left again. They went about their day as if she wasn't there. That made it easier too. Maybe they knew that.

Katey flinched when she heard the front door open and shut, followed by a car door slamming and the sputtering of an exhaust pipe. Curious, Katey forced her stiff limbs to take her to the window. Dustin's red truck cut across the front lawn toward the gap in the trees carved out by their long driveway. Two ruts made by the excessive grind of tires on ground marked the path from the tree line to the house.

In the daylight, she was able to fully appreciate how gorgeous their property was. An endless sea of forest gave a sense of total isolation that stilled the breath in her lungs. She had lived in crowded neighborhoods and subdivisions all her life. They didn't seem that far from town, but with a view like this, they might as well have been dead center in the middle of nowhere.

Katey's stomach suddenly ached with emptiness and gurgled. She glanced to the door, still torn over whether to put off the inevitable a little longer or plunge into the challenge. Bolstered by the beauty of the day, she quietly dressed and grabbed her bath kit before she left the room. The remaining three loups-garous would likely hear her movement, so trying to go unnoticed was pointless. She was the only one upstairs, so she was able to duck into the bathroom without being seen. She shut the door and locked it behind her.

The bathroom was large enough to accommodate an equally large household. The floor was covered in gleaming white tiles, walls a shade of blue lighter than the guest room. Across from the door was a huge shower with matching white tiles, the glass door bubbled and frosted for privacy. Four towels hung across two long bars on the wall. On the toilet lid was a clean stack of a bath towel and hand towel, presumably set aside for her. Katey preferred to shower at night.

The double vanity below the wide, frameless mirror was tidy, much tidier than she thought it would be. Part of the lower cabinetry between the sinks included a stack of four drawers. Nosiness made her peek into one and glimpsed a stick of deodorant, brush, an old fashioned shaving razor, and toothbrush. She closed the drawer, satisfied that those drawers belonged to the loups-garous. No space for her.

Katey set her kit on a cleared spot on the counter. She brushed her teeth and hair, refreshed her deodorant and makeup, then stowed everything back in her bag. She debated whether to take her kit back to her room or leave it tucked in the corner of the counter against the wall. It was out of the way, but would leaving the bag communicate that she claimed some part of the bathroom?

In some effort to break her own toxic way of thinking, she left it and walked downstairs.

Like a skittish mouse, she went slow, looking this way and that for any sign of the pack, any sign of Logan. The living room was empty, and so was the kitchen and breakfast nook.

The view out the spotless glass doors of the back porch distracted her. Splashes of color flowed from the edge of the patio in rivers of flowers and plants. The expansive, well-tended garden skirted along the side of the house and swept a short distance into the yard. A path, lined with stones, wove through the garden toward a stunning gazebo in the distance. She saw a figure lounging on one of the benches, head turned toward the edge of the forest. Katey recognized it as Ben and took a step back from the glass, rethinking the urge to go out to enjoy the garden.

Sounds from another part of the house sent her heart racing. Katey spun and expected to see Darren or Logan appear but saw no one yet. They had to be close by, unless they had left the house like Ben and were roaming the woods. Would they do that so early in the day, in broad daylight?

With greater caution, she stepped into the kitchen. A lone plate of bacon and sausage sat on the kitchen island with a fork and empty glass beside it with the prescription bottle of painkillers from the hospital. She didn't feel the need for them, but they put the extra thought into making sure they were available for her. Had they expected her to join them? Now she regretted her bashfulness.

Katey caught some movement ahead and looked up to see a partial view of the dining room through the saloon doors that only came up to her chest. Darren sat at the head of the table, his back to her. The soft tap of a keyboard told her that he must have been on his laptop. One loup-garou remained missing.

Darren's low growl made her jump. "Logan, don't scare her."

A second later, she suddenly became aware of someone else in the kitchen. She whipped around and found Logan several feet away near the hall that led to the laundry room, hands raised as if he had been caught doing something wrong. He wore a pair of sweatpants and a loose-fitted shirt, perhaps his sleeping clothes.

A smile crossed his face. "Sorry," he half-laughed. "Didn't mean to be that quiet."

Katey took a breath. "Seriously. Wear a bell."

That made the alpha chuckle as he stood and joined them in the kitchen. Like Logan, he still wore pajamas, a pair of flannel pants and a hooded sweatshirt. The look was even stranger than seeing him in jeans. "We made a plate for you, just in case you'd be in the mood for breakfast."

Logan moved to stand closer to the sink, opening up an escape route if she wanted it. "I told him you weren't much of a breakfast person."

"If you don't want it, don't feel obligated to eat it."

Katey caught herself backing up into the counter peninsula and abruptly stopped when she bumped into it. "No, I'll eat it. Smells good."

"Any eggs?"

"This is enough."

The alpha took up her glass and pulled out a jug of chilled water from the refrigerator. "Dustin has gone out. I told him that he would need to go shopping before he comes home. Let me know what you normally like to eat, and he will pick it up for you."

Katey was achingly conscious of Logan's gaze hot on her. "Got any coffee?"

Darren came back with her glass and frowned. "Our condition doesn't allow us to drink coffee, just as we can't have vegetables."

Like French fries, Katey couldn't imagine life without coffee. To never enjoy a good, iced mocha ever again was a new line for the con list. It had been a while since she thought about that list and had completely lost track of the balance.

"But, we have a variety of teas," Darren continued. "None with caffeine, but you're welcome to them." He pointed out a tray and neatly organized box of individually wrapped tea bags, sorted by type. Beside it was an old kettle. She wondered how long they had it, noticing the scratches and dents on the smooth metal body and how the wooden handle's varnish had worn away to expose raw wood.

"Water is fine."

"Any request for something more than what we give you isn't an inconvenience."

Logan hit the nail on the head. Were her thoughts that obvious? Reading the room, Darren waited for Katey to change her mind. Once more, she had a chance to break old habits.

"Do you have chamomile?"

Darren smirked. "Around here, we keep extra stock of chamomile. This one makes it mandatory." He pointed to the younger loup-garou in the kitchen.

Katey looked to Logan. "Your favorite?"

"More like everyone needs it to calm down after I give them hell."

She broke into a tiny, amiable smile as Darren moved to prepare the tea. "It helps chill me out too." Katey took up the plate and pinched a piece of crispy bacon. "Is this pork or something else?"

"It's pork," Logan replied. "The sausage is deer."

Katey changed her mind, put down the bacon and used the fork to pop a piece of sausage in her mouth.

"Logan, watch the kettle while I speak with Katey." Darren set the kettle on the lit range, then motioned for Katey to follow. "You can bring the food with you."

Hesitant, but without the luxury of denying the alpha, Katey followed Darren down the hall with her plate and glass, casting glances to Logan as she did. He gave her an encouraging nod. Katey braced for bad news, but if Logan didn't seem upset, perhaps it wasn't what Katey thought.

Darren brought her to the billiard room. The walls were covered in wood panels and resembled the inside of a bar. A mini fridge sat in the corner beside a mounted rack of pool sticks. The billiard table in the middle of the room looked to be in great condition, the colored balls set inside the triangular mold, ready for a game. In another corner was a small bar-height table with a couple of stools. Katey sat there and waited for Darren's lecture.

"Did you sleep well?"

Katey lied and nodded. For most of the night, like that morning, she listened to the old house creak and settle, and tried to make out the movements of the pack well past midnight. She only found rest when she could confirm they were all asleep.

Darren gave her a look. "First tip about living with loups-garous, lying is pointless. Nearly everyone who lies gives themselves away through some biological cues. Heartbeat, sweating, breathing, all of it can tell us when you aren't being completely truthful. Some of us have learned to control those tells so it's easier for us to lie to one another, but it would be in your best interest to tell the truth all the time."

Katey dropped her stare. Another habit would need to be broken if she stayed. "I was awake on and off through the night."

"That's better... If you need to rest later today, you're welcome to. I don't say that as if you need my permission, but to let you know that you can. When I said you could make yourself at home, I meant it... What I have to tell you now, is that you should be fully aware with whom you share a home."

Darren propped his hands on his hips in that commanding manner as he had in Dustin's classroom. "You know what we are. You know what we are capable of, but you have known us as we are at school. This house is one of the few places we can be our true selves. Here, we will not censor our conversations. You may hear us talk about pack matters that will not go beyond these walls. We may do things, allow our wolves a little freer reign. That may be anything from utilizing our speed and strength to shifting. We don't shift in the house, but partial shifts are not uncommon. It can happen when our most basic needs go unmet, or our more primal emotions get the better of us. Our wolves come forward to take care of us when we refuse to take care of ourselves."

For some reason, that made Katey think of what Logan said the day before, how he had hurt himself through purposeful neglect rather than intentional harm. How did his wolf play into those scenarios? If the wolf was there to protect the man, why didn't it prevent the harm in the first place?

Darren seemed to ignore her pensive look. "You may see things that disturb or frighten you. If your gut tells you to leave the room, listen to it. If any of us begins to lose our temper or you feel our dominance, you get out of the way immediately. We may be extra sensitive on the day of our shift, and if we tell you that it is coming up, don't forget it and give us a wide berth. If, in the unlikely case that one of us finds ourselves in the middle of a shift and you are alone, you go to your room and lock the door. Some involuntary shifts can be more dangerous because it may take us longer to get control of ourselves."

Katey patiently and carefully listened, but didn't touch her breakfast. She thought back to Thursday night and how Logan lost control. That must have been one of those dangerous situations where she should have gotten out of the way. She had been warned a couple of days too late. "You're making it sound like the house could blow up at any minute."

Darren shook his head. "No, but depending on how long you stay, you may have to take certain precautions. Fights don't break out often, and we have settled into a manageable routine with our shifts, so what I tell you may not matter. Still, you need to know."

A thought came to mind, something she probably shouldn't bring up, but it wouldn't be shoved away. "You're telling me all of this because I'm human... If I was loup-garou—"

"You're not and won't be." Darren's voice took on a slicing edge. "Yes, you are human, and by consequence, fragile compared to us. You wouldn't be able to bounce back so easily if you happen to be in the wrong place at the wrong time. I will not allow you to be hurt or killed under my care."

That struck Katey into silence. Darren said some of them were inclined to think that she may survive being turned when no other female could. She must have wrongly assumed that meant someone else other than Logan thought so. Clearly, Darren didn't want to entertain the idea, and he didn't want to discuss it, but she wouldn't toss away her pros and cons list just yet.

"Please don't mistake me. You are safe here. No one wants to hurt you, and I've already informed the pack that they need to be on their best behavior... You may not be part of the pack in the truest definition, but you are in spirit, and have been for some time, though we would never have said so."

A lump rose in Katey's throat and she tried to swallow it back. Darren's words warmed a bit of the ice from her heart, leaving the door cracked for perilous hope to creep in.

"Does that mean... I can stay?"

The lines of Darren's face softened. "Not forever, but you have a place here as long as you need it, whenever you need it. Our door will always be open."

It wasn't the answer she wanted, but she foolishly clung to what he said. *You have a place here.* It almost made her want to run upstairs to unpack and get comfortable.

"Now, I have two requests of you today," Darren continued. "First, make a list of the foods you will eat. Don't be afraid to ask for too much. No, you will not pay me back. Secondly, you need to set aside time to study. I'm not your father, but I am your teacher and I care about your education."

It was then she realized what day it was, and she cringed. "I just remembered. There's a party this evening at the ballroom dance studio where I work."

Concern crossed his expression. "Do you think that's wise after just getting out of the hospital?"

"I feel fine. Besides, I promised Lily that I would be there. I get paid for the hours I help out the guests."

Darren thought on it and then nodded. "Very well. You can make your own judgments. May I request that Logan escort you? We still don't know the full extent of any injuries the doctors missed."

The idea sent a jolt of excitement through Katey's core, but she resisted, knowing Darren likely could sense the change in her. Snagging a few hours with Logan sounded perfect right about now, but her mind wandered to what happened Thursday night, coupled with what the alpha just told her. Logan had spent days in a crowded school without incident. Maybe it was just a fluke. Maybe they weren't as dangerous as Darren tried to communicate. If Logan was a ticking time bomb, he wouldn't have suggested Logan went with her.

Katey only nodded in agreement and glanced to her untouched breakfast, a bit of her appetite returning. "Anything else I need to know?"

"Next weekend, we will be leaving for Alaska. I wasn't able to fully explain the purpose of the trip. For the last few decades, loups-garous from across the country, and some from Europe, have gathered together for the last full moon of the year. Our shifts are not dependent on the phases of the moon, but some of us can be sentimental creatures. We gather to reconnect, catch up, celebrate and grieve the passing of another year... It really is like a reunion of sorts. We'll also be attending a charity luncheon for a wolf conservation organization. We're friends with the founder and bought plates to show our support."

That bittersweet ache returned to her chest. "Sounds nice... I'll be fine here."

Darren appeared nonplussed. "I was going to ask if we needed to purchase another plane ticket and a plate for that luncheon."

Katey sucked in a breath. Once more, she felt the push and pull of seizing the opportunity or slipping into the shadows so she wouldn't be a burden.

"But... I'm not pack. I'm not loup-garou."

"Wives and children also attend. I don't see why you couldn't come along if you wanted. Though, we would likely keep a much closer watch over you. Many loups-garous there may be very young and inexperienced, making them a little more volatile."

That last part went in one ear and out the other. All that mattered was that she wanted to go and they were willing to take her along. She'd have to ask for a couple of weekends off from her job at the studio, but it'd be worth it. Hiding as much of her own inner conflict as she could, Katey gave him a tight-lipped smile and nodded. "I'd like to go, if it won't be too much trouble."

Darren returned her smile, but with double the enthusiasm. "No trouble at all. We'd be glad to have you."

Those words were just the right lubricant to get that switch in her brain to pick a side. They wanted her here, with them. They made breakfast for her, were willing to provide for her, and would keep her safe. For the first time in a long time, Katey felt as if she could breathe, really breathe. The slightly musty air in the billiard room, mingled with the heady scents of the loups-garous, never tasted sweeter. Could this be the closest thing to home she ever had?

CHAPTER 18

Logan paced the length of the living room as he waited for Katey, hands tucked in his crisp, nearly new jean pockets. He wouldn't have put much effort into readying himself for the party, but when Dustin was told of their plans, his grandfather insisted he got at least half-way dressed up. It took him a while to find the black button-down shirt, and wearing it now, the fabric was a little snug across his shoulders.

Dustin came in from the billiard room and clicked his tongue in disapproval. "Tuck your damn shirt in. We raised you better than that."

Logan glanced down at his outfit. "I haven't tucked my shirts in since the eighties."

"Just do it. That looks more formal now."

Logan gave a short, irritated growl before unzipping his fly to do as Dustin said. "Are you going to say I need a tie next? Because if so, you can—"

The sound of light footsteps down the stairs cut him off. He turned so Katey wouldn't see him shoving at his shirt tails.

Dustin gave a teasing whistle. "You clean up good, Katey Kat."

Logan zipped up again and turned about to see Katey standing at the bottom of the steps. His gaze started at her feet and slowly traveled upwards. Strapped, open-toed heels gave her an extra inch of height. Silver embroidered vines and flowers wove elegant patterns across the smooth black skirt that extended to just below her knees to expose shapely calves. Her white blouse accentuated the figure that she always hid beneath big shirts and hoodies. Her brown hair was pulled back, displaying a long, slender neck and giving her facial features a regal, dignified look. Makeup made her green eyes appear brighter and more mesmerizing than they already were. She wore a different perfume, one with a more mature signature that completed the look of someone who could dance the night away.

The Katey in front of him wasn't the Katey he knew. He didn't know whether to like this change or not. His wolf panted after her in the same way, and he wished he could have tugged his shirt over the front of his jeans to hide the effect she had over his body.

Long sleeves were rolled up to her elbows, and he checked for scars. None. Katey was smart enough not to cut in places people could see.

He shouldn't have worried about her mental state. Since she had the talk with Darren that morning, Katey's attitude was so altered, like night and day. Her chin was set a little higher, new confidence written in her posture. She spoke a little louder, asked for things a little more freely, and no longer had that scared rabbit look about her. That talk should have had the opposite reaction. Darren told her that they were liable to explode in a flurry of fangs and claws, and she wasn't the least bit worried. It made no sense. Maybe it had something to do with the unshed tears when Dustin came home with a coffee maker. She didn't ask for it, but he knew Darren added it to her shopping list since she had asked for coffee that morning. The way she thanked them, one might have thought they gave her something far more precious than a kitchen appliance.

Dustin's elbow dug into Logan's ribs and he snapped back to the present. "Have her back by midnight." He turned and strode out the back door onto the patio, leaving them alone in the living room.

Katey's lips curled at the ends and a hint of color rose to her cheeks. "Are we driving separately?"

It took a minute for Logan to force the cotton from his mouth and rubbed at the back of his neck as if that would clear his head. "I'll ride in your jeep if you're okay with it."

"That's fine. I'll drive."

Logan gestured to her feet. "Can you operate the pedals in those?"

She lifted one brow. "If girls couldn't drive in heels, half the population wouldn't be able to go anywhere."

He chuckled at himself and heat pooled down his limbs in embarrassment. "Oh... Right... Ready to go?"

Katey nodded and strode toward the front door. Logan headed her off and stopped her progress. "There's a door off the billiard room that goes to the carport. Don't want you tripping over the gravel."

"Nice of you to think of it, but I promise you, I know how to walk in heels. I just don't wear them that often."

Their nearness, the potency of her perfume and the way she looked up at him behind dark lashes made his wolf turn into a rutting-crazed mess. He cleared his throat and moved away to lead her. The tap of heels on hardwood followed him down the hall and into the empty billiard room.

A rogue thought invaded his mind, no doubt coming from his wolf. Darren still worked on his lesson plans and Dustin likely had left to go check on Ben, who had spent most of the day outdoors. They were alone in the billiard room, and if they stayed quiet, they could have a few minutes to themselves before Darren interrupted. The vision of Katey up on the edge of the billiard table, his hand brushing up her skirt, face buried in the warm spot where neck sloped into shoulder, the sound of a gasp and the utterance of his name from her lips...

Logan's steps slowed, and the rhythm of her heels stumbled.

"Forget something?" she asked.

His nostrils flared and hands balled into fists so tight he thought he drew blood. "Go on ahead. I'll catch up."

She walked out the side door, letting in a sobering gust of winter air. Logan rushed to the bathroom to his left and splashed his face with cold water in the sink. He gripped its porcelain edges and the light red stains smeared on his palms confirmed what he suspected. He looked up into the mirror, meeting crimson eyes that stared back at him.

These eyes may have been just as dangerous as his wolfish gold, but for a vastly different reason. Lust was a new sensation for him. Before Katey, before last week, he only saw his eyes give this warning a handful of times in his entire life.

Like the other night, he had to convince himself that he didn't want that, didn't need that. They weren't mated. It wasn't right. Forest could do as he wished with Lily, but they weren't the same. He had to remind himself that he couldn't have that same level of physical intimacy with Katey, though he couldn't deny how ardently he wanted every part of her, body, heart, and soul. He couldn't have her. Not the way he wanted. Not while things remained the way they were.

That thought, that angry thought, was enough to subdued the need for the time being.

Hard reason forced back the red and blue eyes glared from the mirror. He heard Darren rise from his place at the dining table across the house. He didn't want the alpha anywhere near him, not in this state.

"I'm fine," Logan snarled. The flash of fang in the mirror made him take another long breath. The alpha went still in the kitchen and waited.

Behave, he told himself, *or you'll never have a moment alone with Katey ever again. The pack will make sure of that.*

It took longer than he wanted to compose himself, then left the house without another word. Katey had already started her jeep on the other side of the carport and he hopped in the passenger seat as if nothing happened.

"Everything okay?" she asked as she pulled toward the break in the trees that would lead them to the highway.

Logan steadied his stare out the window, refusing to look her way as long as he thought he couldn't keep his thoughts out of the gutter. He glanced in the side mirror as trees blotted out the shape of the house behind them.

"Everything's fine." Somehow, he managed an even tone, and she bought it. Hopefully he could believe it before the night was over.

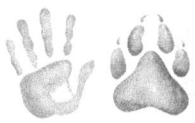

Logan seemed unusually quiet on the way to the ballroom dance studio. Though, it wasn't too contrary to the way they spent most of the day. She stayed in the dining room to study, while he was either in his room or outside, and they only spoke on a few occasions, such as during lunch and in passing.

Katey tried not to read into it, but he repeatedly evaded her efforts to make conversation, and he wouldn't even look at her. She noticed the way he so thoroughly appraised her when she joined him in the living room. Perhaps he disapproved of how she, in Dustin's words, "cleaned up." She admitted it might have been a little over the top, but she had to look the part of a dance instructor, minus the revealing and sparkly dresses as some professionals wore.

She parked the jeep along Main Street and they fell in side-by-side on the cobblestone sidewalk. Contrary to her earlier assertion that she could walk just fine in heels, Katey lost her footing and her ankle kicked sideways, not enough to twist or seriously hurt herself, but enough to throw her off balance. Logan was instantly there to steady her, one hand catching her arm and the other just barely touching her back. Almost falling into him allowed her to get a deeper whiff of his usual wild and earthy scent.

"Thought you said you could walk in heels." His voice dropped, turning gruff with concern.

"I can. Some of these pavers are just crooked and it messes me up."

Katey gained her footing again and realized how close Logan was. Just inches, so close she could reach up and tug him down for a long overdue kiss if she wanted. Her lips tingled with the very thought. The difference in his dress hadn't gone unnoticed. He looked good and sharp, though she would prefer his grungy, dangerous style any day of the week. Katey's tongue darted between her lips as she thought how best to get his shirt untucked, though. It'd look better that way. Should she just grab at the fabric and pull or ask him first. Her fingers tentatively reached for his waistline and he didn't stop her.

"Katey!"

Lily's voice broke her daze. She jumped away from Logan and looked down the sidewalk to see the blonde waving her hand excitedly from the open studio door. Latin dance music gushed into the street and she could see the multicolored lights splash across the cobblestone.

Steadying herself and shaking away the compulsion to take liberties that weren't hers yet, Katey hurried forward to meet her friend, leaving Logan to trail after her.

"I can't believe you got Logan to come with you," Lily said as they ducked inside. "I thought you two weren't dating."

"We're not. It's a long story." And Katey was thankful that Lily would be the one person she could tell everything to. She already knew about loups-garous, though she was still undecided if she'd ever forgive her friend for keeping such a secret from her.

"You know I love a good story, but... we're in mixed company." Lily nodded to the mass of people in the studio. Some, she recognized as current or past students. Others, the ones who danced without form or consideration to what ballroom dancing really was, were likely guests or first-time attendees. They rocked their hips and swayed with partners as if they were in a nightclub. It was the job of the employees to set the tone of the party and give free instruction where it was accepted.

She spotted Forrest's red hair across the room just a second before his head swiveled toward the door. His face pinched with confusion, then smoothed with amusement. Logan entered the studio behind her, indicated by the draft. The studio was warm with the multitude of moving bodies, and Katey knew she'd have to step out several times that night to cool off on the sidewalk.

Forrest wrapped up his conversation with an older couple and crossed the studio floor, weaving his way through the guests to pass Lily and Katey completely. His target was Logan. They clasped arms like old combat buddies and grinned. It was the happiest Katey had seen him in a while.

Lily bent her head to Katey. "Don't feel too bad. I could have been totally topless, and he would have still gone straight for Logan."

"So, they're really good friends?"

She laughed. "Good friends? They might as well be related. You know Forrest is one of Logan's oldest friends, right? They knew each other in Devia." Lily whispered the name of that community as if it were some reverent Mecca for loups-garous. "And Logan stayed with Forrest and his family while he was in Chicago. Do you know about Chicago yet?"

"He mentioned that the guys dropped him off there for a while." Katey was careful of her word choice as they walked toward the podium at the far end of the room.

Lily turned serious, the most serious Katey had seen her since the shopping disaster of their junior year when she got busted for spending hundreds of dollars on her mom's credit card. "Okay, don't talk about Chicago. We don't talk about Chicago. I don't even know that much about what happened, and that's saying something because Forrest tells me everything. All I know is that it wasn't a happy time, so don't bring it up."

Katey glanced toward Logan and briefly met his gaze before he turned away to continue talking with Forrest. Right about now, she wished she had loup-garou hearing so she knew what they talked about. What could have been so terrible that he didn't want to talk about it? The murder of his parents was pretty shocking enough, and he talked about it freely with her the other day. What could possibly have been worse than that?

"Noted... Are they going to stay attached at the hip all night?"

Lily perked up as she reviewed the dance playlist on the laptop. "Oh, probably. We'll have to tear them apart to dance at some point."

The memory of their almost-dance in the wrestling gym had Katey shifting from one heeled foot to the other. They never got the chance to start it, much less finish it. "I don't know if Logan will dance. He's just here to make sure I don't hurt myself."

"Hurt yourself?"

Katey then went into the long story of how she came to be in the accident, leaving out the details she would tell Lily later when they were alone. Her friend's expression went through the whole cycle of emotions from giddy over Katey and Logan getting fresh in the living room, to horror when Mary dragged her out of the house, relief that Logan was there to save her, and then sadness toward the end as Katey lay in the hospital and Mary in the morgue.

By the end, Lily's mouth hung open. "Oh my God, and you're still walking?"

"In heels, too."

Katey stole another glance to where they left Logan. She found him and Forrest seated at a table in the corner, arms folded over the tabletop and face rigid in some terribly intense conversation. They might have been talking about the exact same thing, only Logan would be able to drop his voice low enough to include those more implicating details that Katey had to omit.

"If you're not feeling well or you start to hurt, you don't have to stay. I'll vouch that you were here all night so you can get paid for it."

She shook her head. "I don't need you to cover for me. I feel great."

Lily was still amazed and finally lifted her slender hands as if she gave up trying to understand it. "All right, but the offer is still on the table. Ready to show these people how to dance the right way?"

Katey smiled as Lily tapped a key on the laptop and the music faded from the upbeat club music to a traditional tango. Lily skipped away and made a beeline to Forrest. The loup-garou allowed himself to be pulled to his feet, since he very well had the strength to resist her, and they instantly fell into a feisty tango routine Katey had seen a few times.

Perfectly timed, they dominated the dance floor. The inexperienced guests slipped away to the margins of the room to make way for the students who knew the moves.

Katey and a couple of other instructors who worked at the studio full-time found those guests who clearly showed some interest in learning. Katey could read the room better than some. One girl looked to her date, eyes a little pleading. He was less eager, a line of worry between his brows. Katey saw that exchange all the time. She wanted to dance, but he didn't want to make a fool of himself.

With a genial smile, she approached and began the lesson. They fumbled at first, but soon found the tempo and moved across the floor in the basic tango promenade. It'd take practice, but the couple looked to be enjoying the process and that was the point.

An hour flew by in the same way. Katey gave her full attention to the guests, and Logan didn't move from the seat he had claimed when they arrived. Whenever she looked his way, he either watched the room or watched her. Each time their eyes met, a knot of tension made her pause and she became awkward with whomever she taught in that moment. It then took her a few seconds too long to regain her composure.

Katey only briefly danced with a few guys for the purpose of demonstration or instruction, but she longed to dance with Logan. She wanted to feel his capable hands hold her in any way, to let herself be spun around the dance floor like Forrest and Lily, with a ridiculous smile plastered on her face.

That secret wish must have been etched in every line of her face, because her friend suddenly grabbed her arm. "Your turn," Lily giggled.

Katey nearly fell over as Lily carted her toward Logan. In turn, Forrest hefted Logan from his chair with considerable effort to bring him to his feet.

"Lily, no," Katey hissed. "If he doesn't want to, you can't make him."

"Oh, he wants to," Forrest replied, his voice just loud enough to reach them. "He just won't admit it."

The scowl reserved just for Forrest did not convince anyone.

The four came together, and Katey was all but shoved into Logan's arms. Lily and Forrest darted away, their mission halfway accomplished. The music coming through the speakers softened and slowed. She knew the song. *Come Away With Me* by Norah Jones. It was an easy waltz for beginners or any couple looking for a slow dance.

Katey licked her lips, her body quivering, scared that Logan would walk away, or even worse, that he would take her heart in his hands and do wonderful things with it. It would have been a lie if she said that she never thought about that day in the wrestling gym and didn't wonder what might have happened if they danced. Logan held himself like a professional just before she pushed him away. Now, she was tempted to again. She wouldn't force anyone to be with her if they didn't want it. And by the way he stayed glued to his chair all night, he didn't want to.

"We don't have to," Katey mumbled.

She angled away, inclined to be the first to abandon the opportunity. Better to leave first before being left. That's when his hand grabbed hers and he made her stay.

Gazes locked and no words were needed. Logan was willing. He wanted to. Wanted her. The touch of his skin soothed all her nerves and all the tightness in her shoulders and back slipped away.

One step led to another, and then they were in the midst of the other swaying couples. Unlike in the wrestling gym, Logan did not pull her into the formal waltz frame. His hand dropped to the curve of her waist, elbows relaxed and bodies so close his heat bled through her clothes to warm her core. Her chin was level with his broad shoulders, but she coyly dipped her head, in the perfect place to drown in his scent. Her hand settled on his hard bicep, unafraid to forsake form for intimacy as he did. His muscles bunched, then released under her fingers. Breath stirred the tiny hairs on the top of her head that had loosened from her ponytail, sending goose pimples across her arms, despite the warm air in the room.

Like everything else, their dance didn't follow the box pattern of a waltz. Instead, they swayed back and forth with the music, shifting weight from one foot to the other like they were dates for the homecoming dance.

If Katey saw any other couple dancing like this, she would have instructed them on just how simple a real waltz could be. But Logan knew that already. He didn't want a waltz like that, and maybe she didn't either. This was more personal, more intimate, more free.

Something like relief washed over her and Katey closed her eyes.

"Can I confess something?" Logan's voice rumbled against her ear. "I hate dancing."

Katey snorted a laugh, breaking the mood. "Could have fooled me."

"Dustin taught me a few things a long time ago, but it always seemed like a pointless skill."

"You seemed to know what you were doing last week."

"I was trying to impress you."

"And now?"

His silence made her turn her head to see just how unbearably close their faces were. Just a few inches, and their lips could meet as easily as hands did on the dance floor.

"Now I'm just enjoying you."

A hot, sultry look came into his eyes. Blood quickened through Katey's veins and breathing became a little harder as she moved closer into his space, guided by the subtle draw of his hand across her back pulling her in. She had never been touched like this in her life, not even by an eager student at the studio. To her utter shame and pleasure, she loved it.

Just as Katey wondered if this was the moment they would finally kiss, Logan sent her into a slow turn. When they came back together in the same position as before the turn, reveling in the same nearness, Katey couldn't keep quiet. In a self-sabotaging moment, she asked, "Where is this going?"

Logan turned his head as if he needed to think. She let him, not pushing, patiently waiting for whatever answer he could give.

It felt as if they had danced around the obvious, never getting too near to that crazy idea they had both considered. To mate, to be a couple, whatever it was they could do as loup-garou and human. Katey wanted it. She wanted to be a permanent part of his world, no matter what it took. To mate, to be turned, or both. All she wanted was Logan and she wasn't so sure she could walk away without making that commitment, no matter the cost.

But did he feel the same? She needed to know, and he seemed completely incapable of putting it into words. It infuriated her not to know exactly where they stood. He may not have agreed to a casual arrangement like she assumed, but what was it he wanted from her? He had said before that he had lost his filter and she hoped that it hadn't slid back into place since Thursday.

Logan turned his gaze back to her. The inner depths of his eyes burned, flecks of gold sparkling in the technicolor lights. "Do you think we have a chance?"

It felt unfair for him to kick the ball back into her court, but she knew the answer.

With her next breath came the softest, "Yes."

One corner of Logan's mouth tilted up. "Then it can go on forever."

"But... how?"

His grip around her waist tightened. "Trust me... Trust us."

Katey gave him a look. "You're being cryptic... Romantic, but cryptic."

His smile widened. "Well, one out of two ain't bad."

Katey shook her head and tried not to laugh at the release of pent-up anxiety. It wasn't quite the answer she wanted. How was this supposed to last forever? Did he really think it could? Did that mean he was willing to take the risk that the rest of the pack would not? That also may have meant he was willing to kill her for the chance to have more of this. More dances, more walks through cemeteries, more heartfelt, honest talks, more gazing into each other's soul as if the rest of the world didn't exist.

For one reckless minute, Katey believed such a chance with Logan was worth it. A near eternity with him, with his pack, with a home, was worth the risk. How absolutely masochistic... or suicidal.

The song glided to its endnote. Another waltz song faded into the last. This one was more traditional, more formal. Just when she thought their dance was over, Logan gracefully transitioned them into the waltz frame and lifted his chin.

"I thought you hated dancing?" Katey grinned.

"I do, but I hate it a little less when it's with you."

Before she could reply, he whisked her up into one of the best waltzes she had ever danced. They glided across the floor as if they were in a competition, as if they had danced like this in a thousand lifetimes before. It was as if they were always meant to dance like this and all the stars aligned for this single moment in time. Katey could think of few things that could possibly beat this, even if she lived for hundreds of years.

CHAPTER 19

Logan leaned against the kitchen counter, breakfast plate in one hand and absently pushing his scrambled eggs with a fork in the other. The night before had been... a revelation. Katey thought they had a chance, and she didn't immediately balk at the concept of forever, but only wanted to know how. He knew exactly how, and so did she, even if she wouldn't say it. It was the only way. The only question was when and if they were brave enough to try.

Her miraculous recovery from a devastating car wreck gave him an excessive amount of optimism. She had been pretty beat up when he dragged her through the front windshield of the car, and yet she didn't need a cast or stitches. The small cut on her forehead had completely healed after a couple of days, barely leaving a scar that could easily be concealed by makeup. She hadn't even touched her pain meds. If she could heal that fast, or if she were simply that sturdy of a woman, then turning her may not end in tragedy.

Yet, Logan couldn't shake the images that haunted his night-mares. The ones of Katey's mangled, lifeless body at his feet and her blood on his hands. Since the car accident, the same dream haunted the hours he should have been sleeping. He wished it could have been so simple, so easy to set aside that fear and cling to the prospect that she could be loup-garou like him.

Then, too, he thought of just how much he had hated what he was when he first turned, how he despised the thing in him that robbed him of a normal life. Everything he did was because of the beast inside, and most days he still loathed the creature. He was a different case than some, but even Darren had gone through that phase where he feared the wolf he couldn't control. With training and time, most loups-garous settled into their new lives with a healthy level of acceptance. Could Katey? Or would she inherit too much of him through the bite and resent him for hundreds of years? If that happened, then they'd never have the kind of relationship he wanted, and she would never be his mate.

He tried to tell himself that none of it needed to be decided now. There was plenty of time, and he would still let Kate have the final say. He would not force anything on her. Not mating, and not turning.

"What're ya thinking about so hard over there?" Ben asked. The rest of the pack ate at the glass table in the bay window, discussing the plans for the day and the coming week. Logan vaguely heard the mention of the exams and the trip to Alaska. When he overheard that Darren would be purchasing a fifth plane ticket, Logan had to bottle the shout of joy in his chest so his alpha wouldn't think he had lost his mind.

"Nothing."

Dustin set down his fork. "I can tell you exactly what he's thinking about. How was last night?"

Logan saw the sly look on his grandfather's face and knew what sort of answer he wanted to hear. "Nothing happened, if that's what you're after."

Darren looked at him over the rim of his water glass. "Did you dance or just watch?"

"Danced a couple of times. Mostly watched."

Dustin grabbed at the alpha's shoulder and shook him as if he had heard a wonderful joke. Water nearly sloshed into Darren's lap. "You hear that? They danced!"

Ben rolled his eyes and brought his empty plate to the sink. "Dancin' don't mean nothin'."

Logan shrugged and took a forkful of eggs. He might have been tempted to agree with him, but not this time. Those few dances, his first in years, were unimaginably special. Katey was a talented dancer, and several guests commented on that to their partners.

Darren took up a napkin and patted down the few water droplets that blotted his shirt. "Did you at least have a good time?"

"Sure." Logan took another bite, hoping if he could finish his breakfast fast enough, he could leave the conversation.

"Just make sure ya don't have too good of a time." Ben pinned him with a look. "Don't need to make more trouble for us."

Logan glared. "What the hell is that supposed to mean?"

"I think he's talking about compromising Katey's respectability."

Dustin shot Darren a perturbed look. "For god's sake, man. 'Compromising her respectability' is so outdated." The mocking, over-the-top British accent made Logan smirk. "Just don't knock her up."

Those words wiped off every hint of amusement. "Excuse me?"

Ben folded his arms. "We ain't blind, Logan. It's all over the both of y'all."

He was sure they hadn't been that careful to hide their feelings, but he didn't expect the pack to gang up on him. "And? Are you going to give me 'the talk'? You're over a century late for that."

"You may be consenting adults," Darren said. "But you know the implications of getting too serious."

Dustin ticked off the points on his fingers. "Mates first. Sex later. Much easier that way."

"You're one to talk," Logan grumbled with a mouthful of sausage.

Dustin lifted his hands in conceding fashion and leaned back in his chair. The metal groaned and popped under his weight. "Do as I say, not as I do."

"Katey's too young for that sort of commitment."

Logan snapped another glare at Ben. "Why don't you let her make that decision."

"You should too."

Darren's admonishment held an extra warning. It was enough to take some starch out of him. The alpha had an uncanny way of knowing things about his pack. Some things escaped him, but others didn't. Did he sense the ultimatum Logan had just been mulling over? The poignant look in his stare suggested it.

Footsteps sounded down the stairs and all four loups-garous turned to see Katey enter the kitchen in a pair of soft pajama bottoms and a hoodie two sizes too large for her. The light in her eyes and brightness to her face made him smile and forget how the pack had just counseled him. Her slightly mussed brown hair told him she hadn't made much of an effort to put herself together. So different from the night before, but just as beautiful.

Her gaze fell on Logan first and all four of them sensed the change in her.

Dustin snapped his fingers and pointed toward the stairs. "Logan, go put a shirt on."

They smelled her arousal as unmistakably as he did. Going shirt-less around the house hadn't been an issue before, but he noticed the elder members of the pack had made a point of staying fully clothed in the public areas of the house. Unafraid of what it would do to Katey's comfort, Logan didn't take such precautions.

In passive rebellion to the order, Logan set down his plate on the counter and took his time moving past Katey toward the living room. The back of his hand brushed hers and she drew in a soft, ragged breath. Logan smiled to himself as he climbed the stairs. That probably wasn't fair, but he needed to communicate to Darren and the pack that this thing with Katey wouldn't go away. They wouldn't have a say in anything they did, mating or otherwise.

***

Heavy lidded, Katey forced calm over herself in front of the pack. There was no way she would ever forget the sight of Logan half naked, smooth, perfect skin stretched over hard muscles. Every curve had made her mouth water, from his bold chest to the ridges of his abs and the hollows over his hips that disappeared down the front of his pants. He had looked like something out of a magazine or steamy photoshoot.

Ben mumbled something under his breath that Katey didn't catch before he retreated toward the billiard room. Dustin rose from the dinette table and shoveled the last of his breakfast into his mouth before rinsing off his plate.

It was Darren's strong voice that fully brought her out of the tailspin Logan had sent her in. "Sleep well?"

"Yeah, thanks."

Dustin pinched and blew out his nose as if he needed to clear it of a bad smell. "Fun night?"

A satisfied smile crept onto her face. They didn't dance for long, but what time they shared on the dance floor was spectacular, and rekindled the hope that they had something special. If they took their time and carefully thought things through, maybe they could have it for much longer than a few months, or even a few decades.

"It was." She may not be able to lie, but she could leave out the details.

Dustin slipped her a knowing look, then went down the hall to join Ben in the billiard room. She heard the typical sounds that signaled they were about to start a game.

About that moment, Logan bounded down the stairs and slipped past her. "Hungry?"

"A little."

The skillet of seared sausage was still warm on the stovetop, and an open carton of white eggs sat nearby. Logan set to work pulling a plate, glass, and fresh skillet from the cabinets.

"How do you like your eggs?"

"Over easy." Not wanting to let him take too much control over her breakfast, Katey moved to the far side of the counter where they had set up her coffee maker and toaster.

"What are you doing?" Logan asked as she untwisted the tie from the loaf of bread.

"Making toast." She dropped two slices in the toaster. "You never had toast and dipped it in the egg yolk?"

Thinking on it briefly, maybe he didn't. He was human before the invention of the modern toaster, or even pre-sliced bread. His mother likely made bread the old fashioned way, and any toasting would have had to be done over a stove in a pan, like how most people made grilled cheese in the modern times.

Logan fired up one of the grated eyes on the gas stove and set down the clean skillet. A tinge of some darker emotion crossed his face. "Not really."

"Sorry. I didn't mean to... to do whatever I just did."

He smirked. "It's fine. Just reminded me of what I missed out on."

Katey opened the refrigerator and a gasp escaped her lips. She didn't mean to, but the sight of so much raw meat startled her. The picture looked more like a scene out of some horror movie when the detectives found the butchered victim in the freezer.

They had pushed aside packages of ground meat, chicken, and roast to give her one shelf to claim as her own. That shelf looked far more normal, populated by baggies of vegetables, fruits, condiments, and six-pack of soda, among other things that humans ate. They likely did the same in the pantry and freezer.

To hide her surprise, she quickly grabbed the carton of butter from her shelf and closed the door.

"A little much?"

She hoped Logan didn't see her embarrassment, but the heat encircling her neck would have been a dead giveaway. "You told me your diet was pretty restricted. I guess I just... I don't know what I expected."

With mechanical efficiency, Katey set up the coffeemaker to start a pot while she waited for the toast. Filter, grounds, and water, then it began to percolate that magical brew of caffeine.

"Good God, I missed that smell!" Ben's exclamation echoed down the hall.

She looked to Logan, eyes full of questions. That was possibly the loudest she had ever heard Ben speak.

"The coffee."

"Oh... is it going to be—"

"It's not a problem." Darren came up to dispense his dishes in the sink. "We all miss something from being human. I miss freshly baked bread."

Dustin called out, "Stew, though a younger version of myself hated it."

"Apple pie." Logan cracked an egg on the edge of the pan. Again, that haunted look came over him and she wished she could have hugged it away, but Darren was watching.

"I'd probably miss fries." It wasn't news to Logan, but she hadn't admitted it to the rest of them.

Darren graced her comment with an understanding smile. "Be thankful you won't have to know what it feels like to miss something you enjoy."

The toast popped and she snatched the hot bread between her fingers. It was too late. She had already considered it, and though the restrictive diet of the loup-garou was firmly fixed in the con column of her list, it didn't hold much weight against the "Get to spend the rest of my life with Logan" item on the pro side. So far, that aspect nearly dominated the decision.

"Are you ready for the exams?" the alpha asked.

"I think so." Katey began pulling open drawers to find utensils. Two drawers clattered noisily in her search before Logan opened the third by his hip. "Thanks." She picked out a butter knife.

"You have plenty of more time if you feel you need it," Darren said, "We discussed earlier about spending the afternoon in training, so the house will be quiet and free of distractions."

"Training?"

"In a loose sense of the word."

Logan flipped the egg. "Paintballing."

Before she could stop herself, Katey blurted out, "I've always wanted to try that. Can I come?"

She inwardly cringed and wished she could take it back. It sounded desperate and childish, like a kid trying to hang out with cool high schoolers.

Neither of them seemed fazed. Darren shrugged. "If you can keep up. We use the game to prepare ourselves in the event of a hunter attack. It's important to know how to shoot and avoid being shot."

Katey stood still, buttered knife in one hand. "That's intense."

"That's a reality of our existence." Darren walked away toward the stairs. "As I said, you're welcome to come if you feel up to it and you don't need to study. We have a spare gun."

Katey doubted she could keep pace with the loups-garous. She couldn't match their speed or their precision, and she had never fired any kind of gun. Crestfallen and ready to abandon the thought, she finished buttering her toast just as Logan slipped her egg onto a plate, adding a portion of sausage.

"You should come. It'll be fun."

She took the plate from him, their fingertips brushing in the process. A shiver passed down her spine and she shook her head. "I wouldn't be able to keep up."

As she turned her head to give her attention back to her toast, Logan bent low, his mouth so close to her ear that his breath plumed down her neck. "I'll go slow for you."

His purr made her shiver as she did when he left to put a shirt on. Right about now, she wished he hadn't. It was then she realized they were completely alone in the kitchen. Not much could escape the keen senses of the loups-garous in the house, but if they played it right...

He eased away, but not so far that she couldn't feel his heat. "But I won't go easy. The one with the most shots on them has to do dishes for the week."

Katey didn't reply, but set down her butter knife and closed the distance between them. She pinched the edge of his shirt and pulled it down as if inspecting the design. "Guns n' Roses? Ever see them in concert?"

Blue eyes fixed on her. "Once. Long ago."

Katey let go of the shirt and her shaking hands settled on his hips, feeling the ridge of elastic on his pajama pants waistband. "I like some of their stuff. Favorite song?"

It might have taken him a second to realize she was covering their more sensual behavior with innocuous conversation. Once he did, his hands moved to action, slipping into her half-tangled mass of hair. Fingers curled, but didn't grip. "'Sweet Child O' Mine'."

Katey huffed and let him tilt her head up, rising on her tiptoes at his bidding. "That is such a basic answer."

His voice lowered into a husky whisper. "I honestly can't think of any of the other songs right now."

Katey grinned and let her fingers press into the hard flesh of his hips. "Me neither."

She closed her eyes just as she thought their lips would touch, but as twice before, Logan only touched his forehead to hers and inhaled deeply as if he were taking in her scent. The loup-garou did know how to kiss, right?

A low growl rumbled in his throat just a second before he tore away. She gripped the counter to regain her balance. Darren came down the stairs, fully dressed for the day.

"Are you all right, Katey? You look pale."

She felt her hot cheeks and wondered how she could possibly look pale after a moment like that. "I'm fine."

Logan took up her plate, as steady as a rock, and handed it to her. The coffeemaker beeped and sputtered out the last bit of its brew. Darren passed them both and went to the dining room and his head seat at the table. His laptop and school work was still there from the day before. Clearly, the man had no life outside of work and the pack.

Alone again, Logan gave her a wicked look, as if to say what she initiated was rather naughty. Katey didn't care. Just a bit of fun, and she tried to impart that with a look of her own as she pulled down a mug from the upper cabinet. She hoped for more little moments of privacy, if only to see just how far they could take things before he gave in or the pack caught them.

After a long evening of paintballing in the woods on their property, the pack gathered together to head back to the house. The sun already set the sky ablaze with shades of red and deep purple as night drew in.

Each of them were covered in paint spots, with the exception of Ben, who was a master of the game from his experience serving in three major wars in his lifetime. Katey was the only one decked out in protective gear, while the others wore only white shirts and jackets to keep out the chill.

Katey complained of her legs aching during their walk back to the house, and Logan effortlessly cradled her into his arms to carry her the mile back through the darkening woods. The rest of the pack didn't approve, but it didn't take long for Katey to fall fast asleep in his hold, head nestled against his chest.

They all saw how she did her best to keep up as they dodged and bolted between hiding places for hours, taking shots at one another from the cover of bushes and trees. She was no match for their speed and reflexes, but the others accommodated her handicap by slowing down a bit. Katey even managed to get a few genuine shots on the guys, which sent her into fits of victorious giggles, giving away her position. The practice was not for her benefit, but if it were, she would have failed miserably. By morning, she'd have bruises in those places where the gear couldn't cover. It only reinforced that she needed protecting, or that she needed the ability to protect herself.

Logan watched her sleep, making every effort to keep his gait smooth so as not to jar her awake. He admired her soft features and adored the warmth of her body against his own. The other three kept a close eye on the two. Why they were so concerned, Logan didn't know. It wasn't as if he would do something foolish like run off with her into the woods, though the thought did cross his mind.

Once they arrived home, the pack made their way inside through the side door that opened into the billiard room. They all slipped off their muddy shoes at the door and stripped their shirts so they could be thrown in the wash. Logan only kicked off his boots, being mindful not to jostle Katey too sharply with his movements.

Darren eyed Logan, who stared down at the sleeping human in his arms with a look of complete entrancement. "You might want to take her upstairs, Logan."

Logan's head snapped up as if he had just awoken from his daydream. He nodded, made his way through the kitchen, into the living room and up the stairs. It didn't take long for him to realize the others followed him.

He lowered Katey onto the bed with the utmost care, as if she were a glass figurine, liable to break under the slightest ill-placed pressure. He knew she was stronger than that after the thrashing she had borne during the crash. He then cautiously slid off her dirty jacket and shoes, and unstrapped the gear from her torso.

"She sure seemed to have a fun time today," Dustin whispered from the doorway.

"It's a good thing," Darren replied. "She needed a little fun after all she's been through."

Logan gently pushed her legs under the covers and tucked the blankets up to her chin. From the foot of the bed, he spotted the old stuffed husky toy and smirked. The girl who could send his heart and mind into a state, still slept with a toy. He picked it up and slipped it beneath the covers to join her.

Ben gave a wide yawn and briskly shook his head, much like a wolf would. "Yeah, if ya call shootin' up your teachers fun."

"You should have let her get a couple of shots on you," Dustin snapped.

"Like you were?"

"Of course, I was."

"Ya know if we were actually goin' at our natural speed she would never have gotten any shots in at all."

"That's not the point, Ben," Darren interjected. He turned to Logan who sat on the edge of the bed, crinkling Katey's jacket between his hands and watching her with such concentration. "Logan, are you coming? You need to eat something before going to bed."

Logan glanced up to Darren and nodded, a tinge remorseful that he'd have to leave her there. "Yeah, I'll be right down. Just give me a minute."

Ben was the first to walk away, soon followed by Dustin who only shrugged to Darren in passing, as if to say "What harm would a moment do?" Darren stayed a little longer, then turned away to exit down the hall.

In the darkness, Logan could see her tranquil face and smiled. As if to make up for his earlier blunder in the kitchen, he stood and gently planted a kiss on the crown of her head. When he pulled away, he lingered a moment longer to affectionately stroke the back of his fingers along her soft hair. Logan likened her to Sleeping Beauty and wished with all that was in him that he could have been her Prince Charming to wake her from the spell. He wanted a happily-ever-after for both of them.

"I'll figure out a way," he whispered. "It won't always be like this."

He said it more to himself than to her. He had to believe that they wouldn't be in this weird, stuck spot. One day, they could be mated, or she could be a true member of the pack. He had to believe it, had to give himself completely to such a plan or he'd lose his nerve.

A dangerous, reckless thought came to mind and Logan willed it away as quickly as it entered. If he gave himself over to the wolf, it could do what both of them needed him to do. It had the courage, the drive, the need to make Katey his and his alone. It wouldn't be afraid to turn her.

But that meant letting the wolfish soul have dominion over his body, not in form but in everything else. He couldn't allow that. He couldn't risk her life. If the wolf had control, he could change her, but he may also take it too far. With the blood, the flesh, the carnal closeness, there was no telling what the wolf would do. It was unthinkable.

Still, the idea marked his mind as clearly as the neon splotches of paint on their clothes. The stain was there, and he couldn't ignore it. Perhaps he needed to keep his distance until the strength of such a temptation waned over time. That meant less school, less moments alone, and greater self-control. It also meant no more of those sensuous stolen moments like they had that morning. If the wolf sensed even a bit of weakness in his resolve to wait, it was over. Logan shook his head and rose from the bed to take his leave. The wolf couldn't be let out of its cage. Not even for her. He wasn't that desperate or cowardly... yet.

Hair wet and hanging straight down her back, Katey felt a little bad for hogging the bathroom that morning. If they had woken her up upon arriving back to the house, she would have showered off the remnants of the forest in her hair and across her skin the night before. Now, everyone's routine was thrown off kilter.

Katey poked at the tiny blue and purple bruise on her hip and winced in the bathroom mirror. Its twins colored a spot on her arm and calf. She remembered each of those shots that the protective gear failed to intercept, but she wouldn't have traded the previous evening for quiet time alone in the house. Playing paintball, or training as they considered it, proved to be valuable bonding time for her and the pack. It was as if the ice had been broken, between the running, the taunting, and the laughs. Katey felt just a little closer to them and any reticence on their part dissolved. Even Ben seemed a little warmer toward her than before.

A knock came at the door, and she quickly tugged down her shirt. "Just a minute."

"I need to grab something," Dustin said. "Are you decent?"

Katey gave an affirmative and the door opened. With his tie and first couple of shirt buttons undone, Dustin wasn't quite finished getting ready for the school day. With one hand still on the doorknob, he reached over and grabbed the handle of the second drawer in the stack. Katey stepped back to let him snatch up a razor and can of shaving cream.

"If you need to do that, I'm almost done."

Dustin glanced up, and instead of arguing, let the door swing open the rest of the way to let him into the bathroom. "If you insist. I hate that little bathroom downstairs anyway."

Katey fished out her toothbrush and toothpaste from her bath kit while Dustin used the opposite sink to begin shaving. A moment later, Ben entered. Light brown eyes darted between Katey and Dustin, then wordlessly edged between them to open his drawer and retrieve his own toothbrush.

For a minute, Katey wondered if the whole pack would file into the bathroom by the time she was done. A few days ago, she would have thought this terribly awkward. Now, Katey tried not to smile too wide, lest toothpaste ooze from the corner of her mouth. She knew she wasn't part of the pack, but she did feel closer to it.

Scenes like this, it was so easy to forget what they were. Yesterday, there was no mistaking it. At full speed, the loups-garous were little more than a blur darting through the trees. It was a wonder any of them could get a hit at all. A few times, the shots came from above and she didn't even realize when they had climbed the tree in the first place. Katey wasn't so ignorant to know that, at times, they slowed down and dampened their loup-garou abilities especially for her, and stayed within a certain radius, though she knew that on any other occasion, they would utilize all one hundred acres of land for their training. She hoped there would come a day when they wouldn't have to make concessions for her at all.

Darren paused by the open bathroom door, hands working to fasten a tie around his popped shirt collar. "Looks a little crowded in there."

"Katey said it was okay. Didn't you, Katey Kat?"

With her mouth occupied, Dustin knew she couldn't answer back. He smiled and a bit of shaving lather dropped from his chin onto the counter as he wetted the old-fashioned razor. It was the kind that folded from a sheath and needed to be sharpened on a regular basis. She wondered how old it was, and if it belonged in a museum somewhere because of its age and rarity.

She shot him a look and he chuckled before taking the first swipe on his cheek.

"I'm only in here because the door was open," Ben said before sticking his own toothbrush in his mouth.

Katey spit out the toothpaste. "It's fine. I don't mind."

Darren eyed her, then walked on down the upstairs hall. "If they bother you at all, feel free to kick them out. I'd do the same."

Though his mouth was full, Ben tapped Katey's elbow to get her attention, then pointed to the exposed, golf-ball-sized bruise on her arm. She planned to wear a jacket so no one would ask.

"That's from one of Darren's shots. It doesn't hurt."

Dustin chuckled. "Oh, it's 'Darren' now. Not Mr. Dubose?"

Katey froze, embarrassed by her stumble. "I thought it was okay."

Ben spit into the sink. "He's just teasin'. We don't care."

"Speak for yourself. Maybe I like being called Mr. Keith," Dustin said as he eased the blade along his jawline, crooking his mouth so he could speak without moving too much.

"Only 'cause it gives ya a big head."

Katey rinsed with her own cup and smiled. She enjoyed listening to their banter, even when it got a little serious.

Shuffling footsteps came down the hall and Logan leaned in the doorway. He still wore pajamas, this time in a gray sweatshirt instead of totally topless. His eyes held a bit of a haggard, fatigued look, a sign he didn't sleep at all.

"You not going to school?" Dustin asked as he rinsed away the refuse from the razor blade.

"Was thinking about it."

Katey blanched. It'd be the first time they hadn't at least been within the vicinity for... Katey could hardly remember. The idea of him staying at home crushed her heart.

In a bad effort to hide her disappointment, Katey rinsed her mouth again and packed up her toothbrush.

Dustin narrowed his eyes. "You sure?"

Logan shrugged. "Not like the exams count for anything."

That didn't matter from the beginning. Being with Katey was what mattered, if nothing had changed since Logan told her the truth about his enrollment. Maybe it had changed somehow, and she missed it.

Katey slid past him in the doorway, but his fingers wrapped around her wrist to keep her by his side.

"I didn't sleep well," he mumbled. "Sleep deprivation can make us crankier. I want to keep you and others safe."

Ben guffawed. "Now he cares about safety."

Katey thought about it, then nodded. It made sense, and she could hardly stay hurt when the compassion in his expression begged her to forgive his decision. The last thing they needed was for him to bite someone's head off, literally.

Ben finished brushing his teeth and waited for them to let him pass. Katey moved first and Logan let go of her, but she didn't wander far. Part of her wanted to stay in the hall and waste every second she could afford in Logan's presence. Anything to hold onto a piece of him while she tried to ace her exams.

Logan turned from the doorway and stroked his palm down her arm in an oddly platonic way. Just one heavy handed swipe and he dropped his arm as if he remembered himself a minute too late. No lingering, no gentleness. "You should finish getting ready."

Katey blinked and tried not to feel rejected. "Promise you'll be here when school is done?"

He smirked. "Of course."

Katey tried to smile and accept that as some consolation for being separated from him until noon. Thankfully, it'd be a short day because of the exams. Without even realizing it, Katey had become so addicted to his presence, to knowing he was close by or within shouting distance at least. She would be in good hands at school. The exams were broken up in pairs throughout the week and out of order. Today, she'd have fourth and third period exams. Ben and Dustin could keep her safe, but they were no replacements for Logan. Nothing ever would be.

CHAPTER 20

This was one of the worst decisions Logan had made in a while. It had been over a week since he had spent so much time alone in this house. He had almost forgotten just how unnervingly quiet it could get. Both he and his wolf were driven to the edge of madness with little to do and no Katey to distract him.

No movie, no book, no amount of sketching could keep him occupied for more than several minutes. No matter what room he was in, his eyes searched for a clock and growled when it wasn't anywhere close to noon. He thought to text her, but didn't want to get her in trouble with the pack as she worked on her exams. His thoughts continually drifted back to Katey. Past, present, and future. Her scent touched every public place in the house, following him like a passive ghost reminding him that they were not together.

When the clock struck noon, almost to the second, he pulled out his phone to punch out a quick text.

She beat him to it. His phone buzzed and her message notification popped up.

Missed you today. Coming straight to the house.

Logan deleted his draft, and the next thirty minutes proved more agonizing than the previous hours. Like a lonely, lovesick puppy, he paced the length of the foyer, ears tuned to the driveway, listening for the sound of her jeep. The engine's rumble came and

Logan had to keep himself from dashing out the door and across the yard to intercept her.

Engine cut. Car door slam. The steady pace of shoes on gravel. The door opened and he couldn't hold himself at bay any longer.

Logan charged forward and swept her up into a hug, his arms enveloping her as they spun in the foyer. Katey giggled and held on tight, her feet dangling off the floor. The feel of her body pressed against his finally sedated his restless wolf.

He buried his face in the place where shoulder met neck and found skin around the edges of her skirt and jacket. He breathed in her scent until it consumed him.

"I missed you, too."

He let her down, so her feet met the hardwood floor, but didn't loosen his hold or pull back to meet her gaze. In a moment of startling awareness, he realized the change in his body and mind.

They were alone and likely would be for at least another hour, half an hour at worst. Two ideas warred in his chest, two impulses equally as dangerous fought for his attention. The front of his jeans suddenly uncomfortable and tight, he wondered if she could guess the nature of one of those urges. But there was no way she could guess the second. His lips pressed against her flesh, less than a fraction of an inch from teeth that could become fangs in mere seconds. It would only take one willful decision, one biological catalyst to inject her blood with the right compound to make her like him. He could turn her right there in the foyer and the pack wouldn't be there to stop him.

He didn't know what color his eyes would be if he opened them. Red or gold. Which could he choose? Lust or violence?

Katey's fingers curled across the back of his neck as if to hold him there, asking for whichever way he chose to go. Her breaths became heavy and ragged, the heat and aroma of her arousal like a drug in his manic state. There was no fear, only need that matched his own. A few bounding steps into the sitting room and she could be on her back on the sofa, beneath him. A few vicious tugs and they could be relieved of clothes and...

Alarms sounded in his head that he had to stop, had to pull back, but he couldn't move. He couldn't drop his arms, couldn't pry himself away, couldn't make that plunge one way or another. His wolf prowled forward, ready to take the reins from his human side, and Logan didn't have the strength to stop it.

One sobering sound broke through the thickening fog that wrapped his common sense. Ben's car sped down the drive. They were out of time. He must have left just moments after Katey had and broken the speed limit to get here so quickly. Logan didn't know whether to hate Ben or shower him with gratitude.

Katey wouldn't have heard the approaching car, so with jerky, forced movements, he let her go and wrenched himself free of her hold. He kept his eyes closed and chin down.

"What's wrong?"

He held up his finger and flicked it in the direction of the carport the moment Ben slammed his car door. She heard that much and scrambled away to make it look as if they hadn't just been on the edge of a terrible mistake. Ben would sense the turmoil in Logan, so he turned on the balls of his feet and disappeared upstairs before Katey could blink.

Once safely behind the closed door of the bathroom, he gripped the edge of the counter to steady himself. He wanted to break something, to tear up and destroy anything to expel his rage before it bled on anyone who didn't deserve it. He almost did something he swore he wouldn't. He should have been more alert, he should have known that going all day deprived of her company would affect him that way. He needed her so badly and it blinded him to all reason.

He looked up to golden eyes. Evidently the urge to turn her was stronger than the need to take something else from her. That wasn't a comfort. She may have given signs that sex or a lot of heavy petting wasn't off the table, but if his wolf had its way, Katey could have been in the midst of being turned without consent.

He listened to Ben and Katey exchange a few words in the foyer, then the footsteps up the stairs. Ben didn't bother knocking but didn't open the door either.

"You good?"

"Yeah." The answer came out in a partial growl, though much of his temper had been restored. "Thanks."

Ben stayed on the other side of the door as Logan took deep breaths to push back the wolf one more time. Just like Katey, Ben couldn't have imagined what Logan had been prepared to do in the foyer. He may have only smelled how their need for one another manifested, but he couldn't know what his wolf wanted to do instead.

Logan couldn't let it happen again, but at least he knew that whenever the right moment came, it wouldn't take much to let the wolf have his way with her and take what they both needed. One way or another, the wolf would claim Katey and Logan began to wonder if he would be powerless to stop it.

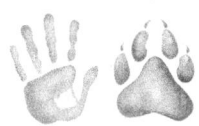

Katey sat onto the floor of the living room, an open environmental science textbook in her lap and her back to one of the sofas as she studied. Logan reclined behind her, sketchbook and pen in hand. Both of them had recovered, for the most part, from that blissful moment alone in the foyer an hour ago. Katey licked her lips as she remembered the way his mouth felt on her neck and all the pleasant tingling across her skin. He must have thought the same thing she did. They could have taken it to any piece of upholstery in the house and wouldn't have been interrupted until the pack came home. It was probably a good thing Ben came home, or they might have taken it too far. Katey may not have minded, but Logan's hesitance, evident in the way he just froze up, was a blessing in disguise. He had enough sense not to even get things started.

Now, they settled into comfortable silence, and Logan hadn't even come close to touching her since he came back downstairs. Ben never left their sight, and she began to wonder if he knew something had almost happened. It was as if they were both on some unspoken lockdown.

Darren arrived half an hour later and sequestered himself in the dining room to grade his exams. Ben graded his own on the opposite sofa, legs propped on the cushion to hold the hefty stack against his thighs, and head pillowed against the arm of the sofa. As he marked up each exam, he dropped it onto the growing pile on the floor with an attitude of carelessness.

The only sounds across the house were Logan's pencil strokes, the two red grading pens striking out the incorrect answers, and her page turns. Occasionally, a loup-garou let out a heavy sigh that didn't necessarily indicate irritation, but perhaps boredom or thoughtfulness. For a while, it was peaceful and Katey liked it.

She jumped when the front door flew open, and Dustin marched through to the living room. He threw his bag on the floor and continued on toward the sliding glass doors like a raging bull.

"I hate Mondays! I hate exams! I'm done! I'm checking out for the next few hours." He threw a fuming look toward Ben lounging on the sofa. "You coming with me?"

The other loup-garou didn't need to be asked twice and bolted to his feet to follow the beta outside, the exams abandoned across the sofa and floor.

Katey turned to Darren, who entered the living room just as the other two escaped out to the backyard and out of her line of sight.

The alpha's face twisted with a look of disdain, like a parent who watched their child run off to do some foolish thing, and knew there was no point in stopping them.

Katey rose to glance over the back of the sofa as Logan did, but he pushed her back down. "Don't look."

Too late. Katey caught just a glimpse of both loups-garous darting across the yard, pulling off their clothes. She didn't see anything compromising, only bare, muscled backs, but she knew their stripping would go farther than that. Her eyes widened.

"Blasted idiots," Darren grumbled as he crossed the room to the door.

"What are they doing?" Katey asked.

"Shifting."

Her body went cold. "Oh." She knew what that meant. Naked bodies morphing into wolves. She hadn't seen them like that yet and her mind tried to fill in the blanks with a mix of horror movie clips. "Is that a bad thing?"

Out of sight, Darren's throat rumbled with a frustrated growl. "No, but they can't just run off to do as they please when there's work to be done."

Logan sat up. "It's not like the exams are going anywhere."

"It's the principle."

"How long does it take?" Katey's voice was soft with shyness.

Darren moved around the couch to enter her field of vision. "Only a few moments." He glanced toward the door. "At least they went into the woods to do it."

Katey took a breath, then asked, "Can I see? Not the shift, but... after?"

Darren's brows arched in mild surprise. She didn't face Logan, but she could tell he stared at her too.

They likely wouldn't understand. Part of her didn't understand her own weird request to see them as wolves either. She had seen the three of them nearly every day for months, but as regular humans. To see them in that other form, to see that other side of themselves, would be like breaking down that last barrier between her and truly belonging with the pack as a human. It felt personal to see them that way.

Darren let out a smooth breath. "I suppose it's only natural for you to be curious... I don't see the harm. Logan, you stay with her. Both of you keep your distance."

Katey vacillated between excitement and confusion when Darren also went out the back door and Logan kept her in place on the floor. "Is it dangerous to be around them when they're shifted?"

Logan shook his head. "No. Ben may be the most unpredictable, but he has a fair amount of control."

Katey closed her textbook and set aside her study materials in preparation to go outside. Her hands shook with eagerness.

"You really want to see them like that?"

"Sure. Why not?"

A hint of discomfort pinched his expression. "I guess you would be curious, just... you seem really excited. It's weird."

Katey turned to look up at him, all seriousness. "Logan, you bunch are the coolest thing that has ever happened to me. When someone has the chance to see some real magic, something different and astounding, they seize it. I'm seizing it."

One end of his mouth curled. "All right. But, it's likely they've shifted into their more... docile form."

"What do you mean?"

"We have two forms." He held up one finger. "The first is a full wolf form. They'll look like any regular wolf, but much larger." He held up the second finger. "The other is a golf-wolf, half-man form. Not like Lon Chaney Jr. makeup style. More like *Underworld* Lycans, but maybe a little less grotesque. You've seen that movie?"

Katey remembered the tight leather and unimpressive special effects, and nodded. "So, today they'll look like big wolves."

"Yeah. But, be aware that's not their most comfortable form. It's easier to move with a more humanoid body than worry about the limitations of a canine body. The wolf also has a bit more control over them in this form. The other form is supposed to be more... balanced for most. However, the full wolf form lets the human half take a back seat, which is likely why Dustin wanted to do this shift. It relieves some stress and can be refreshing once they shift back, despite the pain."

Katey listened and logged it in her memory, just as she had every time she learned a little more about them. "Noted... Are they ready?"

Logan angled his head as if to check with his keen ears. "I think so."

They got up and walked through the garden to the gazebo.

The closest thing she could compare this feeling to was how a child might be just before meeting Santa Claus at the mall. Katey didn't personally have that experience, but saw it from a distance and in movies. She kept her eyes down until the last minute, savoring the butterflies in her stomach and not wanting to embarrass them with her staring.

Logan touched her hand, and she lifted her eyes. Three wolves came galloping out of the woods and she stopped breathing.

She'd seen them before. Her nightmare from last week. There, they had run alongside her in a snowy landscape and circled her in a graveyard, but it was unmistakable. The unique blend of colors in their pelts gave them away. One mostly brown and tan, one silver with highlights of dark gray, and one mostly black with streaks of gray. The only one missing was the all-black one that nuzzled her.

Jaw slack and eyes unblinking, she watched them slow as they neared the gazebo, heads low and ears folded back to show they meant no harm.

They were... beautiful, magnificent, incredible. Katey couldn't believe just how complete the transformation had been, yet she still felt as if she knew them so well.

The silver wolf held himself a little higher, though the brown one was clearly a little bigger. The dark one initiated play with the brown, and the tension snapped. They no longer watched her with golden eyes, but turned on one another to romp and roll across the grass. Yips and a bit of rough play with teeth and claws concerned her at first, but she reminded herself that it was normal. They acted as any other wolf in the wild.

Logan guided her to the gazebo, and they sat down on a bench to watch the fun. Neither of them spoke until Katey could keep words to herself no longer.

"The silver one is Darren, the brown one is Dustin, and black one is Ben." She didn't say it like a question, but like she was stating the obvious.

"Yeah. Our fur lightens as we get older. New loups-garous start out completely black."

Then what did that mean about the wolf in her dream? Was it logan? If she did her math right, he was only a little younger than Ben, but he at least had some variance in his coloration. Was Logan the midnight black she remembered, or did he have other colors woven through his pelt? Perhaps the black wolf was actually a representation of herself. If so, what sort of premonition did that mean?

"I can tell by how they act," Katey said, pushing out that disturbing thought for now. "The banter between Ben and Dustin is like how they're playing now, and Darren carries himself... well, like an alpha. It makes sense."

For the first time, Katey tore her gaze away from the wolves since she first laid eyes on them. It was then she realized Logan had brought out his sketchbook and it rested in his lap. From her vantage point, all she could see was a woman's face in profile. Her face.

"You were drawing me?"

Logan also glanced at his sketch and she saw a sparkle of amusement in his eyes. "Trying. Not as good as the real thing."

He turned it and offered her a better look. He made her look like some sort of angel, or perfect creature. "That's amazing. I mean, it's so lifelike."

"I've had a lot of time to practice."

Katey gave him a reassuring smile. "No, like, you're super talented. You should sell your art."

Logan only shrugged and flipped the book closed before nodding his chin back to the wolves. "So, what do you think of them?"

Katey let him avoid the subject and turned back to the pack. Now, they ran in an epic chase across the lawn, tearing up the sod beneath their powerful paws. They weren't as fast on four wolfish legs as they were on their two human legs, which she thought interesting. Their superhuman speed didn't carry over into their other forms. They were wolves in every respect, except for the human souls and minds within.

"It's awesome. Maybe Darren can shift back and then let you shift so you can take a break too."

She knew asking him to shift would defy Darren's order that she be protected, so it seemed a fair trade but Logan grew rigid, as if hardening himself for a fight.

"No." A muscle in his jaw jumped.

"I'm sure he wouldn't mind if you—"

"No!"

The explosion of anger made Katey flinch under Logan's golden eyed glower. They weren't quite the same gold from the night of the accident, but still vicious and threatening. The soft rustle of grass sounded outside the gazebo before a loud, distinctive growl came from one of the wolves, likely Darren or maybe Dustin.

Logan's nostrils flared as an animalistic rage seethed beneath the surface. The longer she held her place on the bench, unblinking and defiant, the more dominance flooded around them. It wasn't Logan's dominance, that much she knew. She wasn't afraid of Logan, not even like this. He wouldn't hurt her, not as long as some shred of his humanity stayed intact. By holding fast and not cowering at his anger, she communicated that clearly. He wouldn't push her away that easily.

The seconds ticked by and Logan calmed down enough that the blue returned and his gaze softened.

"I'm sorry... I... I can't shift at will like they can."

Katey finally blinked and glanced toward the silver wolf not far from the gazebo. His fur bristled, hackles standing on end to make himself look bigger and meaner. Lips curled up to reveal clenched fangs, ears pricked forward and tail high. He looked just as fierce as he sounded. Dustin and Ben watched from close by, but tensed to run at any moment to assist their alpha.

She took another second to process what Logan said. "You can't? Why?"

"Drop it, Katey." The words held an edge of that residual aggression.

"How come? Is it too complicated?"

It might have been unfair to throw that in his face at a time like this. She had nagged him for trying to evade difficult subjects that way, and he knew very well how she felt about that tactic.

Her remark destroyed the delicate balance. He abruptly stood and made his way toward the house with his sketchbook. About halfway, Darren broke into a run and blocked his path just on the edge of the garden. His order still stood. Katey wasn't to be left alone.

But when Katey left the gazebo to join Logan and reconcile, Dustin cut her off and stood between them, tail erect and amber eyes set, but not threatening.

Some exchange took place between Logan and his alpha that she couldn't understand. She waited patiently as patches of clouds moved across the warm winter sun, casting swift shadows across the yard.

Finally, Logan turned and trudged his way back to Katey, looking like a kid who had been reprimanded for some bad behavior. Darren trotted beside him as he came to stand just on the other side of Dustin.

Logan took a breath that lifted his shoulders. "I don't know why I can't shift at will. No one does. I've tried for over a century, and never came close. I've had some times when I almost shifted outside of my cycle, but it never went anywhere. Some think it has to do with how... diluted my loup-garou blood is, and others that it's a psychological thing. I don't know, and I tried to stop caring a long time ago."

Katey tried to read his expression. Shame, frustration, and a sort of bone-deep self-loathing. He couldn't do what other loups-garous could do. Coupled with his unique heritage and how he inherited the loup-garou gene, Logan was an oddity. An enigma. He was completely loup-garou, but couldn't accomplish an important milestone. He must have felt like a freak among his own peers. Katey could empathize with him that much.

She looked to the wolves before treading closer to Logan. They moved aside to allow it. "Well, clearly you're not over it. Otherwise, you wouldn't have gotten so upset."

"You were pushing."

"I wanted to understand."

"It's not something I'm proud of sharing."

Katey's lips curled together as she thought of what to say next. "I'm sorry I pushed. I didn't realize that it was a sore spot for you... I'm still trying to figure you out, Logan. Just like you're trying to figure me out." She stepped closer. "But next time I push, let your wolf know it's not a challenge. It's an olive branch."

Their eyes met and a little of that woundedness fell away to be replaced by something like pride. "It was impressive how you didn't run."

Katey crossed her arms and lifted her chin. "I don't scare easily. I thought you knew that."

Logan huffed a laugh and slowly closed the gap between them. "I guess I'm figuring you out a little more."

Before they could get too close, Katey felt something big and warm bump against the front of her legs. She looked down to see a mass of black fur wedged between Katey and Logan, an efficient buffer of wolf to keep them apart. With tentative fingers, Katey reached out to touch Ben's pelt. The top layer felt thick and coarse, pillowed by a softer, more dense layer beneath that gave an impression of bulkiness.

Ben let out a pleased sound as she dug her fingers deeper and rubbed.

"Careful," Logan warned in a teasing way. "You might spoil him."

Katey giggled and tried to keep her balance as Ben leaned heavier into her legs. "It's so weird to think that just an hour ago, he was grading papers in the house. I know it's not weird to you, but it's like... my mind can't connect that they're the same people, even though I know they are."

"This is just one side of us. It's like getting to know someone. They put on a face for the world, but can be someone else behind closed doors. Same thing."

Katey's smile faded. She knew all about that sort of life. Every day, she hid her darkness from everyone, but within the confines of her own room, she was someone different, someone she didn't want anyone else to see. Maybe she wasn't so different from the loups-garous after all.

Katey was perfect. The more Logan thought about it, the deeper the talons of poor judgment sank into his mind.

She had no family attachments, but needed them. She had no plans for the future. She accepted what they were and made a real effort to understand their way of life. Though the evidence of the car accident was gone, the bruises from the day before lingered, which didn't make sense but still proved that she was not fragile. She had endured so much, mentally, emotionally, and physically, and survived. That afternoon when he lost his temper, any other sane person would have run for the hills, but she stayed. It was as if she already had the spirit of the wolf within her.

A week ago, he had been only partially convinced that Katey could survive the bite. Now, he believed it beyond a shadow of a doubt. He and his wolf came that much closer to an understanding, straddling the edge of agreement, drastically unfamiliar territory for him. He and his wolf hardly saw eye to eye on anything.

Distracted by that terrifying concept and still reeling by their fight, if it could be called that, Logan kept his distance and poured his anxious energy into sketching. Yet, each time he began a new drawing, it began with Katey or some wolf and ended violently, as if his subconscious tried to warn him of the obvious. He trashed every piece before it could even halfway manifest on the page.

The pack shifted back around nightfall and took fast showers to prepare for dinner. Darren, of course, had choice words for Dustin's negligence, and they went into one of their biting verbal sparring matches. Katey only shrank away from the scene to let the alpha and beta work it out. Again, she somehow knew the right course of action, as if she knew how to let her instinct guide her.

The situation simmered down soon enough like it always did, and the evening was back on track. They voted for a cookout for dinner and Ben elected to grill the brat sausages, beef patties, and ribs. Logan's mouth watered as the smoky aroma drifted through the house from the grill on the other side of the carport. Katey was less distracted, her attention solely on her environmental science exam review. That test wouldn't be until the day after tomorrow, but Katey had voiced her concern that she may struggle with it. Darren offered any assistance she may need, but she hadn't requested any yet. That independence streak may have suggested a hidden vein of dominance.

When Ben came back inside, a pan brimming with steaming meats, the pack assembled to fill their plates.

Katey rose from her spot on the sofa and set aside her books. "Do you ever eat in the living room?"

Logan gave her an odd look as they made their way to the kitchen to fix their plates. "Why would we do that?"

"So you can watch TV while you eat."

Darren barked a laugh. "If we did that, then why bother with a dining room?"

Dustin paused in the doorway to the kitchen with his plate and glass. "I like the idea. Let's do it."

The beta could always be counted on to try the very thing of which Darren didn't approve. Ben, as predicted, agreed, as did Logan.

Darren came back from the dining room, a scowl just bubbling below the surface. "It appears I'm overruled."

Dustin beamed. "I think we should keep Katey around just so we can have a voting advantage."

She turned bashful as she slid a burger patty between two slices of bread. "Sorry."

Darren sighed. "Don't be. We run a democracy in this house... most of the time."

"Some of the time," Ben corrected.

"Every once in a blue moon," Logan said.

Dustin shot them a look. "You both know that's not entirely true. Katey, since it was your idea, you pick the movie."

Ben made a grunt of disapproval. "What happened to democracy?"

"You can still eat in the dining room if you don't like the movie."

The pack funneled into the living room. Darren claimed his recliner, Dustin and Ben on one sofa, Logan on the other, and Katey sat on the floor in front of him as she did earlier that day.

"What's that one movie you said you liked?" Katey asked Logan as she got comfortable. "Something about a falcon?"

Logan grinned, but the rest of the pack groaned. "*The Maltese Falcon.*"

Dustin sank back into the cushions. "God, no. We've seen it like a hundred times."

Ben ribbed him. "Ya can eat in the dining room if ya don't like the movie."

Darren chuckled and set aside his plate to fetch the disc case from their collection to pop it in the player.

Katey looked from one loup-garou to the other in a slight panic. "If no one wants to watch it, that's okay."

"It's all right," Darren said. "It's just one movie and one night."

Katey accepted that, but Logan could tell she regretted the way she so easily bent the pack to her will. Without a bit of dominance, she got her way. Another good sign.

With dinner plates balanced in their laps and glasses on the floor, they watched *The Maltese Falcon*, but not quietly. For nearly the first half, Dustin and Ben offered snide commentary. They faked astonishment at the plot and mercilessly mocked the dialogue, especially the female characters. Dustin's high-pitched, damsel voice made Katey burst into giggles and Logan couldn't be mad at the way they made fun of his favorite movie.

By the time Sam Spade, played by Humphrey Bogart, knocked out Joel Cairo in his office, the pack finished their dinner. Dustin took up their dirty plates and glasses and took them to the kitchen sink. Having lost in their paintball training, he ran the faucet to warm up the water and filled the sink to start a batch.

Below him, Katey shifted, repositioning her legs as if uncomfortable on the hardwood floor. Logan scooted himself up on the sofa, freeing some space on the cushion.

"Come on up," he told her softly. He wouldn't look to the pack for consent.

Her green eyes darted between Logan and the sofa. There was a question there, and Logan answered that it was okay for her to enter the space he had all but denied her since earlier that afternoon. Still, he wouldn't let them be alone, so he knew it was safe for both of them.

Katey sat in the space he made for her. As the movie continued, they edged closer and closer to one another until, by the time Spade and Gutman discussed who would be the fall guy for the murders, Katey laid against Logan, her cheek on his chest and his arm securely around her shoulders. Her hand rested against his stomach and when her fingernails clandestinely brushed just the right spot, Logan had to place his hand on top of hers to stop the movement. Just cuddling this way was enough to tempt him. He didn't need the extra physical attention. The little puff of a laugh told him that she knew exactly what she had done. If things were different, he might have returned the favor by dragging the back of his fingers along the curve of her waist from her hip to her ribs.

He glanced at Darren and knew none of this had gone unnoticed, but the alpha did nothing and said nothing. Ben, who knew what he interrupted when he came home, passed a critical look their way a few times. Dustin, having returned from the kitchen, didn't seem to care.

It didn't take long for Katey's breathing to steady and deepen. A glance down affirmed that she was fast asleep. This was the second time she had done that. It was as if being in his arms was all she needed to feel relaxed and at home. The feeling was mutual.

The movie ended with Mary Astor's character, Brigid O'Shaughnessy, being escorted down the elevator while Spade took the stairs, and the pack turned to see Katey totally unconscious on Logan. They quietly communicated their plans. Darren relented that it was late, and he'd retire for bed. Ben still had exams to grade, and Dustin hadn't even begun grading his own. Darren retreated upstairs and Ben gathered up his exams to take to the dining room. Dustin turned off the TV and bent down to pick up the bag he threw on the floor earlier, likely with plans to follow Ben and leave the living room.

Before he could Logan whispered, "Don't go."

Confused, it took Dustin a little time for him to understand. Logan needed a chaperone. He couldn't be trusted, even if the pack was in the house and any hint of danger would have them on him in an instant. Now, he understood just a part of Darren and Ben's reticence.

Dustin nodded in comprehension and took his seat on the sofa again to grade the exams, then plug those scores into their program that kept track of the students' overall grade.

Time passed, and Logan's muscles burned as he balanced the two of them on the sofa, battling the need to move and risk waking her. Logan watched her sleeping face, how her lips settled into a simple, neutral curve and dark lashes rested against her skin. He kept time with her even heartbeats and brought up his hand to pass lazy strokes over her hair as if she were a dozing pet.

Despite the utter peace she brought with her presence, Logan's chest tightened with tangled emotions. Pure joy became infected by black dread. He imagined life with Katey, sharing these moments of togetherness through the years. Being mates, having children, supporting one another through the easy and difficult seasons that came and went. She made him feel human enough for such mundane things, worthy of love and companionship he had only ever seen in others. Katey made him forget about the beast inside, made him forget that the kind of life he should have had was forever out of reach.

But, in these visions, Katey wouldn't stay the same. She would age, and instead of making him forget, she would become the worst reminder. Mortality would hound her for decades while he never aged, while the wolf kept him alive and healthy. His heart shattered when his projections came to the inevitable end. He could see himself standing by Katey's graveside, alone again.

He squeezed his eyes shut to end the nightmare and came back to the present. Logan was vaguely aware of the house darkening and the movement of the pack in preparation for bed. He glanced to the clock on the wall. It was close to midnight, but he wasn't the least bit tired.

Dustin closed his laptop and sighed at the sight of them on the couch. "You haven't moved in hours."

Logan bit his lips and glanced down to Katey's sleeping form. He shook his head and tried to will away the heartache. "How am I going to do this?" Sorrow stole his voice, but Dustin would be able to hear him when the rest of the pack couldn't.

"Pick her up and take her to her room." When Logan didn't move, Dustin understood his true meaning. "You really love her... don't you?"

Logan was thankful for the beta's discretion. Even though Ben and Darren were already upstairs, no one needed to know the truth. Yes, he loved Katey. He knew that now. Perhaps he had known it all along and had been too blind and stupid to realize his own feelings.

He didn't want to face a world without her. He couldn't have her for just one human lifetime. He needed her for centuries. He needed her there to remind him that he was more than just a loup-garou. He was a man, the kind of man she could be happy with, the kind of man she might deserve. He may not be that right now, but he wanted the chance to become everything for her. He wanted to give her a home, a family, a life she didn't want to hide from or escape. By being together, they could save one another from fates they didn't deserve. No one should have to be alone.

Only one thing kept them apart. One crucial detail couldn't be ignored. That one thing, he knew how to fix.

"Maybe you should talk to some of the Deviants," Dustin suggested. "They've had human mates and can give you a better answer than I could... I'd say ask Darren, but I doubt he wants to talk about that. You know how he is about that subject."

Logan didn't want to be consoled, or to be talked out of anything. They wouldn't understand this burning need to have Katey like this. They could settle. Logan couldn't.

CHAPTER 21

"What do you mean he's gone?" Katey's voice took on a shrillness that irked Darren, but she couldn't help it. Why would Logan leave without warning? Why would he sneak out before dawn, before any of them got up from bed to stop him? Maybe that meant he didn't want them to stop him.

"He does that sometimes," the alpha told her. "He'll wander off for a few hours, perhaps a whole day. He always comes back. Perhaps he didn't want to stay cooped up in the house all day while you were away."

"Can't I call him?"

"I already tried. He left his phone in his room. No one will be able to reach him."

Katey folded her arms and looked out the window over the kitchen sink. Dustin and Ben were already walking out to their vehicles to head to the school. "Can I stay here then? Wait for him to come back? I only have study hall and teacher's aid with Dustin. No exams for those classes."

Darren shook his head as he stacked the last of the breakfast plates. "I'm not so sure I want you two alone together in this house for that long. Besides, there's no telling when he'll come back. You may as well go to school. It's very probable that he'll come back around noon when he thinks you'll be home too."

Did Ben rat them out about what happened the day before in the foyer? Whatever would make Darren hesitant to leave them alone, Katey was unlikely to convince him to be more lenient, so she let out a breath and left the kitchen. Another day without Logan seemed intolerable. She'd take the emotional whiplash of yesterday afternoon and evening over not having him close by. She wouldn't even mind if the pack wanted to give them a chaperone. Anything was better than the aching loneliness that his absence brought. In such a short time, she had become irrevocably addicted to Logan, and she didn't even mind it.

Katey shouldered her bookbag and tried to take heart in the fact that the rest of the pack wasn't concerned about Logan. He'd be back. He wouldn't have abandoned her, not for long. Darren's theory made sense, but she wished he had kept his phone. Just a text message would be enough to hold her over until the end of the day.

Logan circled the same few grave plots, meandering in random patterns as he tried to unravel the mess of emotions and thoughts in his head. Arms crossed and stomach growling, he did the unthinkable and made decisions that would purposefully summon his wolf. He needed the courage, the single-minded drive to make sense of what he had to do.

His gaze wandered to a single familiar headstone, the one that belonged to Robert Croxen. Over a century ago, that alpha made a decision that cost the lives of his townspeople. Though he went down in a blaze of glory alongside other alphas to defend their community, Logan remembered that day and how furious he was with Robert for leading them to the slaughter. He needed to know how a man of such conviction could make that decision without hesitation, without remorse. At the time, Robert thought it best. He didn't even entertain the thought that innocent lives would be struck down that night. Logan needed that same level of bold ignorance to do what needed to be done.

Over and over, he talked himself in circles around the facts, hoping he could drill some level of logic into the matter to make it more palatable.

"I need Katey. I can't lose her. If she stays human, I'll lose her. Not immediately, but eventually... If she's loup-garou, I won't lose her. Not until both of us are old. Centuries together... But, if I turn her, she could die and I'd lose her... But she may not die... If she doesn't die, she'll be mine forever."

Ours forever.

The wolf rammed against his skull and Logan pressed the heel of his palm into his eyes. He didn't eat breakfast that morning, and barely slept at all the night before, after he put Katey to bed. Sleep deprivation and hunger may not have been life-threatening, but the wolf would fight for control of his human body. It only needed more time.

Katey must be ours. Forever. She will not die. She is strong. She is special. Katey will be loup-garou.

Logan snagged on the word "will", when he usually used "could be". The wolf's confidence didn't quite bleed into him yet, but it was getting close. Tremors rattled his body as he pushed back the wolf one more time.

"But if she does die... I would never forgive myself. Having several decades is better than nothing at all."

I will not watch her grow old and wither to dust. Let other females perish before their mates. We deserve better. Katey will be loup-garou.

Logan shook his head. "We deserve nothing for everything we've done." He couldn't believe he was thinking in first person already.

Years in darkness. Years of loneliness. We need a mate. Katey is that mate. Katey will be loup-garou.

Logan roared and kicked at a nearby headstone, snapping it in half. He bent at the waist and grabbed at his hair, the mental anguish almost too much to bear.

Katey will live. She will live for us, and only us. Katey will be loup-garou.

The madness strained to poison his human side and send him into a downward spiral that Logan wasn't so sure he could return from. The wolf surged against him harder and harder with each passing moment. Logic and reason, in one swift torrent, left his thoughts.

Breaths ragged, Logan fell to his knees and felt the cold wash of gold over his eyes. His soul surrendered to the wolf, too weak to fight the one thing he wanted more than anything in the world. "Katey will be loup-garou."

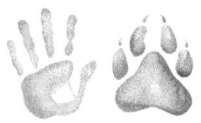

Dustin gripped his classroom doorknob a little tighter. "Are you sure you'll be all right in here?"

Katey sat at his desk, a stack of graded semester exams beside her. She nodded. "Yeah, sure."

"I'm going to go have a quick talk with Darren and I'll be right back. Lock the door if you want."

She waved him off and began to input the exam grades into the computer spreadsheet. The little bit of extra work wouldn't take her long, and he needed something to occupy her while he confronted his alpha.

Ever since Logan admitted that he loved her, Dustin's mind set to scheming. His grandson didn't admit it in so many words, but he wanted Katey in his life, badly. Every decision he made centered around her, and it took Dustin until now to comprehend the entirety of the problem. Logan never did anything halfway. All or nothing. Most of the time, it was nothing. With Katey, he wanted it all and sooner rather than later.

The halls slowly emptied of students as Dustin arrived at Darren's classroom. He waited as the alpha wrapped up a conversation with a student. Once they were alone, he shut the classroom door and pulled the blind as per the rules.

"What's wrong?" Darren asked, leaning against the counter that stretched across the back of the classroom.

Dustin crossed his arms and tried not to look as troubled as he felt inside. "Not sure if it's something wrong, or just... a mild issue. You remember last week when Logan asked us to take Katey into the pack. We said it had to be through mating or through turning her, the latter of which is obviously out of the question, but... I'm beginning to wonder if Logan's close to making a move on that front."

Darren's brows shot up. "You think he's going to form the mating bond with her?"

"Maybe... Or maybe he's going to try and turn her. I've just had this weird feeling for most of the morning like something's off... Like a storm's coming or some other cataclysmic disaster."

"I've felt it too, but I amounted it to the fact that it is, in fact, raining outside." Darren's gaze dropped to the space between them as if in thought. "Logan knows that turning a female is impossible. If he truly cares for Katey, he wouldn't risk killing her. I don't think we have anything to worry about in that respect."

Dustin's face pinched with doubt. "I don't know. Logan's done some pretty sketchy things."

"Those decisions were driven by extenuating circumstances. This isn't the same as what happened in Chicago."

"I know it isn't, but... Last night, he basically admitted that he loves Katey, but what he actually said was, 'How am I going to do this?' I wonder if he meant how he's going to go day to day, knowing he can't have Katey forever. It was a 'How am I supposed to live without you?' kind of vibe." Now Dustin had the song playing in his head.

Darren looked up. "And you think that's evidence that he may try to make her... less human?"

"Pretty much. I wish the little shit kept his phone on him at least, so we could get a bead on him."

"As do I... Perhaps one of us should go home early and wait for him. Where's Katey?"

Katey had fallen into a steady rhythm while inputting the test scores into Dustin's computer. The steady beating of the heavy rain against the window, coupled with the quiet of the classroom and hallway outside was soothing. All day, she had ached for Logan's company. Just a word, a sign that he was all right would have been enough. Each time she thought her phone vibrated in her pocket, she quickly tugged at her jean pocket to whip it out, only to find no notification.

She knew speeding up her work would only lead to mistakes, though she wanted to head home more than anything.

Home.

Katey smirked at the errant use of the word. The house full of loups-garous began to feel more and more like home every day, though she would only ever admit it to herself. Besides the stumbling with Logan, she felt as if her life was finally falling into place somehow. Or maybe it was just the rain.

Just as she was about to enter the last batch of grades, an angry fist banged on the classroom door, making her jump in her seat. Not ten seconds after Dustin left, she had locked the door. The knocking sounded far too aggressive to be Dustin returning from Darren's classroom. Katey took a breath to steady her nerves, then peered out the narrow window on the door to see who it was, but could see no one.

When she opened the door to look down the hall, a gust of cold wind hit her, and a force threw her back into the classroom. The door slammed shut and she was temporarily dazed by the suddenness of the attack.

Before she could even see him, she felt the wave of dominance close around her like a dense fog, so thick and suffocating that Katey had to take a moment to steel her mind against its effects.

When her eyes adjusted, Logan stood in front of her, his back against the door. Katey froze under his vicious, golden glare. His hair and clothes were soaked through, and his face contorted with fury.

"Logan... Are you okay?"

She could feel her hands trembling so she casually slung them in the front pouch on her hoodie as she examined him from head to toe. He didn't look well at all. His complexion ashen as if he just ran a mile, or in his case, maybe a hundred miles. Water dripped from his nose and jacket, dampening the carpet underneath him. His chest rose and fell with rough, shaky breaths.

"No, I'm not okay," he bared his teeth in a snarl. His voice was similar to how it had been that night when he tried to save her from Mary, as if the wolf spoke through him.

Katey backed away toward Dustin's desk to put some distance between herself and Logan. She remembered what Darren had warned her about. "Have you eaten today?" She tried to keep her voice as calm and neutral as possible, hoping that would help to bring him down from whatever this was.

"Don't talk to me like I'm some pup!" he snapped. She could see his slightly elongated canines glistening sharp in the classroom lights.

"Logan, you need to calm down." She bit the words off slowly and sternly, as if she had any right to command him like an alpha.

"You have no authority over me!"

A flash of lightning struck outside and for a moment, Katey saw the image of a wolf growling down at her instead of Logan.

She stopped her retreat and braced her legs like she was ready to stand and fight him. Isn't that what he admired about her yesterday? That she didn't run when he lost his cool? "Logan, I'm asking you to calm down. We're not in a safe place for this."

Logan marched toward her, his eyes glowing gold with some feral desire. Now her fear began to show as he didn't slow down, despite her defiance. She turned in an effort to avoid him, and ran straight into a desk, knocking herself into the seat. Another bolt of lightning struck, and Logan trapped her, one hand on the desk and the other on the back of her chair. She could feel his hot breath engulf her face, its heat radiating down her neck and chest.

"I'm tired of waiting on you to decide. We've done everything we can do to make you feel welcome. We've let you in like you're part of the pack. Do you know how many loups-garous would kill themselves just to be welcomed as unconditionally as you've been?" Terror snaked through Katey as she watched his face warp in blind rage. "We've bent over backwards for you, and you tease me with your indecisiveness. I won't take it any longer. Decide right now. Do you want to be with me? Do you want to be a loup-garou?"

This wasn't Logan, this wasn't even the loup-garou inside of him that needed to feed. It was some desperate part of him that was just as fed up as she was over not being able to define what they were to one another. Were they dating? Were they almost mates? Was she part of the pack? The not knowing, the ambiguity of it all, it had infuriated both of them and this is what it led to.

As clearly as if it were printed across his face, she understood. Logan wanted her, and she wanted him. The only way this could go on forever was if she became like him. She had to become a loup-garou, and they were the only two in the world who knew that it could very well happen.

He had asked if she thought they had a chance. Now was the time to echo that answer.

"Yes."

She could hardly hear herself over the rain, but she knew he could hear everything from the blood racing under her skin to the rabbiting of her frightened heart. Logan's face softened a little, lips closing over wolfish fangs, and he looked normal for the first time since he entered the classroom, but there was still a seething fury and an unnatural thirst in his eyes. Part of her wondered just what would quench that thirst, but either way, Katey was willing and ready. She'd give everything to be with him.

He slowly moved his hands from the desk and grabbed Katey's hips to pull her to her feet. She held tightly onto his arms to steady herself and never wavered her gaze from his flashing bright eyes. In those eyes, she could see her destiny and the future she thought she couldn't have. It was a future Logan could give her, here and now. A future with him, with his pack, with a family, and a home where she could belong.

She could feel the heat of passion and ferocity emitting from him with the dominance. The front of her shirt became damp as their bodies pressed against each other.

Logan leaned his forehead against her own like he did a few times before in that intimate way that made every cell in her body shiver. Katey tried to stabilize her heavy breathing, but it was nearly impossible as adrenaline streamed through her body, preparing her to fight for her life. She gave the tiniest of nods to tell him that she was ready.

Logan drew his damp nose across her cheek and into her hair, inhaling her scent. She could hear each drag of his breath laced with some desirous longing, sending waves of shocks pulsing through her body and converging low in her belly.

He gently brushed her hair out of the way of her neck, fingertips brushing her skin in such a sensuous way she thought she'd collapse. Logan pulled down the collar of her hoodie and shirt to reveal most of her shoulder. Water dripped from his face and hand, cooling her flushed skin as it trickled down her collarbone.

The sound of the pouring rain outside was nearly indistinguishable from the pounding in her ears. Katey shook violently in the throes of both fear and arousal, and squeezed the hard muscles on Logan's arms, moisture seeping from his shirt and into her palms.

His lips brushed against her skin as they did the day before and slid down to the point where her neck and shoulder met. She could feel Logan's throat rumble with a satisfied growl as his teeth grazed across her fragile skin. The lightning clashed once again outside the window, followed by a roll of bellowing thunder that throbbed in her chest.

For that moment, Katey didn't think about anything. She didn't think of how this would turn out. She didn't think that this could kill her. She hadn't even thought about the possibility of becoming what Logan was, and all that entailed. All she thought about was Logan and the nearly endless life they could have together. Katey thought she'd have to be desperate to make a decision like this, to risk her life for the chance to live with him for centuries. In that moment of clarity, she knew she was desperate. She knew she was in love. He was a stalker, he could be obsessive, he had a temper, and it sometimes seemed like he was playing games with her heart with cryptic and vague answers to her demands. Yet, she loved him. Completely and consumingly.

Logan gripped her sleeve to keep the hoodie from sliding up into his face and wrapped one arm completely around her waist. He pulled her in tight, every curve in her body braced against him.

In one rapid second, he sunk his fangs into her flesh and her mouth gaped open as if to gasp, but she couldn't breathe. The bite hurt like nothing she had ever felt before, but she resisted the temptation to scream. Warm blood dripped down her chest and back.

Katey dug her nails into Logan's shirt and whimpered as she felt the venom course through her veins like a burning fire. She gritted her teeth and willed her lungs to keep working. As long as she was breathing, she was alive. Tears spilled from her eyes and streamed down her face, and the breaths finally came in shivering gasps.

Liquid fire streamed from her neck, flowing into her skull and down to her arms and chest, infecting her nervous system. As the venom spread to her heart, internal spurts of explosions crashed through her entire body, detonating in every organ. Katey fell completely breathless once more and gasped for oxygen, spots dancing in her vision. What seemed like hours passed, though it must have been only seconds. The explosions slowly subsided and she could breathe again.

The scorching poison continued its path, drowning her, touching every cell, every muscle, down to the marrow of her very bones. All she could feel was the searing, excruciating pain of the venom infiltrating every part of her. Nothing existed but the pain.

Logan's grip became tighter around her, digging his claws into her waist and arm, piercing the fabric of her hoodie. He had to keep pulling her in tighter as her own body grew limp from the pain and exhaustion. Even with her eyes closed, she felt like her whole world spun out of control. She became lightheaded, her hold on his arms weakening as the venom did its job.

Her head swayed before leaning dully against his. His wet hair felt cool against her flushed cheek and throbbing temples. Her knees began to buckle beneath her. The only thing keeping her upright was Logan. The pain began to subside, and she didn't know if it was because her body acclimated to the pain, if the venom was working, or if she was on the verge of death. Whatever it was, Katey welcomed the reprieve and her eyes drifted shut.

Just as she felt herself slip away, Katey heard the hammering thud of running feet down the hall and the classroom swing open.

"What the...Logan!"

Katey's eyes wouldn't open, but she could tell Dustin was by their side. Another loud thud and Logan finally broke his hold on Katey. They tumbled to the floor, both unconscious.

Darren hurried into the classroom, driven by the stench of blood and loup-garou venom that stretched down the hallway. The change in the pack bond had alerted him to danger even before Dustin tried to call him. On the floor, Katey and Logan lay in a heap, Dustin standing over them.

"I shouldn't have left her alone," the beta muttered, eyes wide upon the blood that stained his floor. "I should have made her lock the door. I should have tried to track down Logan, knowing what I knew." Dustin cursed in the Gaelic tongue under his breath and began to pace.

He had only seen his beta this distraught a handful of times. If it wasn't his duty to remain calm, Darren might have come undone just as quickly. Katey had entrusted them with her safety, and

Logan committed the worst offense possible. No matter if Katey lived or died, he'd be punished. Severely.

Darren closed the door, locked it, and dropped to his knees in front of Katey. He bent low, trying to find a heartbeat beneath the background noise of the storm and Dustin's panicked breathing.

"Her pulse is thready, but it's there... She's still alive, but barely." Darren sat up. "Call Ben. We're taking them home."

SNEAK PEEK INTO BECOMING THE ENIGMA

Darren rubbed at the back of his neck as he sat in one of the dining chairs he had brought into the sitting room, while Ben sat in another, elbows on knees and hands tightly folded together as if in prayer. Dustin sluggishly paced in the foyer just beyond the open French doors, and diligently watched the sleeping figures of Katey on one couch and Logan on its pair across from her.

The loups-garous had loosened their work attire, top buttons and ties undone. It'd been several hours since the attack and neither of them had shown any sign of consciousness. But, as long as the three men could still hear their gentle breathing and strong heartbeats, they knew that there was still hope.

Ben glanced to the clock on the wall, the pendulum swinging with each second that dragged. Dustin blew out a short breath and stopped just inside the French doors. Darren looked at his beta and his impatient, shifty gaze.

"Brooding won't make them wake up," he commented as he unbuttoned his cuffs and rolled up his sleeves. The air in the house was cool, but the sitting room took on a balmy, suffocating temperature.

Ben rolled his shoulders. "What else are we supposed to do? I can't just carry on with my evenin', knowin' that they're like this."

"I knew a loup-garou in Italy that tried to turn his girlfriend," Dustin said, brushing his fingertips underneath his chin with a distant look in his eye. "She was unconscious for nearly a day before she started fading."

"Katey won't fade." Darren had to stay strong for his pack. If he showed the slightest bit of panic, they would latch onto it and begin to doubt themselves and everything they secretly believed from the beginning. "She's strong. She'll pull through."

Ben hung his head and ran his hands through his hair, gripping at the roots. Dustin turned away, his arms crossed and shoulders rigid. Darren swallowed hard and turned his attention back to Katey, who looked to be sleeping soundly. At least she wasn't in any pain... yet.

***

Katey moaned as feeling finally returned to her body. Everything ached, from her muscles and bones to her skin, as if she had been stretched too thin and then pushed back together. She moved her head and pain shot down her spine. She hissed and struggled to open her eyes, but her eyelids felt bruised and swollen. The lights blinded her, and she squeezed her eyes shut again with a whimper. Bright dots danced in Katey's vision as her retinas tried to recover from the sudden assault.

Darren's voice whispered somewhere in the room. "Ben, turn off the lights."

She sensed some movement in the room, and assumed it was Ben obeying the alpha. Beyond her eyelids, she could tell the light directly above them had been cut off.

Katey sighed and blinked for a moment, trying to think, but that, too, made her hurt. She glanced between the three loups-garous and their anxious gazes.

Through the haze and chaos of alien sensations and pain, she could tell she lay on one of the sofas in the sitting room. She squinted around and recognized the old furniture and crystal chandelier in the dining room.

As her foggy mind reached into the past, another face appeared. One distorted with rage and the golden eyes of the wolf staring at her with hunger and distressed longing. Growls and harsh words hummed in her ears, and she remembered exactly what happened.

More pain streaked through her body, but it could do little to distract her from the memory of Logan bent over her with teeth bared in a snarl. Katey found the energy to push herself up, but Dustin gently pushed her back down onto the sofa, his touch like needles jabbing into her flesh. The prickly edges of the bandage tape bit into her skin as it shifted under her clothes.

"Just take it easy. Everything's okay. How do you feel?"

"Don't shout at me," she moaned, her own voice sounding like a clanging gong in her ears.

"I'm not."

"Give her ears a bit to get used to it," Darren whispered from behind Dustin.

Katey blinked hard and raised her hand to her throbbing head, the effort to move expending what little energy she had. "Where's Logan?"

"He's right here." Ben motioned toward the loveseat on the other side of the room.

Katey turned her head and her throat closed up. There lay Logan's limp and unconscious body. His face was blank, as if he were sleeping.

Dustin rubbed his thumb across her tender shoulder, a comforting gesture to her nerves. "Don't worry, we crammed meat down his throat after we brought you two home. He's just resting now."

Katey glanced down to her body, as if to make sure it was still in one piece. "Everything hurts."

Darren took a careful step forward. "It's going to hurt for a little while. But, once everything sets in, you'll feel relatively normal again."

Her thoughts were a tangled mess, searching for an explanation why everything was so sensitive and vivid. Her eyes widened as her mind slowly cleared.

"Am I..." She could barely voice the word, afraid that if she spoke it aloud, her hopes would be dashed to pieces.

The guys glanced to each other and Darren nodded solemnly. "We think so."

AFTERWORD

Dear Reader,

I hope you have enjoyed the first part of this series I have begun. Don't worry, there will be many more novels to come about Katey and Logan's journey together. I encourage you to read on with *Becoming the Enigma* and check out the prequel series, The Legacy Series, which tells all of the backstories for characters like Darren, Dustin, Ben, and Logan. *The Enigma* began when I was a freshman in high school. At the time, I had this weird obsession with everything supernatural. Werewolves, vampires, demons, you name it. I had more monster books than the public library.

Inspiration for this story stemmed from a lot of things that were going on in my life at the time. No, I wasn't dating a werewolf (although that would have been so cool), but I was struggling with depression, thoughts of suicide, self-doubt, and above all I wanted to know what my purpose in life was.

Writing opened up an avenue to vent my frustrations and not only have fun making up stories about people I wish existed, but discovering more about myself. You can thank this book for sparking the fire of creativity in me, because without it, the books that I have already published would not have been in existence today. These characters have been with me for a long, LONG time. They are as close to me as family, in a weird sort of way.

I invite you to check out my social media sites for more updates and sneak peeks into my progress. You can find me at my blog, www.moonstruckwriting.wordpress.com or website, www.sheri ttabitikofer.com

Happy Reading!
Sheritta Bitikofer

About the Author

Sheritta Bitikofer is an author of paranormal and historical fiction. She lives for the deep, engaging stories that enthrall readers from cover to cover. As a wife and mother of eclectic tastes, she can be found roaming Civil War battlefields, haunting her local coffeeshop, or relaxing with a plate of chili cheese fries.

Follow her for upcoming novel releases
www.sherittabitikofer.com

ALSO BY SHERITTA BITIKOFER

Bulletproof
The Nexus
<u>Bewitching Brews</u>
Bewitching Fire
Bewitching Darkness
Bewitching Hearts
<u>Wolves in the Open</u>
Highland Howls
Silver Screen
Mourning Moon
<u>The Decimus Trilogy</u>
The Beast of Verona
Amber Ashes
Saving the Beast
<u>Redemption Duet</u>
The Rose
The Lion
<u>Standalones</u>
Escape
Clouds
Passions
By The Book

www.ingramcontent.com/pod-product-compliance
Lightning Source LLC
Chambersburg PA
CBHW072307020726
47501CB00002B/423